WEST OF JAWS

Book 1 of the Sennenwolf Series

CAPES

West of Jaws

Published by Capas LLC 2023
www.capescreates.com

Ebook ISBN: 979-8-9863167-1-0
Print ISBN: 979-8-9863167-0-3
Copyright © 2023 by Capes. All rights reserved.
www.capescreates.com

Proofread by Ben Wolf
www.benwolf.com/editing-services

Cover design by Jelena Gajic
Check out her work on Instagram: @coverbookdesigns

**Please email capesdoes@gmail.com for wholesale copies. She offers
discounts to indie distributors and bookstores.**

TOTW / INGC

DEDICATION

For the Rat King
(Long Live the Rat King)

SPECIAL NOTE

There are three things you should know about this book.

First, it's pronounced *an-tih-go-nee* (Antigone), *its-if-foh-nee* (Itzifone), and *nih-nih-go-nee* (Ninigone). You get it.

Second, there's an extensive glossary in the back.

Third, this book deals with *adult* themes, like titties and violence and true love and snortable powders. If that line felt a little abrasive, this book isn't for you.

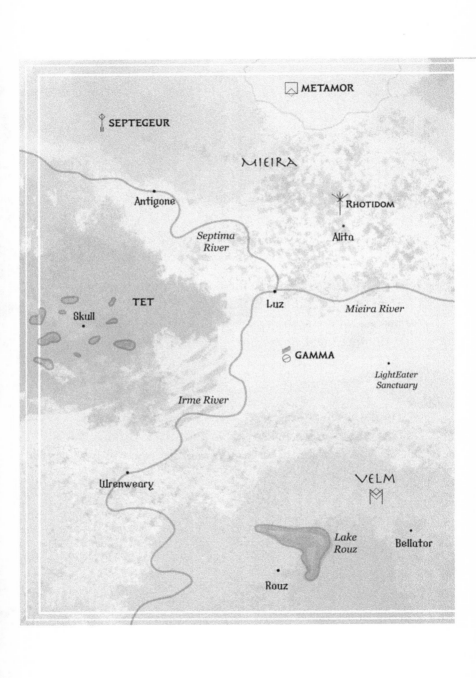

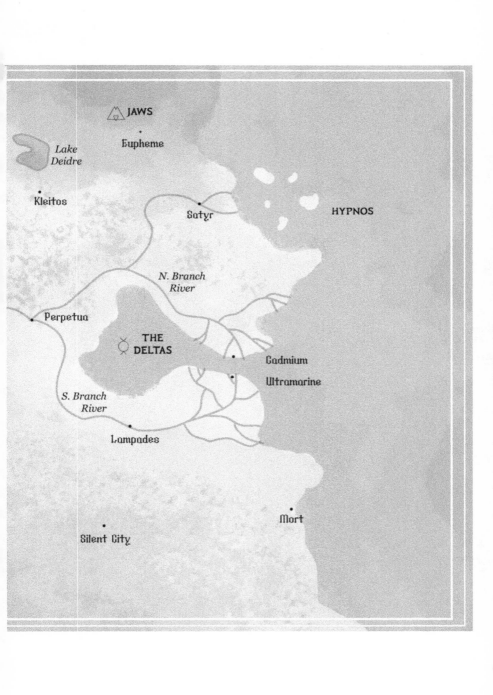

CONTENTS

1. Little Esteban   1
2. An Amazing Personality   16
3. Zhuzhing-Zhazhing   33
4. The Endless Pool of Velvet Fabric   52
5. Lesser Instincts   68
6. Creepy Baby   88
7. Eat Your Noodles   113
8. The Triplemoon, Samsonfang Part I   132
9. Look Away If It's Too Much   154
10. The Pale Squealing Baby   190
11. Tools of the New War   220
12. Brutatalika 567 Sigivald   251
13. It Echoes from the Northwest   274
14. Fragrant Coagulated Goo   306
15. Centerheart   330
16. A Flimsy Thing Like Friendship   356
17. Itzi   383
18. The Triplemoon, Samsonfang Part II   407
19. I Only Have One Left   437
20. Because She Can't   462
21. Are You Watching?   479
22. Deep in Velm   495
23. Deep in Jaws   500

Hi, reader!   507
Glossary & World   509
Acknowledgments   513
About the Author   515

CHAPTER 1

LITTLE ESTEBAN

HELISENT

Honey Heli,
Antigone is everything we always knew it would be. Get here. Fast.
Mint Mili

I splay my body across the dirt road and lay flat.

"Ninigone, can you see what I'm doing?"

Unsure if my appeal is working, I try to conjure a few tears. I'm already covered in tiny flecks of debris, but I'm drunk enough not to care. I'll do anything to shirk this responsibility.

I glance at her through a slitted eye; the witch crosses her arms. "This is me *begging you not to do this*."

Ninigone sucks on her teeth, then she glances at the thin witchling to her left. I don't spare a glance at the newcomer. If I look her way, I'm sure Ninigone will take it as capitulation, and the *last fucking thing* I'm going to do right now is agree to mentor a witchling from Antigone.

The hood of Ninigone's tawny cloak shakes in the wind. Her tone is measured as she stares down at me. "Young Esclamonde here needs a mentor to introduce her to life in Luz. Like the witchling, you once lived in Antigone, which makes me think you'd be a *spectacular* mentor."

I groan and turn back toward the dirt. I know my tantrum won't change Ninigone's mind, but it might make the witchling hate me enough to go home or request a different mentor.

Ninigone turns toward the witchling and lowers her voice. "Don't mind the theatrics, Esclamonde. You'll get used to it."

I rise with a scowl and float into the air, wiggling my cloaks clean. I stare down at the witchling. I don't know anything about her, but I hate her golden eyes, her white hair, her too-large red cloak. How primly she's fit her bottomless bag across her body.

I hover a foot above the witchling. "Do you drink and dance? I don't like innocence, little Esteban."

The witchling gulps. "My name is Esclamonde."

I look at Ninigone. "Is she allowed to talk back like that?"

The witch's stern expression doesn't waver. "Yes, Helisent. Especially when you mispronounce her name."

I stay focused on Ninigone. "Did the Class put you up to this? I give Luz all the magic it needs. You can report back that I'm handling my duties here with *aplomb*."

"I'm Head Witch of Luz. The Class doesn't put me up to anything. I manage myself, *thank you*."

"You still report back to them, though," I mumble. Then I raise my eyebrows and try a new tactic. "Look, I think we can agree this isn't going to work out. And that's not going to look bad on *me*. I'm not Head Witch of Luz. That's your job, which means the mentee is your fucking problem."

"You're making this a bigger deal than it is." Ninigone takes a deep breath that wrinkles her arched nose. "Take her home, let her get settled in, *sober up a bit,* then give her a tour of Luz. Show her how the city works, where she can find what she needs. Guide the witchling with some care and, if I may be so bold, *kindness*. You can start by not floating like that. It's very threatening."

I'm still hovering a foot above Esclamonde. The loose fabric of my velvet peach robe collects around me like soft wings. My nose curls like Ninigone's, my lips pinch into a frown.

Luz's square, brightly painted homes sit in silence nearby. No one is awake early enough to see my little tantrum. Even if they were, I doubt anyone living in Luz's arts district would be surprised. I'm a known quantity after four years in the city—especially in the wide tree-lined streets where other Luzians live a similarly loud and feckless lifestyle.

Still, I study the dark windows of the homes in the hopes someone will wake up, bear witness to this fucking travesty, and hammer home the point to Ninigone that I'm not cut out for this.

Nothing.

With a sigh, I open my hands toward the Head Witch. "I've never done this before. Shouldn't she at least be a *little* intimidated by me?"

"Esclamonde traveled *alone* from Antigone. She arrived thirty minutes ago. Don't you think she's had a hard enough time?"

I snort. "What? Are there bandits in Septegeur and Rhotidom now? The last time I traveled between Luz and Antigone, it was like an extended vacation." I glance at Esclamonde, clarifying, "I met *a lot* of friendly gentlemen."

The joke doesn't land. The witchling adjusts her red cloak with a twitch of her hand. "I'm twenty."

"*She's twenty!*" Ninigone reiterates with a hiss.

I throw my hands into the air. "Oh, my moons, it's a *child.*"

Though first repulsed, I realize the witchling's age could be an excuse.

Luz is home to all five stripes of nymphs: dryads, okeanids, oreads, hesperides, and naiads. Most retain elemental powers from the homelands where they were born, tied to the forests, oceans, rivers, volcanic cones, and stretching plains... but there's one thing all nymphs have in common.

They want to have fun. The not-for-children kind of fun.

I lower myself back onto my feet, clear my throat, and straighten the wild white hairs near my temple. "I live in a *warren*. I can't bring Esteban back to an adult warren with me." I study Esclamonde's wide black pupils. "Do you know *anything* about warrens? Or nymphs?"

She nods. Her voice is small as a sparrow. "Warrens are where nymphs live together. I know a good amount about all five types of nymphs. There were fourteen in my secondary school."

I try not to scoff. "Wow, a full baker's dozen."

A set of wooden shutters clack against a squat home close by. I whip my head to see if I know the being who opens their window to the breaking dawn; unfortunately, the okeanid is a stranger.

She cranes her head over a row of potted flowers. Her cool dark-brown skin is ragged and aged, but her turquoise eyes catch the light and shine like jewels.

I glance at Esclamonde, who studies the nymph like she's never seen an okeanid before.

At her side, Ninigone brandishes a bland political smile at me. She takes the momentary distraction to back away.

As she retreats, Ninigone uses whispering magic to murmur smoothly in my ear, "You'll do wonderfully as a mentor, Helisent. It's time you played nicely with other wielders."

She turns around and heads south along the Septima River, which cuts through the city from the northwest. She studies the calm crystal waters as the long tail of her cloak catches in the wind.

Just so she doesn't think she's gotten the better of me, I

project my voice into her ear through the same form of whispering magic. "You have a piece of food caught in your teeth."

It's not true, but not all magic has to be great. It just has to be cunning.

I turn back around to see Esclamonde and the okeanid staring at one another in a wordless standoff.

The okeanid looks at me. "New witchling, then?"

I nod.

With a grunt, the okeanid jerks her chin toward Esclamonde. "Ever seen eyes like these close up? You can hear the ocean's echo. Come here. I need a light spell. My oil lamps are low. We can barter."

Esclamonde looks to the ground. "I'm a mentee. I'm not qualified to barter yet."

The okeanid snorts. "You don't need a permit to barter, kid. Just something worth trading. Do you know how far from the ocean we are? My magic hasn't followed me here from Hypnos. A closer look at these eyes is all I have to offer." She gives up on the mentee, looking at me next. "What about you? Let's barter."

I float into the air and approach the window with my signature smile. "I can give you all the light you need, dear nymph. But I've seen okeanid eyes before. What spirits are you willing to barter?"

The okeanid ducks back into her house. The lamps inside haven't been turned on—I can't tell if she's out of magical oil or if it's too early for lights.

After a shuffle of wooden furniture and groaning floorboards, she steps back into view in the window frame and squints at a bottle in her hand. "It's some kind of liquor. I'm not sure how much is left."

The okeanid hands me the bottle, then holds up an empty glass cylinder the size of her hand.

Inside the cylinder, a coiled wire runs from one end to the next. The shimmering copper helps store amorphous magic, called dove. Dove, often used to barter by wielders like me, can be used for just about anything—magical oil for lamps is a common request.

I raise the brown bottle of liquor. It's only half-full, but a single cylinder of dove isn't worth much more.

I reach out and tap the rounded end of the glass cylinder. At my touch, golden light fills the glass piece, catching on the wire inside and pooling like rich liquid.

The okeanid winces from the light, then she turns to set the cylinder down. Out of view, it fills her ruddy kitchen with honeyed hues.

"You didn't have to give that much dove." The okeanid sets her burly arms on the window frame and folds them. "I only had enough to barter for what's left of the liquor."

I take a long swig of the sweet brandy and drift back to the ground near Esclamonde. "We're squared."

With a yawn, the nymph looks back at Esclamonde. "Welcome to Luz, little witchling. What are you so nervous about? Ninigone might spin all this bullshit about rules, but there are only two things a new wielder needs to know in Luz—and I'm sure you're already aware of one of them."

Esclamonde nervously looks at me. Eventually, she shakes her head.

"When in doubt, do as the nymphs do." The okeanid lowers her chin. "And *always* step lightly on the triplemoon."

Esclamonde nods. "Always do as the nymphs do, and always walk lightly on the triplemoon. Got it."

The okeanid's turquoise eyes twinkle like the pale oceans in Hypnos. Cast against the midnight hue of her skin, it's difficult to look away—even for me. Esclamonde doesn't stand a chance. The mentee's mouth falls open as she locks eyes with the nymph; the nymph bears a sultry smile as she drinks the witchling's fleeting desita.

The witchling is too young and inexperienced to even register the exchange.

"Esclamonde." I clap my hands, jarring her from the trance. "Let's go. Say goodbye to the okeanid."

Esclamonde chirps a goodbye, which the nymph returns with a wink.

I guide us east toward my warren as the sun rises. We walk slowly; she sticks close to my side, bumping into my shoulder as she stares around with her neck tilted back.

Asymmetrical houses stacked at odd angles fill the residential arts district. Though painted brightly and covered with ornaments, the houses don't look particularly stable.

One of the few things wielders and wolves have in common is how leery we are of nymph construction. Wielders built Antigone by weaving iron between the stone pillars that crane skyward, while the wolves pulled slabs of marble from Velm to carve impenetrable cities.

The nymphs tend to settle for whatever resources are within reaching distance.

"Miss Helisent," Esclamonde murmurs, "I feel a little..."

She feels the haze that comes after desita.

The fourteen nymphs she grew up with must not have clued her in to the workings of desita. It's a feeling brewed between two or more people, a type of collective well-being that is tangible enough for the demigods and their nymphs to feel. To *consume*.

Desita, that collective feeling of joy and bliss, animates the demigods; and what gives the demigods life is then given new animation through the elemental powers of the nymphs.

It is a living system that connects the nymphs to their demigods.

Those are the barest basics. And if Esclamonde doesn't know them, then it means she likely spent most of her life in Antigone's upper tiers. Far from the ground. From the nymphs. From their demigods.

My gut sinks as I realize just how far behind the witchling is. "What—did you grow up in Antigone and *never* leave?"

Esclamonde's voice lowers. "I don't like ground-walking, so I never went to any of the festivals in Septegeur."

"Good to know." *I'm going to kill Ninigone.* "What you just felt is called desita."

"I know what desita is—or I've heard of it." The witchling chatters like a scholar in the making. "It's what the demigods take from the nymphs that live in their territory. They come to festivals to take desita from all who attend—wielders and wolves, too."

"They aren't *taking* desita." I roll my eyes at her phrasing— she must be straight from Antigone, after all. "The nymphs organize festivals to *offer* desita to the demigods. The bigger the group, the better the desita.

"Septegeur is a forest, so it's home to dryads and their dryad demigods. I think there are three. You should keep an eye out for them the next time you go back—the demigods are the real reason Antigone is bountiful. Wielders can build all we want, but without the demigods, the earth suffers. And what good is a city built in a dead world?"

Esclamonde's boots shuffle to a stop on the dirt road. She bites her lip and glances back in the direction of the okeanid's home.

She points to the marigold house, dumbfounded. "My— bliss? *My* desita? I didn't think wielders could feel it..."

"We feel it. You had never seen eyes like the okeanid's before. Your wonder was desita, and she took a bit. It gives them energy. Don't let it scare you." I nod. "The nymphs aren't like us. They put a high value on joy. And the haze will go away in a minute. Desita exchanges always give wielders a little hangover."

Esclamonde pulls a notepad from her bottomless bag and jots down a few lines.

At the same time, I empty the bottle of liquor with a sigh. "And about the ground-walking—I know you don't like it, but wielders don't hover in Luz. We walk like the nymphs and wolves. The only exceptions are for children and adults over one hundred years—and even they use a lilith instead of free-floating. Did you bring one?"

The witchling reaches into her bottomless bag. She pulls out a ratty sitting cushion, which barely squeezes from the bag's narrow opening. The square lilith's white fabric is faded, the red stitching half pulled loose.

Esclamonde smiles as she shows off the shitty lilith. It floats in the air at her hip, as though waiting for her to take a seat. "My grandmother made it when..."

She trails off as I guide us onto the largest street in Luz's northern district, lilith following. Alleys branch out from the wide path, leading like tributaries further into the city. Mature trees line the road, disappearing into the apartments and shops around them. Some trunks act as load-bearing pillars before poking through the roof to offer shade.

As we amble, shutters clack open and wake the canaries. Soon, the birds' high-pitched songs echo through the quiet street. A few shops have already opened their doors. One baker slaps fresh bread onto a cart, while a florist two doors down mists her seedlings.

I stop so Esclamonde can take in the scene.

I can't remember my first time in Luz. What it felt like.

I was already out of wonder by then.

Still, I try. "Pretty different than Antigone, huh?"

She doesn't respond, and I realize she's not focused on the scent of the bread or the birdsong above. Her eyes glitter as she watches a trio of wolves exit a building on the other side of the street.

She takes a subtle step behind me.

I study the trio of tall brawny women, but don't find anything suspicious about the wolves. Each has their blue-black hair slicked back into a modest bun, and each wears three golden torcs—two around their upper arms and one around their necks. One even has loose uncurled bottoms to her harem pants—a style unique to Luzian wolves.

I crane my head toward Esclamonde and whisper, "So you had fourteen nymphs at your school. And how many wolves?"

Her body tenses, causing her knees to hike up toward her chest as her feet lift from the ground. She clasps my arm tightly as she involuntarily hovers into a compacted shape.

"I'll take that as zero." I pause as the wolves head in the opposite direction as us, hoping Esclamonde will calm down. They don't spare a glance in our direction, chatting happily. "But you *have* seen a wolf before, right?"

"Of course, I've seen a wolf before. It was a drawing. Very realistic. I found a book—"

"That doesn't count." I rub my temples with mounting frustration. "Okay, look, what the fuck are you doing in Luz if you're not much of a ground-walker and you're terrified of wolves?"

Part of me wonders if the Class is testing me.

They've kept quiet about my existence since I left Antigone six years ago and Alita four years ago. Suspiciously quiet.

Esclamonde scoots her butt onto her square lilith, tucking her legs under her and letting her red cloak slip behind her. *Wonderful.* She floats at my side as I continue toward the warren.

I try to summon the kindness Ninigone suggested before. "Here's the thing, Esteban—there are just as many wolves in Luz as there are wielders. You can't shit your skirt every time you see one. It's offensive. The War Years ended before your grandmother made her lilith. I know they still talk about Bloody Betty and all that other bullshit in Antigone, but the rest of the world has moved on. Okay?"

As more windows open to the morning, the pastel canaries common to Luz line up along the terraces. They chirp and hop for food, which many residents oblige by tossing out scraps.

Nymphs and wielders and wolves lean from their windows to greet their neighbors, chatting about strange dreams, bartering for breakfast, and predicting the day's weather.

As Esclamonde stares around, her apprehension fades into curiosity.

She shouldn't be sitting on the lilith, but I let it slide. She's certainly a nervous type.

I go on, "And you didn't answer my question. Why come to Luz if you're terrified of wolves and ground-walking?"

Esclamonde tucks her choppy white hair behind her ears. "Because you're Helisent West of Jaws. You're the most powerful witch in Mieira. My mother said so."

I narrow my eyes and study her features. I think back to the years I spent in Antigone and try to assign her features to a family line. She has the arched curved nose and wide eyes all wielders share, but her face is narrower than most.

I come up short. "What's your full name, witchling?"

"Esclamonde Black Rock Antigone."

I try to remember if I knew anyone from the Black Rock neighborhood in Antigone. It was a residential area for traditional wielders who could trace their lineages back to heroic acts from the War Years. Of the Class's six members, three grew up in Black Rock.

At least that explains her fear of wolves.

I lower my voice again. "Here, I'm just Helisent. No West of Jaws. No 'most powerful' of anything. Got it?"

Esclamonde's face tenses. "But you're the—"

"The nymphs place value on joy, on desita, not power. Not intimidation—they're not like the Class, Esclamonde. And I'm like a nymph at heart. All I want from life is a little bit of bliss."

I recite the mantra in my head so often that it sounds weird being spoken aloud. Somehow, it's less comforting.

Finally, my building comes into view. "We're almost to the warren."

As the arts neighborhood bleeds into the market district, the modular wooden homes give way to cobbled, three-story buildings. Arched windows encircle the cobbled edifice where I live in an apartment with seven others. Though less colorful than the rest of the street, and certainly colder, little noise escapes the walls.

I point to the uppermost archway, which is painted peach like my robe. Drooping plants hang from the ledge, and white canary poop dots the painted stone.

"That's home." I grab the witching's wrist before she mistakes it as an invitation to float up. "We take the stairs."

The foyer is frigid and dim in the early morning. Already, a ruckus echoes from the five apartments inside. The witchling hesitates at each doorway, as though she's never heard a lover's quarrel or the high-pitched squeals that accompany a cold bath.

Her face tightens as we reach the landing on the top floor. The sound of sleepy moaning drifts from the seam beneath the door.

Esclamonde stares at me, face tense.

"I told Ninigone I lived in an *adult* warren..." I roll my eyes. "Look, I don't remember what it was like to be twenty, so you'll have to remind me if we're doing something that makes you uncomfortable. There are eight of us. Six nymphs, two wielders. Remember, the nymphs will prioritize your well-being with the same attention and care as their own. If I'm not around, just hint that something displeases you and they'll probably come up with five solutions. Okay?"

Esclamonde moves her gaze to the door handle. "And the other wielder?"

"Oh, his name's Pen. He's from Alita. He's basically a nymph."

She nods. "Okay."

I open the door and then slip aside, quickly shutting it behind me to block the mentee's view.

Like all other warrens, the only walled room in the apartment is the bathroom. The open rectangular space is divided by stacked plants, which crane toward the four massive windows where a few canaries lurk in search of breakfast.

A pile of mats, pillows, and blankets is laid out before the largest window in the center of the room. Toward one end, slack hands and feet poke out from the blankets, twitching now and then; I estimate at least four nymphs lay sound asleep beneath.

The other three are easier to pick out.

Onesimos lays on top of the covers, touching himself as he stares at Zopyros and Pen. Zopyros sits up as though she's just woken, blanket pooling in her lap to expose her freckled pale skin. Pen's wiry white hair pokes out from the blanket's edge as he kisses and nuzzles her breasts. One of his square hands reaches up to caress her back.

Onesimos's expression lightens when he notices me. "Good morning, darling witch."

I clear my throat to get their attention, but all I receive are lazy, invitational smiles from the trio.

Wishing I could join, I stare at the ceiling and break the news instead. "Look, you're all going to hate me, but there's a terrified witchling outside. Ninigone says it's time for me to become a mentor."

The nymphs don't look too surprised. Pen, on the other hand, lifts himself onto all fours and sits back, staring at me as though he's about to scream the word *no*.

I get the worst of it out before he can. "She's only twenty, so... get dressed. And she's from Antigone."

Zopyros, a hesperide, and Onesimos, an oread, look prepared to receive the witchling. Both wear faint smiles, eyes glittering as they stare at the front door behind me.

Pen, on the other hand, crosses his arms. The blankets are pulled back and collected around his ankles; aside from a string necklace, he's naked. "Ninigone made *you* a mentor?

You're a city sponsor. This is way beneath you. How long is the witchling staying?"

I throw my hands up. "These are questions for the ether, Pen. Please just put your cock away so she can come inside and take a bath."

I lean back to open the door and angle my head outside. Esclamonde holds her shoulders as though afraid of losing an arm to the hallway's cool shadows.

I tell her, "You can set your bag down and take a bath. I'm sure you need one. Ready?"

Her eyes widen. "Are you sure that—"

"Yes." I have no idea what she was going to say, but life in Luz moves fast, and she's already behind. I grab the sleeve of her red cloak and guide her inside.

Onesimos smiles and waves from the center of the bed mats. "Welcome, witchling. I'm Onesimos Eupheme Jaws."

While okeanids have dark-brown skin that's cold as winter on the water, oreads like Onesimos have warm chicory-brown skin. His tight curls are the color of burned vermillion, just like his vibrant pupils. His affectatious grin tends to hide their beauty.

Zopyros leans against him. Side by side with Onesimos, her skin looks like speckled eggshells. "Hello, witchling. I'm Zopyros Left Hand Gamma." She points at the door at the far end of the room. "The bathroom is there. Helisent can warm the water if you like. I always ask her to warm mine in the mornings. Aren't baths such a wonderful way to greet the sun?"

Esclamonde gulps audibly as she turns for the bathroom.

Though Onesimos and Pen are covered, Zopyros's breasts remain bared. Only thin wisps of her dark brown hair, dangling to her waist, cover her pink nipples.

"Okay." Esclamonde looks back at the bed mats with every other step. Her red robe catches on the doorframe and she rips it toward her before shutting the door.

A moment later, a shaking breath echoes into the main

room. It's followed by a quick sob, then the sound of running water.

With the stuffy witchling out of sight, Pen extracts himself from the bed mats. His half-hard cock sways with each step as he heads toward the kitchen and pours himself a glass of water.

I stare after him, eager to commiserate about the witchling.

He leans against the counter, takes a long swig, and looks at me. Instead, he says, "Someone's trading information about Oko at Solace. Heard a naiad bring it up last night."

I look at the bathroom door, then back to Pen, then back to the bathroom door.

Fuck.

Fuck, fuck, fuck.

CHAPTER 2

AN AMAZING PERSONALITY

SAMSON

My son,
The greatest action is often inaction; your people will remember all you
never said. Your face is speaking to them, Samson. Your body. Your ala.
Words are nothing. They will not defend against Night. They certainly
did nothing against the wielders.

I stare at the overstuffed satchel set before the door.

My gut drops before my mind catches up to the most probable conclusion.

He's leaving. Probably for good.

I rub the sleep from my face and search the halls for Rex. I can't see or hear him, but his scent drifts from the estate's farthest guest bedroom. I can tell by the scent's density that he's been there since he woke up; only a faint trail of his ala runs from my bedroom to his.

The blue rucksack before the door is meticulously packed, down to its shined buckles and leather straps. When Rex arrived at the Luzian Estate last week, I thought the bag's bulging sides meant he'd stay longer than a few days.

I rehearse a few lighthearted phrases to beg him to stay without actually sounding like I'm begging him to stay.

Look, I know I'm running out of freedom, but I'd like to enjoy my last months with you.

It sounds too needy.

I rephrase. *Rex, what if we just let things be as they are? Just for as long as we can?*

It's too vague.

I clear my throat and take a deep breath. It does little to calm the deepening rut in my stomach.

Here's the truth. *Rex, I'm not prepared for what happens in Silent City, and you're the only being that makes me think I'll ever fill Imperatriz's shadow.*

I roll my shoulders and prepare to face Rex when I hear his feet against the marble floors. Like with most housing in Velm, the Luzian Estate is kept minimal. Sounds reverberate; alas linger and intensify.

I listen closely.

Someday, I'll think back on this time when we could afford the delusion of being young lovers like everyone else in Luz.

Rex steps into the foyer with a sigh. Similar to his tidy satchel, his harem parents are neatly rolled at the ankles, and his long navy tunic smells of fresh cedar soap. Golden torcs hug his biceps, along with a third at the base of his neck. They twinkle as though newly shined.

His blue-black hair is slicked back into a tight ponytail, then looped to conceal its length.

Sneaking out of my bed at dawn is one thing, but tying his hair back is another.

Every rehearsed thought splinters in my mind and shatters like glass.

I sound just as desperate as I feel. "We'll part as friends, then?"

Rex clears his throat, reaching back to feel at his tight bun. "You smelled my hair last night, didn't you?"

"I didn't realize it would be the last time."

Rex heads to the door and reaches for his satchel. With a few brusque movements, he loops his arms through its straps and adjusts its weight on his back.

He sighs and licks his full lips. I try not to stare at his features, try not to feel like they're a part of my own face. "Samson, we've had our fun. Seven years of it, if I'm counting correctly."

"Nine years, if you count our first summer in Mort." I've never considered myself a petty wolf, but I guess there's always time to learn more about myself. A good leader should be honest about his faults—I've found it usually involves learning something the hard way. I am Samson 714 Afador. I am the imminent Male Alpha of Velm. "And I can't believe you're doing this."

Normally, Rex's fixated stare and the blue hue of his black eyes comfort me. Seeing his precise mind at work behind his calm focused features reminds me that I'm capable of the same degree of self-control and insight.

This morning, it feels more like an act of war.

Not only has Rex tied up his hair to lessen the potency of his ala, but now he wants to manage a final goodbye with the same casualty as our earlier partings.

His words, at least, are weighed. "When Night returns, you'll be marched into Silent City and married to Brutatalika or Menemone. I'll be married shortly after. What else do we need to hash out here, Samson? We both know what Velm expects from us."

He's right.

And still...

I glance at the shined marble walls and feel the cold chill of the stone creep into me. Despite the vibrant and bustling city outside, I feel like I'm standing in a tomb.

For a long moment, neither of us speaks.

Finally, Rex says, "I shouldn't have tied up my hair. I just don't want this to be any harder than it already is."

I shrug. Even if I won't have one last intimate scent, I have the remnants of his ala tangled in my sheets. With no visitors expected in the coming weeks, I'll at least have his ghost for the rest of my time in Luz.

I cling to this and let Rex decide when my silence is enough.

With a heavy sigh, he turns and slides the door open. He stares into the narrow courtyard. Lily pads float in a marble basin filled with water, surrounded by ripe grass. It's a far cry from the madness of the city waiting beyond the shoulder-high marble wall.

Luz's cacophony floats over to us.

Echoes of laughter and the hustle of wooden carts skitter through the empty halls behind me. The scents of leaves, freshly baked pies, burning peat, and the musk of healthy bodies are close behind.

Rex looks back over his shoulder. The street's noise fades his question. "Do you know of a place called Soulless?"

"Soulless? No."

"It's on the outskirts of the city, near the watermills and magical processors. It's one of the taverns where wielder and nymph bounty hunters trade information. Yesterday, I had a drink with Ferol nearby. I overheard a naiad bring up a witch named Oko. They were talking about trading what they knew about her at Soulless."

I stare at his profile while my mind chases his words.

Oko.

"Did Ferol notice?" I ask.

Rex flinches, as though offended that I'd insinuate he told Ferol about my interest in Oko. "No. I said nothing." Then he clears his throat. "Goodbye, Samson."

I don't say goodbye.

I watch him step into the courtyard, then reach back and

slide the paneled door shut to seal me inside the frigid marble walls.

It's the only revenge I'll ever level against him—the withholding of that final goodbye.

It won't feel like much at first.

But I know better than anyone how the years will compound that wordlessness into something more poisonous than a seething.

I cry where I stand, then wipe my face clean.

That's the worst thing about the marble walls common to wolves: even a whisper echoes.

I meditate in the interior garden, forgo the meditation for chain-smoking, then make my breakfast. I cry before I eat, and then again after. At least I'm full.

It's not all Rex.

There are a lot of marble things that I can't handle.

By midday, I'm calm again.

I pass the basin of water in the courtyard on my way to the street.

When wolves, wielders, and nymphs built Luz over two centuries ago, my people stuck to the southern outskirts, close to the plains of Gamma, which lead into the towering mountains of Velm.

The first marble buildings erected in Luz have since been converted into schools and housing. Aside from the private estates shared by Velm's Alphas, the rest of the neighborhood's constructions are decidedly Luzian: cobbled stone, wrought iron, and brightly painted wood.

Some like to say Luz was where peace was born between Mieira, land of nymphs and wielders, and Velm, land of wolves.

But that peace quickly took a hedonistic turn. (Some like to say that's how Luz's peace has survived so long.)

I head east from the estate. I follow a marble irrigation canal eastward, toward the markets. I don't know where Soulless is, but the watermills are easy enough to find.

I stare at the trickle of crystalline waters, attempting to angle my face away from the wolves, wielders, and nymphs who hustle by on the street. As one of the most diverse cities in Mieira, I don't often stick out—but wolves who notice me offer at least a nod of respect or a polite smile.

Before I cross a single street, four wolves acknowledge my passing.

My father, the Male Alpha of Velm, has a more commanding ala. As the *Kulapsifang*, or inborn Alpha of my generation, my scent is almost just as noticeable to passers-by.

I light the cigarette I rolled in the estate. The smoke and scent help hide my face and ala. While heading to a seedy tavern in search of information from a bounty hunter isn't strictly forbidden for Velm's upper echelon, I'm running parallel to a line that shouldn't be crossed.

Wolves don't bounty hunt like wielders and nymphs.

Only war bands are permitted to track perpetrators. And when they find them, regional pack leaders decide on a punishment. Eventually, though, that authority tracks back to Bellator. To Velm. To my father and my future throne.

I pause as a wolf steps in front of my path.

His ala wafts over me as I study his wide, pleasant face. Though his scent is powerful, at least past its 400th generation, his upper arms and neck are free of golden torcs. His shoulder-length hair is untied and messy. Rather than navy blue, he wears long white layers.

An unnumbered wolf.

My mind switches to my arms and neck where my own torcs hold me lightly.

I study the wolf's measured smile as I exhale a plume of smoke.

I never know how to relate to outsiders.

"Samson 714 Afador!" The wolf angles his body to subtly block the pedestrians around us.

To his left stands a tall hesperide. Her light-brown skin is speckled with pale marks, like the birch trees that crane near riversides. Though most nymphs and wielders stand at the chest of a wolf, she reaches past my shoulders.

"Hello, good morning—are the demigods smiling upon you today?" The unnumbered wolf's smile expands, as though expecting a genuine response from me.

As a representative of Velm, and the heir to its leadership as the Kulapsifang, I hear unsolicited opinions and advice almost daily. My interactions range a dizzying spectrum. Last week, an okeanid far from home asked to touch my hair. The week before, a wolf from Gamma approached me about reforming a war band.

There are four responses that work on any occasion.

Today, I pick my favorite. "You look healthy."

The unnumbered wolf raises his eyebrows. "What a response. Thank you. I suppose I do look healthy. My name is Gautselin Mort."

Without a generational number (714) or a family line (Afador) to cite, unnumbered wolves name themselves like the nymphs and wielders: after the neighborhood or region where they were born.

He gestures to his companion. "This is Chariovalda South of Gamma."

I turn toward the hesperide. She smiles with twinkling white teeth. "Hello, Samson 714 Afador." She tilts her head, which sends her bejeweled necklaces shifting loudly into new positions. They twinkle like her hazel eyes.

"You also look healthy." I turn back to Gautselin Mort and

fish for a polite way to ask what the fuck he wants. "Have the demigods smiled upon you today?"

"They smile upon me each morning." Though his words are vague, his continued smile is genuine.

Gautselin gestures toward an open plaza nearby; the temple district. Massive stone slabs frame an open space in the triangle where the Irme and Septima Rivers meet to form the Mieira River. It was built for the demigods to observe the city and drink in desita at their leisure. Almost the entire city can pack into the vast space, which is outfitted with bare marble columns that stretch toward the clear sky.

Luz is a common stopover for hesperide demigods that come from the plains of Gamma, for dryad demigods that come from the forests of Septegeur and Rhotidom, and for naiad demigods that crawl out of the Septima, Irme, and Mieira Rivers.

I inhale a deep breath in search of the hypnotic ala of a demigod, but can't find one.

Gautselin says, "A hesperide demigod is on the way from Gamma now. It's bringing a queen."

That explains the group of nymphs frantically sweeping the worn stones. Only the imminent arrival of a demigod, especially one with a queen or king in tow, can spur such frantic work from a nymph.

Chariovalda tilts her head again as she studies the temple district. "The hesperide demigod and its queen will bring a great bounty. I can feel both already. This queen is young; her fields bore grains through the rainy season. She will rule for at least a decade."

The nymph raises a hand and wiggles her fingers toward me. The familiar fragrances of Gamma's plains lift from her fingernails in a magical gust: foxglove, wheat, barley, nitrogen-heavy soil, fetid compost, dry fibers.

Though not a demigod or a Gammic Queen, Chariovalda

has access to some of their elemental powers. To a lesser degree, her magic can also influence the wind and crops.

I make a mental note to study the nymphs more.

The Male and Female Alphas rule Velm; the Class rules wielders. But nymph magic and power are bound to geography and the whims of their demigods. A nymph's magic is tied to the environment where they were born, which means Chariovalda will lose her power if she wanders too far from Gamma.

Still, I'm not sure how a demigod chooses a queen or a king. All I know is that demigods pluck their leaders like fruits from groves then grant them special powers and rites tied to the land. They take them on a tour of neighboring cities to show the queens and kings off, to share their bounty, and then deposit them where they're needed most.

As Chariovalda mentioned, queens and kings perform incredible natural feats, like churning out grains during the rainy season.

Delightful as it is, it has nothing to do with me.

I turn my gaze back to Gautselin. "May you enjoy the bounty of the hesperide demigod and Gamma's latest queen."

He doesn't shift out of my path. "I'm here to offer my bounty to *you*, Samson 714 Afador." *Ah, there is it.* "Chariovalda and I run a pleasure house called Coil. It's located near the watermills. Think: red curtains and mirrors full of starlight. Right now, four unnumbered wolves work there."

I train my face in neutrality.

Even sharing a conversation with an unnumbered wolf grates at me. First, there's suspicion; wolves aren't born unnumbered. Why did Gautselin abandon his pack, his family, and his people to live untethered to the wolves? He may be a criminal.

Second, there's wariness; what does he want from me—to be associated with the Kulapsifang, to have a friend close to the Alphas, to have some tie to his people? Just like I can offer no protection or justice to an unnumbered wolf, I also can't offer them a boon.

Lastly, there's reputation.

As I prepare to become Alpha as the Kulapsifang, I owe my people service. Unnumbered wolves, with no pack, no rank, and no family name, don't count. Unless one blocks my path, I don't acknowledge them.

Gautselin inches closer to me.

I study the gleam of the blue-black irises rimming his pupils. The faint lines of his cream-colored skin. My eyes flash to his neck and his bulging jugular.

"We would be honored if you visited Coil. I'm sure the thought of spending the night with an unnumbered wolf isn't appealing." Gaustelin scrunches his nose as though commiserating. "But we have the finest professionals from across Mieira —wielders and nymphs galore."

I look from the unnumbered wolf to Chariovalda.

Her smile is just as ardent and hopeful as his.

Gautselin takes a quick step away from me, clasping his hands behind his back. "I've kept you long enough. Enjoy your day, Samson 714 Afador. And please consider visiting Coil if you're ever in need of a warm body, a listening ear, or a goblet of liquor."

I step past the pair without another word.

Offers from pleasure houses aren't uncommon, though I've yet to take anyone up. With less than a year of freedom left, a warm body and a listening ear have rarely sounded better. A goblet of liquor, too.

At the last second, something else comes to mind.

I turn back to Gautselin and Chariovalda. "You said Coil is near the watermills. Do you know of a place called Soulless? I'm headed there now."

Gautselin slides his eyes to Chariovalda, then back to me. He offers a casual shrug. "Sure, Coil is near Soulless. We can take you now if you'd like to go. They're on the opposite side of Luz."

I nod. "I would appreciate it."

Chariovalda steps between Gautselin and me as we take off, which I also appreciate. It lessens the impression for passing wolves that I'm conspiring with an unnumbered wolf. Even though I am.

As we walk, Chariovalda wraps a hand around Gautselin's wrist.

With every step, my eyes twitch in their direction and zero in on the light grip of her speckled skin against Gautselin's pale wrist.

He barely seems to notice the touch.

The journey takes a while.

Each time a wolf approaches to greet me, offering something basic like a drink or food, or to make a request for me to pass on to the city leaders, Gautselin shuffles away with Chariovalda. The pair linger close by until the numbered wolves move on. If it bothers them to be wayward outcasts, they don't mention it.

By the time we near the magical processors that precede the watermills, night has fallen. In the dimming light, I can hear and feel the deep infrasound of magic as it toils underground. Powerful wielders offer amorphous dove, which is distributed through subterraneous channels throughout the city for infrastructural needs: running water, street cleaning, construction, trash disposal, storage.

Chariovalda doesn't notice, but, like me, Gautselin continues to glance in the direction where the unsettling infrasound hums.

On the eastern edge of Luz's market district, strings of lamps with magical oil crisscross the narrow streets, casting the dark wooden buildings with golden light. Though none of the structures look fit to last a century, they've already survived two. The planked walls smell of warm earth and spices from the merchant stalls, which sit packed away for the night.

By the time Chariovalda and Gautselin deposit me at Soulless, I haven't thought of Rex in an hour. The pair leave with a goodbye and I watch them go, waiting for the nymph's small hand to encircle his wrist again.

I take a deep breath and turn back toward the bar. I roll another cigarette and light it as I study Soulless from the doorless entrance.

The lights hanging from the rafters flicker, as though running low on magical oil. Nymphs and wielders sit crammed together at the long bar. Puddles of booze and fallen shoes litter the floor at their feet. Before the bar, wooden chairs and tables dot the floor in disorganized clusters. I can't tell the informants from the bounty hunters—or figure out who's just a regular.

No one notices me enter.

I inhale deeply in search of a naiad's ala.

I find a pair of the nymphs huddled together at a table. Their flat light-brown hair pools on the table. Like okeanids, their elemental powers relate to water. The freshwater nymphs have similarly blue eyes, but their skin is almost as alabaster as mine.

I suck down the rest of my cigarette, then head over.

"Excuse me." I squat on my haunches so I'm not towering over the pair. "I'm looking for information about a witch named Oko. Do you know who I could speak with?"

The younger naiad looks away. The elder sucks on her teeth, then she jerks her chin toward the opposite end of the bar. "You're too late. Already traded what I know about Oko— and looks like someone's already bartering for the information."

I follow the naiad's gaze to where a trio barters in the corner.

A lean warlock with an emerald cape throws his hands out as he speaks with a witch. The witch wears an ostentatious velvet peach-colored robe. Behind the swaying robe lingers a young witchling in a red cape.

The witchling locks eyes with me.

She presses her back against the wall.

My attention immediately focuses on her physical signs; her heart rate increases, while her sickly-sweet ala grows in potency. Both are signs of fear. As I approach the group, I try to lessen my bearing and presence.

It rarely works.

I'm second in power only to my father, Clearbold 554 Leofsige.

The witchling grabs a handful of the witch's peach robe, but the witch swats her hand away without sparing a look from the warlock. Her peach robe floats into the air, as though she's lost track of her magic.

She and the warlock don't notice me until I'm a foot away.

By then, the witchling's knees have risen toward her chest. Her compacted body lifts from the ground. I can't remember the last time I saw a wielder get so nervous that they started hovering. I chalk it up to her young age and my terrifying frame.

The warlock offers me a smile when he registers my presence. "Welcome, friend. Would you like—"

"No!" The peach-robed witch spares a livid glance in my direction. She steps between me and the warlock, as though she could block me from view. "We're fucking bartering right now, Itzifone. Look, I'll—"

"How many times will I waste my information on you, Helisent?" The warlock bears his palms to her. "You aren't the only being in this world who's looking for Oko."

At least I know I've found the right informant.

"So?" The witch's voice raises to a screech. "You're going to trade it to fucking Clearbold's son?" She whips her head toward me, baring her teeth. "Hello, Samson 700-something Afador. Can't you see I'm a little fucking busy right now? Look —you're scaring the witchling. She'll be up in the rafters any second now. Why don't you have a seat and wait your fucking turn?"

It's not my first time dealing with a hysterical wielder.

I speak in a neutral tone. "It is for the warlock to decide whether or not to barter with me."

I look at the witchling, who's a few feet out of arm's reach above. I wonder where she's from—at least as far north as Antigone, possibly even Metamor.

I try for a smile as I study her wide golden eyes. "There's no reason for my presence to frighten you, young witch. My name is Samson 714 Afador. I'm the Kulapsifang of Velm—"

"She's not scared of you *specifically*; she's scared of all of you *in general*. Leave her alone." The witch bares her teeth at me again then looks up at the witchling. "What did I tell you? Get out your lilith if you're going to start hovering. Try to look dignified!"

Ah, the witch is a mentor.

I spare another glance at the mentee. Her jaw clenches as she reaches for her bottomless bag and shoves her hand inside without taking her eyes off me.

Itzifone raises his eyebrows with an optimistic grin. "What do you have to offer me, Samson? Let's barter."

Rather than interrupt again, the peach-robed witch turns. Her features strain as she looks from me to the warlock. Like all wielders, she has large eyes and a narrow nose, but her face is wider than most. Her round cheeks give her a younger appearance, but I can tell by her ala that she's at least thirty years old.

What does she want with Oko?

I tell the warlock, "I'm interested in hearing what type of

information you have on Oko. I'd like to find her to have a conversation face-to-face."

I don't give up anything more than that. I've barely put the pieces together enough to know what I should ask Oko if I manage to find her.

The warlock nods. "Interesting. Unfortunately, I can't provide hints about what information I have. I can only barter with you for the information provided by a naiad who ran into Oko near Perpetua. Now, what do you have to offer me?"

I hadn't prepared an offer; I went from Rex leaving me to being escorted around the city by an unnumbered wolf and a hesperide.

I clear my throat. "What interests you?"

The warlock doesn't skip a beat. "I'd like to spend a week in that estate of yours."

I raise my eyebrows. "Which estate?"

Please say Luzian.

"Esclamonde, did you hear that?" The witch looks up at her mentee with a wild cackle. "He has so many estates that you have to be *specific* about which one you're talking about."

The warlock ignores her. "The *real* thing, of course. Bellator Palace—or I guess that's not an estate, huh? I saw it in a book once. Looks very nice. A bit *cold* with all that marble, but they say the peat in Velm never stops burning. Oh! And the furs! What do they say about the furs of Velm...?"

A wielder has never stepped foot in Bellator Palace, but I don't break the news to Itzifone. "Bellator Palace is not my home. I can't offer you hospitality there."

Itzifone nods and chews his lip. "Which palace is yours then? I thought they were all *yours*. The land, the palaces, the furs."

"They belong to the *Alphas* of Velm. As such, they belong only to my father for now. I will inherit them in time."

The warlock's face twists. "So, you can't offer me hospitality in *any* of the palaces?"

"I can offer you one week in the Luzian Estate, but we'd be sharing it."

Itzifone points to his own chest. "Not for me."

Fuck, that ended fast.

He turns his hands to point at Helisent while I wrack my brain for a better offer. "Back to you, witch. I'm decidedly unimpressed by the wolf's first offer."

She snorts. "Well, what the *fuck,* Itzifone. You just said you weren't interested in bartering with me and now you're here *begging* for another offer. Why don't *you* tell *me* what you're looking for?"

The warlock purses his lips as he thinks, glancing from me to the witch. After a long sigh, he offers me an apologetic shrug.

"I'd rather give you the information since I've been down this road with Helisent before. I mean, why keep handing someone information if they don't use it? But, in the end, Helisent has something I'd very much like, and you can't even offer me a week of solitude in the Luzian Estate. Maybe when you're Alpha of Velm, my dear wolf."

Helisent's smile is saccharine, almost threatening. Again, her peach robe collects around her, as though she's only half in control of her magic.

My jaw clenches. I look back to the warlock. "And what can the witch offer you that I cannot?"

Itzifone looks at the witch's ample bosom and says, "An amazing personality." He looks at me and shrugs again. "Sorry, friend."

I clench my jaw and try to find the right words to convey that my search for Oko isn't just personal.

Do you remember Imperatriz, the Female Alpha of Velm? Oko has information about her.

It's too accusatory.

I will give you whatever you want when I'm Alpha if you share this information with me. It's more valuable than you could understand.

Too desperate.

Oko might be the only person with information that can lead me to my mother or her remains.

That's it—

If only I could force myself to say those words.

I look from Itzifone's golden eyes to Helisent's smug grin. I even glance at the terrified witchling watching from the rafters above.

A laugh from the bar jars me.

Without another word, I turn away from the wielders and leave the bar.

CHAPTER 3
ZHUZHING-ZHAZHING
HELISENT

Honey Heli,
Come back next month. As long as you're settled in, papa can't drag you
home again. And chin up—that warlock was asking about you! The
one with the fancy buckles and the weird accent.
Mint Mili

I stare at the two-story marble building and wonder what the fuck Itzifone would want to do in the Luzian Estate.

Gray and brown streaks weave through the beige stone like smoke. Compared to the neighboring stone and wooden structures, the marble estate is otherworldly. In a bad way.

I study it from a wood-shingled roof across the street. From my angle, I can see past the estate's tall marble walls for the first time. A fir tree with shaggy bristles towers over a small pond, its surface unbroken.

Though some find Velmic minimalism austere, I find it cold and lifeless.

Even Samson 700-whatever looks like a vacant vessel as he

sits shirtless beneath the fir tree. His eyes are closed, back straight as though deeply concentrated. His harem pants bundle just below his belly button, where his dark hair trickles down.

The bulk of his muscles doesn't surprise or interest me; even lanky wolves are large enough to be threatening. Instead, I'm curious about his body hair. Unlike wolves, nymphs and wielders don't have nearly as much. Many warlocks, like my father and brothers, don't even grow facial hair.

I *should* be wondering what the fuck he wants with Oko. Or how Esclamonde is doing on her first night out with Zopyros and the other female nymphs in my warren.

Concentrate, Helisent.

I reel back with an unexpected hiccup then balance my half-empty bottle of wine in the roof's steep angles. I rise and float across the street as the foot traffic lessens with the onset of night. Though my magic lets me float discreetly, my peach robe is a bit of a calling card.

I gather the article with my magic as my boots touch down on the broad marble wall of the estate. Near the entrance, I've lost sight of Samson and the interior garden. I scurry to round toward the back, using balancing magic so I don't slip. Even if I wasn't a few drinks deep, I'm not an athletic wielder.

With a sigh, I ease into the garden's light.

On my second step, I freeze with a gasp.

Samson is no longer sitting under the fir tree but standing and staring directly at me.

Fuck.

Growing up, my papa told me not to knock loudly on a wolf's door, or wake them from sleep, or take their food. He never bothered teaching me not to sneak up on a wolf; it's nearly impossible.

My smell. *Ala.* Whatever they call it.

My blood stills as Samson stares at me with the same aloof and unsurprised expression that most high-numbered wolves wear. Nearer, his size seizes my attention. I look at his hands and consider how quickly they could smother me. I can float, I can fly, I can wield magic, but I can't do a fucking thing if something like him catches up to me.

I force myself to look away from his hands.

Past Samson, heavy blue curtains billow at either end of the opened estate walls. Both are pulled aside, showcasing a huge empty room with only bare outfitting. There's a low table and cushions, a small chest of drawers, a thick tapestry—little else. The firelight sconces fixed to the estate walls fill the garden with golden light.

Samson doesn't take his eyes from me as I study the room behind him.

I squat, then I ease from the wall's ledge and float into the grass. "Once, a wolf told me you guys keep everything minimal because of the smells."

Technically, it's rude to *trespass* on the lands and houses wolves occupy. But in Mieiran cities, all is shared. There's no *trespassing* because nymphs don't believe in hoarding. So for all his clout and size, Samson can't complain to Ninigone or Luz's head warlock, Absalom, that I've intruded.

Even though I am, by most standards.

I clear my throat. "He said a potent ala can get into the fibers of clothes and pillowcases and woven jewelry and stay for years. If it was a scent he enjoyed, he didn't mind. But if it was a scent he hated, then it drove him crazy. He said he'd wake up in the middle of the night to the scent's ghost around him. He said it would follow him to faraway places. I guess it makes sense to hold onto only a few precious things."

I keep my back pressed against the wall and wait for Samson's next move.

The cool marble reaches through my peach robe and chills me.

He stares at me with such calm focus that I wonder if he's trying to intimidate me.

Eventually, he says, "There is one scent that follows me no matter where I go."

He gestures to a low table near the fir tree. It's the only area of the estate in eyeshot that looks lived in; atop are a few books, papers, and quills, along with a mug.

"Your name is Helisent," he goes on. "You've been spying on me since we met at Solace. You can sit if you like."

I leave the wall and head to the table without letting myself hesitate. Instinct tells me to leave ample space between us, but I force myself to walk directly past him, within reaching distance, and sit at the table.

He follows and sits across from me.

Last week, I reprimanded Esclamonde for hovering when she saw a wolf. Now I arrange my robe so that I can fly into the fir tree or onto the wall in a split second if those hands move too quickly.

He isn't just *any* wolf, after all.

I raise my chin. "I haven't been spying on you the *whole* time. I'm way too busy for that. Can you imagine?" His lips, fuller than I'd thought they'd be, are set into an unmoving line. I forego my attempts at wit. "I wanted to gauge your character better. You don't give a lot away, you know."

"And that's made it difficult for you to assess me from your hideout across the street?" He glances to the right and looks directly at my roost on the shingled roof.

"You stayed out here even though you knew I was spying." I squint at him. "So you wanted me to see you? You wanted me to...?"

He nods. "To find the courage to say what you needed."

What?

His kindness is like a cold wet thing my hand touches when reaching into the shadows.

Very unexpected and highly unpleasant.

"Right. Well." I glance around the garden. "Do you have anything to drink?"

He raises his thick eyebrows. "Water."

I almost reel back with a laugh, then I realize he wasn't joking. "Fine. Let's get straight to business. Itzifone is a fucking twat and didn't have anything useful to share about Oko. In fact, none of the information I've bartered for in the past year has been that useful..."

There's only one way this alliance might work, and that's if Samson remains ignorant to three facts: First, that I've failed to find Oko for much longer than a year. Second, how far I'd go to bring the witch to justice. Third, why.

So I shrug in a lofty way, letting my robe slip from my shoulder.

I force a hiccup for good measure.

Wolves are prone to underestimating wielders. It shouldn't take a miracle to make Samson useful to me without giving up any of my secrets.

"You want Oko just as much as I do. I saw your face at Solace. Right before you walked away, you were going to try to change Itzifone's mind—what were you going to offer him that second time? I'll wonder for a while."

I run a nail over the grainy wooden table. The books set out are worn; one looks like a journal, its spine handbound.

"Suppose we both want to find Oko..." I continue. "I have the information you need. In fact, I have a year's worth of tips from Itzifone." Technically, it's *four* years' worth of tips. "You'd certainly find them interesting."

Samson pulls a packet of tobacco from under the table and gets to work rolling a cigarette. His chest and shoulders rise with a deep breath, as though he's carefully considering my words. "You want my help finding Oko?"

I roll my eyes. "Reach for nuance, my dear wolf."

He lowers his chin. His blue-black eyes move back and forth as he studies my face. "Wolves don't speak in riddles."

"I'm not speaking in fucking riddles. I tell you I have infor-

mation, I tell you we want the same thing, then you tell me
I'm asking for *help*."

We're speaking the same language, but our words don't
mean the same things.

My gut steels as I glance at the wall where I stepped into
view.

Almost time to cut my losses.

"You're looking for a partnership?" Samson asks. For the
first time since I met him, he looks close to smiling. "To find
Oko?"

"Exactly."

He licks the paper and rolls the cigarette with a deft touch.
"Then why didn't you just say that?"

"Because I don't use my words like bricks to lay a fucking
house, Samson. Don't act like you can't understand. Wolves use
zhuzhing all the time."

Lies in Velms are treated like treachery and liars are
punished with great severity. Still, that doesn't mean wolves
don't lie—they spin their words better than a wielder, they just
don't use outright falsehoods.

A woman walks into a tavern with an ugly dress on and asks
a man what he thinks about it. A warlock who wants to take
her home tells her it's the finest thing he's ever seen, even
though that's a lie. A wolf who wants to do the same tells her
says he's never seen anything like it in all his travels, which isn't
technically a lie even though it's not very honest.

It's just a way to "zhuzh" the truth.

Again, Samson's lips look close to pulling into a smile.
There's a slight twinkle in his eyes. "*Zhuzhing*," he repeats.

Samson's Velmic accent is strong, though he would probably argue it's *my* accent that's more noticeable.

In the last centuries, Velmic language has slowly faded in
favor of the Mieiran spoken by wielders and nymphs. I know
that they call the moons something different. That they call
Samson, the imminent Alpha of Velm, the *Kulapsifang*—or

Kulapsi for short. I think wielders are called *grona* and witches *gronetot*.

The only words I know for certain are a curse: *lekeli Kelnazzar*.

It translates to "dark Night" but means something more like "holy fucking shit." It's got a nice ring to it.

"That's what I said," I insist.

"No, you pronounced it like *zhazhing*. It's *zhuzhing*."

He's got to be kidding me. "That's what I said." I over-annunciate this time. "*Zhu-zhing*."

"*Zhuzhing*." He lowers his head to look at me, then slows his pace as though explaining the word to a toddler. "Not *zhazhing*."

"*Zhuzhing*." I know I'm saying it right; he's just being elitist.

"*Zhuzhing*, Helisent."

"That's what I fucking said—*zhuzhing*, Samson—I know I'm saying it right."

I raise my hands to physically stop myself from continuing the argument.

I close my eyes and imagine the bottle of brandy that awaits me once this interaction is over. "Can we... refocus, please? I'm here to convince you that we'd stand a better chance of finding Oko together. I'm a powerful witch, you're next in line for the big marble throne. What do you say?"

"I don't trust you." He doesn't say it to insult me—at least, I don't think so. He says it with weight and meaning, sucking on his cigarette like a philosopher. "But I suppose we wouldn't need to trust one another in order to work together."

Once, a warlock told me that trust is what the weak cling to when their shaking hands can't hold more.

I wish I didn't think of it so often, but time has proved him right.

I lean onto my elbows on the table and drift closer to Samson's terrifying hands. "When the wielders, wolves, and nymphs built Luz, there was little hope for mutual trust. There was only the desire to work together toward a mutual goal."

Toward *peace*.

I don't say the word; it sounds a bit too altruistic and flimsy for what I'm proposing.

And some might argue that what we once called peace we now know as hedonism.

But Samson nods. "I agree—though I do have one condition. I will respect the confidentiality of your search... if you agree to respect the confidentiality of mine."

Confidentiality? I can never tell the difference between confidentiality and secrecy.

I've been wondering what Samson wants with Oko since our run-in at Solace, but until now, I hadn't considered his search might be just as important as mine.

It bodes well for our partnership; he'll be motivated to find the witch.

But it bodes less well for whatever comes after; I don't plan on sharing Oko once I've found her. And I have no intention of respecting Samson or his search for her when that time comes.

I bow my head. "I don't give a fuck why you want her, just so long as you do."

He nods again. "I do."

"Fine."

Before words can get between us again, I pull my brown bottomless bag from where it sits hidden in a fold of my robe and set it on the table between us. The wood groans as the bag's full weight settles; though the handbag is no larger than my head, it's enchanted to hold all I can stuff inside. My magic carries the bag and manages its mass, which outweighs me at least two or three times.

I snap open the bag's bronze clip and reach inside.

Samson's eyebrows bunch together, staring at my hand as it disappears inside the fabric.

I wiggle my fingers and use summoning magic to find the bundle of folded letters. A small clatter echoes as the bag's contents rearrange to make way. I perk my ears at one clanking sound, which I can't place. Handy as bottomless bags are, it's easy to accumulate more than I could ever need.

At last, the rough parchment floats into my opened hand.

I pull it free, set my bag back on the ground, then offer the stack of notes to Samson. "This is everything I've collected on Oko."

He glances at me before reaching for the notes and unfolding the first. His face scrunches as he reads my script, cigarette hanging from his lips. "All this says is 'Itzifone said Oko stubbed her toe really bad in Alita and had to go to Ultramarine for treatment.' It's dated from last year."

"Yeah, *Samson*, it might sound like much, but when you put all the information together, it's... you can *glean more clues*..."

I chew my lip and try to remember how Onesimos talks about the tips. He's the only other being who knows about my search for Oko. Though neither of us is a scholar, he's helped me stitch together a few ideas over the years.

I can't seem to remember them now, but... "There's a trail that the clues are leading us down. And then there are the things the clues *don't* say. Reading between the lines, so to speak."

I'm a powerful witch.

But I'm not athletic, and I'm only instinctually shrewd when my back is against the wall. Assuming I'm not blackout drunk.

Based on Samson's dumbfounded expression, he's putting this together as we speak.

He folds the note and sets it aside, then reaches for another. "This one says, 'Itzifone said Oko was seen near the northern edge of Tet. She had a saiga with her. The saiga looked unhappy.'"

I tap the parchment where it reads "unhappy." "See, that

one doesn't sound like much, either, but what would she have been doing with a saiga? They're only unhappy when someone uses them as pack animals. So we can guess she was using the saiga to carry a bunch of shit. But why do that near Tet? No one goes near the lakes anymore. Definitely not wielders."

Samson blinks at me for a moment, smoke curling around his face, then he reaches for the third note.

"I'm not going to stay here all night while you go through them." I don't have the patience or gumption for that. "Take your time, write down some ideas, and I'll come back in a week to see what you've come up with. Then we can start looking for her."

Samson puts out his cigarette, then he takes a long drink from his mug. "I assume we'll be leaving Luz."

"That's the idea—follow wherever the clues take us. Are you..." I glance at the garden, then to the empty estate at his back. "Are you allowed to leave?"

Though I don't know much about the Kulapsifang and Velm's customs, I know Samson is somewhere in his free years, between his education and the start of his leadership. And I know it all ends soon with a wedding to the imminent Female Alpha of Velm. When it's Samson's turn on the marble throne, he'll oversee the war bands that handle disputes in their realm, attend diplomatic meetings around Mieira to represent the wolves, and, at some point, father the next generation's Kulapsifang.

Or so it once went.

Things might be different since Imperatriz 700-something Afador disappeared seventeen years ago. There hasn't been a Female Alpha at Clearbold's side since then—just some stand-in whose name I can't remember.

"I can travel freely," Samson explains. "I have my freedom until I'm thirty."

I study his features, which are almost a composite copy of Clearbold's: strong jaw, straight and semi-flat nose, thick eyebrows with sharp-set eyes. They're the strong features that wolves find attractive, but they're not soft. Like his hands, they're threatening.

This face has no compassion; this face hides a mind that thinks of how to dominate; this face doesn't weep.

"And when's your thirtieth?" I ask.

"The next coming of Night. Eight months from now."

He looks older than twenty-nine. Part of me wants to tell him, since I'm pretty sure alas denote age and he must realize I'm almost thirty-five. I manage not to, and it seems like a good start to our partnership.

"Fine, then. I'll come back next week ready to leave." I nod toward the stack of notes. "That's everything I know, including what Itzifone told me the other night. You're better off picking a place to start."

"And what about the witchling? The one from Solace. You're a mentor now, right?"

I roll my eyes. "I don't think the mentorship is legal. I mean, the witchling came here *looking for me*. That's not how it should work. It should be random. You probably know the rules. Is a witchling allowed to just walk into a fucking city and pick out a mentor?"

"I only communicate with Ferol and Victina," he says. Like Ninigone and Absalom do with wielders, two wolves oversee their kind in the city. "I can't speak to the rules Ninigone and Absalom enforce for wielders."

"Whatever. I'll figure it out." Annoyed with the memory of the clinging, terrified witchling, I stand with a huff.

Like muscle memory, my magic smooths out my robe. It's much too large for me, but I like to think it adds to my reputation for brightly-colored nonsense. I also tidy my long strands of white hair, which tend to cling to the velvet.

"We're squared, then?"

Samson also stands. "We are."

He tucks his hands behind his back, and my eyes once

again linger on the blue-black hair of his chest, of his lower abdomen. His muscles have a faint outline. I've seen plenty of wolves with sharp lines that define their bulk, but Samson looks... softer. Like there's a thin layer of fat over his muscles.

I turn away, though it grates to turn my back to him. I try to look casual and unhurried as I return to the wall then float back onto the ledge.

With the estate's lights at Samson's back, he looks like another faceless feature of the courtyard, just as shadowy and hulking as the fir tree.

High above the estate's roof and the lights of Luz, the three moons shift into view from the horizon.

Marama, the largest of the moons, is nearly full. Its pink-gray hue fills the world with silvery light.

Laline, half the size of Marama, is only half-waxed. Its greenish light is dim and alluring.

Cap, the tiny crimson moon forever trailing its larger cousins, is only a narrow crescent.

I forget what the wolves call them. Marama is *Vicente* and Laline is *Abdecalas*. What's Cap to them? Something with an S.

I file the question away for the boring periods of silence Samson and I are soon bound for.

With a sigh, I tell him, "I'll meet you here one week from now."

The Samson-shaped shadow nods. "I'll smell you."

It sounds rude, but I know he doesn't mean it to be, so I leave without another word.

The next day, Onesimos and I lounge on a blanket in the temple district. Overhead, the sun twinkles in the empty, cerulean sky.

An ecstatic crowd fills the ample space between the huge stone columns. Merchants wheel their wooden carts between the groups, which toast, eat, and cheer to the arrival of a hesperide demigod and its new queen. They arrived from Gamma this morning.

In the center of the buzzing plaza, the happy demigod lounges on its side. It takes up a large portion of the space; its head rests near the union of the Septima and Irme Rivers, but its feet extend out of view where the first marble tower marks the start of the temple district.

In terms of demigods, which are all giants, this one is large. Though we missed its entrance into the city, it likely stands around forty feet tall, twice as tall as most Luzian buildings.

Its features closely resemble the hesperide nymphs of Gamma. They have round faces with slim eyes and lips. Like most of the plain-dwelling nymphs, braids separate the queen and demigods' thin straight hair. The queen has olive skin speckled with pale marks, like a moss-covered boulder. Unlike the queen, the demigod's skin glows with a sickly blue hue, semi-transparent and slightly aglow.

The pair glance at each other as the queen stands in the demigod's cupped hand.

And the crowd stares at them with delight.

The demigod and the queen break eye contact to gaze across the plaza with a similar glint in their eyes.

Humming desita fills the air.

It intensifies as a band begins to play folk songs and the passing crowds rush forward to lay gifts before the demigod. In response, the demigod also gives back.

Its long braids, tangled to its waist, shift in a breeze none of us feel and send the scent of foxglove into the air. Now and then, the demigod pulls tufts of tallgrass and green snakes from its hair. Then a trickle of bees buzzes skyward from its ears. The demigod wipes its pointer finger on its tongue to collect their honey, which the being offers to a few squealing youngsters; they jump to scoop the honey where it drips from its fingers, as large as their tiny bodies.

"How I miss the oread demigods," murmurs Onesimos at my side. "Have you ever seen one?"

I snort, reminiscing. "I'll never forget it. The oread demigod came to Eupheme when I was visiting. It opened its mouth in the central plaza and threw up enough garnet and tourmaline to bury half the crowd. I think I still have a scar from where one scratched me—they weren't polished."

The hesperide demigod regurgitates the nurturing gifts of its land, but not all regions are as fruitful and pleasant as Gamma.

The oread demigods that wander across the volcanic cones of Jaws, where Onesimos was born, imbue their land with minerals like magnesium and iron, along with jewels like garnet and tourmaline.

Onesimos smiles. "People still talk about that. I think the city council used the garnet to build a statue in the demigod's honor." He stretches across our blanket with a yawn. "This demigod's queen looks young. Wonder how long she'll last."

The queen in the plaza has the knowing gaze of a leader with years of experience, but we're too far away for me to gauge her precise age.

Though some nymphs grow up dreaming of being appointed a king or queen by a passing demigod, the position isn't lasting.

I study the hesperide demigod. Its dress is soft, like worn cotton, pooling near its abdomen. "Did you ever meet a queen or king in Jaws?"

Onesimos tilts his head as he thinks. "Once when I was really young. They don't last long up north. The queen we see right now will grow wheat and barley in Gamma with a little added *oomph*. But in Jaws, the kings and queens don't grow crops. They pull minerals from the cones. And working with magnesium, zinc, and iron is a lot harder on the body. The king I met ruled for four years before the oread demigod came and took him back."

Took him back.

I look from the hesperide demigod to its latest queen. The nymph looks drunk on bliss. Many queens and kings look similarly dispossessed by ecstatic desita; I suppose they'd have to be, doling out precious magic to their homelands until it leaves them empty and dying.

I glance at Esclamonde next. She observes the chaotic scene from the flat top of a stone column high above. Her red cape catches in the wind like a streak of blood, made brighter by the background of clear sky.

I wonder if she can feel the desita. If she's gotten used to how the light trance shifts her consciousness for a few moments, like a buzz from a fine brandy.

I can feel Onesimos's gaze linger on me. He asks, "What's it like to be demigodless? I always romanticized it. It must be freeing. You belong to nothing, and nothing belongs to you."

"I don't feel demigodless." I study his face, wondering if that's a private epithet he's kept for me. *Helisent West of Jaws, Demigodless*. "I know I'm not a nymph, but I feel like the demigods belong to me. And I belong to them. After all, I feel desita. Maybe not like a nymph... but still."

"Sure, but you only feel that way because the demigods have asked for your help before." Onesimos runs a hand along the top of his fluffy vermillion hair, pressing a few wiry strands into place. "What about the wielders who aren't powerful enough to attract the attention of a demigod?"

Demigods interact with us to deliver kings and queens, or to search for desita—and other times, they ask for help.

In my case, they ask for magic.

I reach for one of the veggies set on a plate between us. "They don't *always* acknowledge me. I've been ignored by demigods way more than I've been noticed—and even then, I felt like I belonged."

Onseimos jerks his chin toward Esclamonde. Her hand

moves in her lap, likely taking notes on the festivities. "What about her?"

I still don't know how to feel about the mentee, and the days aren't improving my attitude. "Her family is from Black Rock, Simmy. She barely knew what desita was. Who gives a fuck what she thinks about demigods?"

Onseimos's vermillion eyes shimmer as he stares at the witchling. "I wasn't talking about that. I was talking about what you plan on doing with her when you leave next week."

When I outlined my plans to find Oko via Samson last night, Onesimos only nodded.

Since then, he hasn't broached the topic—not even during our late-night bender, which ended only hours ago when Esclamonde woke up and started squealing about a demigod's arrival.

I weigh his words.

My hunt for Oko far overshadows my job mentoring Esclamonde. My hunt for Oko far overshadows any repercussions the Class might think to level at me for abandoning the mentee.

I glance at Onesimos. "I didn't know anyone except you when I moved here. She'll be fine."

"So you're leaving her in our warren, then?" He munches on a green apple, expression calm and unreadable.

"Pen enjoys bothering witches. I'd hate to leave him high and dry."

Onesimos smiles briefly. "And I enjoy watching him bother witches."

For a long time, he doesn't say anything. He picks at our spread of raw fruits and veggies. As I teeter between being drunk and hungover, none of it looks appealing. I pinch off a piece of pastry, but even that goes dry in my mouth.

The crowd cheers as the demigod releases handfuls of barley, oat, and wheat grains. The cacophony distracts me as I look over my shoulder to watch the rush to collect them.

With a sigh, Onesimos goes on, "I can't decide if you're an idiot, a genius, or just in way over your head with this little plan of yours." He takes another bite of his apple, studying me as he chews. "But I know if you leave the city with the wolf, you won't be back for a while."

"Don't talk like that. I'll come back in a few months at the latest."

"You started clearing out your bottomless bag." Onesimos glares at the leather bag, whose edges now fade. "Wielders don't do that unless they're preparing for a long journey. How old will I be when you come back? What if I go back to Jaws before you return to Luz?"

I raise my eyebrows, shocked by his words. "Simmy, I'll be back before you return home. Like I said—"

"I'm almost forty, Helisent."

"Don't say it like that!"

The nymph kings and queens don't last long in their positions because of the magical demands put on them... but even the average nymph faces a similarly short lifespan compared to wielders and wolves.

I set aside our meal and scoot over to Onesimos. I tuck myself against his side so we face the demigod together, resting my head on his shoulder as panic bubbles in my heart. I can't imagine the warren without Onesimos; I can't imagine his face with any more wrinkles, his hair with any more gray strands.

I use magic wrap him in my robe's velvet fabric so we're cocooned together.

"You're being dramatic," I reason. "Most nymphs don't go home until they're fifty."

"I don't want to go back home as an elder." He turns to stare at me, then he raises a hand to stroke my face. "I want to enjoy life in Eupheme before all my lights dim. I told you you'd hate me for it someday."

To be fair, he did say that. And I had argued I wouldn't be sad.

Then we went to Luz and started a warren.

I bite my lip to clamp down on my tears.

Most nymphs return home at age fifty to enjoy their last years where they were born. Simmy, an oread with a hearty love of Eupheme, wants to make sure he has time to *really* enjoy his senior years.

I'll live on to my one hundred and fortieth year along with other powerful wolves and wielders. I'll spend half my life weighed down by all the love the nymphs left in my heart then took with them into death.

Onesimos wipes away the tear that slips down my cheek.

He smiles. "Say goodbye to me, Helisent. Don't just leave and pretend things won't change. You can do that with everyone else. Not with me, my darling witch."

That's the thing about Simmy. I've never had to explain myself to him—which is good, because half the time I can't tell what I feel, and what I want, and what I need.

"I don't want to leave you behind." I nuzzle into his shoulder further and take a deep breath. His skin is warm like the volcanic cones of Jaws, soft as the silks of Rhotidom. "I don't want to leave the warren, either."

"Who would want to leave our warren? We've built a good one. The *best*, some might say. But you won't find Oko staying here."

Onesimos smiles again, ignoring my mounting sobs. He cranes his neck to gesture to Esclamonde. "I'll hold onto my favorite parts of you through the witchling. I'll teach her how to hold her liquor. How to be helpful without letting anyone know she cares for life, or love, or beauty."

I look away from the stupid fucking mentee as I attempt to swallow the lump that's in my throat.

The hesperide demigod catches my gaze. It tilts its head to meet my eyes.

The demigod winks at me as though we were long friends, then shifts its attention to Onesimos. It's enough to send me into another fit of weeping, while the oread smiles and waves.

"The demigod is saying goodbye," he whispers in my ear. "It's saying good luck. It's saying never forget your favorite oread."

When I finally look up, tears gild Onesimos's hickory skin with amber streaks. He doesn't wipe them away. He's never been afraid. Not like me.

CHAPTER 4

THE ENDLESS POOL OF VELVET FABRIC

SAMSON

My son,
There are parts of Velm the wolves will not show you. Unseen, they are
still yours. Find them.

I t's easy to believe the witch is an idiot.

It's easy to believe that she's like fire: thoughtless, shameless, powerful. All is well for the being who knows how to beat a sword into shape with her flame. All is lost for the one who doesn't smell the smoke before the wildfire catches.

Still, I try to make sense of the stack of notes she leaves behind. After all, this is the destiny I've accepted until my day in Silent City arrives.

I spread the remaining notes across the low table in the Luzian Estate's dining hall. With the ghost of Rex's ala, I sip my tea and attempt to make sense of the witch's haphazard scribbling.

"Itzifone said three naiads saw Oko harassing a phoenix in Gamma."

"Itzifone said Oko rented an apartment in Perpetua under a false name."

"Itzifone said Oko bartered a large portion of her dove in Kleitos."

"Itzifone said two okeanids stole a pouch from Oko in the Deltas."

"Itzifone said one merchant in Alita bartered for a sad saiga from Oko."

None of it leads anywhere definite. I set the disappointing notes aside and study the only conclusions I've been able to make so far.

First, Oko doesn't go south to Velm or northeast to Jaws or east to Hypnos. She's been seen as far east as the Deltas, but she otherwise sticks to Rhotidom, Gamma, and Septegeur.

Second, she uses saigas for transport rather than the usual wielder combination of cushioned liliths and bottomless bags.

Third, she's interested in the phoenixes. Multiple notes mention sightings near phoenix nests in Gamma, as well as a report of the witch harassing one of the great raptors.

Like the rest of the clues, it's barely anything to go on.

I sip my tea and stare across the neatly arranged scraps of parchment. Now and then, I rearrange their order in hopes of gleaning a new insight. The three bare conclusions hold tight, even as I scour the clues well into the night.

Eventually, I stand and head into the garden.

Even in the last dregs of this winter, Luzian nights are as warm as Velm's hottest months. I stretch in the soft grass, then meditate. Now and then, I glance at the wall where Helisent entered the estate last week.

I don't smell her ala or notice her bright robe strewn atop the roof across the street, but my eyes keep switching to the spot, expecting to see her.

Part of me thinks she'll return and cancel our arrangement, or sniff out whether I'll be helpful, or attempt to manipulate me.

She doesn't.

I lay back in the grass and I stare up at the brightening

faces of the moons Vicente and Abdecalas. Far below is Sennen, crimson and eye-catching like freshly drawn blood.

I sigh, feeling hours from sleep.

If the witch is an idiot, then what does that make me for agreeing to her plan?

The next morning at dawn, Helisent's ala wakes me.

Her potent scent, bitter like all wielder alas, has an alcoholic twang. My gut sinks; the only way I can smell clear traces of alcohol in a being's ala is if they're well and truly inebriated.

I sit up where I fell asleep in the grass and turn toward the wall.

Helisent sits atop the marble barrier with her legs dangling over the edge. They extend half the length of her robe, which pools in the grass below. In the early light, the velvet fabric shimmers like light on water against her olive skin.

Her bright jewelry clanks together as she hikes one leg over the other and hiccups. "My warrenmates came to see us off." She jabs a thumb over her shoulder. "They're waiting out front. Can they come inside? They always wanted to see the Luzian Estate, and I said you're actually—"

"No."

I stand before she can take the idea any further.

The idea of nymphs who don't believe in personal space running through the estate would send Clearbold into a fit of rage. They touch everything, sniffing and tasting and discussing as though unaware of how long an ala can cling.

Helisent frowns grandiosely, then she hiccups again.

"It isn't *my estate* to offer tours of," I amend. "I'll meet you out front. Please wait for me there."

I turn and head inside, listening to the noisy clank of her glass and bronze jewelry as she leaves. I retrieve my bag, tighten the leather straps over the odd angles, and then go to the washroom.

The reality of my decision to leave with Helisent hits me as I spread oil on my palms and pull my hair into place. I try not to dwell on the fact that I don't know Helisent, or the witch we're hunting down, or even whether Oko can answer my questions about Imperatriz's disappearance.

Worse, we don't have a clear destination yet.

I look at my reflection, wishing I saw more of my mother in my features.

"I have to keep trying," I tell whatever piece of her spirit lives in me.

Then I head into the foyer. Like Rex last week, I tug my satchel into place, look back once, then leave the estate. I pass the marble basin of lily pads before the scent of the warren hits me: liquor, incense, scented oils, semen, and river water.

Samson, what the fuck are you doing?

I open the gate and greet the group of giddy nymphs. They crane their heads to see past me, as though they'd be able to see through the estate's impenetrable walls. As they shift around, I tally two hesperides, two dryads, one naiad, one oread, and one warlock—no sign of the red-cloaked witchling.

Only the warlock ignores the estate to study me instead.

His pale golden eyes work over my body.

Like Helisent did the other night, he watches my hands. Then he turns to her where she lingers to the side of the pack. He joins her as she searches in her bottomless bag for something. The oread heads to her side, too, gently holding her wrist as she and the warlock fish around for something in the bag.

The rest of the warren assails me with questions and comments.

The hesperide with freckled skin says, "Helisent can warm the water for your baths. Do you bathe a lot? She doesn't mind doing it. She's very helpful."

The dryads are close behind. One has glimmering amber eyes, which are like shined gems against his tawny skin. "We gave her the best produce we could find. Remind her to eat it today or tomorrow."

The other dryad nods. His thick turquoise hair is separated into three tattered braids. "She'll forget about it."

The hesperide jumps in again. "Oh, and don't eat the bitterroot. You won't like it. It's too sour, even for nymphs. What types of foods do you enjoy, Samson 714 Afador?"

They go on and on like a drunken horde of curious school-children. While the scent of liquor is strong, their vibrant energy hints the group favors dextro. While uncommon in Velm, nymphs and wielders enjoy the stimulant. But there's a fine line between appreciation and addiction, and I have no idea where that line sits in relation to this warren.

In relation to Helisent.

Off to the side, the warlock and the oread help the witch tug her square lilith from the bag's narrow opening. They dust off the plush cushion before setting it flat in the air.

Helisent rears back with laughter as the pair help situate her. Between her curvy legs and the endless pool of velvet fabric, it takes a moment.

Unsure of how to shake the lingering warren, I approach Helisent on her lilith. Metallic ornaments dangle from its bottom, catching and twirling like noisy wind chimes.

Though I dislike magic, I'm glad she'll be traveling by lilith.

If she walked, I'd spend my days with my neck craned down. Judging by our brief interaction the other night, her height barely reaches my chest. But on her lilith, she can float at a height that puts us at eye-level and makes me feel less like a terrifying giant.

The witch raises her white eyebrows. "Ready?"

I glance at the warrenmates around us. "Whenever you are."

The nymphs come to offer their final goodbyes, pinching Helisent's calves where they dangle from the lilith, kissing their palms and squeezing her hands, and baring ecstatic smiles. Only the oread lingers a moment longer to tie a string of glassy volcanic beads to the clasp of her bottomless bag.

Helisent scrunches her shoulders together then waves goodbye to the group. "I gave Ninigone extra dove, so just go to the processors if you run out of magic. Have Pen send word if she starts catching an attitude."

I glance at a crooked fig tree to the left, trying not to react to the information.

While I've come to realize through her ala and attitude that Helisent is likely powerful, the idea that she might sponsor Luz with her magic is unexpected. If she *is* a city sponsor, I'm not surprised she felt irate at Ninigone's decision to stick her with a mentee.

Wielders who offer their dove freely to help power a city's fundamental processes, from clearing irrigation canals to lighting the streetlamps through the nights, are vital pieces of Mieira's urbanized areas. Even some Velmic settlements have started relying on wielder dove for similar purposes.

Wielders who sign on as city sponsors are goaded with gifts from local councils—free housing, unlimited access to markets, and public commemorations. They're not saddled with responsibilities like wide-eyed mentees.

Is Helisent one of Luz's sponsors?

I try to see her in a new light, try to take her more seriously.

She smooths her robe and lifts her chin to address the warren one last time. "Try not to forget me. Not that it's possible."

I take a few steps down the road in case the group wants their privacy.

I wouldn't really know how it works.

The closest I've come to a warren is a war band. I spent my formative years learning the basics of fighting, tracking, punishing, and judging in Velm's rural outposts. Aside from my wayward affair with Rex, there's little resemblance between my war band and Helisent's warren.

A moment later, her lilith approaches me with a few high-pitched jingles.

She sniffles and wipes her eyes, face angled away from me.

Unsure how to comfort Helisent, I forgo any attempt and start planning our journey instead. "Based on the notes you left, I think we should head to Gamma. I'd like to interview the nymphs who live near the phoenix roosts. Oko has been spotted nearby multiple nests. I'm sure someone will remember her. What do you think?"

She spares a glance at me. "Can we talk about this when I'm done crying?"

A dozen responses, some comforting and some dismissive, float through my head. I settle with, "Should we stop walking until then? Journeys are useless without a destination."

Her breaths begin to stutter again. "No. Whatever. Just lead the way."

We're only a block away from the rushing Irme River that runs north from Velm. Though not a direct path to Gamma, it's the easiest route to leave the city.

I lead the way, and Helisent keeps up, lilith jangling at my side.

It doesn't take long to get used to the sound of the metal pieces or the scent of Helisent's brandy-soaked ala. For how intoxicated her scent hints that she is, she doesn't fall from the floating cushion or hiccup her way into sleep or slur her words.

She just sniffles and wipes her face and looks away from me.

I decide to ask about dextro later.

An hour outside Luz, infrequent travelers move north and south along the Irme.

The wolves who pass greet me and make offerings. I left

Luz with only basic food supplies but have already been gifted fresh meat, fresh bread, and plenty of herbs. By the second hour, I politely decline the rest of the offers; my rucksack isn't bottomless like Helisent's bag.

Only two wolves spare a glance at the witch.

Their reticence doesn't surprise me; just like some wielders remember the War Years in Antigone, many in western Velm refuse to let its memory die. Those in the east have had an easier time moving on since their fields weren't stained with blood. Most of the battles from the centuries-long conflict took place in the hilly plains where we walk now.

Wolves hold onto blood feuds; the fangself doesn't forget the ala of a perpetrator.

I wonder when their coldness will bother Helisent enough to broach the topic.

But if she notices their indifference, she doesn't mention it.

We push on as the sun moves from east to west above us, and the pale faces of the moons slowly come into focus. I head inland at dusk to find a place to stay well off the road. Nothing carries farther than the ala of the Alpha line, and I don't appreciate uninvited visitors—no matter how well-intentioned they are.

For the first time today, Helisent has an opinion.

"I hope you don't expect me to sleep on the ground." She points toward a midden of oak trees that stick out amid the rolling fields of northern Gamma. "Let's camp there for the night."

Her mention of the ground directs my attention to her boots. I make our first attempt at small talk after a day of wearying silence. "What's the longest you've ever gone without touching the ground?"

She snorts as we head toward the darkening patch of trees. "I lived in Antigone before I moved to Luz. I probably went longer than a month without ground-walking. You'd do the same if you lived there. Have you been?"

Antigone is the only wielder-built city in Mieira. When they crawled down from Metamor Plateau hundreds of years ago, they made their first settlements amid the towering rock pillars of Septegeur's forest.

Antigone is an impractical and magically bent city that's half-carved and half-strung between the massive pillars, high up and far from the ground.

Far from logic.

Just the idea of it terrifies me.

"Septegeur is one place I've yet to travel," I admit. "Although I suppose I'll have to make the trip soon enough."

"Wait for the dry season to go. The rainy season was unbearable for some wolves. Most of the city is built from iron and copper, which smell strongly in the rain. So if you have to go during the rainy season, stick to the top levels. One through four would be best. Anything below the fourth level starts to smell *really* intense—for wolves, at least."

As we near the oaks' coverage, her lilith sinks toward the ground. She steps into the grass with a shuffle of her boots. "So what now? I know cooking magic and fire magic. I can make us something."

I set my rucksack down with a groan and lean back to stretch. At the onset of the quiet night, the trip feels more intimate than it has all day. "I have my own food. I can prepare the fire. It would be helpful if you could light it."

In the sheltered cove of oaks, there's less wind and sound. Our alas pool between the trunks and canopy overhead. I get to work to ignore the stillness, collecting firewood and setting up a pit with the spare light of an orange-and-purple dusk.

Once I've collected the wood, Helisent snaps her fingers to start the fire. I'm not sure how it works—all I see is a snap of her tiny fingers, then a flame combusts between the kindling I set out.

Magic has always been vague and spine-tingling to me—

especially the idea of wielding something that can't be seen or quantified.

Tales of seethings have done little to help. According to whispered legends, a seething curse occurs if a male wolf comes into contact with a witch's most intimate ala, whether on purpose or by accident. The tales I heard of seething curses hint that they alter the thoughts and impulses of the wolf affected, tying his attention to the witch.

It's so thorough that his dreams at night revolve around the witch in question.

Spending my waking hours with a witch will likely be hard enough. The risk of a seething curse only adds to my apprehension of magic.

I head back toward the river to wash. When I return, Helisent prepares a spread of food before the healthy fire. With only the light of Vicente and part of Abdecalas overhead, the bright streaks of flame help me sort through my own supplies.

Halfway through our wordless meal, Helisent offers me a raw carrot. "My warren packed extra stuff for you. I can't eat all of this. It will rot soon."

I glance at the spread of carrots, turnips, radishes, and quinoa on her wooden plate. It looks like what my food used to eat.

Helisent looks at the carrot in her hand, then at me. "I know you're not supposed to take food from a wolf, but I didn't think it was bad to offer food."

I take the carrot, unsure what to do with it. "Thank you."

We both look at the bright orange root.

She says, "Just set it close to the flames if you want it cooked."

I don't want it raw or cooked, but I don't tell her that. I set it near the coals and hope she'll forget about the carrot, then turn back to my meal.

"I was thinking we could follow the Irme for two more

days," I explain, "then cut east into Gamma. It should put us close to the westernmost phoenix nest. We can ask for directions to the next from there."

"I actually thought of something way smarter—I have incredible ideas when I'm hungover. No one ever talks about that." She gnashes into the bowl of quinoa, filling her cheeks before she goes on. "While I see your point about going to Gamma and checking out the phoenixes... I was *thinking* a better idea would be to cut *west* into Tet. You know, to go to Skull."

The idea is so fucking dumb, I wonder if she's been leading me along.

Does someone want to isolate and target me? Wolves and wielders haven't worked together for any common goal since the era of rumored peace before the War Years. Still, there are few motivations someone could have for a statement so horribly misguided.

Go to *Skull?*

I leer at her. "No."

She takes another huge bite of quinoa. "Here's the thing—we're going to go on a wild goose chase for this witch. You saw my notes. We're grasping at straws here. But last night, Zopyros said she'd been dreaming of her dead cousin, and it reminded me of something. Do you see where I'm going here?"

I set down my plate and take a deep breath, preparing all my strength and logic to stop her idea before she can say the word *ghost*.

"I've never been to Skull or Tet, and I have no plans to change that. Your magic won't work if we run into a magical sink in Tet—and you won't last a day if you have to walk."

Her mouth slowly works to swallow the bite of quinoa while her eyebrows bunch. "What the fuck? I'd last a day walking. How weak do you think I am?"

I use her comment to further distract her from Skull. "Let's find out tomorrow. We'll see how far you get without your lilith as we travel *south on the Irme*."

"What if we did that while traveling *west* to Skull? Think about it. Close your eyes."

I stare at her animated expression with disbelief.

She rolls her eyes. "Fine. Don't close your eyes. But—*just imagine* we go to Skull, we find a desperate ghost, and we convince it to haunt Oko. I met a warlock at Soulless who knows of another warlock who regularly deals with ghosts to find people. He's the most successful bounty hunter in all of Mieira."

"Kierkegaard?" I ask.

Her face lights up. "Exactly. You know him—"

"No one *actually* knows Kierkegaard. He's just a myth. Everyone thinks they've met a friend of his, but none of it's real. And that's because *no one is dumb enough to go to Skull* and start bartering with ghosts."

"Sure, but what if we *pretend* to be dumb enough to do it? We'll be in and out. Maybe we'll even run into the real Kierkegaard."

"No, Helisent."

"So you're not going to eat the carrot *and* you're not going to listen to my ideas?" She swivels toward me, craning over her plate to bare her eyes into mine.

With the bright flames close by, I make out more of her features than in the estate's courtyard or Soulless. Her wide cheeks are smooth, her cheekbones high. Her eyes are almost bulbous—I wonder if she can see more than I can with such massive pale-gold irises. The rest of her is buried in bright and noisy jewelry, which smells heavily of copper, stale thread, and nauseating perfumes.

She puckers her lips as she takes a deep breath as though summoning her patience.

"I'm going to need you to dig deep and find that place in your heart where you *don't* think I'm a silly drunken witch who has tons of dextro in her bag. Good. Now that you're in that tiny crevice of good faith, I'd like to remind you that there are only two GhostEaters in Mieira. If we can convince a ghost to haunt Oko, then we just need to find the GhostEaters before Oko asks one of them to reverse the haunting."

To my great surprise, the idea starts to make more sense as she goes on.

"Even *better*, both GhostEaters live in the Deltas. One lives in Ultramarine and the other one in Cadmium, last I heard. So, we go to Skull, then double back to the Deltas. We split up to cover each city, keep tabs on the GhostEaters, and then report back when one of us catches wind of Oko."

Helisent returns to her original seat before her plate. She picks at her meal, glancing at me as she awaits a response.

I stare at the fire. I wrack my brain for a solid excuse to avoid heading west, but the idea is better than anything I've come up with in the past week.

Though wildly dangerous, it's reliable.

"To reach Skull, we'll have to walk through half of Tet. What happens if we run into a sink and you can't use your magic?" I ask.

As a wolf, I won't really be the one at risk in the vast land of quagmires, fog, and endless lakes.

She rolls her eyes then hikes up one of her legs. Her white suede boots look old, though their soles aren't particularly worn. "I'll fucking walk, Samson. These aren't just for show, you know."

I avoid the urge to roll my eyes like she just did; though Helisent has soft curves, there's certainly muscle beneath it. "I'm talking about your bag. You can't carry it without magic. You also haven't considered how you'll *feel* without your ability to wield magic. Will you still trust me, or will you watch my hands day and night? Will you sleep on the ground by my side, or will you try to climb a tree and sleep there? Or will you not sleep at all?"

She falls quiet, then says, "That's a good question. I definitely don't trust you... but I'm also not actively suspicious of you. Does that make sense?"

It's probably the most honest thing she's said to me. "I understand."

"What if we found grimoire before we go? Tet or not, it would probably help us set up a..." She stares at me, looking for the word; I stare back, waiting. "A foundation, I guess."

I nod. "So long as we can find a village before we reach Tet. There aren't many west of the Irme River."

She smiles. "Does this mean you agree with my plan?"

"For now, yes. But let's see how I feel tomorrow. And after we find grimoire."

Her smile turns devilish. "Fair enough."

After dinner, she leans back to study the canopy overhead. In the night, the shifting leaves are little more than fluttering shadows that rustle in the wind.

After a moment, I realize she's picking out a spot to make her bed for the night.

In the deepest parts of Velm, they still call wielders birds. This is the first time I've seen one build a nest; she approaches the trunk of the largest oak, then scampers up the side of it, half-climbing and half-floating. She walks along the primary branches to find a place she likes while her robe spills between them and catches on small twigs.

With a sigh, she sits down and unloads a bundle of twigs from her bag. The dozen or so birch sticks don't look impressive until she taps one. Then they start to weave together and lengthen. The pale twigs work around the branches to create a base for her nest, then they intertwine along the sides to build a bowl-shaped shelter.

My stomach clenches as the reeds twine and warp and grow.

I hate magic.

Maybe I don't hate it.

I just don't understand it.

Helisent spares a glance at my hands every hour, but I'm just as leery of her tiny little fingers and how they bend matter and command impossible things. It's just as suspicious that simply inhaling the wrong *scent* of the witch might leave me with a seething curse; even her ala contains magic.

For now, I'll have to settle for what I can glean from the grimoire.

At dawn, I rise.

I meditate with my back leaning against one of the smaller oak trees.

I stare out into the vast plains of western Gamma and control my breath. It does wonders to soothe my anxiety about my companion, though her loud snoring distracts me.

As the sunlight buries the faces of the moons, I round the circle of oak trees to stare westward. The view looks similar to the golden plains of Gamma, but far in the distance, I know what awaits us.

The wall of fog that leads into Tet.

With a sigh, I head back to the oaks and prepare breakfast. Helisent doesn't wake up; I eat through her snoring, pack my things, then wonder how I should wake her.

Throwing a rock seems a bit callous, but I can't scale the oak tree. Even if I could, I don't think intruding on a sleeping witch would be wise. I call up to her, raising my voice incrementally, then move on to clapping when that doesn't work.

Slowly, my temper builds.

She's delaying our journey, she's left her items all over ground, she hasn't helped rebuild the fire this morning. *Does she not plan on washing or eating?*

"Helisent!"

With a gasp, she sits up in the nest. Her long white hair is messy, and her eyes don't look open.

"Good morning." She faces the east, then flinches from the light. "It's *dawn*. Why'd you wake me up?"

"We'll get nowhere if we start our days late."

"What about *dawn* seems *late* to you?"

One week ago, I was staring at Rex's packed satchel and trying to figure out how to beg him to stay. I don't know what other conclusions to draw, just that that moment seems disproportionately far away, like him leaving me is a blurred memory from childhood.

"Oh, *relax*. I see that expression you're making. I'll be right down." She doesn't think I can hear her when she mumbles, "Helisent, what the fuck have you gotten yourself into?"

At least I'm not alone in my doubts.

CHAPTER 5

LESSER INSTINCTS

HELISENT

Honey Heli,
Hope you and Anesot are enjoying Hypnos. Oko won't leave me alone.
I think she misses him how I miss you. (Do you think they used to date?
Don't tell him I asked you that.)
Mint Mili

A week into our journey, I'm getting better at waking up at dawn.

Based on the way Samson watches me collect my things with his hands on his hips this morning, he would probably disagree.

I scuttle around the firepit in search of a sock, then a fork, then a scarf. "You know, anyone who knows me would find this kind of behavior extraordinary. *Rushing* in the *mornings*? What a horrible way to live."

Samson lights his cigarette. "Really?"

That's what he says when he's not interested in listening to me.

I clip my bottomless bag shut then hoist myself onto my

lilith. My magic sets my robe into place while I work a comb through my hair. Normally, I'd stare in my handheld mirror while brushing my hair, but Samson has shown great disdain for my vanity.

We head out of the clearing of trees where we camped last night and head west. For days, it's been our only direction.

"Yes, *really*, Samson." I finish brushing my hair with a *tsk* then tuck my comb back into my bag. "You rely on order too much. Take a cue from nature. Get wild."

For a while, there's only the sound of my jangling lilith and the scent of his cigarette.

I can't stand that he ignores me so easily.

But Samson keeps his eyes on the western horizon. Yesterday morning, the brackish fog of Tet came into view, a wall of gray extending upward. It doesn't stop at the cloud line but nearly blocks out the sun, clogging the sky.

He's been even quieter since then, which doesn't make sense considering it's *my* magic at risk in Tet.

A half-hour later, we pass into a thin forest of evergreens. The wooded patches, emerald like the forests of Velm I grew up hearing tales of, dot the low prairies west of Gamma.

Though sparse, the trees are towering giants. Reddish needles litter the ground, cracking under Samson's boots.

"A wolf's dedication to order isn't a commentary on nature," he says.

I glance at him. It's not the first time I'd thought he was ignoring me only to realize he'd been thinking quietly.

"It's the way we hold ourselves accountable for our behavior. Wielders don't use complex forms of magic until they're a bit more mature, but a wolf will phase from birth. Order is what separates us from animals who can't control their lesser instincts."

Lesser instincts.

That's a polite way to describe how the wolves turn skin on the triplemoon, when Marama, Laline, and Cap are all round and shining. I've heard wolves with high generational counts also turn skin on the doublemoon, when only Marama and Laline are full.

When *lesser instincts* like rage, bloodlust, and domination are enough to send them transforming into wolves as tall as the buildings in Luz.

Order seems like a flimsy thing to stave off such powerful inclinations, but what would I know about self-control? A sack of full bottles jingles someplace inside my bottomless bag. Even larger is the sack of empty bottles.

I glance at Samson's hands where they're clasped behind his back. "So you swap your natural inclinations for order. Then are you sure you know the *real* you? I can't tell if you're *trying* to be quiet and austere, or if you're just..."

Just as he is now: walking with his chin up and staring straight ahead, thinking and worrying of nothing, not where his journey will lead to or away from.

I go on, "Or if you're just at peace. Or is that what you want me to think?"

"It is what I want you to think. It's what every being should think when they look at me. Control, tranquility, vision."

Now and then, little comments like this remind me *who* he is. That I'm walking beside the imminent Male Alpha of Velm. The Kulapsifang. Not a man, nor a being, nor a companion, nor a wolf, but a symbol of Velm that's been carried in a single, unbroken line for 700-something generations.

I lower my voice to a whisper. "I won't tell anyone if you want to be something else. At least, for a little bit."

He whips his head toward me.

I flinch, wondering if I offended him.

Then something grabs me by the abdomen and hoists me into the air.

I clench my eyes and scream blindly, too startled to call on my magic.

I calm down when I see the semi-transparent bright-blue fingers of a demigod around my waist. The hand doesn't squeeze the air from my lungs but holds me up before the great being's face, twenty feet above the towering trees and Samson below them.

The dryad demigod blinks at me. Wet, tangled hair half-covers its face, a few strands caught between its thin chapped lips. Even its narrow eyes are half-closed as though sleepy or confused.

"Hi there," I say. Quickly, my shock turns to anxiety; this isn't a healthy demigod. I look down at Samson, who stares dumbfounded from the ground. My empty lilith floats at his side, hopelessly small from my vantage.

I call down to Samson, "It's okay. Don't worry."

Part of me flushes with embarrassment; if the wolf didn't believe I was powerful before, he's in for a reality check now. Aside from truly unforgivable acts committed against the land or their nymphs, there's no other reason for a demigod to snatch a passerby.

I turn back to the great being.

It brings me closer to its face. I stare as its nostrils flare around my robe, wondering if the dryad demigod can gauge my power by scent. Unless I'm in my form with my horns out for all to see, there's no simple way for another being to determine the depths of my magical stores.

"Helisent, what have you done?" Samson calls up from below.

I lean over the demigod's thick fingers to return his accusatory glare. Of course, he assumes I've degraded the demigod's territory and will now be punished. He forgets he's been at my side this whole time. I try not to take it so personally.

In Velm, power is tied to austere morality, to spotless reputations.

For wielders, life is much less transparent.

I roll my eyes back to the dryad demigod. "Don't mind him. We're just passing through. If I can be of service, just direct me to your needs."

Typically, I've interacted with demigods at desita-filled festivals. But I've also had a few run-ins with demigods in need of help. I've never minded sharing my magic with the great beings. Like Onesimos said, wielders are demigodless, but I find great comfort in serving the nymphs.

I am a magical resource, like a river or a sun.

Still, that doesn't mean my run-ins with demigods are easy. While they seem to understand language, they never speak.

I pat the being's blue-hued finger. "You look a little worse for wear, my dear demigod. Show me the way. Also, I can't help but notice how undignified I look right now, being held like this. What if I float beside—"

With a jerk, the demigod turns and starts walking with me in tow.

The evergreens in the thin mossy forest reach the being's hips. But its lower body doesn't shift between the trees as it walks. Instead, its legs disappear into the canopy, bleeding into the trees in a half-real way that gives me a migraine.

I see a flush of transparent light around the demigod's thighs, then treetops, then the forest floor below. Its grip remains tight enough that I can't turn to see if Samson follows us.

For the next ten minutes, I'm trapped in the walking demigod's bobbing grip. Eventually, a muddy pond comes into view amid a clearing of parched tall grass. A few dead trees crane over the murky body of water, their trunks hollow and blackened.

The demigod sets me down at the pond's shoreline, then it kneels at my side.

I shake out my robe in the brown grass. Behind me, someone else shuffles into the brittle fibers. Samson heads toward one of the dead trees, keeping a healthy distance from the demigod.

To my great surprise, he didn't leave my lilith behind. Less to my surprise, he seems to be using a stick to drag the cushion by one of its metal ornaments.

I roll my eyes, but the demigod ignores his arrival. It looks from me to the water then taps the surface with a finger.

I stare at the bog and wait for something to happen. Usually, the land responds to the touch of a demigod—even to the thought of one, I would imagine.

A breeze shifts the tall grass around us and sends ripples across the pond's murky surface.

I crane my neck to glance up at the great being. Unlike the hesperide demigod who brought the Gammic Queen to Luz, this demigod's cotton layers are ripped and wet, just as lackluster as its thin hair.

I gesture toward the pond. "You have to show me the problem. Once, in Rhotidom, another dryad demigod needed help stopping mudslides after the rainy season. It showed me how it wanted the boulders stacked to fortify the mountainside. If you don't show me what's wrong, I'm going to have to guess— and nobody wants that."

The demigod extends one hand over the pond, clenches it, and then opens its hand. It repeats the process; a tight fist that slowly opens.

I turn to Samson and call, "Do you have any idea what that could mean?"

He looks just as suspicious and stunned as before. He shakes his head, eyes on the demigod.

The great being leans toward the pond. It sticks a hand into the water, then brings it back up to perform the same clench-and-release gesture with its fist. As with the canopy on the walk here, its body doesn't submerge beneath the surface and then crest—it bleeds into the muddy water in a fizzle of blueish light, as though the pond is an extension of its body.

It clicks.

"There's something stuck?" I ask.

In response, the demigod uncurls its fist to demonstrate *opening*. Then it lowers its hand back into the pond.

"There's something stuck *under* the water?" I go on.

I float to the edge of the pond and collect my robe around me, avoiding the mud and tall grass. I set my hand on the demigod's shoulder. Sometimes, touching a demigod will provide a burst of insight—a scent or an image or an itch. Nothing this time.

"I can't swim," I say. "Give me a minute."

While I hover at the demigod's shoulder, I plunge sensing magic into the water.

While my magic is non-physical, I can still feel what it encounters—and I hate the slick and muddy bottom, the fluttering tendrils of hydrilla. As I work, the demigod twitches as though my magic tickles it.

Eventually, I find a tense patch of mud. There's something caught beneath that wants to escape. I probe a bit further with sensing magic and realize it's more water.

I raise my eyebrows. "Your spring is clogged. Nothing too dire—you were being a little dramatic back there, don't you think?"

But the demigod isn't cajoling. Its face is pinched and serious; I wonder if it's in physical pain from the blocked spring. Or is it the land? And what is pain to land?

"Get ready, dear demigod." I gently shift the mud that's blocking the trapped water, but the sludge is rockier than I thought. I push and pull rather than rip aside the tacky earth. As soon as the first veil of mud tears loose, a massive torrent of clear water shoots up from the pond.

I bellow as a flash of blue light crackles around us. I rush backward while in the air, half-tangled in my robe. Within seconds, water rains down in puddles, smacking against the pond's surface and flattening the tall grass on the shoreline.

I'm too late to shield myself from all the muck, which spatters against my robe and hair in heavy globs. *Gross.* With a sigh, I get to work drying and cleaning my robe with magic.

I look around as I flare out the velvet layers and dry their wetted ends.

Samson hustles over, still dragging my lilith at the end of a stick. His wide blue-black eyes run across me. "Are you okay?"

I reach for my lilith. "Sure. Just a little water."

I climb into place on the cushion and stare at the pond's undulating surface. Water gurgles up from below, leaving its surface choppy. The demigod now hunches in the pond, its skin fizzling with blue where it touches the water. Only its eyes, forehead, and hairline stick out.

It studies me and Samson with slow-moving eyes. Already, its hair is drier and fluffier than the wet matted mess from before.

I wave to the great being, then turn to Samson. "What should we ask for?"

His eyebrows pinch together. "You want to *demand* something from a demigod? Are you sure that's a good idea?"

I tsk. "The last demigod I helped gave me a bag full of rubies. *Rubies*, Samson."

He sighs as he turns in a circle to study our surroundings. The woods where we started our day are almost out of sight, the emerald trees fading into the pale hills. "We're near Tet, so if we want to find grimoire before we pass into the fog, it would be helpful to know where the closest village is."

"That's a good idea. I'm glad you're starting to contribute." I clear my throat and look at the blue-tinted being, huddled in the pond like a mischievous child. "We're looking for grimoire, my dear demigod. Where's the closest village where we could find it?"

A hand rises from the water to gesture to the northwest. I squint toward where the horizon ends in a tangle of forest. Just before that, I make out a few trails of gray smoke from narrow chimneys.

"Thank you." I bow my head.

Samson does the same. "Farewell, dryad demigod."

The demigod lowers its arm below the water, then its face.

In its wake, a few large bubbles pop at the surface as freshwater from the spring unleashes below.

We head in the direction of the village. For the first time, our silence feels comfortable.

When we arrive at the outskirts of an unimpressive cluster of huts and wooden buildings, I start my search for the village's tavern.

We barely make it past two hesperides with speckled birch-bark skin before a pair of wolves barrel around a corner. Unlike the traveling wolves who passed us along the Irme River, these men aren't bearing gifts for Samson.

It's the opposite. The elder man stops before Samson and bows his head. A wolfling, gangly and awkward, stands just behind his shoulder. They both pant lightly, their cheeks rouged. The younger has muddied ankles, as though he's been running barefoot through the muck common to this region.

The elder speaks quickly, "Samson 714 Afador, Kulapsifang, my pack needs your help."

I slide my eyes to Samson. He stares ahead with the same vexed indifference as usual, but his tone is warm. "I am here."

I am here.

The words lodge in my head as the elder wolf goes on at a breakneck pace.

"This village is shared between my pack, hesperides, and naiads. A warlock came last week, and now we've realized our seedlings are missing. Planting begins soon, Samson 714 Afador, but there's no war band close by to call on. We ask that you send the pack leaders from Luz, or one of their representatives, to track down the warlock responsible. We ask for the full return of the stolen seeds."

I slide off my lilith as the wolf's tone changes. I wish my robe was slightly less audacious, especially as two naiads pass. The women carry baskets full of bright crops on their heads, balanced with a hand. They bring out the green in their pale eyes as they slide disdainful looks my way.

The elder wolf chatters on about the seeds, the quantity stolen, and where they might be now. So many details—but I'm not sure what a warlock would want with seeds. We don't plant and harvest like the nymphs and wolves; we barter.

I slip away without a word.

I glance back once. Samson hasn't moved, staring at the elder wolf as he continues to detail the travesty of the lost seedlings.

I am here.

I wander through the plain village with the understanding Samson can follow my ala through the dozen or so dirt streets with ease. Even if he can't, I'm sure he'll know to check the village's single tavern.

Inside, two fires in the center of the long structure fend off the burgeoning night outside. Near the fogs of Tet, wet cold endures longer than in other parts of Mieira. The groups of hesperides and naiads lining the communal tables huddle for warmth. A scurrying waiter delivers overflowing mugs to the nymphs, chatting and joking with them.

At the far end of the tavern, a trio of wolves notices my entrance. The three women look over their shoulders, eyes narrowing on me.

I ignore them; they're Samson's problem, not mine. I inhale the scent of ale-soaked wood and let my body relax.

Home sweet home.

I head to the bar, happy to find barrels of ale, bottles of liquor, and empty glasses galore. I eye a glass pitcher full of sparkling liquid: bitterroot brandy.

The waiter slides behind the bar and bares a large smile at

me. The naiad's skin is light olive like mine, his blue-green eyes darker than the sky-eyed okeanids.

"What's your poison, then?" he asks.

I smile back, relieved he doesn't seem to share the village-wide disdain for wielders. Still, I keep my guard up. (My papa taught me this long ago: a good bartender exacts revenge by not cutting someone off and letting them make a fool of them-selves; this will be the only way to tell that you have displeased them—and you won't remember it.)

"Bitterroot brandy please." I snap my fingers when he turns to fill a glass. "And grimoire."

The naiad pauses to look back at me. "I see. And what do you have to offer in exchange?"

I wave my hand. "Name your barter. I'd like a full bottle of brandy, so no skimping. Plenty of grimoire, too."

The bartender sucks on his teeth and glances across the crowd, then to the patch of fading sunlight beyond the entrance. "My warrenmates are due back tomorrow. Haven't done *any* of the laundry since they've been gone. How quickly can you have everything washed, dried, and folded?"

I open my mouth to tell him twenty minutes, but Samson's deep voice sounds over my left shoulder. "You want washing, drying, and folding for two servings of grimoire and a glass of brandy? Be reasonable."

"No, no, no—he's talking about the *bottle* of brandy." I wink at the naiad and ignore the Samson-shaped figure looming over me. "In which case, I can have all your laundry washed, dried, and folded in no time. Where is it?"

The waiter claps his hands with delight, then hustles from behind the bar. "Follow me. It's out back."

Samson leers at me as I turn. "He didn't specify how much laundry he had."

I leer back. "Do you think this is my first fucking barter? Go say hello to the lady wolves. They've been staring daggers at me since I got here."

I follow the naiad from the back of the bar. Outside, a mound of clothes, sheets, and rags sit in a festering pile beside an empty washing bucket. The nymph looks sheepishly at me, shoulders hunched. I glance back to make sure Samson didn't follow; he certainly wouldn't approve of the devastating mountain of dirty laundry.

The naiad rolls up his sleeves then glances from the bucket to the mound of clothes. "I haven't seen a wolf with a high count travel with a wielder in... well, ever."

"Well, you're not in the right place for that, are you?" I jab a thumb over my shoulder toward a stack of firewood. "My super-great-grandma probably killed a prominent wolf over there." I point in the opposite direction toward a few scraggly bushes. "And the wolves probably got their revenge just over here. Do the villagers here still howl about Bloody Betty? It kind of seems like they would."

The naiad's face tightens. I know it's a little forward to bring up Bloody Betty, a centerheart witch who was abducted by Velmic wolves and became their greatest battle-winner. Still, I find it strange that the beings who live exactly where the War Years were fought are the least likely to acknowledge the conflict.

I suppose I can't judge the naiad. Samson and I haven't brought up the War Years once since beginning our journey.

I change the subject, glancing at a circle of stones nearby and praying it's a low well. "So is that the water supply? I can't wash all of this without a good amount."

The naiad gestures to the well, then he walks over. He lays one hand on the stone lip, then stares into the shadowy abyss below. His lips twitch, as though speaking; I've heard some nymphs have to *tell* their elemental magic what to do. How adorable.

In a few seconds, sloshing water echoes from the well.

The naiad offers me another sheepish grin. "I called up the water—do you mind drawing it? I need to get back inside."

I wave him back toward the bar. "Go on, then. Get my brandy ready."

His smile triples in size. "You're a gracious, gracious witch."

"Don't forget it."

Once the naiad is out of sight and the door to the tavern has clanked shut, the washing, drying, and folding takes around fifteen minutes. Washing magic is one of the first forms wielders learn; in fact, most of our early studies cover life's mundanities.

In addition to making activities like washing, storing, and organizing easier, it's good sense for wielders to learn service-based magic. First, it makes bartering for anything a breeze—especially for wielders without magical dove to spare for longer-term spells. Second, it puts nymphs and wolves at ease to know we care about pulling our weight. Third, it gives us the ability to self-determine; unlike nymphs and wolves, we don't tend to travel in packs.

I wait outside for another fifteen minutes just so the naiad thinks I'm going the distance for him.

When I head back inside, Samson has a place for us in the corner opposite the female wolves. He takes up almost the entire bench on one side of the table. His burly arms are set in front of him, one hand lifted to toy with one of the candle's tiny flames.

It's the first time I've seen him truly lost in thought. His features are relaxed, the reflection of orange flames dancing in his black pupils.

He notices me with a start. "That was quick."

"It took longer than your business with the wolves." I raise my eyebrows as I slide onto the open bench. "What will you do? Send word back to Luz for Ferol or Victina to send in a bounty hunter?"

"Wolves don't use bounty hunters. Each city has a pack leader —they call on war bands, which are regulated by Velm, to go and handle conflicts." While he explains, I reach for my bottle of brandy and pour myself a glass of rich liquor. "And I won't send word back to Luz. His pack can handle that on their own time."

I take a long sip of brandy. "So you didn't do anything?"

I am here.

That's what he'd said.

Samson tilts his head. "I always help. It's my duty, Helisent. I sent the pack leader south toward Wrenweary. The packs there will have enough seedlings to spare—a little from each village will replace his original supply in no time.

"Once they've replaced the missing seeds, they can send someone to Luz to ask for a war band to be dispatched. But even that won't be straightforward. Because it didn't happen in Velm, the war band will need to work with the Class to punish the warlock responsible."

Samson's eyes return to the flickering flames, dangling from the top of each pale candle.

"Since I'm not in a war band, I can't start that process. And that's not what this pack leader needed. Every conflict has two solutions: one is mundane, one is emotional. The mundane issues must be addressed first—and swiftly. Justice comes later. Wolves consider it a type of emotional vindication. And emotions are always secondary to survival. So first we replace the seeds for the planting season, and then we search for the warlock responsible."

I don't really know what to do with his wisdom.

Like his observations from the garden of the Luzian Estate, it's extremely unpleasant to encounter.

The naiad returns with a hulking goblet of ale the size of my bottle. He sets it on the table, then squeezes my shoulder. "Thank you, darling witch. The wolf has the grimoire. It's all I have left."

"We're squared," I say.

The naiad scuttles away, disappearing amid the noise and

hustle. With nightfall, the tavern begins to fill with chatty villagers.

Samson guzzles his ale. When he's taken his fill, he sets his mug down and reaches for the tin of grimoire. Despite how fragile and small the container looks, his thick fingers deftly open and separate the marigold-colored powder.

He lifts the tin to snort half the powder, then offers me the rest. I lower my nose and inhale the rancid, overly-sweet grimoire, then sit back with a sound of disgust.

I'm used to snorting dextro, which gives the body an ecstatic kick of energy that lasts for hours. Though a bit bitter, I'm accustomed to dextro's tangy drip at the back of my throat. Grimoire, used to snuff out lies from a conversation, is less relevant to my lifestyle. I collect lies like shiny things; I stack them on a shelf in my mind.

We sit in silence and sip our drinks. I avoid the urge to gag at the grimoire's taste and scent.

"Let's see if it worked," Samson says a moment later. He looks at me, squaring his shoulders from across the table. "My name is Helisent—"

He barely gets out my name before leaning to the side and sneezing. The booming sound is loud enough to startle everyone in the tavern, who suddenly fall silent and swivel toward our table.

This time, I attempt a lie. "My name is Samson 700-something Af—"

Before I can finish the falsehood, the grimoire kicks into action. I sneeze so fast and hard that my forehead slams into the bottle of brandy and knocks it off the table.

Samson grabs it before it can shatter on the ground.

I clench my eyes; it feels like half my brain shot out of my nose. "Holy fuck."

Samson smiles as he sets the bottle back on the table. He bites his lip as though attempting to hide his amusement. "Are you okay?"

As soon as I lean back to laugh, Samson also lets out a few low chuckles. I prod the tiny lump on my forehead. "I'm fine. At least we know the grimoire works."

"Yes." Without wasting any time, he pulls a piece of parchment from his satchel and reads from it. "I'd like to begin by asking how many horns you have."

Our short-lived camaraderie shatters into a thousand pieces.

For a long moment, I watch the candlelight shift across his features. Part of me hopes he'll crack a smile and chalk it up to a bad joke.

He doesn't.

I flick my hair over my shoulder and straighten my velvet robe. "Go ahead and ask, then."

"How many horns do you have?"

"Go fuck yourself, Samson."

He falls utterly still, hand on his mug. "I'm not trying to pry, but you're powerful enough to attract the attention of a demigod. I've never personally met a wielder with enough magic that a *demigod* would feel entitled to their services. Based on your reaction, it wasn't the only time it's happened. And you mentioned leaving extra dove at the processors in Luz when saying goodbye to your warren. I'm guessing that makes you a sponsor of Luz."

What the fuck? Has he been taking notes on me?

I try to remember what I said to my warrenmates outside his estate. The memory is a blur of half-remembered sentiments, dextro, and a multi-day hangover.

I sip my brandy. "Wielders aren't like wolves. We can't smell our generational counts. And we certainly don't show our horns to strangers."

"I see. I don't need to see them; I was just wondering how many you have."

"That's *so* offensive, Samson. That's like me asking how many nuts you have."

"Two."

"You know what I mean. And *no*. I won't be talking about my horns. I told you I was powerful when we first met, and you had your proof today when the demigod needed help with the spring. Stop asking for more."

"That's fair. Your turn."

I take a deep breath to formulate the question. Asking for information like Samson did is one way to play with grimoire, but I've always preferred an existential approach over specific details.

I study his features and ask, "Would it please you to harm me?"

To his credit, he doesn't hesitate. "No." He glances at his notes. "Will you trust me in Tet if you temporarily lose your magic in a sink?"

It's a complicated answer. I move the bottle of brandy to safety in case I don't phrase my words well enough for the grimoire. "Probably not. But I'll do my best to trust you. I like that we laughed together when we sat down, but I *hate* that you just asked about my horns. Two steps forward, one step back."

He nods. "I can respect that."

"And if I lose my magic in a sink in Tet, will you do everything you can to ensure my safety and well-being until my magic comes back? And will you protect me against selkies? I heard there are some in the lakes in Tet."

Once again, he doesn't hesitate. "Yes."

"Why?"

"It's my turn to ask a question."

"Just answer it. Why would you do that for me? I can tell I annoy you, and that you think I'm stupid, and that you're judging yourself for ending up here at my side."

He sighs, then he takes a few long sips of ale. Like I did, he seems to be phrasing his answer precisely. "You do annoy me, but I find you less foolish by the day. Your idea about Skull is our strongest option—and I think it will work. I also think that my chances of finding Oko diminish greatly if I don't have your help."

His words surprise me, as does the gentle tenor of his voice. Compared to the high-pitched shouts and rowdy laughter from the tables around us, sitting in front of Samson and listening to his unwavering words feels...

I don't what it feels like, but I don't hate it.

I raise my eyebrows. "Your turn."

"I'm sorry I asked about your horns." He glances past me, toward the bar, then shrugs. "I know wielders don't show their true forms often, if at all, but I didn't realize it was offensive to ask, too. I won't bring it up again."

"Do the wolves really keep sets of horns hung in Bellator?" The question slips out before I can stop myself. I try to amend it quickly, so he doesn't think I'm trying to instigate a fight. "I heard rumors that the Alphas of Velm still keep some mounted in their great halls from the War Years. A merchant from south of Gamma told my village about it once."

For a long time, Samson stares evenly at me. "I don't like that question."

That's a yes, then.

"Were the horns red or gold?" I can't help myself.

Having a highly ranked wolf like Samson—nonetheless the Kulapsifang—cornered in a tavern with a nose full of grimoire is an unlikely yet serendipitous scenario. And these questions have been building since we pierced the hilly plains where the War Years were fought.

"I heard they're red," I continue. "All of them. And they're all sets of four—the most powerful wielders. I even heard there's a six-horned set. That's why there are only gold wielders left. The Alphas hunted the red line into extinction."

Once again, he looks at me for a long time before responding. "Do they still wear our hides in Antigone?"

"They're kept far away from the public, but I've seen a few and felt one."

It's just as offensive as him saying they use wielder horns as letter openers in Bellator, but something compels me to keep pushing—to cross every boundary now so we don't accidentally overstep in the cold light of day.

For good measure, I add, "I wish I hadn't touched it."

I remember the oil in the fur, the thick roots of the blue-black hide of a wolf felled in its form during the War Years. Compared to the sable and saiga hides common throughout Mieira, the wolf's hide felt...

Predatory.

"The horns are also kept out of public view," he says. "And there's no six-horned set. Only four horns. I don't even think having six horns is possible, but I guess you'd know more than I would about that..."

Indeed.

I down my glass of bitterroot brandy, then refill it. "It feels like purging, doesn't it? All the things we can't say to one another about the War Years even though we still feel..."

I glance at his hands. One lightly holds his mug, while the other is curled near the end of the table.

"Feel what?" he pushes.

"A fear that isn't ours, I suppose."

"Do you know my name?"

I snort, surprised by the question. "Well, I've been assuming it's Samson, *Samson*."

"I meant my generation. My number. You've never said it. You always call me 700-*something* Afador."

"Let's see... I remember Imperatriz 713 Afador..." I squint as I reach back into my memory and try to verify the former Alpha Female of Velm's generation. Samson's *mother*, I remind myself. She was more active than Clearbold within nymph and wielder communities before her disappearance. "Which means you'd be Samson 714 Afador."

Samson's eyebrows bunch together. "You remember my mother?"

I search Samson's face for some trace of his matrilineage but find only Clearbold's features. The Leofsige line. How unfortunate.

I nod. "I saw her once. She came to Alita when I was little. I think she was promoting the Northing. She gave many gifts to the Rhotidic Kings and Queens, and to the Head Witch and Warlock."

Uncertain what to do with his strangled expression, I keep chattering. "Right, I guess you don't really know who I am. You only know that my name is Helisent. My *full* name is Helisent West of Jaws."

He nods. "Samson 714 Afador."

"Nice to meet you." The words slip out before I can gauge whether they're true.

He returns my smile. "It's nice to meet you, too."

For a second, we sit tensed, as though waiting for the grimoire to snuff out our lies; it doesn't.

I hadn't realized any genuine part of me thought it was nice to meet him.

Based on his calm surprise, neither did he.

CHAPTER 6

CREEPY BABY

SAMSON

My son,
Velm relies directly on what you think; the wolves will rarely ask how
you feel. That doesn't mean you shouldn't know. Secrets are dangerous.
Especially those we try to keep from ourselves. In the privacy of your
heart, all feelings are safe, Samson. Forever.

The fog of Tet looks different than it did in my youth.

As Helisent and I pass through the heavy vapor, I consider grabbing one of the dangling ornaments from her lilith. Losing track of travel companions is one of the region's primary dangers.

Along with vast patches of hidden quicksand.

And magical sinks that leave wielders powerless.

And caves prone to flash floods.

And a lack of doting demigods to offer help.

And a city of ghosts.

And a dizzying series of lakes that no being has ever successfully mapped, which could also be filled with four-eyed selkies and their whispers.

The fog warps in gradients of deep gray and beige, hiding the world twenty feet in every direction. It smells of stagnant water, mud, evergreen needles, wilted grass, moss, and rotten fish.

As we walk, Helisent's small warm hand takes my forearm. I half-drag her and her lilith as she clamps down.

I try not to look at the hand in bald surprise and discomfort. She's not familiar with Velmic custom and has no idea that touching only precedes one of two things: sexual intimacy or a brawl. Even brushing against a wolf with a high generational count is regarded as disrespectful; a wolf should always be in control of their body.

I glance at her fingers, their olive tone rich compared to my pale skin.

It's not uncommon for nymphs and wielders to overstep Velmic boundaries—not out of a lack of respect but rather a lack of understanding. Nymphs often hold each other's wrists as they walk, sleep crammed up against each other, and sniff and pinch one another as though to make sure nothing's changed. And wielders are apt to do as the nymphs do.

I try to let it go.

Helisent chatters nervously. "Holy shit, Samson, imagine if we hadn't snorted all that grimoire before we got here. I'd be convinced you brought me here to murder me. No offense. This just looks like a prime location to make someone disappear."

I'd be offended if it weren't so true.

With each step, I take a deep breath. One of the only ways we'll know a threat is coming is if I smell its ala before it parts the fog.

"Do you know much about the magical sinks?" Helisent's voice lowers to a whisper, as though afraid of attracting attention. Part of me wants to tell her she can speak as loudly as she wants—if anything is going to give us away, it's the jangling of her lilith's metal ornaments. "You said your war band came by this region when you were younger."

"We weren't studying magical sinks. The only time we came *really* close to Tet was when we were looking for a lost flock of sheep."

"Oh, how scandalous and dangerous. Did you find the sheep, Samson? All of them?"

She looks serious aside from her pinched mouth.

In our two weeks together, I've started making sense of her expressions. This one is eighty percent devilish interest and twenty percent ribbing.

It's an acceptable proportion to warrant an answer. "We did find all of the sheep, Helisent. Thank you for your concern."

"And did you punish the sheep for running away? Was there justice for the shepherd?"

I've also started taking less offense to her deep misgivings about wolves. How I misunderstand her magic, she misunderstands my culture. "No, we didn't punish the sheep for running away. We punished the wolf who led them from their pasture and killed the shepherd."

"Killed the shepherd? Why?" With each question, Helisent drifts closer to me. Her hand renews its grip; I can't tell if I'm intrigued by the touch or dismayed.

My arm will be marked with her ala now that she's held it for a few minutes. I'll also be more attuned to her scent now that she's left it on me. My fangself will be able to smell her from greater distances and with greater distinction—and I'll remember her scent even when phased into a wolf.

Into Samsonfang.

"The shepherd had enough peat for Night, but another wolf didn't. I'm not sure if you understand what Night is... in Mieira, your winter is cool and rainy. But in Velm, we have a long and sunless and snowy winter. Night lasts up to eight months."

"Samson, everyone has heard of Night in Velm."

"I see. Excuse me, then. At first, the killer wanted access to the shepherd's peat... but when he wandered close to the shepherd's home, he recognized his scent. The wolves' grandfathers had been in conflict, which meant the pair were part of that blood feud as their grandsons. They tend to—"

"A *blood* feud on behalf of their grandparents?" Helisent cuts in. "I thought blood feuds were personal."

I've seen a blood feud started over food stolen off a plate. I've seen a blood feud for such a useless cause be rekindled after generations of peace.

Helisent has heard of Night, like all Mieirans. But she doesn't understand how demanding it is. How the will to survive takes an unfathomable and violent shape in some.

Weary of her mistrust, I take care with my explanation. "A blood feud can run on for generations. Some think they're genetic; a wolf will inherit a predisposition toward certain alas from their parents. But I think it's a matter of self-control and circumstance.

"The killer we were tracking had gone to the shepherd's home to steal his peat. He was desperate for the bricks— nothing more. But that desperation quickly turned violent once he realized he had a blood feud with the shepherd.

"We were called to find the sheep, which he set free as a distraction. When word spread of the murder, we went to find the killer next."

It's like I explained in the village when we snorted grimoire: first comes the practical solution, and next comes justice.

"But why aren't peat stores communal? Don't you freeze if you can't make a strong fire that lasts until morning? I heard the snow buries some houses. The wolf wouldn't have been looking to steal peat if he had enough for winter."

Is she... defending the murderer?

Happy to avoid explaining the punishment we dispensed to the killer, I go on, "It's possible. But the offender didn't have enough stores because of his own failures. Velm is rich in peat. It's usually laziness that prevents a wolf from collecting enough to last through Night. It's not like it is farther north..."

Our seasons are unrecognizable in Mieira.

Helisent grew up with a frigid and rainy winter; a warm and rainy spring; a dry and heat-filled summer; a dry and wind-swept autumn.

I grew up with Night, which is broken by four fragile months of warmth and sunlight—a summer that never lasts long enough.

The witch reels back with a loud squeal. I have no idea what the sound means; her yowling has indicated delight, wrath, and awe on separate occasions.

This time, it looks to be awe. "*Night*. Do you remember what snow is like? I heard snow is whiter than even the palest wolves."

The question brings a smile to my face. "Of course, I remember snow. And it's much whiter than skin. When there's a fresh drift, it can be bright enough to blind you. And it looks like a lot when it falls, but snow is made of tiny, tiny flakes. Snow is really just soft jewels, piled together."

I associate the pale drifts with my mother, Imperatriz. With the happy months we spent west of Rouz, where the valleys are narrow and the mountains steep and their tops blasted with gusts of world-ending snow.

Long ago.

Helisent smiles, golden eyes twinkling. "That's very poetic, Samson."

"The Female Alpha of Velm said it first, not me."

Helisent's warm hand slides from my arm and resettles in her lap. With a sheepish grin, she glances at me. "I keep forgetting that you're the Kulapsifang. That you're so important."

I wish I could say the same about her.

With each day, her magical power becomes more apparent.

In the past, the only time I'd gauged the infrasound of powerful spells was as Samsonfang. Phased under the triple-moon or doublemoon, all of my senses are enhanced—I didn't think my ears could even register the low bass of magic without having turned skin.

Since leaving Luz, I've heard it four times with Helisent. Three times, a deep humming encircled her nest like a hoard of bees while she slept. The palpable buzz kept me up until dawn, hand resting on my satchel with my throwing ax tucked beneath.

The fourth burst of infrasound occurred when the dryad demigod snatched her off her lilith the other day and she panicked.

She tilts her head. "And is it cold? I've never felt snow."

"It's very cold, very pristine. As soon as the weather warms, the snow melts... but if it's *too* cold, snow becomes ice. Nobody likes ice." I take a deep breath and pretend I'm not so far from home. "What I like most is the scent of snow. It smells pure— pure in a way I can't describe."

Helisent fidgets with the volcanic glass beads on her bag's clasp. "Pure in a way you can't describe..." She repeats the words in a high-pitched voice. "Those are the best descriptions, Samson. Something you feel you can't describe. Try it, then. Tell me what pure snow smells like."

There's nothing else to do.

We stay on the topic for most of the day. It seems to distract us both from the unending haze of fog that bends around us like a sphere, trapping us within an uncertain, murky depth.

The search for Skull in Tet is a specific type of hell.

The fog doesn't disband—not during the first traces of bright dawn or at the onset of the cooling night. We find lake after lake as we run into their muddy shorelines, then we follow the sandy mud to round the body of water.

All we find past them are more treeless expanses.

Then more lakes.

Tet's only mercy is its lack of selkies.

On multiple occasions, we circle back on bodies of water several times before realizing our mistake. With each day, we walk closer together and speak less. At night, we count our supplies to flesh out a plan of retreat.

That's not the only uncertainty; Helisent has no tree to build a safe nest in. Instead, she weaves her magical birch twigs into a conical shape that she sleeps under. We handle almost all of our routines side by side so as not to be separated: brushing our hair, preparing our meals, drying out our damp layers near a fire that runs on our lessening stores of peat.

I start to fear a seething more than ever before because we spend so much time side by side.

Exactly how much of her intimate ala would I have to inhale to set off the curse? Would a wayward whiff be enough, or would my head need to be directly between her thighs?

I've taken to holding my breath when her velvet robe and dress hike up toward her thighs.

But as we push further west into Tet and fail to find Skull, a city of ghosts, a new fear kicks in. I start to wonder if we'd recognize the limits of Mieira. If we're walking into a nether-world without recourse.

It doesn't really matter.

I'll go as far as I must to find the witch who might be able to lead me to Imperatriz.

And Helisent seems just as hellbent.

On our sixth day in the maddening fog, Helisent decides to fly above the vapor to scour the distance.

I wait for her on the ground and try not to wonder about

the likelihood she'll abandon me. Ten minutes later, she parts the fog to return to my side on the muddy hilltop.

Her eyes widen with joy. "I wish you didn't hate magic so much, Samson. I could take you to the place above the clouds. It's so beautiful there. It reminds me of Antigone. Some mornings—"

"Did you see anything helpful?" I've started feeling less guilty about interrupting her diatribes; she seems used to it, too.

"What? Yeah? Of course. I found Skull. It's that way." She throws a hand westward. "*As I was saying*—some mornings, in Antigone, you could see above the clouds right from my apartment window. The clouds would make these little round stepping stones. One witch told me it's because of the stone pillars. They're tall as mountains, skinny as rivers. They do something weird to the warm and cold air. It makes the clouds form in a strange way."

"Really?" I glance in the direction she indicated. "Any word on what Skull looks like?"

Her chin drops as her features fall still. "Oh, you won't like it, Samson. It was green. A foul type of green."

What the fuck does that mean?

I turn with a roll of my eyes. Helisent's jangling lilith takes off in my wake.

I guide us west and pause intermittently to let Helisent drift above the cloud line and refine our path. Her descriptions of Skull become less promising as we near the city.

At first, it's foul green. Then, it isn't a city at all, and then it's made of walls of green fire. Lastly, it's nothing more than a horrible tangled pit of cave entrances that each project a sickly green light that parts the fog as it rises skyward.

It sounds like madness until we finally find a cave entrance.

The grotto starts with a few loose dark pebbles that advance into steep descents of jagged unstable boulders. Unlike the rest of Tet, the cave entrance is free of fog—as is the space above the dark rocks. The clear air forms a tunnel that reaches into the sky and, true to Helisent's word, glimmers with a staticky peridot light.

The asymmetrical cave below looks like a tunnel of black carved into the earth. At its deepest point, a green light shifts and shimmers.

"Have you ever seen a ghost?" Helisent asks as we approach the first grotto.

"No. I've heard descriptions, though."

"They're green, right? Kind of like the demigods—only half-forms. You know, the first time—"

The witch reels back with a world-ending shriek.

I flinch as her voice barrels into my ear and leaves it ringing. My body locks as I prepare to lower my inhibitions and give the chattering wielder a piece of my mind.

And then I see it.

A toddler with transparent green flesh waves at us from the cave's pitch-black center. It makes a few wordless high-pitched noises as though excited to see us.

The hairs on my arms stand on end as a chill shoots up my spine.

I suck down a deep breath only to realize the green-glowing toddler has no ala. There's only the cave's scent of ancient stone, dark mold, and tepid water.

Helisent lets out a breathy sob. "Why the *fuck* did you listen to me? What kind of Kulapsifang are you? Just following a witch into Tet when she says it's a good idea to barter with a ghost in Skull. I mean, Samson, my dear wolf—"

"Take a few deep breaths."

She's never in charge of her own emotions. I wonder if it's as exhausting for her as it is for me.

I pull my eyes away from the toddler to make sure she's calming down. "Remember that you can always breathe an emotion away if you control your breath. Try the exercise I taught you the other day."

She sucks down a breath from her stomach. It's forceful enough that I can see her belly moving beneath her peach robe.

"Good." I nod. "Stick with that for a minute."

I leave Helisent's side to take a step into the grotto. The tiny ghost waves its hand and makes more optimistic sounds. My ears pique at each whistle-like noise; similar to Helisent's deep, humming infrasound, this is like an itchy, ear-splitting *ultrasound*.

I wonder...

I glance back at Helisent. "Your magic makes a very deep sound, but this feels like the opposite. Leave your bag up there. I think this is a sink. We'll collect it when we leave."

Her eyes flash from me to the grotto below. "When we leave what?"

I look toward the cave and its terrifying ghost. "Leave Skull."

She makes a few noises as though she may argue, but then she slides from her lilith and gets to work stuffing it into her bag. Helisent fixes her hair then shrugs off her peach robe. It's one of the few times I've seen her without the large luxurious garment.

Beneath, she wears a strapless beige dress that matches her boots. It's sinched above her breasts, free-flowing to her calves. She keeps her jewelry on—the bangles around her forearms and wrists and ankles, the dangling earrings with fringy ends, the drooping necklaces that smell like copper and old thread.

"Close your eyes," she says. "If my magic doesn't work at all, you'll see me in my form."

I brace my hands on a rock, then turn around.

I hear her take a fragile breath, then hear her boots scuff against the rocks.

She gasps, then I hear more shifting. "Fuck. You're right. Just let me figure out how to hide my form—I don't think the sink can nullify *all* my magic."

I wonder idly how much *all* that magic is. Since our conversation in the village, I've started to assume she has four horns. I prepare myself for seeing them should things go awry in Skull.

Behind me, her infrasound whorls and flares like a group of migrating birds in flight. Then it snuffs out.

"You can open your eyes. I need a moment."

I turn to find her slouched near her bag and robe, set in the muddy grass.

She eyes the cave as she explains, "I can hide my form, but only barely. I won't be able to use any magic."

I nod. "Is there anything you'd like to tell me before we do this—in terms of being magicless, I mean?"

"I'm not very strong and I'm not very balanced." She rolls her eyes like she hates to admit something I've already figured out: her magical might makes up for a lack of physical strength.

Her plump curves and unblemished skin have faint outlines of muscle. The other day, she also made a point of walking for most of the day and made it farther than I would have thought. Still, I would never peg her as the type for physical labor, and she wouldn't likely forgive someone who did.

She clears her throat. "And I really think I should have a drink before we do this."

"You already had your morning brandy. I'm strong enough to help us both navigate the cave."

With a huff, she looks from her robe to the closest boulder. She steps from rock to rock with an uncertain gait. One hand holds her flowing dress, while the other reaches straight out to help her balance.

Though her pace is tedious, it doesn't slow down as we near the entrance. She steps into the cave's sharp precipice of shadow at my side. Before us, the toddler's features come into view.

It only heightens my unease.

Though small as a four-year-old, its green-glowing semi-translucent facial features are warped. Some, like the button nose and huge eyes, are suitably infantile. But they're accompanied by forehead wrinkles and smile lines that hint it might not be young at all.

It smacks its tiny hand against the rock with a wicked smile.

At least the ghost's green shimmer helps light the rocky cave tunnel.

I look back once toward the milky light outside. From within the cave, the fog of Tet comes into stark detail. Rather than the abstract shifts of gray and beige fog, I now see bodies in the mist.

It's as though the fog is actually *made* of half-invisible beings that stand shoulder-to-shoulder, packed together—wolves, wielders, nymphs.

My gut steels.

Again, I drink the air for a hint of their alas but find only the putrid scent of fog that's followed us through Tet.

No wonder the fog never fucking parted—it's not fog.

Holy shit.

Helisent's right. I'm a fucking idiot for following her into Tet.

I take a few deep breaths like I instructed Helisent to do. Then I shift into place behind her, hoping to block her view of the fog, and focus on the tiny ghost with renewed suspicion.

If the beings in the fog are actually ghosts, then what the fuck is this thing?

Helisent kneels before the toddler. It stares at her with wide eyes, a wrinkly smile on its face.

"Hi, baby ghost." Like she did with the dryad demigod, Helisent speaks to the peridot-shimmering being with an affectatious tone. "I'm guessing this is the entrance to Skull, your city. We're here to barter with a ghost in exchange for a haunting. Would you like to haunt someone? Do you know any beings who would be willing to do so?"

The toddler throws out its arms in a plea to be picked up.

Helisent giggles before her voice drops to a more serious tone. "See, I think you're full of shit, little one. I think you're using a child-like form to hide the nature of your power. The more innocent the cover, the more sinister the trick. That's what us wielders always say." She winks at the toddler. "Shall we be honest with each other, my dear ghost?"

Ultrasound flickers from deep inside the cave's shadows. I flinch from the high-pitched ringing as it clangs between the cold rocks.

Though Helisent doesn't seem to notice the flare of sound, the toddler does; it turns to stare into the cave's innards.

Rocks shift in and out of place within the shadows. A trace of rushing water also echoes out to us.

Then a voice sounds from the cave's shadowy belly. "Leave the creepy baby alone! If you're looking to barter for a haunting, step inside the cave. You're not really *inside* Skull until you've let the shadows engulf you. And you can't barter with a *real* ghost until you're inside Skull. Don't be fooled by the baby. Seriously. He's being punished."

The toddler holds out its arms to Helisent once again, whimpering a high note.

Helisent straightens with a tsk. "I fucking knew it. S-i-n-i-s-t-e-r. That's how you spell sinister, Creepy Baby."

With a sudden shift in mood, the toddler hisses loudly, then it leaps from the boulder and sprints farther into the cave. It jumps from rock to rock swiftly, without any second-guessing. We stare wordlessly at the trail of pale green light the ghost emits.

I nod toward the cave's innards, which remain semi-illumed with green light. "Shall we?"

She nods, then takes off navigating the uneven spread of obtuse rocks. I follow at her side in case she slips as we round the curved tunnel toward a gate. Thick bars run from one end of the circular passage to the other to form a sturdy blockade. Like the ghost, the gate's metal shimmers, semi-translucent and green.

Creepy Baby perches on one of the bars with a vibrant pout. Its facial wrinkles are more pronounced now; there's even stubble on its chin.

This is such a bad idea.

On the other side of the gate stands another green-hued ghost. This one looks like a normal adult hesperide with long braids and a wide-set mouth.

He says, "Don't worry, the creepy baby doesn't bite. We yanked out his teeth years ago. Come on, then. You're nearly there." The ghost looks from the toddler to me to Helisent with a contagious smile. "I hope the junior ghosts outside didn't bother you."

Helisent glances at me. "Junior ghosts?"

My skin crawls as I think of all the fog we've inhaled in the last week. "You don't want to know."

The adult ghost steps forward and opens the gate. The metal groans as though it hasn't been touched in ages. The nymph holds it aside and gestures for us to come in. "Welcome to Skull, welcome to Skull. We don't have to travel far, just step beyond the bars and we can barter. Otherwise, the creepy baby will bother us. He might even get a junior ghost involved. Who knows?"

Helisent and I slowly approach the gate.

Unfortunately, her deft ability to gauge Creepy Baby's lies doesn't seem to be working on this new ghost. Like me, she eyes the glowing nymph with every step. Though its features look like an average composite of male hesperides, his pupils flare with flashes of bright green light and emit pulses of ultrasound.

My gut tells me he's just as untrustworthy as Creepy Baby, perhaps just more convincing.

But if he can help us find Oko...

And if Oko can help me find Imperatriz, or her remains...

Helisent steps over the threshold, then she looks back at me.

With a sigh, I also pass into Skull.

As soon as my boots hit the rocky floor, another clang of ultrasound echoes from within the cave. The adult ghost shuts the gate behind us with a loud clank, leaving Creepy Baby on the other side, then he turns to guide us farther into the cave. At least now the ground is flat, covered in tiny pebbles.

But to my surprise, the cave gets smaller the farther we journey. The ghost glances back now and then with a pleasant smile.

Helisent walks closer to my side as we continue; without her lilith, it feels like I'm escorting an adolescent. While she's taller than I'd once expected, only the puffiest wisps of her tangled white hair reach past my chest.

"So why are you punishing Creepy Baby?" Helisent calls up to our host.

"It's a long story. Mostly just ogling. A bit of gnawing."

"Gnawing? I see." Helisent cranes her neck to look up at me, eyes narrowed with suspicion. She mouths the word *gnawing* like a question.

I shrug. I also have no idea what it means in this context.

We continue in silence, following the ghost's green-hued light. Eventually, a wall of black comes into view, and I anticipate a sharp turn. Instead, the ghost continues straight until we reach a dead end.

With a flourish of his long tunic, our guide turns back to us and sits down on a flat rock. He gestures to the pebbled ground a few feet before him. "Have a seat. It's time to barter."

Instead of sitting down, Helisent looks around at the unimpressive tunnel of dark rock. "This is Skull? We grew up hearing tales of a *city* of ghosts."

The ghost smiles with a sultry indifference. "And I grew

hearing tales of witches with *horns* and wolves with *fangs*. Looks like we're all being let down, aren't we?"

With a gentle tsk, Helisent sits down. Without her magic, she looks unsteady; she pulls her knees to her chest and wraps her arms around them. Her shoulders shiver, causing her jewelry to jingle. Does she usually use magic to warm herself? Does this feel *cold* to her? At most, it's brisk.

I take a seat at her side. Though the ghost is out of reach, Helisent is close enough for me to grab in the event of an unpleasant surprise.

She clears her throat, then starts, "You already heard the basics. We want to barter with a ghost to haunt someone. What could we offer to sway you, my dear ghost?"

"Well, a few details might be nice. Who would you like me to haunt? What's the nature of the haunting—to compel them to do something?" The ghost pulls a small ledger from his tunic and uses his fingernail to scratch something onto the paper. "Or to punish them in general? Such as through the use of sleep paralysis, late-night moaning, the moving of furniture, hiding of precious items, and so on."

Helisent glances at me. "We need our target to be haunted sufficiently enough to seek out a GhostEater."

The ghost reels back with a scoff. "A *GhostEater*. What wielder came up with that? You know they don't eat us, right? They just send us back here."

The ghost hisses again as it scribbles on the ledger with the end of its nail.

"What kind of being is it?" the ghost continues. "You know, some nymphs don't actually mind the hauntings. One desperate fuck like you two came here asking for help a few decades back. I sent one of my scariest agents to haunt the target out of hiding, and the fucking oread fell in love with the ghost. Tell me how that works?"

Once again, Helisent glances at me.

We never decided how much to share about our mission.

In fact, the only binding element of our agreement was not to pry into the other's motives.

The ghost lifts its finger from the ledger. He looks at both of us as though doubting our intelligence. "I do hope you both realize the witch here could use tracking magic to locate your target, right?"

"I'm well aware of tracking magic, *thank you*," Helisent cuts in. "We're after a witch. Will you help us or not?"

"Of course." The ghost snorts. "I brought you back here, didn't I?"

I take a deep breath to summon my patience. "Well, then, you should have a barter in mind."

"Oh, look, the Kulapsifang has a voice." The ghost puffs out his shoulders and lowers his voice to a performative rasp. "'Well, then, you should have a barter in mind.' Well, yeah, I do. I charge the same for all haunting services."

Rather than anger, another wave of chills crosses my body.

I never said who I was, and I know the average nymph can't smell wolf alas, much less differentiate them according to power.

"And that is?" I ask.

"It'll be phoenix ash. Yes, yes, yes. A nice hearty load of phoenix ash."

"Why would you phrase it like that?" Helisent asks.

I cut in before she can derail the barter; she doesn't seem to register the fact that the ghost knows I'm the Kulapsifang when I didn't clue him in.

Hoping to speed up our bartering, I ask, "And how will you verify that you're haunting the correct target?"

"I need you to help me do that, of course. You'll tell me the characteristics of the witch, as well as a few precious items she carries. I use both to ensure I have the right being." The ghost wags his head back and forth, and green light shifts across the coarse walls. "I'm guessing you didn't bring any phoenix ash with you?"

I raise my eyebrows. "Correct."

"You'll leave it in a remote place for me. I'll collect it. If I don't find it... well, you know who I'll be haunting next."

Helisent shrugs. "Fair enough."

I turn to her, stomach dropping. "Can you describe Oko? I've never seen her, and I have no idea what sort of items she'd be carrying."

With a nod, she turns back to the ghost and cranes her neck, as though hoping to glimpse the ledger he scribbles on. "She's a few inches taller than me. She has two scars that you'll want to look out for." She runs two fingers from her ear down to the center of her throat. "Big fucking scars. You won't miss them. She wears the scent of lemongrass. Can you smell things?"

Once again, I try not to look as surprised as I feel.

I'm searching for Oko because she was mentioned in a letter that I found in one of my mother's trunks. It hinted my mother had been meeting with Oko around the time of her disappearance seventeen years ago.

But Helisent seems to know the witch on a more intimate level.

Her vendetta is personal.

Part of me is relieved; she must be motivated to find Oko. The rest of me panics; nothing is more dangerous than a wielder who has been wronged.

"Yes, of course. This nose isn't just for *show*." The ghost glances up from his frantic scratching to glare at Helisent. "Go on. Any jewelry or pets or special tunes she whistles?"

"She wears moonstone—necklaces, rings, earrings, all of it. Moonstone. She hates animals and ground-walking. She did whistle quite a bit, but I never knew the songs. They didn't seem familiar... so if you hear her whistling an unfamiliar tune and she has any of the other traits I listed, you've probably got the right witch."

The ghost raises his eyebrows. "You have a strong memory of her."

She doesn't spare a second for the comment. "Where do you want us to leave the phoenix ash?"

The ghost's eyes flicker with green light; another clap of ultrasound clangs. Now that we're seated at a dead end, I wonder where the sound comes from. It sounds like it emanates straight from the black rock around us.

A trickle of water falls from the cave's upper crevice where the wall meets the ceiling, as though a tiny seam separates them.

"Leave the ash on the southern shore of the Mieira River as soon as the lights of Perpetua come into view. Set it between a rocky outcropping to shelter it from the wind. Store it in red fabric. I'll know it's for me."

I look from the trickle of water to the ghost. "And you're *certain* Helisent gave you enough details to find Oko?"

The ghost nods again as he reviews his notes. "It's all here. Moonstone, lemongrass, two scars, unfamiliar songs. It'll take me some time to find her and then haunt her with enough force to drive her to a GhostEater, so don't go rushing out of here expecting a quick miracle."

Helisent swivels to look behind us. "Fair enough. Are we squared?"

I follow her gaze and realize there's only a pit of darkness at our backs—no hint of the green-glowing gates or Creepy Baby. The tunnel must have curved, blocking out the light.

The ghost hunches its shoulders as though apologetic. Once again, the light in its green eyes flares, bringing another dizzying clap of ultrasound.

Like the ghost, Helisent and I rise to our feet.

"We're squared," the ghost says. "Just so long as you two make it out alive."

In unison, we demand, "What?"

Multiple fissures crack along the walls, spraying freshwater across us.

The ghost tucks his ledger into his tunic. He presses his back against the cave's dead-end wall. "Why do they always call Skull a *city*? Just because you live inside something, that doesn't make it a *city*."

The cracked seams in the wall burst, gushing massive torrents. It quickly soaks my clothes then pools on the ground, filling the small gaps between the pebbles.

I step forward and the ghost leans back farther. His green-hued form disappears into the black rock, as though he doesn't have a physical body—just a mirage of light.

Helisent lunges forward, as though prepared to grab the nymph. "What the fuck does that mean? Where are you going? You're the only source of light!"

"Yes, well..." The ghost leans back even farther, leaving us with only the barest wisps of peridot light. "If it makes you feel any better, the gate was just an illusion."

What?

And then the ghost disappears into the wall, abandoning us in a gulf of utter blackness and rushing water.

Holy shit.

Helisent screeches, kicking off my own panic.

I lunge to find her before we get separated. As soon as my hand wraps around her shoulder, her screaming doubles in volume. "Don't touch me!"

I retract my hand and take deep breaths to locate her ala. I step forward, tracking it to where she's pressed herself against the wall. I can sense her adrenaline; her heart rate increases, and her sweat becomes more potent. As adrenaline hits my system, it increases my ability to smell and sense her; her pheromones, her pumping blood, her breathing.

It's all a visceral, attention-grabbing mix of panic.

"Helisent, take a few deep breaths—"

"I can't swim!"

I summon a few large breaths to calm myself. It's almost impossible as the rushing water fills the cave, rising to my calves and driving my instinct to flee—with or without the witch in tow.

"It doesn't matter if you can't swim. *I* can swim, Helisent. Wolves are born knowing how. I can guide us from the cave— but I have to touch you to take you with me, okay?"

I reach for her again. This time, her nails dig into my flesh as she swats me away.

Right—she's afraid of wolf hands.

Enough that she's willing to die right now.

She starts hyperventilating. Her ragged gasps cut above the sound of rushing water that fills the darkness and rises to my knees.

"I can carry you from the cave." I raise my voice to cut above the competing sounds. "You won't have to swim."

"Don't touch me!"

Frosty water fills the cave swiftly, soaking my boots and pants as it rises to my thighs.

My heart rate rises as I prepare for a race toward safety. "If you don't let me grab you, you're going to drown alone in this cave. I don't want to die right now—and I'm guessing you don't, either. Just feel my hand. Stop freaking out. It's a fucking hand."

I don't know that it'll help her, but I know we're running out of time. The water is at my thighs, which means it's likely at her hips.

I repeat, "It's just a hand."

Gently, I extend my hand toward where her ala shivers. Her warm and rushing blood has quieted; she's cold now, shivering with shock. Her ala smells of weak physical signs—not enough dopamine, not enough endorphins.

My hand knocks into something cold. Then a series of frigid fingers start to pinch and feel at my hand as though verifying I'm not carrying a weapon.

I don't want her to panic, but... "We need to go *now*. Can I pick you up?"

"I can't swim," she sobs. "What if you drop me?"

Holy fucking shit she's stubborn.

And what does she think will happen if I don't help her?

"I won't drop you. Wrap your arms around my neck and hold on. I'll carry you—I'm right here."

Her hands release mine and then flutter toward my chest. Her fingers press against my chest, my jaw, then find my neck. She comes forward, her entire body soaked with icy water and shivering, and wraps her arms around me.

She squeezes and bares down. Her breath is warm against my collar as she weeps and stutters. I press her to my chest with one arm. In the utter blackness, it's desperate, awkward chaos. Rather than use her legs to grip me, Helisent compacts herself into a tiny shape against my chest, making her weight harder to manage.

There's just one second of idle wonder as I adjust my grip and prepare to flee—I've only been with wolves just as muscular as me, and every part of Helisent that I touch is yielding and soft.

And her ala is around me, brighter and more complex than ever before.

You're about to drown in a cave, Samson. Not now.

The water rises. As soon as the frigid currents hit my balls, I brace myself against the wall and start scrambling to backtrack toward the entrance.

"Keep your head above the water, Helisent." I use my left hand to follow the wall to avoid getting lost. "I can hold my breath. You stay above."

At first, the water level helps me move easier. It half-buoys me, rushing at hip-level as I hustle along the wall. But the water rises at an ungodly pace, accented now and then by flashes of ultrasound.

Soon it's at my navel. The currents roil with whirlpools, sucking me away from the wall and dragging me backward.

Helisent's desperate breaths hiccup against my neck.

By the time the pale fog of freedom comes into view, the water surges to my upper abdomen. The rocks slide out from beneath my boots. I crane my neck to keep Helisent above, but the water finally hits her.

She claws at my shoulders to keep her head above as water rushes against my chest and drives us back into the darkness. Her knees barrel into my collar, then her breasts and necklaces cover my mouth and nose.

Her warm body buries me in the cold water.

A frigid current drags me back into Skull.

My fingers manage to grip a jagged portion of wall. I use my other hand to grab a fistful of Helisent's dress. My face submerges as my boots search for solid ground to push off of, then I leap with all my might toward the foggy light of Tet.

The water surges as I push Helisent above me to keep her at the surface.

But she clings to me rather than let go, and her body folds at a strange angle over my shoulders and head. I gulp down a huge breath as I crest the surface, only to realize my face is near Helisent's thighs.

Her dress is tangled and collected near her waist, creating a perfect funnel that sends her most intimate ala straight toward my nose and mouth; musky and sweet—not bitter like the rest of her ala.

I plunge my face under the water, hoping it might lessen the intensity of the scent I just inhaled.

Fuck.

Fuck.

Fuck.

Not a seething.

I kick off from the rocks again, pushing Helisent away

from my face toward the grotto's entrance. We clear the cave's shadows and scramble toward the light.

Outside of Skull, there's little sign that we survived a flood. Already, the torrents slow, then begin to recede back into the cave. Clear water laps against the rocks as though it were a peaceful brook. Only the echoes of rushing water hint that the mayhem continues.

Helisent pants and coughs as she clambers toward the flat ground where she left her bag and robe. Her white hair clings to her bare shoulders like her pale dress clings to her body.

I brace myself on the rocks, collapsing onto my back to gulp fresh air. My muscles ache as I lay on the rocks, too heavy and exhausted to move. I stare up into the circular green-hued air that breaks the fog like a tunnel into the sky.

I glance around at the mist that lines the grotto. I'm thankful I can't see the outline of foggy ghosts, just the bland tendrils of formless mist.

Still, I try to make myself wonder about the junior ghosts, about what Skull is if it's not a city, about whether Creepy Baby was a ploy.

I close my eyes and focus on answering these questions.

But my mind doesn't wander far from Helisent's ala, snapping back to the blend of her skin, her copper jewelry, her pheromone-ridden hair. The triangle between her legs where her seuxal ala is most potent and clandestine.

I try to calm myself down.

Who knows if the rumors about seethings are even true?

Clearbold said a seething is how a witch claims your mind; magic takes root first where thoughts are weakest. In dreams.

A member of my last war band, Pietrangelo, said a seething gives a witch access to a wolf's memories. This is how she commands them; she builds dreams from the shredded edges of distant recollections.

Even if they are, Helisent won't know what happened. I definitely won't tell her.

I open my eyes to find the witch buried in her peach robe. She throws her head back to chug from a dark bottle of brandy, surrounded by a halo of foggy ghosts I can no longer see.

Fuck.

CHAPTER 7
EAT YOUR NOODLES
HELISENT

Honey Heli,
I get it—even if they don't. Do your thing. Be happy. After all, the
world needs more red witches, doesn't it? And Anesot always wanted
daughters. They'll come around.
Mint Mili

Once we pass through the final veil of Tet's fog and re-enter the wide golden fields of Gamma, I think of my life's problems less and less.

One month into our journey, we're back where we started: south of Luz on the Irme River. We continue east toward the Deltas, where the warming weather coaxes the first seedlings toward the clouds. The world is a menagerie of endless plains and their early growth, of unfathomable clear skies.

The vastness of it stuns me each day.

Judging by Samson's relaxed demeanor, Gamma's splendor pleases him, too.

The night after our escape from Skull, we washed, ate, and slept in silence. Samson accepted my apology for clawing at his body like it was a flotation device devoid of feeling. And he accepted my admission that his freakishly large hands don't frighten me anymore.

He never would explain the junior ghosts.

I don't mind.

With each day spent in casual travel to Cadmium and Ultramarine where the GhostEaters live, my life centers around two increasingly simple concepts:

First, finding Oko and having my vengeance.

Second, hashing out a friendship with Samson, the Kulapsifang.

It all fits together surprisingly well.

So well that I think I might be a fucking genius.

One of the many dirt roads that cut through Gamma leads us to a sprawling village.

Broad thatched huts dot the rolling hills before us, with a few two-story wooden buildings at the settlement's center. Ripe green farmlands surround it; grain plots, groves with fluffy canopies, and enough clucking chickens and huffing saigas to enchant any traveler.

Like most central Mieiran hubs in Gamma, the village has large wolf and nymph populations. On the outskirts, I also make out the flowing capes common to wielders—first a pair of warlocks, then a lone witch.

My nose twitches as we pass the first thatched buildings.

I smell...

"Foxglove!" I sniff with all my might, rocking back on my lilith. "The hesperide demigod who brought the Gammic Queen to Luz—this must be where they found her. Can you smell it?"

Samson doesn't glance up from the parchment in his hands. "Really?"

"Yes, *really*. Can your huge nose not smell it?"

He looks up from his parchment, brow furrowed. "I smell foxglove, goldenrod, blue star, grama, switch grass, coneflower, and dropseed." He holds up the note. "We should pick up all the supplies we need here. Did you review what we have in your bag?"

Along with a few extra smiles, Samson has also started sharing his supplies with me—in exchange for storage in my bottomless bag, of course.

He goes on, "We should barter for peat and grains. I also need another rolling mat."

He doesn't comment on the fact that I at least smelled the foxglove. For me, it's an accomplishment. The more time we spend together, the more I realize how weak my senses of scent, taste, and eyesight are compared to his; I didn't smell any of the other plants he mentioned. I've never even heard of half of them.

With a sigh, I unclip my bag and shove my hand inside. I use summoning magic to call on our peat supplies and tug them free. "Is that why you've been sleeping like shit—the rolling mat? You've woken me up like three times since we left Skull. It looks like you're fighting someone in a dream."

Samson falls still. He glances around at the distant horizon of windswept plots. "Yes."

I zero in on his features from my lilith. I can tell by his twitching jaw muscle that he's considering his words carefully. "Samson! Are you *zhuzhing* the truth right now?"

He takes the peat bricks and studies the crumbling pieces. "Am I doing *what*?"

I roll my eyes. "You know what I'm talking about. Stop pretending I say it wrong. Did you think I wouldn't notice you're sleeping poorly?"

I rise from my lilith to hover at eye-level with him. Though he still watches me perform magic with vague suspicion, he's accustomed to my floating now. Like I would do with a friend to emphasize a point, I drift horizontally and let my magic buoy my robe aloft so that I'm five times my normal size. Maybe bigger.

Samson barely slides his eyes over me, still focused on the note. "You look like a huge bird when you do that."

"You're zhuzhing the truth right now—I just can't tell why. Do you not want me to know what's keeping you up at night?"

With each of my words, his expression hardens. His eyes narrow to slits, his jaw clenches again.

I study the dark bags beneath his eyes from a hand's length away then float back down to my lilith. "Your consternation piques my interest greatly, dear wolf."

"That wasn't me zhuzhing the truth. That was me avoiding your question. Zhuzhing is more direct." He reaches for my bag to slip the wrapped peat bricks back inside. "It's your turn to barter for peat and grains. I prefer rice, but quinoa will do. I'll go see about a bed mat."

I arch an eyebrow. "Maybe I'll also try to find driproot so you can sleep at night."

"You're so thoughtful, Helisent."

I set my lilith moving toward the village again. "Don't start with the sarcasm or you'll never get rid of me."

Before we find the local market, we're stopped multiple times.

First comes a gaggle of nymphlings. The hesperides and naiad children stop in a dead sprint when they catch sight of Samson, their bare feet kicking up dirt. They nearly break their necks staring up at him, then again clawing at one another to ask him for gifts.

One hesperide with curls of chestnut hair to his butt asks for snow. A naiad missing her front teeth asks to touch his hair. He has no snow, but he obliges their reaching, sticky fingers by lowering his head. Then two shouting oreads join the group. Unlike the others, they fixate on my lilith's metallic ornaments.

Oreads love metal. Onesimos once said he could smell it in my blood.

Unsurprisingly, the youngest oread notices the string of volcanic beads Onesimos tied around my bottomless bag. Though I hate the noise and nonsense of littelings, the girl's tight vermillion curls and soft features remind me of Simmy. Like him, her wide smile hides most of her simmering red eyes and, as with Simmy, I move my head for a better vantage of their color.

The next run-in is less pleasant.

As with the village west of Gamma, male wolves step forward to greet us—four rather than two this time. Their leader is just as barrel-chested and solemn as Samson, while the three wolves behind him are slightly less attentive. The first two men, both with narrow faces and large eyes, look outright frightened. The third's nostrils keep flaring, eyes darting around.

Their golden torcs shimmer in the early afternoon light, twinkling against their pale skin and dark layers.

One of the frightened wolves seems to be missing one of his.

I wouldn't have noticed were it not for how tediously Samson cares for his own. Until now, he's worn long-sleeved tunics and harem pants, so I've rarely seen his upper arm torcs. But beneath the Gammic sun, with spring on the horizon, he now wears a single tunic that exposes his armbands.

The nervous wolf grabs his arm where the torc should be.

Their leader bows his head to Samson. "Samson 714 Afador, son of Imperatriz 713 Afador, my pack needs your help."

"I am here."

My ears perk at the words. Even Samson's expression looks remarkably similar to the one he wore when presented with the last village's problems.

It reminds me of the cave in Skull. What I remember most about almost drowning has nothing to do with the water, my panic, or the scrapes the rocks left on my body. It was

Samson's voice. I don't dwell on his words or what he kept saying while the darkness filled with rushing water. Just the sound of his voice. The lack of panic or emotion.

That's how he sounds now.

I am here.

The pack leader doesn't spare a look at me. He lowers his voice to explain, "The triplemoon approaches, and tempers are already high among my pack. Last week, Malachai passed through. There was a dispute regarding a meal late at night. One of my wolves has been stripped of a torc."

The words mean little to me. I know Malachai is Samson's brother—or at least he's one of Clearbold's descendants. Being stripped of a torc after a late-night dispute over food is a topic I know even less about.

Samson steps forward and angles his head. "*Malachai* stripped a wolf of a *torc*?"

The pack leader nods once, tensed with anger. "My pack would be grateful for your intervention, Kulapsifang, son of Imperatriz 713 Afador. I invite you to dine with us now so that I can plead for leniency."

Samson turns to me. I'm already sliding from my lilith and opening my bottomless bag to continue alone on foot.

He says, "I'll find you later. Have you traveled here before? Where will you be?"

I shrug. "I'm sure there's a tavern close by with my name on it."

Before I turn away, the pack leader addresses me. "A band often plays at the tavern near the textile market. I apologize for interrupting your plans, friend of Samson 714 Afador. I hope you enjoy your time here. Our village is peaceful and bountiful."

Friendly acknowledgments from wolves, high-ranking and unnumbered alike, aren't entirely foreign. In Luz, I have many unnumbered friends—and even a few numbered acquaintances.

But I've never been close to the respect like what the pack leader offers me now. I've joked with wolves, drank with wolves, worked with wolves—but I've never grazed the togetherness that seems to define life in Velm. This feels quite close to that.

I wish I were handling it better.

My mouth falls open as I stare at the older wolf. He reminds me of Samson, from his baring to his tidy layers to his slicked-back bun. "That's great—you're great. Thank you."

I hustle away before any of us can register my nonsense. I don't dare look back, taking two turns onto adjacent streets.

From there, I make quick work of acquiring enough peat, rice, and driproot to please the big bad wolf, then I beeline to the tavern near the textile market. To my great delight, there are musicians inside preparing their hand-carved instruments.

I wonder if I should have asked for the pack leader's name. I'm not part of the Class of wielders who rule our people from Antigone, nor do I plan to be, but making connections with reasonable wolves should probably be part of my agenda.

I order the tavern's largest ale for Samson, then a bottle of brandy for me. I sit at the bar and chat with strangers about the musicians, who take turns playing for the meager crowd. By late afternoon, I move on to Samson's untouched ale. Then I realize I'm out of dextro. By nightfall, the ale is gone, too.

By the time Samson ducks into the tavern, I'm starving. And buzzed.

I rush to meet him, relieved that he's carrying a large meal on a wooden tray, then guide him to our place at the bar.

He sits and sets his meal down without a word. His eyebrows bunch when he notices my ravenous gaze set on his plate. Steam wafts from the rump of fragrant roast. Beside it sits a full loaf of bread, a pile of legumes and vegetables, and a mixed rice dish.

I look from him to the food as he digs in. "Samson, I got

you an ale, and then I drank it. If I get you another one, can we share the food?"

I lean closer and offer him a saccharine smile, but he doesn't look up from the meal. He focuses on the food, then puts his elbow on the table to block my access.

"Samson, are you pretending you can't hear me? Just a piece of bread? *Please*. For the love of the moons. I got us rice instead of quinoa, too. Just like you asked."

His blue-black eyes shift from the meal to meet mine. "Why didn't you eat? You've had all day to eat *several* meals."

"Because I was drinking and then I was full and then I was dancing and then I was waiting for you. Why won't you share? We share all the time at camp, and—"

"It's different. You aren't taking from my plate when we eat together. We're both taking from a communal bowl."

"How is that different? Just imagine your plate is the communal bowl."

He shakes his head, nostrils flaring. Though his words are direct, his tone is polite. "I haven't eaten all day. I've been in meetings to calm the male wolves down since Malachai's visit. *Don't touch my food*, Helisent."

"You saved me from drowning in a flash flood, but you won't let me have a bite of your bread?" One month into our little adventure and the nuances of wolves still baffle me. "What the fuck, Samson?"

He exhales through his nose as though summoning patience. "Would you rather it be the other way around?"

"Well, aren't you a fucking philosopher?" I groan as my mouth fills with saliva. The scent of the rich food distracts me, as does the warmth that wafts from his plate. "Fine then. Don't share."

I slide from the bar and find the naiad server. When I ask for another ale to barter with Samson for some of his food, she offers me a meal instead.

The naiad tucks her brown hair behind her ears, her blue-green eyes darting across my features with urgency. "The high-ranking wolves don't share food, lady wielder. Malachai was here last week. He caused quite a stir when someone took from his plate that was sitting close to his. The villagers still talk about it every day."

I roll my eyes. "Right, well, what do you have? Anything that won't cause conflict amongst the wolves will do. Noodles, maybe?"

I sip on my brandy next to the kitchen until my noodles are ready then sidle back onto my stool next to Samson. I make a show of dressing my meal with extra spice, hoping the scents will bother him. But he remains hunched over his meal, thinking only of chewing, swallowing, arranging another bite, and starting all over again.

Eventually, my curiosity outweighs my stubbornness to keep our feud going. "So who's Malachai again? Sounds like a bit of a drama king."

He pauses from his food long enough to say, "He's Clearbold's second child."

A brother, it is.

"I thought the Alphas only had *one* child so there was no competition. How can you be sure whether you or Malachai is the *true* Kulapsifang?"

This gets Samson away from his fork. He looks at me, eyes wild. "*I'm* the inborn Alpha, not Malachai. In each generation, *one* Alpha is born from the previous Female and Male Alphas. Imperatriz 713 Afador was the Kulapsifang before me; as her sole heir, I'm my generation's Kulapsifang.

"My father, Clearbold 554 Leofsige, fought waricons with other males of similar generational numbers for the right to become the Male Alpha of Velm. For the right to marry my mother, Imperatriz."

Part of me wants to joke about Clearbold. I hate him almost as much as I hate Oko... but I respect Imperatriz. She was a proponent of the Northing and envisioned a future in

which more wolves would mix with nymph and wielder populations. To this day, some still dream of the Northing.

But Imperatriz was far ahead of her time.

Her ideas are still revolutionary.

(And she is gone.)

In addition to the Northing, she also spoke of a Southing,
in which nymphs and wielders would start to inhabit Velm in
larger numbers. So far, most nymphs and wielders haven't
wanted to. Not under Clearbold, at least.

But I'd rather not talk of the Male Alpha—especially when
I'm starting to like Samson's company.

I ask, "So, are female wolves currently fighting waricons for
the right to marry you?"

He nods as he returns to his meal; half the food is already
gone. "It's down to two wolves, so there's only one series left.
It will be fought before Night comes. I'll marry the winner
around my thirtieth this winter. We'll share the responsibilities
of leading Velm. Eventually, we'll produce the next
Kulapsifang."

Produce.

He says it with such nonchalance that I wonder if it really
doesn't bother him.

Nymphs tend to avoid marriage because they only live until
their sixties. There's little need to settle down when life passes
so quickly. And even after bearing children, being a 'parent' is a
loose definition. I met a hesperide in Luz once who said she
had seven fathers and two mothers and four demigods to look
after her.

Wielders are more like wolves.

We want to know exactly how our power will be passed
down.

Our lineages are gendered. A witch inherits her power
from her mother, and, once her mother is dead, all of her
mother's power is split between her female descendants. The
same for warlocks and their sons.

The wolves' power isn't gendered, but many couples marry and go on to have one child. It lessens competition for resources in Velm, where the climate can be unforgiving. Or so I've heard.

Wielders, on the other hand, tend to have one child because conception is rare—and so is long-term monogamy.

"But you won't be the *real* Male Alpha of Velm until Clearbold is dead, right?" I clarify. "That'll be like a thousand years from now."

"Alphas don't have children until they're around fifty years old. When I'm that age, Clearbold will be one hundred—that's when I'll take his place as Male Alpha. We stagger the generations so there's less friction. My great-Alphas are all over one hundred. They live peaceful, secluded lives deep in Velm."

I set my fork down. "And how does Malachai fit into this?"

Samson scoffs. "He doesn't. Around seventeen years ago, Imperatriz vanished. Not many speak of her reign anymore, but I'm sure you heard of her disappearance at some point. There's never been a missing Alpha—dead Alphas, traitorous Alphas, unmanageable Alphas, sure. But never one who just *disappeared*.

"No one knew whether the loss indicated some fault in the Afador line. Some think she deserted her post. Others think she was killed. Either would indicate a pretty serious issue with her position as Alpha, so Clearbold decided to bare another child just in case I turned out to be a bit..."

Samson glances at me, as though expecting me to finish his sentence.

I don't. I'm wondering what Samson thinks happened to Imperatriz; he didn't seem convinced with either option he just put forth.

He goes on, "In case I turned out to be weak, I suppose. Malachai 555 Leofsige is below me in line for Velm's title of Male Alpha. Depending who you ask, his mother is either

Clearbold's concubine or the Female Alpha of Velm or just a necessary symbol. It changes in every region, so I don't—"

"Helisent West of Jaws. *There you are.*"

Samson and I turn around.

A witch in a burgundy cloak approaches us from the tavern's entrance. A vibrant grimace pinches her nose as she beelines for me. I glance from her to the cowering warlock behind her. Absalom, Head Warlock of Luz, steps into the light with an apologetic expression, hands tangled in his dark robe.

The witch spares a glance at Samson before she sets her golden eyes back on me. "Where *the fuck* is my daughter?"

A daughter? What?

My gut drops when I realize she's talking about the mentee.

For fuck's sake.

Instead of addressing the witch, whose hands are tensed and ready to cast magic, I glare at Absalom. "Are you fucking kidding me? Absalom, I thought we had an agreement. I told you, I left little Esteban in the warren—"

"You *left* Esclamonde in a *warren?*" The witch throws her hands into the air.

As though thoroughly disinterested, Samson turns back to his meal. I wish I could, too.

Rather than ply me with a smile, Absalom sets a hand on the witch's shoulder. He angles his head toward her and speaks in a calming tone. "We were notified that Esclamonde is being cared for. In fact, there's a warlock in the warren—"

"How dare *you*." The witch ignores Absalom to seethe at me, her burgundy cloak flaring in response to her temper.

I offer an apologetic smile to the rest of the tavern's patrons, who have all turned to stare at us. Even the musicians have stopped playing.

The Antigonian witch steps toward me. Her tight white braids gleam against her scalp. "You accept a position as a mentor and then, a week later, *abandon* a witchling in a city like Luz?"

The more her features come into focus, from her narrow face to her round eyes to her olive skin, the deeper my rage runs.

I glance at Samson and wonder if he'd take offense to a slight act of wrath.

"I never accepted the position," I tell the witch, tossing my hair over my shoulder. "Go talk to Ninigone."

"You're a fucking *brat*, Helisent! You were useless when you lived in Antigone, and you'll be useless until you crawl back into that hovel you called home." She sucks down a breath before pushing on, "You and your whole fa—"

The witch croaks and clutches her throat as I stiffen my fingers and use smothering magic to silence her.

It's a complex spell; I use smothering magic to block the sounds that bubble in her throat, but I only apply it when she attempts to speak. If I use smothering magic while she inhales, I'll block her intake of air and kill her.

Which I don't intend to do.

It's an interesting thought, though.

Absalom is familiar with my little trick. He lowers his voice as though painfully aware of the silent audience that watches us. He even hunches his shoulders. "Helisent, please give the witch her voice back."

"Absalom, how *dare you* lead this witch to me? I *told* Ninigone it wouldn't work out with Esteban. Don't you and her talk about this shit anymore? You're supposed to be a team, unified under the wisdom of the Class. Do you think they'd find this very dignified?"

Absalom's golden eyes twinkle with nervousness. "Look, I understand—"

"It was rhetorical." I point to the ground next to my stool. "Come here."

I beckon Absalom forward while Esclamonde's mother

holds her throat and attempts to look distinguished while half-choking. The tavern's patrons look from her to me, then to Absalom as he slinks forward.

The warlock bows his head near Samson's shoulder first. His voice is quiet and exhausted. "Hi, Samson. Sorry to interrupt your meal."

Samson barely turns away from his plate to grunt a hello.

Absalom turns to me next. He has the sort of symmetrical boyish face that beings of all stripes adore, which makes up for his lack of backbone and the fact that he's lazy in bed.

He clears his throat and starts, "Helisent, to be fair—"

"I didn't call you over here to hear your excuses. I don't care that the Class looked at your horns and thought you'd be a noble little warlock and look after Luz—do you know why that doesn't particularly matter to me? Because the Class means *nothing to me.*"

I clap him on the back and drag him closer, using holding magic to add a little extra *umph.* "And now you talk about what's fair. Do you think that interests me? If I were interested in what's *fair*, I'd want a lot more than brandy and warm bodies. Don't you think so, *Abby?*"

The warlock gulps. His hands untangle from his black robe and press together to plead with me. "I have *no* idea what to do with this witch. Her brother is Ethsevere—the oldest member of the Class. She has me by the balls here, Helisent. One little peep from Ethsevere... and all my hard work the last three years...

"She stormed into Luz last week, found Itzifone, got him talking, figured out you'd left, then tracked you using something Esclamonde must've taken—"

"The witchling *stole* from me?" My gut steels, my attention focusing on that single fact.

"It was an earring," Absalom explains. "It's a little murky where she got it from."

My temper snaps.

I direct my smothering magic toward Absalom next. The warlock grips his throat with a wet gasp. Like small fires burning in separate places, I stoke my spells against the witch and Absalom, tend to them, keeping them chugging all in time.

My chest shakes as I inhale a deep breath and try to push back at this feeling—

This feeling that Absalom and Esclamonde and her stupid mother are conspiring to *track* me because they feel they're *owed* a slice of my magic...

It's one thing with the nymphs. With the demigods. With all those who also give back to me when they're done taking.

I hate wielders.

I think I hate the wolves, or just everyone in general, but it's really my own kind.

"Helisent." Samson's voice cuts above the noise in my head.

I'm shaking; my lips tremble while my eyes fill with livid tears. It's so fucking *dumb*—everyone in this stupid tavern is looking at me and judging *me* because Absalom and Ninigone haven't kept their promises—they take my magic and use it to light Luz and then double back and say that I abandoned a child in a warren—and then *steal* my things to track me down like a free thing that's being fucking hunted—

"Helisent, take a deep breath like I taught you—"

"Not now, Samson."

I could scream at him, too—how fucking dare Samson confuse this for some sort of respectful wolf dispute? How dare he think that I'm afforded any fucking sense of respect or honor for the power I carry? In my world, it doesn't make me the Kulapsifang.

It makes me a target.

I pretend Samson hasn't left his meal to stare at me, as though prepared to pull the warlock from my grip, from my magic.

My hand tightens around Absalom's cloak. My magic waits

at the ready as I bend my neck toward him and grit out the words, "Absalom Metamor, turn around and take this witch back to Luz. Make sure she takes her daughter back to Antigone with her. Make sure they know I will find them in Black Rock when my journey has ended, and *I will break the hands that stole from me.*

"In exchange, Luz will have all the light and power it needs. It is *my* city, right? Isn't that what you told me when you brought me to your bed four years ago? That you would take care of the Class and *make sure Luz was my city?*

"I remember it like it was yesterday. Don't you, Abby?" I clap him on the back again. "Now goodbye, my dear warlock."

Absalom doesn't try to speak through my magic. Without even a look of surprise, he straightens his back, then his robe, and turns to collect the witch. He takes her by the arm and heads for the door.

Though the witch looks back twice, a curse on her lips, she eventually turns and follows.

The patrons look from the trail of their cloaks to where I sit. Samson, still hunched over his food, also watches me.

I wait for him to slide from his stool and remove himself from my presence. I can't imagine it bodes well for a public leader like him to be seen with an angry witch. Still, for a long time, he looks at me without a word or any type of expression; it's as though he's said something to me and is awaiting a response.

This morning, I felt like we were friends.

Now I feel like we're just as unsteady as when we met in the Luzian Estate's garden.

Samson says, "Eat your noodles. You'll feel better. You've been drinking all day and haven't eaten."

I'm still too angry and embarrassed to eat, or move, or think beyond the reddening rage that fills my mind. I pick up my utensils and prepare a bite, but that's as far as I get. My jaw clenches as I stare at the plate.

This is the truth about me, one that I like to hide with lies: I hate everything in this world.

I hate everyone in it; especially everyone behind us who pretends to go back to their drinks but really stares at me, the unstable witch, in waiting.

I hate myself.

The unstable witch inside.

She's crying now. I can hear her sobbing echo from the northwest.

Samson nudges my plate of noodles closer to me with a knuckle. He whispers, "When people are watching me and I wish they weren't, I go back to a memory I like."

Ah, he's trying to help, but he doesn't know my mind.

He doesn't know the things that lurk in my memory.

His voice almost falls out of range as the chattering and music kick up again. "I imagine myself with my mother. We're in a valley west of Rouz. Night is coming, and we're happy. Think of a memory that makes you feel understood."

I think of a memory.

It doesn't make me feel particularly happy or safe, but it was the last time I felt *understood.*

I'm staring at a witch. We almost look like twins; our blood-red horns are the same size and shape, our faces nearly symmetrical with wide cheekbones and round eyes. Her lips and eyebrows are thinner than mine, but everyone can tell we're sisters.

We're touching each other's horns and making silly faces in a handheld mirror and laughing about the time Yngvi shit his pants at a festival.

It's a stupid memory.

I wish I could throw it away.

But there's Milisent, giggling as she tries to brush the wisps of white hair that grow between our horns. And there's me, Helisent, trying to dodge her touch without any idea that one day she would die like Andromeda.

(Because of me.)

"Should we get out of here?" Samson asks.

I wish I could throw it all away.

I wish I could throw it all away.

I wish I could throw it all away.

"Helisent, can you hear me?"

"I have fucking ears, don't I?"

Samson finishes his meal hastily, then he turns his attention back to me. I'm descended deep inside, listening to the witch scream from the northwest. I can never pay attention when her wailing starts to echo.

Samson doesn't seem frightened by this.

He taps on my plate each time I drop my fork, encouraging me to keep eating. I pick at the meal bite by bite until it's gone. I have no idea how long it takes.

When the bowl is empty, Samson guides us out of the tavern. I have no idea how he barters for anything, unless him toting the unstable witch to another place is a sufficient trade for my meal.

I'm too angry and distraught and full of the wayward sound of a witch crying to notice I walk instead of float. Samson, once again, doesn't seem phased by my reticence—though I guess it's less trying than almost drowning in a cave.

We don't make it far before more wolves step in front of us. One of them looks vaguely familiar; I wonder if he met with Samson earlier today.

A small group guides him through the village while I follow on foot, sticking to the outskirts of the pack. Rather than set up camp outside the village or barter for lodging, Samson follows them to a long, smoky dancehall.

He takes me to the corner and helps me climb onto an unused table. All the while, male and female wolves huddle around him. They offer him all sorts of things I can't quite make out in the dim shadows of the thatched hall. And

Samson stands at their center as though he was born to be their sun.

A female wolf brings me a bitterroot brandy a while later. She sets the towering mug at my hip, bows, then ducks away. I offer a limp wave in thanks.

I wish I had the wherewithal to observe the casual encounter better—especially when the wolves drag Samson onto the dancefloor.

But sometime between my first gulp of brandy and my third, my eyes tear up.

Usually, this is when Onesimos drags me home and tucks me into bed.

I sit unnoticed on the table in the corner for a long time. It's just as well. The female wolf comes over to refill my mug a few times. Bless her heart.

Samson comes over later to help me down, then he guides us from the hall. He says goodbye to the group of wolves, who look to be our age, then leads us away from the village.

Outside is brighter than the dancehall as the almost-full moons of Marama, Laline, and Cap soar above. Their glowing faces project light across the fair plains of Gamma.

A mix of pink and silver and green and red.

Samson sets up camp beneath a large curved tree.

I clamber up into the canopy and weave my nest. With a few final sniffles, I prepare to lay down. At the last second, I realize Samson isn't setting up his bedding below the tree. Instead, he watches me with his arms folded, walking backward as though hoping to see into my nest.

I stare back at him.

"Go to sleep," he says. "You should also drink water. Do you have any?"

I'm too tired to tell him to mind his own business.

I sniffle again, then I fall into my nest.

Into oblivion.

CHAPTER 8

THE TRIPLEMOON, SAMSONFANG PART I

SAMSON

My son,
Bite hard enough the first time, and there is no need for a second bite.
Many times, there isn't a need for the first. Wolves run on instinct. It
can be sudden and powerful, but it is rarely unpredictable. Predict it.

Despite my hopes, seethings are real.

I dreamed of Helisent the first night after surviving Skull... and every night since.

In the daylight, I can't discern her sexual ala from the rest of her scent; it all blends together, thankfully. But the scent is logged in my mind, where my fangself constantly sorts through the world's sensory details.

In the daylight, it makes little difference in our mission.

But at night, having a full repertoire of her pheromones gives her priority in my psyche. Like the legends of seething curses hinted, we're dragged into one another's dreams.

The myths also stated that the dreams would be of a sexual nature. After all, a seething occurs only if a male wolf is exposed to a witch's sexual ala.

But in my dreams, Helisent has been fully clothed and on her best behavior.

Which is good, because I'm not *me* in them.

I'm a child, aged around twelve years old. It's sometime between my mother's disappearance and Clearbold's demand that I bring a wooly's corpse to Bellator Palace.

In the seething dreams, Helisent talks to young Samson beneath a thick yew tree. She touches my hair and cleans my dirty hands with water and asks me questions.

"Are you scared about what your father will do?"

"Do you miss her?"

"Are you sure you're strong enough to do this?"

The answer is always yes.

And then I wake up on my bed mat to the infrasound of Helisent's magic and snoring.

The days following Helisent's run-in with Absalom and the Antigonian witch are quiet.

I avoid the topic so she can have the space and peace to reflect on what happened.

Beyond that are several pressing questions.

First, I'm not sure how she relates to the Head Witch and Warlock of Luz—or even the Class. Wolves rely on pack hierarchies based on centuries of Velmic tradition. Nymphs have demigods and the kings and queens they appoint.

Five hundred years ago, wielders showed up on Metamor Plateau demigodless and anarchical. The Class is the only group responsible for doling out rules to Mieira's wielders and holding them accountable for their misdeeds—and it was only formed at the behest of wolves and nymphs after the War Years.

Judging by the scene in the tavern, the Class has a very loose hold on authority.

Unless it's Helisent who can't be ruled.

But she wasn't the one who broke their rules—it was the Antigonian witch who acquired stolen goods to track Helisent.

I may be subject to unwarranted meetings and responsibilities because of how far my ala carries, but I was born into the position of Kulapsi. And it's one I benefit from greatly: palaces, estates, gifts, praise, respect, devotion, and all the resources to get me through Night.

What is Helisent offered for her power?

And why doesn't she fear the Class—or even seem to respect it?

I don't have the gumption to ask her directly. And I'd hate to contribute to a similar episode of lashing temper followed by hours-long despondent weeping.

For now, I have my own power to worry about.

We walk one of the wide paths that lead east toward the Deltas. As the world waits for spring, the earth bloats as though anticipating release. Beneath our feet await the quickest-growing crops in Mieira, which will soon blanket the rolling hills.

A few gusts of winds are still twinged with cold. I inhale into every current, searching for a phoenix's ala or the scent of its ash.

I glance southward, wishing I could see the indigo outline of Velm's towering mountains.

I take a long drag of my cigarette. "The triplemoon is in two nights."

Helisent whips her head toward me. It's swift enough that her lilith shifts, which causes its metal ornaments to jingle. "Oh?"

"I'll be gone for a day or so," I explain. "I don't phase below the sun, but tensions can be a little high the day before the triplemoon. Even when I can't see them, I can feel that the moons are full."

She fidgets with the volcanic rocks attached to her bag. Since we left the village, she's hardly dropped them. "I heard wolves avoid each other when in their forms. What happens if you run into a stranger after you turn skin? Do you..." She makes a claw with one of her hands, then swipes at me with a weary smile. "You know..."

I'm guessing she's talking about fighting.

I take another drag. "A wolf in its form is directly tied to the whims of its fangself—and a fangself *always* wants to assert itself. It's worried about survival. Wolves start meditating young to curb those fears." Added testosterone and dopamine make our fangselves nearly unstoppable; they also endear us toward brutality. "A calm mind is less likely to become violent when we've turned skin.

"Meditating helps us avoid phasing when we don't want to —especially on a doublemoon. It's not necessary to phase on a doublemoon, but the fangself usually wants out, like I said.

"But so long as a pup is raised correctly, they don't need to avoid anyone on the triplemoon. A well-rounded community can run as a unified pack. And most communities *are* well-rounded. A wolf's first pack is their immediate family. The eldest female and male are the group's alphas."

I'm giving Helisent a romantic vision of life in Velm.

I don't mention the disasters that occur when rival packs accidentally meet outside Bellator, Wrenweary, Mort, and other larger settlements. (A fangself will not forget or forgive a blood feud.)

I also leave out unnumbered wolves and the dangers they face under the triplemoon. A wolf's ala changes when they've lived outside a pack for a few years. It makes them an easy target.

I can't remember how many corpses I've found battered in Velm the days after the triplemoon—and even in the southern region of Gamma where we travel now.

"I guess I shouldn't poke fun at you for meditating every morning," Helisent says with a sigh.

I hadn't realized she'd noticed me meditating. "Is that an apology?"

"No. I'll build up to it someday." With another sigh, she drops the string of volcanic beads. "So what happens if you meet a sexy wolf? Can you guys make fuck in your forms?"

I roll my eyes at "make fuck."

I criticized her usage of "fuck" sometime last week, but she argued "make love" was too emotional. "Make fuck" is her horrible attempt at a compromise.

"No. Never. Sexual encounters aren't common—or expected."

She pinches her lips, staring ahead with a repressed giggle. "Why is that? I saw a... never mind."

She saw two animals having sex and wondered if it was close to what wolves do in their forms. I'm happy she backs out of that question.

Helisent continues in a measured tone, "Why not have a little fun in your form? In your fangself. Whatever you call it. Aren't you curious what it would be like?"

Here are the things a wolf wants while in its form: to roam, to put its scent everywhere in order to claim a territory, to dominate anything that walks inside that territory.

Male, female, juvenile; it doesn't matter.

The longer a wolf's generational line, the stronger those instincts become.

Aware that Helisent is watching me with optimistic curiosity, I search for a more neutral explanation. "Even after they were married, Imperatriz and Clearbold didn't share a territory when they phased. We're not..." We're not romantic. We're *wolves* almost five times my size. "My fangself is interested in establishing a territory and protecting it. Sometimes eating. Sometimes exploring. Not love."

The snicker she was holding in finally peals from her lips. "I never said anything about *love*. You know, the more I get to know you, the more I think you might be more shy than you are brooding."

Brooding? Seriously?

Do I come off as brooding?

There's a growing part of me that can't gauge whether Helisent and I are friends yet. Is it just her appearance in my dreams that gives me a sense of camaraderie?

I glance sidelong at her. "Maybe if someone promised me a city like Absalom offered you, I'd be more open-minded."

She smiles knowingly at me, eyebrows arched. "Why would someone promise you a city when you were born in a Palace?"

The witch's words from the tavern float through my mind.

You'll be useless until you crawl back into that hovel you called home.

Helisent hasn't brought up her family. And why not?

"And I didn't sleep with Absalom because I wanted a city." She tsks. "You wouldn't understand."

If she's interested in baby-faced men like Absalom, then I definitely don't. He couldn't even grow a beard.

As though my statement bothered her, she backtracks further, "I was really naive as a witchling. I grew up near a little oread settlement. When I moved to Antigone, I didn't know anything about wielder politics. Turns out there's not much to know—just so long as you're comfortable backstabbing and showboating and manipulating."

We pause as an elderly wolf couple turns onto the path from an adjacent road. They turn toward me immediately, beelining until they stand before us. The male hands me a spare brick of peat, then his partner offers a bundle of rosemary.

They both bow their heads, and I bow mine.

I enjoy offerings from older wolves. They don't mince words; they just shove things into my hands and move on with understated smiles.

Helisent stares into the distance to politely ignore the exchange. When the couple has passed, she tucks the supplies into her bottomless bag, and then we continue.

I study the soft veins on her hands as she clips the bag shut. "And how many years ago did you move to Antigone?"

Since the seething dreams started and I became more acquainted with her ala, I've settled on an age estimate between thirty-two and thirty-five years old. Like the long-lived wolves, wielders age at a similarly slow pace, often living to their one hundred and fortieth year. It makes selecting a concrete age almost impossible.

"I moved to Antigone when I was twenty," she chirps. "Just a few little years ago..."

"Your ala tells me—"

"How *dare* you age me by my ala. Are you even *sure* this is my scent? A bit of smelling magic and you'd never know the difference."

I can tell she's not using scent magic; it always sticks out like a toxic perfume. Hoping to encourage her, I start, "I'm twenty-nine and you are..."

She raises her chin. "Twenty-eight. Wow, don't you feel old?"

I study Helisent in the hopes of gleaning one last clue. I know that wielders are vain, but being in her mid-30s isn't old. She's barely one-quarter of the way through her life.

Golden sunlight glitters off the beaded necklaces that cover her chest. Her messy white hair is half-pulled back, twisted and tangled from the wind. Faint lines mark her tawny skin near her eyes and mouth.

I lean a bit closer, dragging in a huge breath through my nose just to be sure I didn't miscalculate her age range.

I didn't. I round up in the hopes of over-estimating.

"You're thirty-four," I say.

The lilith stops moving as Helisent gasps.

I turn back to find her glaring at me, mouth open and one hand flat on her chest.

Who's brooding now, little witch?

"Someday, you'll be thirty-five," I go on.

The lilith starts moving again. She barely spares a look in my direction as she continues at my side.

I stare at her, wondering if I've upset her or simply started one of our long episodes of banter. They've become more common in the last week.

At last, she says, "Whatever, Samson. You'll be settled in Velm with a wife and a throne by the time you're my age. I'll be old, but at least I'll be *free*."

This time, I stop. Helisent floats down the road with her arms crossed, glancing back once as though ensuring I'm suitably upset.

Which I am.

Because she's right.

Two female wolves remain as candidates for Female Alpha: Brutatalika and Menemone. They'll fight a waricon series later this year, then I'll walk into Silent City with the winner at my side. Clearbold will marry us between the white marble columns, then he'll carve our names onto one of the pillars that line the empty platforms.

After, my wife and I will walk into the palace I was born to inhabit.

And then my life ends.

It will start again the next day; first it will die, though. I'm very aware of that.

With a sigh, I return to Helisent's side. She searches my face with a slight bend to her eyebrows. It takes me a second to realize it's an expression of pity.

She goes on, "You know, you're lucky you met me. We balance each other out." She splays an arm, as though scripting a headline. "You're the public face of everything that's balanced and fair. Samson 714 Afador, Kulapsifang of Velm—a hero for the future of Mieira. And I'm the one that can do anything behind the curtain. The whisper of power that no one can ever *quite* make out. What do you think?"

I hadn't realized that Helisent envisioned a future between us beyond finding Oko. I hadn't realized I cared, either.

"I'd like that." I glance south toward Velm. "Imperatriz was dedicated to the Northing. It's something I'd like to undertake when I'm Alpha, and I'll need plenty of help along the way."

"I can take you to Jaws," she says with a devilish smile. "Lake Deidre is one of my favorite places in the world. Not even the selkies can ruin it. There wasn't a single wolf there when I went last, but..."

The idea sets her off on one of her breathless diatribes. I follow her arguments, but when they stop making sense, I enjoy the unspoiled view of Gamma.

The sun twinkles like a jewel overheard.

Hidden in its splendor are three whole moons.

That night, I dream Helisent and I are sitting in the yew tree.

I'm twelve years old with a lanky boyish frame. My feet and palms are laid flat on a wide branch, grasping the coarse, flaky bark. Bright red berries dot the fluffy yew needles that layer the canopy.

Helisent sits on an adjacent branch wearing a red cape instead of her peach layers. With a giggle, she turns and floats onto another branch. Her white hair, like her red cape, catches on small twigs and needles.

Terrified of being left alone, I leap after her. "Miss Helisent, wait up."

"Oh, relax, little Samson. I'm right here." She passes onto another branch, red cape floating around her waist. Her feet are bare, her toes and soles dirty from climbing. "I'm just looking for someone."

She's looking for someone?

My heart surges with hope. "For Imperatriz?"

I want someone to look for my mother. I want someone to bring her back to Bellator.

Helisent stops as though confused. Her eyebrows bunch as she looks over her shoulder to study me. "Imperatriz? She's gone?"

I nod. "Yes." I don't know where she is. "The wolves are..."

Weeping. Shouting. Whispering. Searching.

Speculating...

"Where is she, Samson?" Helisent asks. The longer she stares back at me, the more a deepening pessimism takes root in me. The witch doesn't know where my mother is. No one does. "Where is the Female Alpha?"

My chest shakes as a lump grows in my throat. "I don't know. I need—I miss—"

"I know." Helisent nods. Her panicked expression makes me believe that she understands.

But in the next second, I'm distracted by something else. "Miss Helisent... your face..."

My head tilts as I study her.

A breeze shakes the fluffy emerald needles in the yew tree. Its scent fills my lungs, along with Helisent's ala. There's something wrong with her face as she blinks her large eyes—but what is it?

She reaches up and pinches one of the red, fingernail-sized berries. With a wicked laugh, she says, "They're poisonous, you know."

I wake up with my next breath.

I stare up at the massive faces of the three moons amid the twinkling stars. Rather than the pink-gray mass of Vicente or the trailing green of Abdecalas, my eyes shoot straight to the small blood-red sphere in the navy sky.

Sennen.

I blink, staring up above.

That's what it was—

Helisent's irises in the dream weren't golden but rather a bright infuriating red.

Not a golden witch, but a red one.

My eyes shoot to the pale twigs of Helisent's nest. With the wind howling over the plains, I can barely hear her snoring or smell her ala. It grates at my nerves to not see, smell, or hear her clearly; Samsonfang wants access to each sense.

I close my eyes and take a few deep breaths.

Sennen isn't quite full, but with each passing second, I can feel more sunlight illuming the glory of the tiny red moon. It will be full later today before being revealed by the night.

I'm mostly Samson now.

Mostly.

The part of Samsonfang that slides into my mind focuses immediately on the witch.

How many horns does she have? It is the only reliable way to know how strong she is; all wielders lie.

I talk to Samsonfang, and he communicates back through wild rushes of instinct.

"I don't know how many horns she has, but I trust her. Helisent is our friend."

Friend? She is not part of our pack. She smells like liquor and old jewelry, not like a wolf.

"She's helping me look for someone who might know where Imperatriz is."

The enemies of your enemies are not friends. They are also enemies.

"She's an ally, then."

This is appropriate. Her magic can end worlds.

Samsonfang's sudden capitulation regarding the witch is even more alarming than his suspicion of her.

I open my eyes and stare at the nest. With a pause in the rushing winds, Helisent's light snoring echoes out to me. Next comes her ala.

"What do you mean, her magic can end worlds?"

Bring her to me. I will tell you how many worlds it can end.

"There's no reason for you two to meet."

And why not? I am the Afador, not you.

"Samsonfang, we are both—"

Velm loved Bloody Betty. All of Velm.

I stand up rather than try and fail to steer this conversation.

I push away thoughts of Bloody Betty and centerhearts, but they linger close. During the War Years, Velm managed to get ahold of an infant wielder. As a centerheart, the witch couldn't use her magic against those she loved—only in their service.

I don't look up at Helisent's nest as I pack my things.

I'm sure she's heard about Bloody Betty. About the witch the wolves raised and manipulated into a weapon; one that couldn't be turned against them so long as Betty loved her wolves.

(And she did. Until the very end.)

Dawn peeks over the horizon. I glance back once at Helisent's pale nest and wait until I hear her snoring, then I mark the campsite with urine. She won't be able to smell it with her tiny nose, but any wolves who come near our camp should smell me and be deterred from bothering her.

As the Kulapsi, other wolves tend to avoid me on the triplemoon—either out of fear or respect.

Satisfied that the camp smells like me, I push north with a quick pace to put miles and miles between me and the camp.

I spend the day repairing my supplies and preparing for the coming moons; I imagine Helisent takes the day off to drink and nap. During the final moments of light, I stare westward where the sun hangs like a boiling speck of metal above the horizon.

Before it's fully set, the light of the moons churns my mind.

I pace a small stretch of trees where I tucked away my bag. I mark the spot with my urine like I did beneath Helisent's nest.

And then the panting begins.

A wolf's greatest secret isn't self-control, but the wild chaos of turning skin. Samsonfang beats at my mind, my form, until my body struggles to take in enough air.

After the panting comes foaming.

I hunch before a sturdy maple tree, gripping the soft bark for support as I scoop the foam from my mouth. If I need to, I can swallow it, but it tastes like the foul things that flush through my system; testosterone, adrenaline, dopamine.

Then comes the knockout.

I fall forward and sag against the trunk. My hands go slack and fall to my side, then I curl over my knees into a compacted shape.

In the seconds before I leap into my four-legged fangself, my body goes numb. My mind fragments with illogical thoughts, just weak enough for Samsonfang to barrel through.

I only have the strength and sense to haul air into my lungs and spit out the foam that clogs my airways.

A wolf's second secret is the unimaginable pain of phasing. Most of what Samsonfang does and thinks will be forgotten when I return to my usual form; the memories of what he does take time to turn into clear recollections.

The memory of this pain, though, never seems to fully take root.

That world-ending pain stays forever behind a foggy glass.

And when it ends, I'm not a man sagging against a tree.

I wake to bright sunlight in my eyes.

I smell sweat, dirt, pollen, sable fur and blood, dewy grass, and scat.

I sit up with a groan.

Though Samsonfang made it back to the thin patch of trees, the real me is sprawled out ass-naked twenty feet from the closest coverage. It takes me a second to blink away the black splotches from my vision and then find the maple tree where I left my bag.

I take a few deep breaths as I stand, checking for any onlookers.

I guess this might be a wolf's third secret: the indignity of waking up naked and trying to figure out where I am while casually brushing dirt off my dick and pulling leaves from my hair.

I pause mid-step when I sense a male wolf's ala in my vicinity.

It's distant and faint, coming from the southeast where I left Helisent.

I rush back to find my bag then tug on my pants, tunic, and torcs. All the while, I reach back for Samsonfang's memories. It's a half-remembered blur of running across the plains, voracious howling, rubbing my scent onto the world, pissing my scent onto the world, hunting and eating sable, avoiding another wolf's territory—

Oh.

Oh, shit.

I trailed a strong scent back to its territory, then ran along its outskirts to mark the region as mine. I had stuck to the northern edge of the territory, but Helisent's nest would have been directly within those boundaries.

I had left my scent around camp to prevent other wolves from bothering Helisent; I hadn't realized our camp sat directly within a pack's territory.

I hustle back toward where I left her yesterday morning.

I check my jaw for loose teeth and cut gums, but don't find any sign of dominative biting. I check my neck and body for any other signs of a violent meeting—again, nothing.

The journey back to the campsite takes a few hours; I

continue to pick up on the male wolf's ala with each field I pass. Though Samsonfang's memories are held behind an opaque threshold, they return incrementally, like distorted images shifting back into focus.

Their alas pool as I near Helisent's nest, grating my nerves and setting my instincts back on edge.

The original male scent splinters into four unique alas.

Did these wolves approach my camp this morning after phasing back? And why?

Samsonfang, though sleepy and satiated, perks his ears up.

How high was the tree? How far up did she weave her nest?

And, again, why did these wolves come to my camp? What made them think they were welcome?

Helisent's ala is accented with mine now that we've traveled together for over a month; it should have been more than enough to deter any wolves from bothering her.

My guest.

My heart rate accelerates as I crest each hill and find no sign of Helisent's birch-twig nest.

I am her only connection to Velm—I am the link that binds her power to my people—

My chest shakes with relief when Helisent's broad nest comes into view. She sits at the edge of the woven twigs. Her white hair is down and tangled, angled like she's peering over the nest's ledge. I suck down a breath to verify her ala doesn't smell of blood; it doesn't.

It smells of adrenaline, though.

I count four wolves beneath her tree. Their heads are tilted back as they stare up at the witch. I can also make out scratching marks along the tree trunk.

Even their simple presence, their bold posturing, would be enough to set a wielder or nymph on edge. Scratching at her tree would have been a needless act designed to frighten her.

Worst of all, they can smell my ala around this camp; it does nothing to deter them.

Even if it's *their* territory, I marked the camp as *mine*.

And as the Kulapsi, whatever I mark is *mine*.

Their territory, even if only for the duration of the triple moon, becomes *mine*.

Which means intruders are unwelcome.

There aren't many motivations that would compel wolves toward this type of disrespect. In fact, they're typically only undertaken strategically.

In tandem, the wolves catch my scent and turn their heads. Their leader is in his mid-fifties with a high generational count, someplace above 450 and below 500. His sons, in their late teens and barely more than pups, stand at his flanks. The last wolf has a very low count, likely a few generations removed from an unnumbered couple.

I crest the final hill and pick up my pace.

Helisent finally notices me. She faces away from the wolves, eyebrows bunched and mouth tense. The wind shakes her white hair as she points to the four wolves and pulls her robe tight over her shoulders.

She calls out, "Samson! I swear I didn't do anything. I don't know what they want. I..."

My body fizzles with wrath; each of these males is challenging my place at the top of Velm's hierarchy by stepping onto my territory, my camp, by leering at my guest, my friend. And there is no room for this type of challenge—

This is *mine*.

This camp. This witch. Where the sun rose behind me, wherever it rests when it disappears.

Mine.

As I switch my focus from Helisent, I find relief in knowing I've already seen her lose her temper with Absalom and the Antigonian witch.

Hopefully, it makes it slightly easier for her to bear witness to what comes next.

Don't judge me, Helisent.

Remember my hands are safe.

The eldest wolf raises his chin when I switch my gaze to him. My chest rises and falls with huge breaths as I try and fail to calm my temper.

"Samson 714 Afador." The eldest wolf steps forward to meet me.

I pass Helisent's tree and round on the wolves. My pace and bearing cause the three pups behind their leader to retreat. The brothers stick together, backing up a safe distance behind their father. The unrelated male retreats at a quicker pace, as though prepared to turn and flee entirely.

Look—he will run.

"I'll handle this, Samsonfang," I murmur.

Chase him if he runs. Kill him if he runs.

"Don't run," I yell to the lone wolf.

I'm barely in charge of my mind. Barely keeping a handle on what I'm saying out loud and what Samsonfang is compelling me toward and which one of us is actually in charge.

I meet the elder wolf. I haven't decided what to do as our chests touch and my momentum forces him backward; he can either back up, strike me, or fall down and let Samsonfang have him.

Let me have him.

I watch the thick veins in the leader's jugular shift as he moves. My hand shoots to his neck. I don't seize him—I just grip forcefully enough to gain control of him and keep forcing him backward, farther from Helisent and our camp.

As though unsurprised by my reaction, the wolf continues his retreat at a steady pace. The other pack members revolve around us at a safe distance.

I study his round face and slim features, then search his ala for a familiar note. I find nothing. "Who the fuck are you?"

"Invidio 499 Kelberg." His round face squishes with a quick smile.

Though we're out of earshot, I'm guessing Helisent can still see us. I try to unclamp my hand from his neck, but my entire body is rigid—waiting for a quick movement, waiting to unleash.

"And where do you want your waricon?" I ask.

There can be no other explanation for Invidio's posturing and challenges: he wants the honor of fighting the Kulapsifang. Of the dozens of waricons I've fought, this is the third to stem from a conflict rather than a thought-out invitation.

There are only three reasons to call for a waricon.

First, to determine pack hierarchy where generation counts are too convoluted.

Second, to host exhibition competitions for the public to enjoy.

Third, to resolve feuds, like the one Invidio just started.

"My village will host the waricon. It is two days southeast on foot," Invidio says. His blue-black eyes break across my features with fascination. "I apologize, Samson 714 Afador. There's only one way for me to know if you really killed the wooly at age twelve. If the Afador line isn't spoiled, after all."

Some wolves feel my mother's absence wasn't a coincidence. Some believe she abandoned her post.

Some have even hinted it might have been from the lacking of her inborn pup.

Rather than watch him grow and fail, Imperatriz 713 Afador fled.

"And the pups?" My hand tightens around Invidio's throat, preventing him from shifting while I look away to study the wolves around us. I file through their alas to search for the same notes of tree bark that mark Invidio's hands; as the pack leader, the other wolves are apt to do as Invidio does. "Are they prepared to fight a waricon?"

Invidio's eyes narrow. "You want the pups to fight?"

This is one of those times where I'm not sure where the real Samson ends and Samsonfang begins. Samson doesn't want the pups to fight; Samson knows the brutality of the waricons. Samsonfang wants them to fight; they will all lose and be shamed and weakened, and even that might not be enough.

There's only one way for me to know...

My voice shakes. "They were at *my* camp, weren't they? *My fucking camp, Invidio.*"

I wonder if Invidio brought the pups because he feared facing me alone. Or did he think I'd be defenseless, easy to pick off if the rumors about Imperatriz's inborn Alpha turned out to be true?

"What did you think would happen?" I shake my head, vision shaking. "Call them over."

Unable to move his neck under my grip, Invidio slides his eyes to the left, then to the right. His sons approach first. Based on their focused and tense expressions, their fear has been replaced at least partly with anger. Their eyes are glued to my hand as it holds Invidio's neck. The other wolf takes longer, as though convincing himself to approach with each step.

I clench my jaw and release Invidio. I shove him backward with more strength than is necessary, then switch my attention to the juveniles.

I want to know which motherfucker clawed at Helisent's tree.

I start with the youngest son. I yank his hands to my nose; his fingers and nails are clean. The wolf beside him, Invidio's second son, also has clean hands. But the last has long fingers that reek of flaked bark, bunched under his dirty nails.

The wolf's lips press together, his nostrils flared and his chin lowered.

My hand tightens on his wrist. "You clawed at the tree where the witch slept."

The pup's voice shivers. "I did."

"And are you prepared to fight a waricon for it?" I ask.

I can smell adrenaline bleed into Invidio's ala, at last. As the pack leader, anything that happens to his subordinates today falls on his shoulders.

The pup looks at the ground as he answers. "If you challenge me to a waricon, I will have no choice but to fight in one."

Invidio speaks evenly from a few paces away, attempting to assuage my rage with a bit of logic. "I came here to challenge you to a waricon. To make sure you were motivated to win. He was just doing as I did, Samson 714 Afador."

I look at Invidio. "Then he'll fight in the waricon, *just as you do*." I turn back to the wolf, holding his wrist in the hopes that he'll heed my words. "A pack follows its leader. Do you want to go where Invidio goes? Your generation count is low. You have time to decide what your future will look like, and which pack is worthy of your life."

Too frightened to speak, the pup stares down at our feet.

I release his wrist.

With a gulp, he steps immediately behind Invidio to join the other pups. Of the four wolves, only Invidio meets my eyes. The bunch in his brow hints he may have finally second-guessed his actions—he will stand a chance in a waricon, but the wolf I challenged won't fare nearly as well.

Invidio's regret might be enough to satisfy me, but it won't be enough to satisfy the customs of wolves.

Of Velm.

Invidio puffs out his chest with a bow of his head. "My village will wait to receive you."

He takes the first few steps away while facing me. After one last measured glare, he turns and takes off with his young pack in tow.

I follow the wolves until I'm sure I won't catch their alas in the wind, then I turn back. It takes me a moment to find the tree where we camped; all the canopies are empty; Helisent must have dismantled her nest.

Eventually, I untangle her glimmering peach robe from the warm hues of morning.

She sits on her lilith, brushing her hair with thoughtful strokes.

I prepare an explanation and sketch an apology, but her tentative smile grows as I approach. I avoid the urge to check over my shoulder as it becomes wider, more dazzling.

Her golden eyes twinkle. "Nice hair. You never wear it down."

I reach up and realize my dark waves are tangled in a heap, dangling to my chest. With a curse, I tug it back into place. A messy bun will have to do for now.

"Are you okay?" I ask.

She nods, a smile still hanging from her lips. "Believe it or not, I've met a few fussy wolves in my day. These ones weren't particularly scary. Interesting throat-grab, by the way. You really just went for it, huh?"

I ignore her teasing and hope she's just as forgiving about this next part. "The wolf's name is Invidio. I challenged him to a waricon. I'm expected in his village in a few days time."

My gut twists; I challenged the pup, too.

I was justified in doing so, but...

"A *waricon*?" Helisent claps her hands together with a gleeful squeal. "The naked oil fights?"

"We're not *naked* and it's not *oil.*"

"Oh, I see. You're just mostly naked and it's something just as slick as oil."

I can't concentrate on her joking right now. I'm too tired and upset with myself. "Helisent, I need you to do me a favor."

"Wow, this is quite the morning. Do you want to grab my throat next? Should I grab yours?"

"I need you to track someone."

She tsks. "How mundane."

"I don't want to walk alone into the waricon."

Helisent's amused expression falls. "Tracking, huh?" She

studies me from head to toe for a long moment, hairbrush falling still in her hand.

Is it in bad taste to ask her to use tracking magic when she nearly committed an act of wrath for the same recently? And especially when I've shown disdain for her magic up until today?

I explain, "It won't reflect very well on me if I enter a waricon alone, and there are two wolves who must be punished for scratching the tree. I know someone who will come if I send word."

Hopefully.

Helisent shrugs a shoulder. "So long as you have something that belongs to them, I can track anyone."

I glance at my satchel, packed near the cold firepit. Ideally, I would ask her track down the four wolves who once composed my war band—but I've only kept something personal from one of them.

"I do."

Helisent tucks her hairbrush into her bottomless bag, then she extends her empty hand toward me. "Go on, then. Hand it over."

With a sigh that reaches my core, I head to the satchel and tug at its leather straps. I take out my spare clothes, my journal, my spare rolls of leather for boots. Bunched at the very bottom of the bag sits a marigold hair tie.

His ala faded from it a long time ago, but I got used to having the tie with me.

Just in case, I guess.

I chew my lip and stare at the tie before I hand it off to Helisent. Now, her ala will erase any trace of his that remains.

She holds it up and studies the piece. "Who's the lucky wolf, then?"

"Rex. Rex 543 Kaneling."

CHAPTER 9

LOOK AWAY IF IT'S TOO MUCH

HELISENT

Honey Heli,
I left some extra dove at my bedside. You can always use it for household chores when your twin misses my twin. By the way, my twin misses your twin. And I miss you.
Mint Mili

Rather than start our day's journey, we stay at the camp amid the golden plains.

I glance eastward. I'm anxious to make it to Cadmium and Ultramarine before Oko can seek out a Ghost-Eater. Still, the ghost in Skull mentioned he'd need time to drive her out of hiding with a haunting; we have time to reach the Deltas.

I switch my gaze to the south, where the four wolves' tall silhouettes fade into the horizon.

With a sigh, I slide off my lilith and study Samson's faded hair tie with mounting suspicion. No one holds on to such a useless thing unless it carries emotional significance. Aside from doubt, frustration, and a keen love for his mother, I've yet to see Samson's *emotional* side on display.

He follows me to the clear patch of dirt beside the firepit with his hands on his hips. He looms over me and blocks out the blush of morning light as I kneel and prepare to track Rex 500-whatever Kaneling.

I crane my neck to study his scrunched features. "I don't need your assistance to track someone, Samson."

He shuffles into a sitting position beside me. Like his ruffled debris-ridden hair, his tunic and harem pants are wrinkled. Dirt encrusts his bare feet and ankles. But he doesn't seem to notice his state of disarray. Instead, he's staring at my hands as they test the fabric of the hair tie.

"What will you do with it?" he asks.

Seeing that Samson isn't in a state for my usual joking, I strive for patience. "I'll show the tie to my magic, and my magic will find its owner. My magic can leave a note, if you like. Can you take a page out of your journal to write a message?"

He reaches for his satchel. "That's a good idea."

Then he pauses with his hand around his bundled parchment. He chews his lip, glancing at my hands again. "Look, I know it's probably... wrong that I don't feel comfortable being around magic—especially now that I'm asking you to use it as a favor."

Fear of magic is more common than anyone admits. Even Onesimos bristled when he felt the depth of my power, at times.

Samson clears his throat. "But the wolf we're looking for— Rex—he also isn't very comfortable with magic."

I raise my eyebrows gently. "Samson, we're friends, aren't we? Just tell me what you're thinking."

"I'm worried it will bother Rex if your magic... touches him."

I tilt my head; Samson doesn't understand magic at all.

"I doubt it will *touch* him. If you give me the note, my magic will track him and then leave the note at his bedside or someplace he's bound to see it. My magic won't throw him in a bag and drag him back here kicking and screaming." I shrug. "That'd be kidnapping magic. It's nasty business."

His mouth presses into a thin line.

I try for a sweet smile. "Samson, I'm joking. I don't know kidnapping magic."

He glances at the bundled paper in his hands. "Maybe I'll handle this alone."

I try to blink my way back toward patience, but my frustration quickly mounts. "Well, that's fucking offensive. Is my magic really that scary? It does *nice* things, you know. It starts your fires, stores your supplies—all kinds of shit. And I got over your fucking big dumb hands, didn't I?"

For a long moment, Samson studies me with a blank expression. It reminds me of how he looked at me when I flipped out at the tavern: cautious, thoughtful, calm.

We're going to get nowhere like this. "What if I explain how magic works? If you become Alpha and you still don't understand it, you'll just be another version of Clearbold."

He glances south, as though expecting to see the wolves returning.

I frame my explanation in his silence; I've yet to describe how magic works to anyone. For how many beings I've seen be made uncomfortable by my spellwork, no one has ever asked me to describe it. Not even a nymph.

"I think of my magic like a twin," I explain. "It can do absolutely anything—but I have to explain how something works, step by step, detail by detail, before I can create a spell. From there, my magic will handle things itself... but only after I've explained the topic from every angle."

Samson's eyes narrow, as though he's about to start with questions.

Before he can, I reach into my bottomless bag and pull out

one of my birch twigs. "To do weaving magic, a wielder first has to learn how to weave. Technically, I know how to weave by hand—even though I'm not very good at it. My magic, or my magical *twin*, let's say, is much quicker and more accurate. My magic learned the basics of weaving from me, then got better at it."

He sits back and relaxes, gaze drifting from my bottomless bag to the pale birch twig in my hand.

"And what about tracking magic?" he asks. "Can *you* actually track someone?"

"Like I said, my magic is a lot more powerful than I am. It only needs a physical item, a former possession, to find its owner. When I learned how to track, I was practicing with..." With Milisent, my sister. My best friend. "...a close friend in Antigone. I was in my late teens; she was in her early twenties. We learned all the toughest spells together—tracking, heating, scaring, building, digging, welding, fighting, seducing."

The city was ours.

We were the youngest sponsors Antigone had ever seen. The first red witches to sponsor the city for decades.

"To learn tracking magic, we'd hide from each other in Antigone. It's a huge city—very complex. Remember, I told you there are twelve stories to the city. We'd leave tiny clues for each other to find. Sometimes, it'd take a whole week to find her."

I remember how it grated not to have Milisent in our apartment. That was my first taste of loneliness.

"Eventually, we got really good at picking out even the tiniest clues the other left behind. A fallen piece of jewelry, a familiar perfume, a window left open. We only ever learned how to track each other, but from there..."

I glance up to see if Samson is putting it together.

He isn't.

"From there, my magic had learned enough about tracking to figure out how to do it itself. I'll show my magic the hair tie and then, like an animated twin, my magic will go to Rex to leave him a note. It'll find him how I used to find my friend in Antigone."

Eventually, Samson nods. "Is that why there aren't many wielders who know healing magic?"

"Exactly. First, we'd have to learn how to stitch wounds and apply salves. No fucking thank you." I throw my hands up. "Right, I probably should've mentioned at some point that I don't know healing magic. So don't get hurt. You'll be shit out of luck."

He nods again. "Good to know. And what about other types of wielder magic? We were taught there are only three kinds, but you just mentioned a ton of different spells."

"You're talking about the *categories* of wielder magic, not specific spells. Spellwork falls under the category of skilled magic. Aside from skilled, there's also instinctual and panic magic.

"Instinctual magic is what we're born being able to wield. It's mostly floating—even babies can do that. Climbing, hovering, lifting objects. It's all instinctual.

"And panic magic happens when we don't know what we're doing and our magic takes over. It only happens when shit hits the fan. Like, imagine a mother doesn't know tracking magic but then she loses her child. Her magic can basically... figure it out anyway, just running on a *need* to find the baby.

"Panic magic will also kick in if we're in danger while unconscious. It's never pretty, but it'll get the job done."

Samson nods. "And panic magic makes you lose your memory."

The tiny pieces of magical knowledge he's gained make little sense to me—it's none of the fun parts, only the scary and dangerous aspects of wielding.

"We only lose our memory if we're wielding powerful panic magic. A mother who uses panic magic to find her child might only lose a month's worth of memories, but they'll come back eventually. Only a really insane act of magic would wipe someone's memory for a longer period of time. Even then, I don't know that memories are ever permanently lost."

Now that we're on the topic, Samson seems highly interested. He leans toward me, forgetting about the bundle of parchment in his hand. "How do you start our fires? You just snap your fingers and—flames. Does that mean you can actually make a friction fire?"

I almost want to laugh. "Me? Rubbing two sticks together like a madman? No. That one I learned from Onesimos."

"You can learn magic from a nymph? I thought nymph magic came from the demigods and wielder magic..."

I'd love to hear his opinion on the origin of our magic.

Like the nymphs take their power from the demigod that oversees the lands where they were born, wolves also claim to draw their phasing power from their single neuter demigod, Hetnazzar. The blue-black wolf wanders Velm, howling through the nights before running freely through the forests and moors. Unlike the nymph demigods, Hetnazzar doesn't select kings and queens, nor does it imbue the land with magical power.

Or so it goes; I have no idea what the demigod does, and I've yet to venture into Velm for a chance to find out.

And if Clearbold takes after his demigod, Hetnazzar is the one being whose attention I don't know that I'd appreciate.

"I don't know where our magic comes from." I shrug. "Think of it like this... magic in *any* form is like having a twin. For wielders and nymphs. In the case of me and Onesimos, our twins..."

How do I describe sex magic to someone who doesn't understand magic or, based on our conversation from the other day, casual sex?

I do my best. "Onesimos taught me to wield fire while we were physically intimate. When two beings are involved like that, their magical twins also become closer. Not physically close, but... spiritually, I guess?

"People's magical essences, their magical twins, become friends. They teach each other things. I guess you could technically say that there are four types of magic, then: instinctual, skilled, panic, and sympathetic magic. That's how we learn from the nymphs. Sympathetic magic."

My magic was the size of a city, Onesimos's a shoebox.

But Simmy never feared I'd lose control. My twin, neither.

"Simmy said his twin was trying to show off for mine. That's why it taught mine fire magic." Based on Samson's tense expression, that might've been too much information. But... I miss Onesimos. And I'm not ashamed of what we did.

His discomfort quickly passes. He goes on, "I suppose it's a bit like my fangself. Samsonfang can be stubborn and willful, but it's astounding what he knows and intuits."

"And what sort of things are those?" I glance over his body. Based on his dirty layers exhausted baring, Samson in his form is positively maniacal.

If there wasn't the ghost of the War Years that fills my mind with images of hulking wolves gnashing their teeth into the soft bellies of my ancestors, I'd probably have gone to spy on him during the triplemoon.

All I heard was a single howl, loud and clear enough to leave my skin rippled with goosepimples.

"I already told you what wolves do on the triplemoons." He rubs his face with both hands; this isn't exhaustion, but something more like regret. He looks up with a sigh. "Thank you for the explanation. I don't know why I didn't just ask a while ago. I need to eat and rest. I'll write the note first. I'm sorry to send us off track for the next few days."

I shrug. "We're still ahead of schedule. Who knows if the ghost has even found Oko yet? And I've always been curious about the waricons."

He pauses his search for his quill, hand shoved inside his

satchel. "Helisent, you can't come to a waricon. Wielders aren't permitted. Neither are nymphs."

"What?" I snort. "Those motherfuckers scratched at *my tree*."

I'm going to the waricon. I don't actually care about seeing the wolves punished as much as I care about seeing Samson all oiled up and panting—

Wait, what?

Woah, woah, woah.

Take it easy, Helisent.

I backtrack as though I could erase the idea of watching someone rub oil across Samson, starting with his calves then moving up to his thighs—

Oh.

Oh, holy fucking shit, that's not good.

I hadn't realized I was *that* interested in the oil. Or Samson.

I clear my throat and stand. "Samson no one wants to see your stupid fucking waricon anyway. Just write the note and take a nap."

I pretend not to notice his look of hurt confusion. Then, once he's finished scribbling across the parchment, I stick out my hand.

Ten minutes ago, I'd planned on reading the note to try to glean more information about Samson's relationship with this Rex and why he'd have an old hair tie in the bottom of his bag.

Now I hope they're lovers and that Samson never spares a sexy thought for me.

The only thing dumber than convincing the imminent Male Alpha of Velm to help me find Oko would be falling in love with him along the way.

I pinch the tightly folded piece of paper and breathe my magic into it with a quick whisper. "Find Rex 543 Kaneling immediately and give him this note. Don't touch him. He doesn't want to be touched by us."

And then I throw the square into the brightening sky. It catches in the wind and takes off to the southeast, sailing through the air on invisible wings.

Rex is the first wolf to make me wish I could scent alas.

What I would give to know what kind of scent accompanies such a handsome face.

Samson sucks on a cigarette while we watch the wolf approach from the southeast. At our backs, Invidio's shitty little village starts to wake with the dawn.

I listen to the morning chatter from the hesperides and naiads, as well as the lower-toned grunting from wolves. It barely distracts me from the warmth that wells in my mind and body. Rex looks like he was carved from stone, unsullied by the mundane world. His eyes are sharp and set, his lips plump and pink enough to make up for his too-sharp cheekbones and jaw.

Then there's the way he walks, the way a few loose strands of dark blue hair slip from his temples and flutter in the wind.

"Good fucking moons, Samson—I want to lick him where he sweats."

Samson throws me an unamused glance, exhaling smoke into the wind. "He's close enough to hear you. So are the villagers behind us. Wolf ears, Helisent. Don't forget."

He reminds me once a week, but I continue to forget just how much stronger a wolf's senses are than mine.

"Well, then, Rex, I hope you're ready for this." I amend my statement. "Meeting me, not the licking."

My last comment finally breaks the dead stillness of Samson's expression.

Since we arrived at Invidio's hilly village, he's been stony and reticent. It takes me back to our first interactions when he treated me with a similar disconnect. I'm surprised to see the same presentation for Rex. While I haven't broached the topic of the hair tie with Samson, I'm still assuming the pair were once lovers or once almost-lovers.

Rex keeps his eyes on Samson until he stops before us. "Samson 714 Afador." Then he looks at me. He holds out the note I sent to him with the tracking spell. It's folded as precisely as when I'd sent it. "Witch."

He says it like a curse. It's almost enough to make me flinch.

This is how it usually goes; I'm incredibly attracted to someone only to be made a fool for it later.

I snatch the note from his hand and prepare a nasty retort, but Samson speaks first. "Helisent West of Jaws." He also says it like a threat; I like that.

Then he turns away and heads north toward where we're camped outside the village.

Shortly after our arrival, a swarm of nymphs came to welcome us to the village and offer lodging. But the offers were half-hearted; the hesperides with speckled skin and naiads with blue-green eyes had anticipated Samson's decision to remain outside Invidio's direct territory.

When I asked why we couldn't stay in the village, Samson said it would bother Invidio to have his scent lingering days after the waricon. When I asked why again, he said I'd get it later.

After the troop of nymphs came a caravan of wolves.

The male wolves arrived with the same calm, fatalistic expression that Rex now wears. The elders had thinning white hair that hung loose in their buns. At their sides, juvenile wolflings carried thick bundles. Although they ignored my presence, they didn't seem surprised or upset to find a witch at Samson's camp.

One of the wolves had even left a bundle at the foot of my tree.

When we unwrapped them later, I was shocked to find mounds of bitterroot. Samson, on the other hand, felt it was a lacking gift—especially considering I was traveling with the Kulapsifang. He'd expected more gifts for me. Better ones.

(I think there may be a bit of warlock in him, after all.)

Samson guides us out of earshot of the village's loneliest huts, toward the outskirts of the hills where we're camped. I glance south one last time. I've never been so near the frontier of Velm; this is the first time I've seen the towering mountain range that shelters the cities of Bellator and Rouz.

They look like indigo giants looming amid the hazy clouds. I can't even see their peaks, only the gray-white trails of snow that fall below the cloudline.

I look back, hustling on foot to keep up with the wolves as they amble. The smoke from Samson's cigarette spread over my head like fragile clouds.

Once we're a safe distance from the village, Samson begins, "Have you heard of Invidio 499 Kelberg?"

Rex ducks his head toward Samson and speaks in a low voice. "More and more often. I was north of Silent City to help with a search—we were tracking someone from this village, actually. We ran into Malachai, who was looking for the same wolf."

I follow, attempting to move silently so they'll forget I'm here.

I've yet to see Samson in his natural element.

His voice takes a harsher tone than I've ever heard before —run-in with Invidio included. "*Malachai*? What does he have to do with Invidio?"

"You know how it is in the east. Malachai and Emerel are promoting the Leofsige line everywhere," Rex explains. "Malachai's been to this village multiple times in the last five years. He's building alliances, and it looks like Invidio and his pack support the Leofsiges."

The Leofsige line is Clearbold's; it's the same generational title he passed down to his spare heir, Malachai. But I've yet to hear about the Female Alpha of Velm who's standing in for

Imepratriz. Though I think it must be Emerel, I'm too nervous to ask them, afraid they'll remember I'm here and ask for privacy.

With each step, he and Rex pick up their paces and drift closer together. I'm already starting to breathe heavily in their wake, but I don't want to float with Rex nearby.

Witch.

Eventually, Samson says, "That would explain Invidio's actions, at least."

"Your letter didn't mention why a waricon was called. What happened?" Rex asks.

Our camp finally comes into view as Samson explains, "I left Helisent West of Jaws on the triplemoon. They came to our camp at sunrise before I got back. There were four. I challenged both that had scratched at her tree."

I didn't appreciate Invidio and his little wolfling scratching at my tree, but it had been clear they weren't trying to harm me. Just bother me, maybe make me a bit uneasy.

Until seeing Rex's reaction, I hadn't realized how big of a deal it was.

"*Lekeli Kelnazzar...*" The wolf, who seems to hate me, turns on his heels. He looks past me, toward the village. "Why the fuck didn't you challenge all four of them, Samson? *They walked into your camp?* They bothered *your guest?* We should wait and send word to Riordon, Berevald, and Pietrangelo. We'll handle every single wolf who thought they could trespass on your camp."

Rex takes a quick step back and takes a deep breath, as though calming a rage before he goes on. "I mean, what the *fuck* Samson? I'd do a lot more than challenge them to a waricon if they came into my fucking camp while I wasn't there. Clearbold should be notified that—"

"No. I'll handle it. The pup is yours. Invidio's mine." Samson sighs. "And I would also like to send word to our war band, but we don't have enough time to spare. The last I heard, Riordon and Pietrangelo were as far as Wrenweary. Berevald might be farther south than Mort at this point."

"Fine. We'll handle it—just us." Rex scoffs. "But I'm biting twice, Samson. If you give these fucks an inch, they'll take all of Velm. Especially with Malachai waiting in the wings."

Samson does a doubletake over his shoulder when he glances back and sees me. Rex does the same a moment later.

I've already planned it out. I bite my lip as though uncertain then glance back at the village. "Should I just wait at the tavern?"

Samson checked it out with me yesterday. It's far from the wolves' residential area. We even spotted a few wielders passing through the neighboring inn.

I go on, "I'll stay there until tomorrow so you guys can... get out the oil or whatever."

Based on the quick glance Samson and Rex share, I was right to think they were lovers.

I raise my eyebrows. "Not like that. Good luck." Samson nods, though Rex still seems to be avoiding eye contact with me. "I'm glad you're here too, Rex. Not for me—obviously."

I offer them a stupid smile then scurry away. I duck into a gulch that precedes the first thatched huts in the village, then use smothering magic to block my scent from the wolves.

I've been practicing the spell with Samson over the last week.

I'd drift out of sight, then duck to hide as I used smothering magic to hide my scent. Samson never made it more than ten steps before turning around, nostrils flaring as he searched for my ala. But no matter of sniffing revealed my spot.

Time to really test the spell.

I slip off my bright robe and hustle back to camp. I take the opposite direction as Samson and Rex, hoping I won't miss out on too much of their conversation while I double back— and crossing my fingers that they haven't switched to the Velmic tongue.

The pair sit in silence as I sneak into the shadows of a squat tree.

Rex knocks two pieces of flint together above a pyramid of kindling. To my great luck, he addresses Samson in Mieiran. "The witch's note found me in the middle of a public meal. Her scent was all over it; so was yours. Malachai was in the same village, so I'm sure he's heard of it, too. I'd be surprised if he didn't come."

Samson unwraps the linen bundles the wolves left for us the other morning. Aside from my bitterroot, they also brought a small mountain of fresh meat, tough stalks of herbs I don't recognize, and jugs of cedar-scented oil.

Rex leaves the growing fire to help Samson sort through the contents.

Samson flips and angles the red meat with a deft touch, then uses his throwing ax to cleave through it. "I'd expect nothing less from Malachai."

"You *should* expect more from him. There are rumors in Mort that you didn't kill the woolly mammoth, Samson. And people aren't necessarily whispering about it anymore."

Kill the wooly?

I know high-numbered wolves face a series of trials as juveniles before they're considered adults. Killing something would be a prime way to prove worth to other wolves—but that's the extent of my knowledge.

Samson separates the bones from the edible flesh with a few grunts. He tosses the bones into a separate pile with a rugged crassness he doesn't display around me.

With a huff, he glares at Rex. "The wooly's skull is still in Bellator. What does he think about that?"

"Everyone's seen the skull in the palace. But there's still enough uncertainty left from Imperatriz's disappearance to keep people on edge—and to keep wolves like Malachai talking. For all your enduring silence, people may start to ask questions. The last I heard, Malachai was hinting that Clearbold would have been *incredibly motivated* to hide your inability to kill a wooly."

With a start, Samson stands. He chucks the throwing ax into the slab of meat at his feet; it sinks in with a loud *shunk.* "Malachai thinks Clearbold sent me into that forest with nothing but a fucking throwing ax *three years too early* and then *lied* about the fact that I brought home a wooly's corpse? Malachai's just bent out of shape because he barely managed to do it at fifteen years old."

I'm starting to wonder if they're talking about the wooly mammoths that wander through the Velmic valleys.

I heard there aren't many left of the massive, shaggy elephants—which would make sense, especially if wolves kill them as juveniles as a rite of passage.

Does that mean Samson *killed* a wooly at age twelve with nothing but a throwing ax?

"It sounds like that's exactly what Malachai is implying. He wants everyone to think Clearbold lied to save your hide." Rex looks up from where he separates the fibrous herb stalks, eyebrows raised.

"And what the fuck did you say?" Samson asks.

"Malachai knows better than to talk like that when I'm in earshot." Rex watches Samson as he paces around the firepit. "I heard others stood up for you. Berevald was there. He told Malachai and all who would listen that Clearbold sent you alone into the woods three years too soon to *prove* there was nothing wrong with Imperatriz's line."

Samson's eyes are wild. He shakes his head as he stares around, pacing with sharp turns. For a moment, my gut sinks into my toes; what if he's caught my scent?

But then he says, "They'd believe that was the truth if Clearbold hadn't remarried Emerel. If he hadn't bothered to make a spare with her."

Emerel must be Malachai's mother, then.

Part of me wonders if they're too loyal to see the truth:

that Clearbold may have sent Samson into the forest hoping he'd die. Hoping he'd restart Velm's most powerful generational line with the name Leofsige.

Instead of Afador.

Clearly, Samson's heart hasn't been broken enough in this life; only pain teaches us to see truth. Even I know that.

"You should have told Clearbold the whole story, Samson." Though Rex's words are dire, his tone is gentle. "Then there'd be no question. There wouldn't have been an Emerel or a Malachai. Clearbold would have known you were the rightful heir of Afador if you'd told him Hetnazzar was there when you killed the wooly."

What the fuck?

Ten seconds ago, I wondered if Samson was critically naive. Now I realize he's keeping secrets from me, too—demigod-sized secrets.

What are you, Samson? Kulapsifang and King of Zhuzhing?

He didn't say a word about his own demigod while interrogating my relationship to the demigod west of Gamma. And now I'll never get to criticize him for it because I'm eavesdropping.

I roll my eyes.

Rex goes on, "It's too late to speak your truth now. The wolves won't believe Hetnazzar stepped in to help you."

Samson kneels before the meat and starts hacking again. "It doesn't matter if they believe me. Hetnazzar will come for me. The demigod will come back when I'm in need again."

"Is that what you're doing with the witch? Hoping something with an ala as powerful as hers will catch the attention of Hetnazzar?"

Rex watches Samson for a long moment, and Samson ignores him.

It's a deceptively intimate exchange; my mind switches back to the nature of the hair tie.

Rex forgets the supplies spread before him. He brushes the

hair from his temple with the back of his hand. "I can't even smell your ala. It's all fucking tangled with the witch's scent."

Ex-lovers, it is.

Samson slides his eyes to the wolf. "You have to be kidding me. Do you remember our last exchange? You said that anything between us would compromise the future of Velm."

"And how does the witch factor into that?" Rex scoffs. "A wielder will compromise the future of Velm more than I ever could. Everyone else might see you as all rules and customs, but I know the truth. You're—"

"She's looking for Oko, too."

For whatever reason, Samson's words take the joy out of eavesdropping. Rather than feeling like I know him better, I feel like an insignificant piece of his life. I remind myself that we're budding political allies who will both have an influence on Mieira in the years to come.

That's a lot for any witch and wolf.

I should be happy leaving that as it is.

Rex asks, "And how's the search going, Samson?"

Samson's hacking starts to pick up a rhythm. "Sometimes I think you're only interested in my life when things start to go well."

"Remember the storm in Lampades? Was I there for you because things were going well, Samson? What about now? Is this me, coming to ruin your life when things are going really well?"

Rex is a piece of shit.

And I don't want to wait around to see if Samson is also a piece of shit.

With a sigh, I turn and sneak back toward the village.

At the tavern, the hesperide bartender remembers me from yesterday. He already has a bottle of brandy ready for me.

I wake up on a wooden table with no idea where I am.

I knock into an empty bottle and send it to the floor. It doesn't shatter; it hits something with a hard *thump*, which is followed by a curse. A second later, someone groans awake.

I try to open my eyes, but a wave of nausea has me sinking back onto the tabletop. Eventually, I coax one eye open and manage to glance around.

I'm relieved to wake up where I remember drinking last: the dusty tavern in Invidio's village.

I'm less relieved by the howling horn that sounds in the distance. The high-pitched wailing goes on and on.

I clamp my hands over my ears as I break out in a feverish, hungover sweat. "Someone make it end."

It doesn't. The horn stops just to start over a second later.

Eventually, I push myself onto my elbows. A dozen snoring nymphs dot the open tables and floor around me. Though it seems I'm the only one in the impromptu warren without a blanket, I suppose my robe is enough.

I force myself into a sitting position as the horns stoke a hungover rage in me.

A hesperide sits up from the bench that's half-shoved under my table. He blinks his large hickory eyes at me then glances at the window near the table. Mist hangs between the thatched buildings, backlit with pale light.

"Did someone curse your village or something?" I study the hesperide. My mouth is fuzzy, my stomach empty.

The nymph collapses back onto the bench. "It's a waricon. The wolves here are fucking crazy, Helisent."

Fuck.

The waricon. It's probably already starting.

I flick my hand to set my magic into motion—hair-brushing, face-cleaning, all the morning basics.

The hesperide sits up and watches my magic work with a tilted head. His thin brown hair is tugged back into a high ponytail; the baby hairs near his temple flair out.

I ask, "How do you know my name?"

His eyebrows bunch together. "You don't remember me?"

I have no idea who this hesperide is, but no one likes to hear that so early in the morning.

I wink. "Just kidding. Do you have any food, my dear lover?" Were we lovers? Seriously, who is this guy? "I want to go watch the fight, but I'll pass out if I go on an empty stomach."

I can't remember if Rex or Samson fights first—but I'm likely missing out on the sheen of oil in the early morning light.

With a puzzled expression, the hesperide extracts himself from the table's bench and steps over the sleeping bodies toward the bar at the far end of the tavern.

I finish the basics of grooming, use smothering magic to hide my ala to sneak to the waricon, and then head to the door. The hesperide meets me there with a wrapped bundle.

"We made a meal last night." Once again, the nymph eyes me with a suspicious bend to his brow. "You also told me to remind you that the wielders and nymphs spy on the waricons from the northern edge of the grounds."

The blaring horns start again, loud and brutal enough that they send a shiver up my spine and fresh nausea clanging through my stomach.

The hesperide makes a pensive sound, then gestures south-ward. "The wielders never like the sound. Just head that way and stick to the trees." He leans toward me and sets his nose against my shoulder, inhaling deeply. "They won't catch your ala. You hid it well. But you don't need to hide *too* much— Invidio knows nymphs and wielders come to watch the wari-cons here. I think he likes it."

I glance at my robe where the nymph stuck his nose. "Wonderful."

"Ah, you can follow them." The hesperide gestures behind me to where two wolves and a nymph walk together. They part the mist on the narrow street, stepping in tandem. "That's Chariovalda, my sister. They came from Luz to..."

I'm five steps ahead of him.

I sprint toward the familiar hesperide with brown skin speckled with pale marks, with long brown hair tangled into thin braids.

I haven't seen a friend in over a month of travel and hadn't realized how much I missed home.

"Chariovalda!" I shout. She raises her head with a smile right before I stop in my tracks, brace myself on my knees, then spit into the dirt. "Wait. Hold on. I might throw up."

Chariovalda reaches me. She runs her hand down my back with a giggle. "Helisent, my dear wielder. I see you met my brother."

I take a few deep breaths and clench my eyes. "Yeah. Super nice guy."

Please don't ask me his name.

Then her tone changes. "A witch came to Luz looking for you a few weeks ago. It was about your mentee—I didn't know Ninigone made you a mentor. Seems a bit foolish to ask a sponsor to babysit."

"Chari," the female wolf cuts in. "I'll carry the witch if she's too hungover to walk. We need to go. We'll miss the first bout."

I straighten and raise my chin. I stare up at the unnumbered wolves. Gautselin, owner of Luz's sexiest pleasure house, looks down at me with a crooked smile. After traveling with Samson so long, I find Gautselin doesn't look quite as threatening; he has a healthy layer of fat, an easy and wide smile, and free-flowing hair that's pinned back with a clip today.

"Good morning, Helisent." Gautselin bears one of his winning smiles at me. "I hope the demigods are smiling on you today. What the *fuck* are you doing here?"

The wolf at his side looks less thrilled to see me. Her blue-black hair is cropped and choppy. Something about her curved lips looks familiar. "Let's chat at the waricon. The horns stopped—it'll start soon."

Gautselin waves a hand, glancing at her. "It's just Rex and the pup now. I've seen enough senior wolves bite the little ones to know how it'll go."

He sinks on his haunches to speak with me. Even among the unnumbered wolves, Gautselin is a warm presence who values understanding and, above all, joy. He constantly hunches, and squats, and lowers his voice so the nymphs and wielders around him feel more comfortable.

He *touches* people, too.

"It'll just be a bunch of screeching," he explains, fixing his attention on me. "Don't worry—it's not all from pain. Most of the noise is from the shame of being bitten." He nods toward my bottomless bag. "Did you want to get our your lilith or do you want Elvira Ultramarine to carry you? She'll really do it."

I study the female wolf and wonder if it'd be like being carried by Samson in Skull.

Elvira is just as tall and broad as her male companion. Unlike wielders and nymphs, male and female wolves are the same size. The women have slightly softer angles, but even their breasts are smaller and more muscular than any nymph or wielder I've ever met. Their wide hips are the only hint that they're capable of carrying and birthing new life.

"Elvira Ultramarine. I've heard of you before." I narrow my eyes as I study her face. Though her lips are thinner than most wolves', her eyes are brighter. Almost *bluer*. "You live in Luz, right?"

She raises her eyebrows. "Helisent, did you forget about the time your warren came to Coil?"

I scan my memory. "I've never remembered a single night I spent in Coil. No offense. I'm sure you're one in a million, Elvira."

She snorts, running a hand through her short hair. "Don't

worry. You mostly drank in the corner and yelled at Onesimos for something he did earlier that night."

What I would do for another night like that.

"Sounds about right." I stuff my hand into my bottomless bag and tug out my lilith. I hobble onto the pale cushion.

Chariovalda leans close to me. She groans. "I walked two days with these long-legged freaks to make it on time. Please let me on."

I scoot over to make room for her, then use lifting magic to help her settle onto the lilith at my side.

She waves goodbye to her nameless brother and he waves back, then we take off toward the fighting grounds.

Like they've attended waricons here before, the group heads straight for the hilly forest outside the village.

First, I hear drumming. The instruments are common to wolves and found throughout Velm, where hand drums range in size for individual to group usage. Based on the quick booming beats reverberating beyond the next hill, the wolves here are using multiple group drums.

I'm glad I'm here with Chariovalda.

No matter the number of years put between my life and the War Years, I'm keenly aware this is the sound that preceded death for my ancestors.

Chariovalda and I float behind Gautselin and Elvira as they lead the way. Their pace picks up as we crest the final ridge that leads to another forested hilltop. This one is denser than the other areas surrounding the village, providing shelter for the uninvited guests to watch.

Their numbers are greater than I would have assumed, especially considering Samson said it was *forbidden* for non-wolves to spectate.

I make out at least two dozen beings on the hilltop through the trees. More come into focus as we scale the gradual incline.

Halfway there, Gautselin and Elvira stop. I grab Chariovalda's wrist as my lilith almost runs into the wolves' backs. Gautselin turns back toward us, as though prepared to grab us.

Elvira stares at him, her lips pinched together and her brow tightened.

What are they sensing?

I follow her gaze and look over my shoulder.

All I see is the pleasant forest, moss-ridden and sleepy as the shivering drumbeats echo from the waricon grounds.

Then something barrels over a leafy fern and runs into Gautselin. The massive figure knocks the unnumbered wolf to the ground. The pair topple over one another, flattening the saplings and bushes in their path.

Elvira brushes past my lilith to join the skirmish as the pair grapples down the incline. She moves just in time to meet a second wolf, who also rushes toward where Gautselin struggles on the ground. Elvira gets the upper hand for a second, shoving the second wolf off-course with a loud grunt.

It takes a few seconds to put things together: my friends are unnumbered wolves, just as uninvited to this waricon as me.

The wolves tackling them must be numbered and displeased by their arrival.

I raise my hands, but my reaction is slow.

That's the thing about magic. It can do almost anything—so long as a wielder is levelheaded (and sober) enough to call on it. And to make the right call when things start moving quickly.

In the seconds it takes me to decide that halting magic will be enough to freeze all four wolves in their tracks without harming them, the second intruder has turned around and slapped Elvira across the cheek. He's growling something in Velmic that I don't understand.

By the time I get around to casting my halting magic, the first wolf has landed multiple hits to Gautselin's cheek. The second wolf has Elvira by the throat, similar to Samson's hold on Invidio; guiding more than crushing. Still highly unpleasant.

And then I cast the spell.

All four wolves stop mid-movement.

Gautselin's cheek is bloody where he lays pinned beneath his aggressor. Elvira has one fist cocked back and leveled at her opponent, who still holds her throat.

Get it together, Helisent.

"Elvira, Gautselin—please move behind me," I say.

I tighten my hold on Chariovalda's wrist, worried she'll go tend to Gautselin and further piss off the numbered wolves. Then I release Elvira and Gautselin from the spell.

Elvira yanks her neck free from the attacker's grip. Instead of turning away, she adjusts her fist, fingers flexing into a tighter position. I stare at her, prepared to send more halting magic toward her fist if she decides to strike her halted attacker.

Gautselin slides out from the wolf's grip by shimmying along the ground. He doesn't look nearly as shocked as I would have imagined. He stands, dusts off his white layers, then uses the edge of his tunic to dab at his bloody cheekbone, then his bloody lip. Then he runs a hand through his hair to shake out the debris.

He steps over to Elvira. He doesn't touch her but levels an exhausted and knowing look at her.

Elvira growls, fist trembling where it's held aloft. Then she lowers her hand. She turns away with Gautselin, angry tears pooled in her eyes and teeth gritted.

I stare at the halted wolves. One remains braced on the ground on his knees. The other still has one hand extended, gripping the air where Elvira once stood.

Once Gautselin and Elvira stand behind me, I address the still-halted wolves. "My name is Helisent West of Jaws. These are my friends you're assaulting. I'll release you from my magic in a moment. If you don't plan on apologizing to me, Chariovalda—that's the nymph—and my friends, *Gautselin* and *Elvira*, then I suggest you leave. The next spell I cast will not be so kind."

I lift the spell.

My stomach clenches when the pair straighten and I make out their features. I'm happy that I at least contain my gasp as the first wolf looks at me—at first, I think it's Samson. But this wolf's eyes and brow are less severe. His jaw, too.

He looks young. But that doesn't stop him from stepping past his companion and squaring up to me with a look of violent disdain.

I clench my jaw to avoid retreating.

Then I place a barrier spell between me and the wolf. My eyes shoot to his hands, which straighten out his tunic with quick tugs. They flex at his sides next.

The wolf looks me up and down. "Helisent West of Jaws."

Malachai 555 Leofsige.

I don't say that. Instead, I arch an eyebrow. "Yes, wolfling. And who the fuck are you?"

"I am Malachai 555 Leofsige. I'm here to intercept the unnumbered wolves. They aren't allowed to watch waricons. Tell your *friends* to leave."

"In *Velm*, they aren't allowed to watch waricons." I raise my other eyebrow. "But the last I checked, we're in Mieira. That means there's no place nymphs and wielders can't walk. So I think that means you and your friend should *fuck off.*"

Malachai inches closer. My eyes keep shifting from his face to his hands, from the likeness of Samson to the fear of death. "I am the son of Clearbold 554 Leofsige and Emerel 524 Ledselin. I don't take orders from witches."

I could kill you a thousand times over.

It was the first thought I had when I met Clearbold. It didn't come as quickly with Samson, but it did, eventually.

That's the thing about these wolves—

I could kill them a thousand times over.

My devilish smile probably says as much.

I try to keep in mind that the waricon is starting, that my friends might not be interested in leveraging this skirmish into a full-on fight.

But I am a witch, after all.

I lower my chin to leer at Malachai. "Is that a challenge, wolfling?"

The drumbeats stop suddenly, making way for the calming sounds of the forest. Birds chirp in the canopy overhead, while small creatures scuttle through the brush. Pleasant chatter echoes from the crowd spying on the waricon over-head. No one sounds disgruntled or concerned, which makes me wonder if the drums disguised the sounds of Malachai's attack.

The wolf scowls back at me. "No, witch. It was a reminder."

For a long time, neither Malachai nor I shift.

I'm not nervous anymore, I'm just waiting.

When the time is right, I raise my hand and shoo him back in the direction he and his cohort arrived. "I think that's all for now."

My father taught me the trick long ago. He said, *"Honey, just wait until your enemy is about to leave, then shoo them. It'll piss even a nymph off. Don't do it to me, though. You'll break my heart."*

It takes Malachai a while to turn away; his nostrils flare as though he's studying my scent. Then with a quick pivot, he and his cohort head back over the trampled fern where they emerged.

Once they've disappeared amid the trees, I glance behind me.

Elvira and Gautselin also stare after the pair with hard expressions.

"Should we stay and watch the waricon or...?" I ask. "I can't really tell if I took it too far or not far enough."

Gautselin's eyebrows shoot up as he smiles. "I'd rather stay off Malachai's shit-list—just in case. So it's great you feel comfortable harassing him. It feeds my soul. It really does."

Just in case what?

Elvira directs her loathsome gaze at me. "Well, it doesn't feed mine. I could have handled that. Now those two know my ala *and* my name. Stay out of my business next time, Helisent."

With a tsk, she turns and continues up the hillock. She takes her place toward the back of the crowd, which has fallen silent. She rolls her shoulders then runs a hand through her spiky hair, as though still full of adrenaline.

My stomach twists.

Did I just make life harder for her? I make a note to ask Samson about the politics of unnumbered wolves. About the likelihood of Malachai seeking out Elvira in the future for a round two.

Gautselin takes a step back to fall in line with my lilith. He sets his hand on Chariovalda's leg. She pats his hand and studies him, staring at the blood on the corner of his shirt and then the bruising welt on his cheekbone.

He whispers over to me, "Elvira will shake it off in a few days. She tends to direct her anger at the first thing that makes eye contact with her."

Chariovalda also offers me a hopeful nod.

Still, I feel like an asshole as we scale the hill. Rather than join the crowd at the hilltop, Gautselin leads us along the hill's slope. To my surprise, the crest doesn't continue on to a rolling decline—instead, there's a steep drop-off, as though someone dug a massive portion out of the hill.

Gautselin lays on his stomach near the ledge. I take his free side as Chariovalda settles into the soft grass on his opposite. A few ferns and bushes hang around us, offering added coverage as we spy. The rest of the spectators hang near the hill's highest point, peering down with blatant curiosity.

Beige sand covers the cleared pit below. A square portion in the center is outlined with stones. Within, Rex and one of

Invidio's wolves wrestle with one another. Each wears a minimal navy-blue layer of fabric at their hips, which only partially covers their butts. Their skin gleams with a thick coating of oil.

In the center of the sand pit, they grapple with one another. It's much slower than I thought it would be, as though they're locked into a hold and determined to make it their last move.

Their grunting drifts up from below. Though at least fifty wolves surround the square boundaries of the fighting area, they're dead silent. I scan the wolves in navy clothes, attempting to pick out Samson from the crowd, or even Malachai. But given the similar hair color, hair styles, and cotton clothes, each being looks hopelessly similar to the next —even down to size.

I elbow Gautselin. "Where's Samson?"

Gautselin raises an eyebrow as he turns toward me. "Samson 714 Afador? And why are you looking for him? Last I heard, he hated magic and had never made a wielder friend."

I roll my eyes. "He just needs time to learn more about magic. He let me use a tracking spell to get Rex and tell him to meet us here so that—"

"What, what, *what*?" Bless Gautselin, he even talks like a nymph. "Are you *here* with *Samson*? Is that why you got so sassy with Malachai before?"

"We're traveling together. That's how I ended up here in the first place. The village's pack leader, some guy named Invidio, scratched at my tree on the triplemoon. Samson's gonna bite him in the neck."

Like Rex did, Gautselin pauses. His expression darkens.

He speaks slowly, as though in an effort to understand me correctly. "Invidio came and scratched at your tree where Samson was also camping on the triplemoon?"

I love how scandalous it is. Gautselin wasn't at all startled by the fact that Malachai showed up out of nowhere to beat him simply for existing. But the idea of a numbered wolf impeding on Samson's campsite...

"Yeah. The wolfling scratched at my tree, too. That's why Rex is here. He's fighting him on my behalf."

Gautselin turns away from me. "Chari, did you hear that? *Samson* is fighting a *waricon* for the honor of a *witch*." He whips his head back to me. His childlike wonder sits juxtaposed with his growing shiner. "Are you... are you *lovers* with Samson 714 Afador?"

It takes me a long time to find an answer to that. I can't really say why. A solid *no* should be more than enough. "Gautselin, don't you think that's a ride I wouldn't survive?"

"What? Why's that?" He gives me the onec-over. "You know, the rumors about wolf cock aren't true. They're reasonably sized."

From his other side, Chariovalda calls, "It's true, Helisent. They can also be trained to use them very well."

Gautselin goes on, "Plus, you're not really a novice when it comes to that kind of thing."

"I beg your fucking pardon, Gautselin."

"You can *peg* my pardon all you like, Helisent."

Gautselin smiles at me with an irreverent giggle, and I smile back. My moons, how I've missed sexual banter.

But the next second, Gautselin's features grow solemn. "Look, I don't mean to be uselessly crass, but the idea of the Kulapsi shacking up with a witch is something wolves have dreamed of. I mean, maybe not all of them. I can only speak for the unnumbered wolves... but it would mean a lot to us if something like that happened."

I watch Rex and the pup wrestle. What started with a deadlock has evolved into a livelier fight. Though Rex continues to pin the smaller wolf, his target keeps writhing free. Sand sprays into the crowd as their bodies crash into the ground.

I glance at Gautselin. "And why would that mean a lot?"

He keeps his eyes on the action below. His words are slow and thoughtful. "One day, Samson will be the 714th consecutive Alpha of Velm. You can trace the Afadors all the way back to the first time we turned skin under Hetnazzar's gaze. Since then, there's been... well, close to no change.

"What I know about my own people is that we have always prioritized survival. Then came the War Years, which set us back centuries with wielders and nymphs. All the good either kind had done in Velm was forgotten amid the bloodshed.

"The centuries since then have been about rebuilding. We're doing as the nymphs do, just like wielders are. We're doing it for peace, to build a future in which the Northing might exist. That wasn't just Imperatriz's goal—it was something her mother, the Kulapsifang and Female Alpha Sutnazzar 712 Afador, also pushed for.

"But it all came to a screeching halt when Imperatriz disappeared. The wolves are fucking *Southing* under Clearbold. Samson could change that. Samson might look like he's all Leofsige, but he's Afador at heart. He's... He's..."

I am here.

I scan the wolves below for another sign of Samson. Nothing.

I clear my throat. "Yeah, I get it."

Gautselin nods. "You know, before he left Luz, I jumped in front of him and asked him to come to Coil sometime. He was on his way to *Solace*. No other Kulapsi in history would've dealt with an unnumbered wolf jumping in front of their path. But Samson spent a whole five minutes letting me invite him to Coil—and then *he* asked *me* for directions to Solace.

"I mean, you saw what just happened with Malachai, and I didn't even bat a lash in his direction. Wolves like him target us because they're unchecked and we're unprotected. Samson would never do something similar—he's cut from a different cloth. He could change the future of Velm, Helisent."

"You know, that's where we met. At Solace."

Gautselin laughs without humor. "What I'd fucking barter to know what you two are up to right now."

"Go on, then. Make me an offer."

Gautselin knows better. "Fuck off."

We turn back to the action.

It goes on much longer than I thought it would. By the time Rex finally pins the pup and bites his neck, the sun is high above us and I'm reaching for my second bottle of brandy. The shout that peals from the younger wolf's mouth when Rex finally bites him is just as cringe-inducing as the horns used to announce the waricon's start.

Rather than a screech, like Gautselin said, a low bellow starts before Rex has even released the wolf's jugular.

It looks so intimate.

With a passing glance, I would assume the pair were lovers. That Rex lowered his mouth to his neck for a kiss.

Then Rex stands. Red blood fills his mouth; it falls from his lips, down his chin and neck and chest. It stands out amid the muted brown rocks, the wispy grass around us, the pale sand.

The surrounding wolves rush into the square once Rex has stepped past the stone perimeter. The pup rises and hurries after Rex, as though unable to stay down and accept the fight's conclusion. Three male wolves pin him as the bellowing continues, drifting into the sky from far below.

The wolves take the juvenile to one side of the grounds.

Rex heads to the far side of the sanded area. There, a lone wolf waits for him. My breath catches when I realize it's Samson. He raises a dark towel to help Rex clean his face and upper body of the blood.

The crowd disperses and reveals three massive drums. Female wolves sit down and surround the taut hides, picking up drumsticks before they begin a rhythmic beat like before. The sounds are so striking and loud that it's hard to pay attention as the wolves prepare for the next fight.

Once Rex is clean, Samson sets a jug of oil between them. They reach into its narrow opening to scoop oil, then rub down Samson's limbs with quick motions. The pair's mouths move, as though they're speaking as they work. They glance to the other side of the grounds, where Invidio's pack coats him in the same gleaming oil.

My attention catches only briefly on Samson's bare flesh.

I tally all the parts of him I haven't seen yet: his upper legs, his hips, his butt.

Then I stare across the crowd.

I count how outnumbered Samson and Rex are; the only beings convinced of a wolf's self-control are other wolves.

And if Malachai and Invidio are looking to undermine Samson's claim to the throne...

Eventually, Samson steps into the square. Rex stands close to the stones, prepared to jump in.

Invidio steps into the square from the other end. They look to be the same size, though Invidio's muscles have cleaner outlines. I can count his abs from here.

I glance sideways at Gautselin. "Do you think Samson will win? I mean, he has to, right?"

Gautselin slides his eyes toward me. "He's the Kulapsifang. It's physically impossible to be stronger than him. Well, maybe not stronger in terms of brute strength—but certainly in terms of endurance. Only Clearbold could best him in a waricon, and even that might not happen since most of Samson's power is inborn from Imperatriz's line."

Below, Invidio strikes himself in the chest, as though summoning his might and courage. He shouts a few times, too, as the women sit back from their drums.

Samson stands at the other end of the square, hands ready and waiting near his abdomen.

"Why would Invidio challenge him to a fight if he knows he won't win?"

Gautselin laughs again, low and humorless. "For the honor

of fighting the Kulapsi. Maybe for the chance to reveal a crack in Samson's façade. Some wolves think Malachai should be Velm's next Male Alpha."

Malachai and Rex can both get fucked. "So I've heard."

As though for my sake, Gautselin murmurs, "It won't be pretty, but he'll be okay. Just look away if it's too much."

Look away if it's too much?

I stare down with renewed interest.

With a cue I can't see or hear, the wolves take off toward each other. Even that shocks me—I'd never imagined Samson could move quickly given his bulk. The wolves meet in the center of the square with a series of loud slapping as they vie for position.

Then comes grunting.

I can't tell which tones are Samson's. The sounds are deep growls sprung from the usage of brute force, along with quick pants. If I thought Rex and the pup looked evenly matched, this is a fight in slow motion.

The pair don't break or disengage where they're locked in the center of the square. Their legs drive deeper into the sand as they vie for a stronger hold and attempt to twist the other. Eventually, blood begins to drip into the sand, streaks coating their arms as they dribble downward.

"Why is there blood?" I ask. "Did Samson already bite him?"

Gautselin snorts. "No. Invidio probably broke his nose. It's a shitty move some wolves pull at the start of a fight to try to get an advantage. It makes it harder to breathe. The pain sucks, too, but it's mostly about making Samson breathe through his mouth."

In the next second, Samson turns his head in our direction. His stomach pumps in huge breaths, expanding then collapsing, and he exhales a fine spray of bright-red from his blood-filled mouth.

I study Invidio with mounting rage.

Why didn't I just handle this?

I'm more than strong enough—and it's not like Invidio came to my tree while still in his form. Wielder magic may be useless on a wolf that's turned skin, but Invidio was a man when he walked to my camp.

I fish around for a third bottle of brandy in my bottomless bag. I'm right to anticipate a long fight.

Hours pass.

As dusk breaks, their panting and grunting merges into a terrifying, forlorn, and urgent sort of breathing. Gautselin was right—Samson doesn't necessarily look stronger, but his strength endures longer than Invidio's.

Their deadlock breaks and then they meet again. Samson knocks Invidio's hands away from him, then rushes forward to knock his opponent onto his back. Samson falls down to pin him, and the pair grapple on all-fours.

Samson slides an arm around Invidio's neck, then bears down to hold him from behind. His legs wrap around Invidio's torso while his arm squeezes tight.

Invidio claws at Samson's arms while his face and neck redden.

After a long moment of struggling for breath, Invidio finally slackens.

Samson pushes against Invidio's dead weight to get out from beneath him. I wonder if he already bit his neck—part of me expects Samson to stand up and limp away and that will be that.

But I don't know wolves as well as I think I do.

As Invidio fights to gain his sense again, Samson sets one hand on his cheek to force half of Invidio's face into the sand. His other hand sweeps Invidio's arm around his back to prevent him from rolling free.

Samson lowers his face toward Invidio's. My gut clenches as his jaw opens toward the pack leader's pale neck.

It's not a quick bite, like Rex and the wolfling. He gnashes into his neck, as though keeping him in place.

Invidio reawakens with a deafening cry.

I scoot a bit closer to Gautselin as streaks of thick blood pool around Invidio's head and neck and chest.

It's *a lot* of blood.

I guess I've never seen violence this close.

Heard it this loud.

I don't like how Samson looks when he stands up. When he leans to the side to spit blood onto the ground. When he stares down at Invidio for a long time, as though waiting for him to get up.

I don't like how Samson looks when Invidio finally does get up, and Samson pins him again, and bites him again, and then there's more fresh blood spilled across the sand.

The fresh blood is redder than Cap.

Redder than my seven fucking horns.

My father told me the story long ago. He said, *"Honey, once upon a time, a wielder wanted to scale Metamor. As a lone warlock, this was an impossible task. Rumor has it the wielder was a bit of a drunk and from a line of golden warlocks with two horns so small their short hair covered them both.*

"But he tricked his magic into scaling the mesa's face by falling in love with it. He created great works of art regarding the rockface and the clouds that engulfed its heights. Slowly, his magic fell in love with Metamor.

"One day, it carried him to the world above the clouds. To Metamor Plateau.

He built a home with terraces and spiral staircases. He tended a garden that grew grapes to make wine. He carved folk heroes into the wooden beams. He chanted on the triplemoons. He lived a happy life.

"Alone."

As though his image has been fuzzy and slightly blurred this whole time, Samson finally shifts into focus.

That's what I've always sensed in his shadow—not the reticence of wolves, or the conservative gaze of leaders, or the solemn charge of great power, or the quiet nature of a shy (possibly brooding) heart.

It's loneliness.

Invidio stays down after the second bite.

No wolves rush into the square as with the first fight.

Samson stands and watches him for a long time, a sheet of blood covering his mouth, chin, neck, and chest, oozing toward his legs.

Eventually, he turns and limps out of the square.

Only then does Invidio's pack rush in to help the fallen wolf. The pack leader jerks and grunts; a moment ago, I'd wondered if he was alive.

Rex doesn't touch Samson. He doesn't pick up the dark towel to wipe away the bright red blood. Samson doesn't stop to clean himself up, either. Rex grabs his satchel, then follows him from the grotto as he walks into a tilting sunset of bright pink and orange streaks.

I finally make out Malachai, too.

He stands near the entrance of the grotto with four wolves flanking him.

They turn as Samson passes, angling their bodies in his direction as though prepared to challenge him next. They don't, and Samson and Rex disappear into the bright dusk.

CHAPTER 10
THE PALE SQUEALING BABY
SAMSON

My son,
The first drum all wolves know is their own heart. My heart made
your heart; our drumbeats are the same, Samson. Together, we are
home. We are Velm.

Helisent and I are in the yew tree in a seething dream again.

This time, her irises are blood-red instead of golden, and I'm very aware that it means she's a red witch.

I'm still a child around twelve years old, nervously following her from branch to branch. The sap from the yew's rough bark makes my palms and soles sticky.

Helisent half-climbs and half-floats through the canopy, pulling aside the drooping yew bundles and their bright-red berries.

Helisent faces away from me as she climbs and I follow. She chatters loudly, "Do you have to bite your enemies twice? Always?"

I'm not sure how to answer.

Imperatriz imparted her knowledge of the world to me, but it's quickly being buried by Clearbold's version of life.

I vaguely remember what Imperatriz told me: there's usually a way to avoid biting in the first place.

Now all I can really remember is Clearbold's new stance on biting. I repeat his words. "If a wolf challenges you to a wari-con, you bite them once. Then you wait and see if they stand up. You have to keep biting them until you see the light in their eyes go out."

I don't know what it means yet.

"What?" Helisent sounds aghast, her voice low and disapproving. "Like to kill them?"

"No. Not the light of life. The light of defiance. We're wolves." That's the easiest way to explain it. That's how Clearbold explains it to me. I don't know what it means yet, but I will someday. That's what Clearbold says, too.

Helisent turns around. Crouched on a thick branch, her red robe droops around her, slipping toward the ground. It's a lot of red amid the cool emerald-azure shadows: the berries, her eyes, her robe.

She tilts her head, as though preparing to tell a secret. Her eyes twinkle like the full Sennen moon, smallest and brightest of the midnight planets. "Did you ever see Hetnazzar bite someone? It's the biggest wolf of all. The demigod of your people."

I wish she wouldn't have brought up Hetnazzar.

My demigod.

In my memory, only flashes remain—even though the incident must have been recent for young Samson. I was in the forest with my throwing ax. I was south of Bellator, where the thick canopy leaves the ground blanketed with shadows even during the day. Cold clung to my body after spending days in the forest alone. My numb hands shook.

A wooly had backed me against a rockface—

The beast was large enough to live inside.

Its curved tusks smelled of bone, fiber, sap, and bark. Its thick brown fur smelled of oil, natural debris, soil, and a heavy wild musk. Its panting spread clouds of condensation over me.

There was a wolf, too—

Large enough to swallow me whole.

Its fur was black and blue like night on the ocean east of Mort. But it didn't smell like a wolf in its form. It smelled like snow. Pure snow. And its growl came from within the mountains, shaking the boulders and the trees straight from their roots.

I gulp a breath as I stare at Helisent. "It bit the wooly. It brought the wooly down."

"Hetnazzar?" Helisent turns around and settles on the branch, as though intent to listen to my story. "Your demigod?"

"Yes. Clearbold sent me to kill the wooly, but I was cornered, and my ax fell, and I couldn't climb the boulders. Hetnazzar came for me. Then I dragged the wooly's head back to Bellator. I didn't... I didn't tell anyone."

She drifts closer to me. With each passing second, her expression falls. At first, she looks aghast, and then she looks afraid. "It must have been a lot of blood."

It was.

"It was red like your eyes, Miss Helisent."

I jolt awake with a gasp that's loud enough to frighten the birds from the canopy.

It takes me a minute to get my bearings in the dead of night.

I look around to make sure Helisent isn't nesting in the tree above me or drinking near the firepit. She isn't.

I lick my lips and take a few deep breaths to investigate our camp. With a broken nose, I'm relying mostly on my mouth to help me process scents. Neither Malachai nor Invidio have encroached during the night. Though the fire is

low, I can see Rex's outline where he sleeps across the
fire pit.

With a groan, I adjust my bed mat. My entire body feels
heavy and dehydrated. The exertion from the waricon
yesterday drives a sharp pain through my head.

It's enough to distract me from the vision of Helisent that's
becoming increasingly clear.

The one with red irises.

I'm glad Rex doesn't slip away at dawn's first light.

It's not for emotional comfort—at least, not all of it.

Since he arrived and saw Helisent at my side, he's been
punishing me with small comments. It's been confusing, if not
a bit satisfying. We've done a similar routine before, in which
we part ways only to find ourselves in contact again.

But didn't he leave me *in Luz?*

*And didn't he claim to do it out of a desire to respect our responsi-
bilities?*

After washing last night, we sat down near the fire to apply
the healing salves left by Invidio's pack days before. When we
finished, he handed me his marigold hair tie.

"In case you need to find me again," he'd said.

Still, while he hasn't slipped away with the dawn this morning, he also isn't planning to stay.

I wake to find him packing his satchel amid thin shifts of
fog. The valley is cold and dewy; even the dirt is damp with the
caress of frost. It reminds me of Velm, where Night has yet to
relinquish its hold.

Rex tightens his satchel's leather buckles, holding one end
with his incisor. He sets the bag down and watches me from
the other side of camp. Then he studies the empty tree where
Helisent's ala remains coiled, as though half-expecting to
see her.

I try to find a way to ask him to stay for the day.

You've made your point about our futures. Just stay one more day, then we'll go back to ignoring each other.

It's too cold.

Stay one more day and pretend with me.

It's too...

It's not what I want anymore.

With a boldness that tastes like Invidio's blood, I say, "If you're not in a rush, stay until Malachai shows up. I'm sure him and his little war band will come say hello before they leave the village."

I don't say *please.*

Rex made the choice to come here, then stay last night after resetting my nose; he might as well stick around a bit longer. And at some point, regardless of our tangled history, we'll fit into the traditional roles of Alpha and pack member. He'll listen to me not because we once held each other in the mornings, but because I'm the leader of all Night touches in Velm.

I go on, "I know you and I have a long history together, but I've always factored you into my inner circle. It's you, Riordon, Berevald, and Pietrangelo. I'll need all of your wisdom to help me figure out what to do with Malachai—especially if he's in a war band rallying support for the Leofsige line."

Rex's features don't move. It's a tightness I recognize. It's the mask I put on when the things I think and feel are no longer relevant.

Eventually, he says, "I understand. I'll stay."

"Thank you. For coming, and for staying."

He glances at the tree again. "And where is your witch?"

My witch. I study the pale sky above the shadowy canopy, still dark with night. Hopefully, she's making herself useful; it's a thought so improbable I almost laugh.

"I don't know. She left a note saying she'd be back when I'm rested."

"And how will she know when you're rested? Does she do magic on you?"

"No. Not that I know of, at least." I think back to her explanation of magic as a powerful twin. "I guess she'll just send her magic to check on me."

"And what does that mean, Samson? You're traveling with the strongest witch I've ever smelled. By a *long shot*."

"Rex, you and I haven't smelled many wielder alas in the first place. I don't want to be unprepared when I start building my court. Luz is still as far north as I've been. I'm going to rely on the power and opinion of wielders just as much as the nymph kings and queens."

"I see. That's what this is about? Building trust with..."

Rex trails off. I open my mouth to gulp in a few huge breaths. With my nose broken, it takes me a moment to process Malachai's ala as it drifts to us from the village's direction.

His ala sets my senses on fire.

With every year I age, the instincts that urge Samsonfang to run free on the triplemoon condense into something... richer. Something more difficult to ignore. It's not an instinct as much as a grating compulsion to dominate and put down anything that challenges me.

And just Malachai's scent is enough to threaten my place as Alpha.

His ala is similar to mine; I recognize threads of his musk from Clearbold, our father, our Alpha.

And then there are foreign traces that come from his mother, Emerel. Those are the bits that stoke a rage in my chest. It's the same type of wrath that sends me back to the throat of an enemy that won't *stay down*.

Malachai wasn't allowed in Bellator Palace when I lived there.

It was only half because he didn't *belong* in the Palace.

And it was half because his presence filled me with a

boiling desire to pin the juvenile to the cold marble and bite deep enough to drown him in the warm thick blood that's half-scented of a foreign female, of a traitor, an imposter. Of Emerel 524 Ledselin.

I was thirteen years old when I first caught her pup's scent.

I hadn't seen my mother in a year, but I heard her voice in my memory when I beheld the pale squealing baby.

"Kill him, Samson."

Imperatriz tells me the same now.

The wolf in my memory, the Female Alpha Afador who stood with me in Rouz and beheld Night's dead shadow warping through the steep mountains, is watching me again.

I can almost smell her ala, as though she's still alive somewhere, standing upwind a thousand miles from me.

Rex says, "Try to get your bearings, Samson. He's approaching quickly."

Rex kicks into action as I sit frozen on my bed mat.

He ties his hair up, then shrugs on his tunic. I don't bother with either. My patience dealing with Malachai has lessened greatly in the last year. It's likely the same for him now that he's seventeen years old. He's mature, nearly as large as me, with the same driving instincts that all wolves of high generation counts are born with.

Except he isn't the Kulapsifang.

And he knows it.

I stand up and head toward the edge of camp where their alas drift to me.

Rex glances at me, as though to make sure I've collected myself. I try not to groan as I shake out my arms and legs. Even my spine and ankles and fingers feel sore and battered after the waricon.

Then Malachai and his four-man pack part the thin mist.

His companions have the antagonistic flashing eyes of males who want to prove their strength. I file through their alas quickly. To my surprise, Malachai hasn't surrounded himself with wolves of similar 500 rankings. Instead, they're all in the mid-400s.

Did he choose this pack? Elders often assign a juvenile to their first war band—and they're careful to select its leader. As Clearbold's son, Malachai is the default leader; but he should be surrounded by wolves of similar generational counts who will challenge his authority with opinions and ideas.

The wolves around him now aren't likely to do the same with significantly lower generational counts. They're likely to bend to his ala, his whims, his version of leadership.

Malachai doesn't enter our camp.

He stops around ten feet away near the tree line. Like the rest of his pack, he stares at me with an even, set gaze.

I inhale deeply and realize he smells of Invidio—strongly enough that he likely just visited the pack leader. I raise my eyebrows. "How is Invidio?"

Malachai tucks his hands behind his back. His shined torcs catch the milky light, flashing. "Does it matter how he's doing? He challenged you to a waricon, and you gave him what he wanted."

I remember the pack leader's words from our run-in.

There's only one way for me to know if you really killed the wooly at age twelve.

If the Afador line isn't spoiled, after all.

I ignore the memory of Invidio's skin and sinew parting between my teeth.

The traces of his thick blood that slipped down my throat before I released him.

I study the males posturing around Malachai. I save my calmest and coldest gaze for Clearbold's second son. "What he wanted was to understand whether or not I have a rightful claim as the Kulapsifang. There are rumors I didn't kill the wooly. Rumors the Afador line has been compromised."

Malachai tilts his head. "And who had the gall to present you with these rumors? They sound very serious, Samson."

He's always asking questions. He's always standing just as close as he dares and watching, tallying, observing, interrogating.

I won't have to bother with it for much longer.

My life will end the moment my name is carved into one of the marble columns in Silent City alongside either Brutatalika or Menemone's name... and so will any chance that Malachai becomes Male Alpha.

And that's worth it for me.

I approach Malachai and his four-man pack. The other juveniles have enough sense to back up, like Invidio's subordinates.

Malachai doesn't budge. We inherited the same jaw and lips from our father, but the rest of his face belongs to Emerel. Part of me is jealous; I wish I could see any trace of my mother when I looked in the mirror.

Another part of me is glad. If Malachai looked as much like Clearbold as I do, it might be difficult to hate him so thoroughly.

I stop in front of him, nearly close enough for our chests to touch, then I fill my lungs with his ala. I can smell more hair on him, can pick out the wash of pheromones in his system even with my broken nose. Every time we meet, he's larger and more imposing. Muscle and strong tendons wrap around his arms; they twitch as I study them.

And then I stare at his lips, at the flashes of teeth hidden behind them. "Wolves don't wage war with flimsy words. Do you think they'll carve your rumors next to my name in Silent City?"

Malachai raises his eyebrows. "Wolves don't wage war with witches, either. Who is Helisent West of Jaws, Samson? And why does a witch who reeks of your scent conspire with unnumbered wolves?"

Helisent's image reels through my head.

She blinks her massive red eyes as she stares at me in a dream.

I push the thought away as fast as I can.

Conspire with unnumbered wolves? Great.

I narrow my eyes. I have no idea what he's referencing, but I don't let that derail my confidence. I plod on like I'm sure of myself. "What, are you still frightened of wielders, Malachai? Still don't know how to handle the unnumbered wolves?"

His jaw clenches, lip pulling up in a grimace.

Part of me is worried he'll back up and retreat or finally attack me after years of aggressive posturing. It won't be a pretty encounter. Samsonfang went into hiding the morning after the triplemoon, but I dragged him back into the light yesterday at the waricon.

Samsonfang is lingering close.

He's not sure if it's safe to rest; it isn't.

Malachai doesn't yield a centimeter. "You have bigger issues to worry about, Samson. The more I think about it, the more I wonder if Clearbold wanted to protect you. If he sent you into the forest outside Bellator to bring back the wooly too early, knowing he'd cover up your failures with a skull big enough to drown the rumors. If he pretended you killed that wooly to protect Imperatriz's legacy. If it's true, Velm will suffer for Clearbold's leniency when you prove to be an inept leader."

Kill him, Samson.

I angle my head toward his throat, shifting an inch. "And if it's not true, Malachai, then *you* will suffer for Clearbold's leniency. For your mother's *leniency*, too."

For the fact that Emerel walked into the palace where my mother lived, where my mother was born, where her mother was born, where her mother's father was born—back and back and back until the earliest Afadors. For the fact that Malachai's whore mother slept where my mother slept, where her mother slept, where her mother's father slept.

Where I will sleep.

I go on, "And so will every wolf that believed the rumors you spread about my claim as Alpha. About *Imperatriz's* claim as Alpha."

He nods with a faint smile on his lips, as though he's enjoying my anger, enjoying my doubts, enjoying the fact that my ala must smell of exertion after a grueling waricon.

"Imperatriz isn't Alpha, Samson." Malachai barely moves his lips to speak. "*Emerel* is the Female Alpha of Velm. You always forget."

I smile the way Helisent does to insult others, and then I reach for the cruelty of her clever observations. "Your mother isn't Female Alpha of Velm, Malachai. Your mother is who our father fucks when he feels lonely."

Malachai's smug calm fades into a mask of rage.

He's never expected me to growl an insult at him.

Now that we meet alone, without the watchful gaze of Clearbold nearby, he's treated me with more casual defiance than ever before.

I've been the one who never responded—and only because the threat he posed to me was barely palpable. Now the danger of his presence in Velm increases along with his bearing and strength. With each year he grows, so do his plans to overthrow my place on the marble throne.

The hairs on my body stand up.

I lower my voice to a baritone. "Try to bite me now, Malachai, or turn around and take your war band back to wherever you're stationed. And keep in mind that you have *no* authority to strip a wolf of a torc. Word has spread quickly of your tantrum in a village in Gamma. I'm sure you understand how poorly this behavior reflects on the Leofsige line. So try to bite me or leave. *Choose.*"

Will he do it?

I stand and prepare for him to close the distance between his teeth and my neck. Though I'm exhausted from the waricon, Samsonfang refuses to back down.

With painstaking slowness, Malachai turns; he doesn't want me to think he's fleeing or backing down. Rather, he's obeying me in the loosest terms.

It gives me momentary satisfaction as the rest of his pack lower their gazes and turns to follow him. Rex comes to my side as they file away from our campsite, slipping between the trees and hanging fog.

Malachai turns back to glare at me one last time.

Rex and I don't move until they're out of sight.

Without Helisent looming by, I head to the outer rim of the camp and pee. Instinct has compelled me to mark our campsite's territory before, but I've only done it when I was certain she was snoring in her nest overhead. It's not exactly viewed as civilized by the nymphs and wielders.

But with Invidio's intrusion so recent and Malachai's ala drifting through my camp, I'm glad it's Rex here instead of Helisent. He won't judge me.

In fact, he heads to the opposite side of the camp and pees along the northern edge; two scents are stronger than one.

And Helisent, like on the triplemoon, won't register it with her lagging sense of smell.

With a sigh, I sit before the fire pit and prepare breakfast. Rex stays and helps me cook, then we eat the rest of the meat and grains offered by Invidio's pack. Our silence is peaceful, though I can't tell if it's just exhaustion that hangs between us like the thinning fog.

He keeps his silence until he slings his satchel over his shoulder. "Let's do a pack goodbye."

His unexpected words bring a smile to my face.

Like we did in the old days when our war band wandered through the plains near Wrenweary and, before that, the coastal moors surrounding Mort, we lean close and angle our heads. It's a quick embrace; our chests touch, our heads angle around the other's neck so our noses sniff once behind the ear.

His ala carries so many things: memories, regrets, hopes,

and the cold edges of responsibility. But just a passing scent is simple. It's familiar, like a piece of home.

"Do you see our packmates often?" I ask. I haven't seen most of our five-man war band since we disbanded three years ago. Since then, most have gone on to find partners and permanent packs—at least until I become Alpha and call them back into my inner circle.

Rex says, "I see Berevald and Riordon more than Pietrangelo, but we all keep in contact. I think Berevald will want to stay close to home south of Mort. He built a homestead there."

"Send my regards when you see them next. I'll be north of Velm for the next few months."

"I will." Rex backs up a few steps. "I'll speak of your exchange with Malachai." He nods. "Imperatriz would have approved." He glances at the tree where Helisent set up her nest, features strained. "You'll make a good Alpha, Samson."

They're the kindest words he's ever spoken to me.

I wish I had something to say back.

Nothing comes to mind as I watch Rex leave camp, heading southeast in the same direction as Malachai's pack.

I spend the next two days wondering if I scared Helisent off.

Though I couldn't smell her ala during the waricon, I'm certain she watched.

Since then, I've prepared arguments to convince her that my hands aren't dangerous again.

Now I wonder if she'll even give me the chance.

There's also the possibility that Malachai scared her off. I couldn't exactly interrogate him about his run-in with Helisent and the unnumbered wolves, but I know it wouldn't have been pleasant.

I loaf around camp and apply the salves left by Invidio's pack. On the second morning I wake alone, I wonder if

Helisent might have continued toward the Deltas without me. In terms of travel, she's much quicker than I am.

If that's the case, I'm fucked.

I doze off that evening with an uncertain future.

I wake up to something cold and bitter on my tongue.

I sit up to a torrent of wayward giggling.

I cough on whatever was poured in my mouth. Ale.

I squint at the figure reeling with laughter at my side. Helisent.

A goblet of ale teeters in her grip. "You're welcome, Samson."

I look around at the dark campsite as the moons hang overhead. The low fire is bright, casting warped orange flashes around the camp. I stare at the witch, attempting to gauge whether her irises are golden or red.

Whether I'm dreaming or awake.

Helisent's knees and shins lift where they're folded inside her velvet robe. She floats toward me and holds the goblet to my mouth, eyelids half-closed as she laughs.

"You're half-asleep—look at that face. Just take a drink. I brought it from the village. From the tavern. It's really good for ale. I don't even like ale."

Dreaming or awake?

She pushes the goblet against my lips. I reach up to prevent her from knocking into my broken nose, then I take a gulp. The ale tastes too real for this to be a dream, from its hoppy flavor to its bitter scent.

While I sip, she goes on, "I found a phoenix nest. It's on the way to Perpetua. How's your big scary body? Can we keep moving tomorrow?"

I squint at her features and realize her irises are golden—awake. "Sure. I'll be a little slower than usual, but I'm happy to get back on the road."

She nods then lowers herself and the goblet. "Okay. I'd

offer you a lift on my lilith if you weren't so fucking stubborn about magic."

She hiccups with the ale in her grip. The liquid sloshes over the sides and soaks into her peach robe, darkening the velvet. But it doesn't look like she notices. Her face scrunches with a pout as she looks at me.

She reels with another hiccup. "Samson, are you okay?"

My heart rate increases; she must have watched the wari-con, and now she'll want to discuss how deeply I bit Invidio. Twice.

She whispers, "I saw Malachai."

My back straightens. "I'm fine. My nose will heal soon—Invidio's pack left salves, which help. And I heard you met Malachai. He told me you were with unnumbered wolves. Are you..."

Are you okay?

Are you afraid of me again? Did Malachai hurt you? Did he intimidate you? Did he hurt the unnumbered wolves?

"Am I what?" she asks.

I clear my throat. "How are you?"

"Fine. Malachai is an asshole. You were right. All things considered, I think I handled it really well. It's also possible I handled our run-in poorly. Do you ever feel like you can't see yourself clearly? Like everyone else knows what's going on except for you? Oh, and you didn't answer my question."

I'm still half-asleep, my body still half-dead from the wari-con. I'm in no condition to follow Helisent's wayward logic. "What question?"

She leans toward me, setting her drink down while her white eyebrows bunch together. "Are you *okay*?"

"I'm fine, thank you."

"Okay." She chews her lip. Her hands tangle in her peach robe, which lays around us in a heap. "Samson..."

Just say it, Helisent—you don't feel safe traveling with me, you can't fathom the barbarity of wolves, you think I'll be just like Clearbold.

Whatever you have to say.

She opens her arms to me. "Come here." Her lower lip juts out as she peers at me from beneath her bunched brow.

I stare at her to gauge what she wants.

Her robe parts to reveal her pale strapless dress and her dizzying array of necklaces. Her ala drifts out to me, complex and deep; it fills me with familiar comfort like Rex's did.

A feeling that I realize is a safety born from routine.

She wags her hands to beckon me forward. That also looks strange; wolves welcome people with their fingers facing upward. Helisent's hand is angled down, which looks more like shooing than welcoming.

I raise my eyebrows. "You want a *hug*?"

She nods frantically.

I lean forward and wrap my arms around her. Aware of how much larger I am than her and that she just saw me commit violence, I set my hands loosely around her. Hopefully, she can feel my warmth without feeling trapped.

This near, I wonder if she can smell me.

She throws her arms around my neck and tucks her head against my collar. She holds me with an inebriated snugness. She angles her legs against my thigh, while her breasts push against my upper abdomen.

I'm glad my broken nose offsets the potency of her ala, which hangs around me like the fog of Tet.

I can't tell what her play is right now. I remind myself that she has lived in a warren for years; physical touch to her isn't always a prerequisite to sex like it typically is with wolves. Maybe she just needs a friend.

"Did you watch the waricon?" I ask, shifting a bit with discomfort. "I didn't see you."

Aside from sexual embraces, I've never been held for this long or this close.

Part of me is surprised at the strength of her grip. I tally the weight of her chest and breaths, the strands of scent that define the textiles of her robe and dress and jewelry, the precise warmth that emanates from her body.

"Yeah, of course." Her breath smells like ale and honey. Her head rests at a dead weight against my chest at an awkward angle.

"I see."

She pulls back, floating into the air so we're at eye level. Her wide golden eyes work over me, lips parting slightly. "Your nose looks a lot better."

"It should be back to normal in a week or so."

"I'm sorry I don't know healing magic." At last, she sits back. Her velvet layers fall back toward the earth, no longer suspended aloft.

One of her hands rests on my forearm. It seems like she's forgotten it's there. I'm not sure how non-sexual physical intimacy goes. I glance at her hand, its olive skin silky and rich against my pale tone. Then I try to brush it off again; for wielders and nymphs, a touch like this would be normal.

"Don't worry about it," I tell her. "I wouldn't have accepted healing magic after a waricon. I think it's right to feel a bit of pain."

She snorts. "What a wolf thing to say."

She pats my forearm twice then returns her hand to her lap. With a loud yawn, she curls up inside her piled robe.

I glance at her round shape beneath the velvet. "Did you eat today? You should sober up and get a good night's rest if we're going to start moving again tomorrow. And what's this you said about phoenixes?"

She points to a conspicuously large bundle laid near the fire pit. I reach for it and realize it's a full meal. A tendril of delicious steam floats out as I unwrap the items, which have been preserved in a broadleaf.

My stomach growls at the scent of the warm food.

Helisent cackles, then she leans forward to slap my calf. "The tavern-owner was right. You know what he said to me when I ordered the food? He said, 'Helisent, if you give a wolf a good meal, they'll look at the food like nothing else exists. And then you'll know what their face looks like when they're full of joy.' I've seen it, Samson. I know what your happiness looks like now."

I'm barely listening to what she says. My mind has switched from her ala to the roasted meat.

"Thank you."

She pulls another package from her bottomless bag, proportionately sized for her. "He made me my own. He's used to dealing with wolves so he made sure we wouldn't have to share anything."

She gets halfway through her meal before she falls asleep bundled in her robe. One of her hands twitches where it lays slack near her forgotten meal.

I wake her up hours later before I return to my bed mat. She startles in a semi-conscious rage, swats the hand I used to rouse her, then clambers into the tree with a highly unlikely speed. The first time she did it, I'd been offended; now, I just watch on with wonder.

She sits hunched in a ball on the highest branch, leaning against the tree trunk. She's not even looking while her birch sticks weave into a nest. Then she falls into the bowl-like shape, one bare foot hanging over the edge.

We spend the next two days on foot, following the Mieira River as it flows east.

On day three, I begin to wonder if Helisent actually found a phoenix nest or if she was in a drunken stupor that left her confused and convinced.

She squarely denies this. "No, *Samson*, it wasn't a drunken stupor. I saw the LightEater, and then I saw the phoenix nest in a Gammaface."

I stop in my tracks at the mention of the LightEater.

I stare across the rolling plains of Gamma. The first pocks of ripe green rise from the soil, accenting the tired fields with color.

I ignore the splendor to search for any sign of Helisent's latest nightmare: the LightEater.

A pit deepens in my gut. "And why didn't you mention the LightEater when you brought up the phoenix?"

Since surviving a near-drowning in Skull, I'm less afraid of the LightEater than ever before. Still, I *am* afraid.

The being, not a nymph or a wolf or a wielder, has sat in the same spot in Gamma for centuries. A lovestruck group of doting nymphs monitor the being, waiting for it to wake up, or move on, or even blink.

All the while, the LightEater attracts wayward strands of lightning. He got his name for his supposedly insatiable appetite for the electrical charges, which pool along his body before being absorbed by the being's skin.

I comb the southeastern horizon for any hint of the Light-Eater's home; it's best to wait for the dark of night to follow the trails of lightning to the boulder where he sits.

Helisent tugs on my wrist to get me moving again.

"Are you *scared* of the LightEater?" she teases from her jingling lilith.

"I don't *understand* the LightEater. No one does. Not even the nymphs that tend to him know what they're doing. It would be foolish not to be at least a little bit scared."

She makes a pensive sound. "They don't actually tend to him—he doesn't need anything. He doesn't eat or pee or talk or move. Just sits there like he's asleep, collecting lightning. All the nymphs do is sit around and wait for something to happen.

"I knew a hesperide who lived at his sanctuary for a while. She said each new leader thinks they're going to crack the code and get the LightEater to wake up. The last one got a bunch of lassos and tried to move him, but I guess the lightning burnt up the rope within hours. It's been centuries—no dice. I think they worship him just in case he turns out to be important."

She almost makes him sound like a demigod.

I study her curious expression. "I didn't realize you knew so much about the LightEater."

"I *don't*, Samson. I met that hesperide once, then I showed up the other day after I found the phoenix nest. I had gotten a little lost on my way back to you, and it was the only place to stop and barter for food and directions." She looks at me, as though making sure I'm listening. "I saw the LightEater, too. It was crazy. The lightning—" She moves her hands around her body, "—covers his whole body. You think he's going to die, but he doesn't."

Technically, the LightEater sits right on the border between Velm and Mieira. As such, I should probably be more familiar with its existence, fruitless as it may be.

I make a mental note to assign his study to a member of my inner court. With each week, Helisent's place amid my council becomes even more certain. Mysteries like the Light-Eater will be treasured by wielders like her.

For now, I'm more worried about the phoenix.

"And where was the phoenix nest in relation to—" I move my hands around my body like Helisent did a moment before, "—the LightEater."

She cackles loudly, then she flings a hand southeasterly. Her vague directions bring to mind the weeks we spent lost in Tet. "The phoenix nest was that way. A bit off the river. I was flying, so it's a little hard to gauge from the ground."

She moves her hand to hold my forearm. Since we shared our first hug the other evening, she's touched the same spot on my arm in casual conversation. Like it did in Tet, the spot has started to smell like her.

Now she pinches my arm for emphasis.

I raise my eyebrows. "What?"

"We could fly to find the phoenix nest now. It would save us time. Then we could relax in Perpetua for an extra day. There are always concerts there."

"I'm a ground-walker. I was born on the ground, and that's where I'll stay." I clear my throat. "It's not because I don't trust *you*, Helisent. I need more time before I'm comfortable with magic."

She shrugs. "I don't take it personally, Samson. My twin probably will at some point, though."

Her *twin*.

Her *magic*.

Does it feel *things—independently of Helisent?*

I glance at her as though I'd be able to see its ghost lingering around her shimmering robe, her messy hair, her dangling boots. "I'll keep that in mind."

With a sigh, I turn my gaze back to the rolling fields of Gamma.

More than seedlings dwell beneath the dirt here. As Mieira's most fertile region, demigods dot the landscape; sandstone figures in their shapes also grow from it. The figures, called Gammafaces, slowly claw their way up from within the rich soil.

Shaped like hesperides and large as demigods, the silent Gammafaces act like memorials for the region's greatest kings and queens.

They closely resemble those who have served the plains with their elemental magic. Most believe the Gammafaces grow from the plots where these kings and queens die—one last spell tied to the land.

After reaching their full height on two legs after decades of slow tree-like growth, the Gammafaces start to deteriorate. Crack by crack, limb by limb, the sandstone figures fall back to the earth.

Whether whole or growing or degrading, hesperides prize the Gammafaces as residences.

We pass a handful of half-whole structures with wooden platforms and rooms strung between their limbs. Bright decorations litter the planks, along with oil lamps and clothes hanging from lines. Laughter and chatter echo from some, while the scent of rich meals drifts from others.

Dusk falls.

We pass impromptu camps like those we usually erect. Travelers pepper the roadside, where groups cook over small fires and lay out their bedding.

Each wolf, whether alone or with company, offers me a place at their fireside. They also offer food, water, layers for the cool night, and, in the case of two elder males, more salve for my nose. Only one asks for a spare brick of peat for her fire, which Helisent extracts from her bottomless bag.

The female wolf, around Helisent's age, stares at the witch for a long moment before she accepts the crumbling brick. The wolf looks down at the peat, back up at the witch, and then at me. "Thank you, Samson 714 Afador." She looks at Helisent. "Thank you..."

Helisent blinks at her; she tends to stay silent for the duration of these exchanges. As though uncertain, she says, "You're welcome."

The wolf doesn't look away. "I was waiting for your name to thank you by your name. The peat came from your bag."

Helisent's head tilts. "Oh. Well, that's new. I'm Helisent West of Jaws."

The female wolf bows her head. Her lips twitch, as though fighting a smile. "Thank you, Helisent West of Jaws."

The wolf ducks back toward her camp. Helisent swivels to study the stranger but doesn't bring up the exchange again. Shortly after, we turn off the road to make our own fire and shelter.

Before we set up camp, Helisent points into the distance
with a gasp.

I squint at the tiny silhouette of a crumbled Gammaface,
stark against the last pale smears of orange sunlight. At her
beck, we beeline toward the structure where she swears she
saw a phoenix nest.

I drink the rest of my water and try to ignore my aching
legs. While it's not late into the evening, exhaustion from the
triplemoon and Invidio's waricon weigh on me. On and on we
walk beneath the light of the moons until I'm in a half-asleep
state of mindless trudging.

Vincente's pink-and-gray face beams silver light across the
plains, accented by Abdecalas's greenish hue. Sennen, closest
to the land and smallest, is only half-full. Its blood-red color
doesn't shed light; instead, it captures my attention again and
again, nestled amid the silky stars like a warning.

I search the hilly expanse for any trace of the phoenix.
Even the Gammaface is hard to make out with only moonslight overhead.

Then I hear is the trail of a long, pained cry.

I slide my eyes toward Helisent. "If I remember correctly,
you told me you'd found a nest *without* a phoenix in it."

"That's true, but it didn't have any ash in it. It should
now." Helisent's voice is soft and small compared to
phoenix's next cry. "Why does it sound like that, Samson? Is
it in pain?"

"They don't have any natural predators, so I'm not sure
what could hurt a phoenix." Even during the height of the War
Years, the great creatures, around the size of a demigod,
ignored the affairs of wolves, wielders, and nymphs.

While they don't seem to mind the trading of phoenix ash,
used for medicine and sterilization, they're also not shy about
halving intruders with a snap of their sharp beaks. Aside from
infrequent sightings of demigods and phoenixes together, the
raptors live of their own accord and will in Mieira, untethered

to the affairs of the nymphs and wolves who also populate Gamma.

Helisent's hand clamps down on my forearm. "Samson, I don't like its crying."

"I think what we're hearing is more of a battle cry, Helisent. Why don't we camp for the night and try to find a less angry phoenix tomorrow?"

I have no idea what to offer even a happy and calm phoenix in exchange for its ash. I turn, eager to escape the raptor's sound of distress.

But Helisent stares in the direction where the cries echo. Now and then, a flash of lightning offers an extra slice of light. Though we haven't seen it yet, I'm guessing we're close to the LightEater's sanctuary.

Eventually, one magnificent ray provides a bare outline of the Gammaface. The only discernable remnant from the sandstone figure is a half-crumbled head, neck, and shoulders. One fingerless hand also juts from the dirt, extending toward its head.

A few more flashes of lightning sear through the air. That's the other eerie thing about the LightEater; the lightning isn't accompanied by thunder. Which makes me wonder if it's lightning at all.

On the horizon, I see a shuffle of pitch-black wings atop the rockface and a series of branches that resemble Helisent's curved nests. Whether angry or in pain, I'm certain the phoenix doesn't want any visitors.

"Helisent... why don't we at least wait for daylight?"

Moonslight traces her features as she shakes her head. "Wait? I don't mind if you hang back. I won't be in danger. I'm sure I can fly better than the phoenix."

Ever since learning her panic magic can act of its own accord no matter how drunk or discombobulated she is, I've grown less concerned for her safety during her many wayward adventures.

Still...

"Just because you're a little bird doesn't mean you can outfly a phoenix."

She snorts. "Do you really call wielders *birds* in Velm?"

"Only in the deep south. Past Bellator."

She looks away from the phoenix to stare at me. She feels at the ridge on her nose. "Is it because of my nose?"

"No—not at all." Actually, it's probably her wide eyes more than it is her arched nose, but I don't mention that. "It's because of the nests and the flying and the observing. Also, the obsession with shiny things. And darting around from place to place all the time."

"What, Samson? And you don't piss around our camp at night like a big dumb animal?" She raises her chin defiantly. "I saw you once, you know."

I'm glad it's dark enough that she can't see me blush. Did she see my penis? Was it a regular pee or a marking pee? There's a big difference.

She twists to look in the direction of the phoenix nest. "So are you coming with me or not?"

Too abashed to argue with her, I follow her jangling lilith as she heads toward the phoenix.

As we approach, its anguished cries lessen.

In their place comes the sound of scratching.

A shiver shoots up my spine when we wander close enough to the creature to make out the deep jagged claw marks along the sandstone. The phoenix sits half-balanced on a nest woven between the Gammaface's crumbled head and a half-extended hand. It uses its marigold beak to pull itself into place before shifting into another position.

It limps across the nest, as though incapable of finding a comfortable position.

Helisent gasps. "She's hurt, Samson."

She?

I don't know what makes her think the phoenix is female

or gendered at all. I stare at the mass of burgundy feathers, uncertain where the phoenix's neck and torso and wings and feet start and stop. I tilt my head to search for the scent of blood but only find the raptor's dizzying ala of oil, feathers, scat, and simmering embers; the last isn't an indication of a fire catching, but a note common to all phoenixes.

As the wind shifts, the raptor notices us.

Its cries double in depth and volume; these are warning calls.

I grab Helisent's arm. My fingers encircle her supple skin to prevent her from continuing on toward the nest.

She pats my hand. "She's just hurt."

"A hurt Samsonfang is the most dangerous version of me, Helisent." I keep my hold on her arm. "We're likely stressing the phoenix out just by being here. Let's come back tomorrow."

She shakes her head, features tensing. "I can't leave her, Samson."

I take a deep breath. "I know you think I'm being cruel, but the phoenix will help itself in the morning. It will know what to do—where to go, what to eat, all of that. You and I can't figure it out, Helisent. We don't know enough about phoenixes—or, at least, I don't."

Part of me wishes we did, as the phoenix starts to move around the nest again, screaming in pain, in fear, as it tries and fails to relax.

I go on, "Tomorrow, we can leave offerings after we take ash for the ghost."

"Go and make camp." Her words are cold and harsh. It's such a quick shift in mood that I do a double-take to where Helisent scowls at me. I immediately release her arm. "I'll meet you there tomorrow."

I glance from the roaring phoenix to her. "Helisent—"

"You would take its ash and leave it to suffer like this—all because you think you don't understand it? When I was little,

I went to stay in Alita for a while. A wolf came to see us. A very important wolf. She said that *all beings* that live and breathe want the same thing."

Helisent's wide golden eyes are the fourth and fifth moons tonight.

She remembers?

She bores her eyes into mine and waits for me to finish the sentence my mother spoke long ago as she built a foundation for the Northing. For how often I remember Imperatriz's words, it's been a long time since I've spoken them aloud.

I recite, "'All beings want safety, love, and possibility. The rest are details.'"

Helisent nods. "The phoenix, too, Samson. Go and make camp. I'll be there in the morning."

I make it around ten steps before I turn back. Sleepy and hungry and frustrated, I follow Helisent as she ventures toward the phoenix. But I stay back and spend the night a safe distance from the witch and the raptor.

I watch their trials, sitting with my back against my satchel.

First, Helisent rounds the Gammaface. This draws more feral cries from the phoenix. It follows her, craning its neck over the ledge of the nest. At one point, I stuff my ears with pieces of fabric to dull the ongoing roaring.

The phoenix's wrath does little to deter Helisent. She wanders closer and closer. The moons are high above, their light paltry, when Helisent finally ascends the Gammaface, half-floating up its cheek. The phoenix lunges to meet Helisent, opening its sharp beak.

A scream rises in my throat as I prepare for the phoenix to swallow her whole.

But Helisent climbs toward the nest's edge like she's never known danger, like she didn't almost drown us both in a cave for a fear of water and darkness a month ago.

At the last second, the phoenix clamps its beak shut.

And in the next, Helisent sets a hand on the rounded end, patting it.

From there, I enjoy short-lived peace. I even doze off. But a short while later, I'm jarred awake by the sound of Helisent's yelling.

I stand and rush toward the Gammaface, wondering who hurt who. Then I realize she's not in danger, but calling out for assistance.

"Samson! Did you use all the salves Invidio brought us?" she bellows from the nest.

"No," I shout back. "Should I bring them over?"

"Don't come here! You'll scare her!"

I stay put and extract the jug of salve from my bag. I stand again when I see a velvety, peachy silhouette soaring through the air. Given how much more space her robe occupies than her body, it looks like an amorphous blob drifting toward me horizontally. Then I untangle Helisent's face and white hair from the velvet and moonslight and shadows; like a bird, her eyes flit around me in search of the jug.

It almost slips from my hands.

I've never seen her *fly* before.

Floating, hovering, float-climbing, and just about every variation between—but *flying*? No.

How hopelessly mundane the rest of us must seem to her.

As though she's swimming through the air, her body follows her head's momentum in a relaxed motion. It's almost like a snake. Her arms slide out from within the robe as though to offer balance as she descends toward me.

She lifts the jug from my hands. "Thanks. You can go back to sleep."

"Wait, what are you going to use it for? It's topical only. Don't use it on an open wound."

"It's not a wound. Her little bum is hurt. I don't know what happened. She lost all her feathers. It looks like a bruise, but I'm not sure." She glances back toward the quiet nest, eyebrows bunched. "I rewove her nest so she can at least sit comfortably. She has more room. I just... who would hurt a little phoenix?"

It's not *little* and I'm not even sure what *could* injure a phoenix.

"It looks like someone bonked her good," Helisent continues.

I rub the sleep from my face. "What the fuck does that mean?"

"Hit her." She tilts her head, still hovering in front of me at a horizontal angle.

"Oh. Okay. Well, I certainly hope not."

She waves me back to my bed mat, but I watch her robe dangle and tilt as she flies back to the nest. There's another period of angry shrieking. This time, I also make out Helisent's argumentative shouting, though I can't tell what she's hollering at the raptor.

I stay up and keep watch for as long as I can, half-curious and half-worried. Eventually, I nod off again.

When I wake up, I'm alone. The vast, pale sky above extends just as far as the horizon of rolling hills. Only the Gammaface, its sandstone speckled with moss and bird shit, sticks out.

The phoenix sits hunkered in its nest. A few burgundy feathers shake in the wind above the woven rim. Close by is a slip of peach-colored robe, caught and tangled amid the thick branches.

Uncertain how to rouse Helisent without angering the phoenix, I pinch my lips to whistle a high note. It doesn't work on the witch. With a sudden rustle, the phoenix wakes up. The bird raises its head to peer down at me from the nest's ledge.

Unlike last night, it doesn't look upset or shocked to find me here.

It just looks tired, familiar exhaustion in its roving, bright orange eyes.

Though I've seen huge burgundy phoenix feathers from the ground before, I've never seen the finer facial plumage. Like the bird's cadmium eyes, tiny vibrant feathers rim its beak and skull. Some are pale and silver, others gold.

It clicks its beak together, head tilting as it angles its eye to study me better.

Helisent pops up a second later. Her white hair is a wiry mess, her robe slipping from both her shoulders. Still, she smiles and holds up a fabric pouch that looks to be filled with lumps.

"A hearty load of ash," she announces.

I roll my eyes. I'd forgotten about the ghost's phrasing.

Helisent disappears again; I'm not sure what she does in the nest as the phoenix shifts back and forth. It ruffles its feathers with a low hoot, then Helisent clambers into sight atop the nest's perimeter.

She walks toward the phoenix's head, then sets her hands on its beak. She says something, but I can't hear her. Then she hover-climbs down the half-standing Gammaface. Without a nose or lips, the face resembles an oblong egg more than a face.

We head back toward the Mieira River, then continue eastward toward Perpetua.

I ask her a few questions about last night, but Helisent seems distracted and tired. She glances back toward the Gammaface and phoenix often. From there, our collective exhaustion leaves us both in a wordless stupor.

After lunch, we rest and chat, then we carry on until the moons brighten overhead.

When night falls, the lights of Perpetua ignite in the distance.

We wrap the phoenix ash in red fabric then lower it into a crevice of high rocks near the river. Then we keep walking toward the lights of Perpetua.

CHAPTER 11

TOOLS OF THE NEW WAR
HELISENT

Honey Heli,
Is he in Antigone yet? He said he'd take the northern route back from
Lake Deidre so he wouldn't pass by Yngvi and Yves's apartment. I
can't believe they aren't playing nice yet. Should we start betting on
who looks like an asshole when it's all figured out?
Mint Mili

Ecstatic nymphs fill the streets of Perpetua.

I can feel their desita pool between the cobbled streets like smoke.

Even on the outskirts of Perpetua, their numbers are shocking.

Tight groups chatter while sharing food and drinks. Based on their scuffed boots, they've traveled from great distances. And based on how packed the streets are surrounding the city's amphitheater, they're here to see a show.

I told Samson Perpetua hosts the best concerts in Mieira.

Most of the happy nymphs are oreads, with tiny markers of the Jawsic cities where they come from: Eupheme, Lake

Deidre, and other smaller unnamed villages like those I grew up in. I search the groups for a sign of Onesimos, convinced he may have come to join in the festivities; he may live far from home, but he's a proud oread.

But every time I whip my head toward a lanky male oread, their vermillion hair is either too short or too tidy. Their smiles aren't wide enough, don't hide enough of their red irises.

I clutch the string of volcanic rock he tied to my bag; once I have a moment away from Samson, I'll send a note to Simmy. He would have mentioned planning a trip to Perpetua before I left, but I could use a spare hug and piece of advice from my favorite oread.

And I'll need all the luck I can get if he is in the crowd. Even if my letter finds him, it doesn't mean he'll be able to find me.

Not only oreads fill the streets. Perpetua sits on the cusp of Gamma's plains, home of the hesperides, and the unending stretch of marsh that defines the Deltas, home to naiads and okeanids. And like oreads, okeanids have rich brown skin, only theirs is tinted with cool tones that reflect their ocean eyes.

When searching for oreads proves too trying, I move on to searching for nymphs close to Onesimos's age. But even that's a mixed bag—elders carry children on their shoulders beside groups of rowdy teenagers. Happy adults like Simmy are the least represented in the group.

Samson and I pierce the crowds in the direction of the amphitheater. The massive venue was dug out of a hill, similar to the waricon grounds near Invidio's village. Wooden tiers form large steps toward the central platform, allowing groups of all sizes to see the stage.

Much like Luz, Perpetua was built on nymph, wolf, and wielder ingenuity. Along with wooden tiers, smoothed marble and load-bearing iron rods support the sides of the amphitheater.

At the top of the steps, Samson turns to gaze across the madness. "I forgot how much like Luz it is here."

I glance around with a nod. While the wide streets and stone constructions are grander than even Luz's temple district, it has the same sensation of mismatched glory.

I let the volcanic beads slip from my hand. With a sigh, I try to imagine myself living in a place like this. "It's a little flashier than Luz, but... I could make this work."

Soon I'll need to.

This search for Oko will end someday; I know how it ends, too.

What comes next is less certain for me.

I'm a sponsor of Luz, along with Antigone, Eupheme, Lake Deidre, Alita, and other portions of Rhotidom and Jaws. My roster of magical debt is extensive; my dove toils in the cities year-round to handle mundanities that make urban living possible.

For all my nonsense, head wielders like Ninigone and Absalom need me. For all my untamed rambling, the Class would be drained of magic if its members attempted to replace the dove I offer to cities across Mieira.

My father taught me the balance long ago. He said, *"Honey, no one minds that the flower is poisonous if they've never seen it before."*

Perpetua and the Deltas will be next.

One day, I'll walk into this city as a stranger; one day, I'll leave it as a sponsor on my road to Ultramarine. To Cadmium.

"Make it work?" Samson asks. "Make what work?"

Did I say that out loud?

I shrug with a demure sigh. "Just as a home, I guess. Warrens don't last forever, Samson. That's called *marriage*."

Samson raises his eyebrows, then takes a step closer to me to get out of the way of a frustrated merchant pushing his cart through the tight crowd. "Right. I need to go and speak with the pack leaders. Will you stay for the concert? I'd like to come back and watch."

"Speak with them about what? The waricon?"

He nods. "I'll leave a statement for Clearbold about the waricon—and about Malachai stripping a torc from a wolf in Gamma. Local pack leaders may also want me to help settle any outstanding disputes. Clearbold can't be everywhere at once.

"Oh, and since we're in a large city, pack leaders will have plenty to offer me—is there anything we need to pick up? I'm running low on leather. I'd also like a new tunic."

I study Samson. His nose is nearly healed—only greenish hues linger on its ridge.

Aside from that, he's more finely put together than he's been on our entire two-month sojourn. He's shaved his face clean of stubble. His tunic and harem pants are tidy and smell of cedar soap. His hair is tied back, every blue-black strand in place. Even his torcs look brighter, as though he shined them.

I'd wondered what the fuss was for.

I consider the contents of my bottomless bag. "Do pack leaders hand out brandy? I know better than to request bitterroot."

"No. I might be able to swing some ale, though."

"Gross. Save it for yourself."

He sighs through his nose. "Fine. Anything else you can think of?"

"No. I'll get us a spot somewhere around here. I'm sure you can smell me." I bow with a mocking smile. "Don't let me keep you from your pack leaders, my liege."

Such comments don't make him uncomfortable anymore. In fact, he sketches a mocking bow back to me. "Little bird."

He's called me that multiple times since seeing me fly the other night. I hadn't even realized I was doing it until I got close enough to see his wide eyes and parted lips, trickled with moonlight.

I watch him step lightly through the crowd. As soon as he's gone, my adventure with the phoenix rushes back into my mind.

With a shaky breath, I sort through all the ways I feel fucked up and stupid; it's all been piling up over the last few days.

I keep thinking I'll get older and all my fears and uncertainties will wane—they don't—not even a little.

The first thing that floods my mind is the phoenix's pale, dimpled skin. The dark purple-and-green bruise where its feathers had fallen out—maybe been ripped out.

The second thing that floods my mind is its cringe-inducing shrieks, first of pain and then of fear. Its hiccupped breathing after I reformed its nest into a more comfortable shape.

Then the creature's labored breathing after I finally sang it to sleep.

I didn't actually *help* the phoenix.

I just left its pain for another day. I just helped it get through a night, and that's never enough.

Night always ends in a new day.

Dawn is pain.

And then there's Samson and his big stupid hands and how much I love the smell of cedar and how I open my eyes in the mornings and think, *Oh, is Samson awake? I wonder if he's already making breakfast.*

And then he's already finished cooking food and he also poured me my morning brandy even though he hates that I get drunk by noon.

And I think that's cute.

Even though he spat out a mouthful of blood like it was a drink that displeased him.

Even though Clearbold will march him by the scruff into Silent City at the year's end and marry him to the next Female Alpha.

Even though that's what he *wants*.

And here I am, this dumb wayward witch who never got it together even though she had everything laid out for her, and love from her family, and all the magic the world could distill into seven horns.

"Excuse me, lady wielder." An elder okeanid grabs my lilith with a weak grip. I look down, happy for the distraction. "I need to barter for magical oil. My lamps are running low and it's already getting dark. I'm here with my family."

She turns and gestures toward the amphitheater's packed tiers; I can't see who or what she's pointing out amid the pleasant hustle.

She smiles wide to reveal crooked teeth. This close, her mahogany skin doesn't hide her extensive crow's feet. "I can offer you a bottle of pear wine."

I hold out my hand; I'm already backtracking on being happy for the distraction. "Pear wine? Hand it over. And how many cylinders do you need filled with dove?"

She murmurs to herself as she fishes around in her woven bag. Items clank together before she pulls out a dark bottle filled with light liquid.

Her cerulean eyes twinkle as she hands it to me. "From last year's harvest. The pears were planted north of Hypnos. Our lands are infertile, so our fruits are smaller. This also makes them sweeter."

I raise my eyebrows. "And how many cylinders, dear okeanid?"

With a groan and a shuffle, she hoists up a bag full of oblong shapes. It falls against my lilith, throwing it off-balance before my magic steadies me.

"Oh, just..." She studies the bag with an overly casual sigh. "A few here and there. There are thirty in my group, lady wielder. We require a lot of light."

This is what she really means: *I'm old as dirt and my nymph senses are tingling around your magic. I know you have enough to spare me and my family some light, even though all I have to offer is this bottle of pear wine.*

I'm sure her family is bogarting a barrel of it.

I roll my eyes. "Fine."

With a coy smile, she leans toward me. I reach past the taut straps of her bag and touch one of the cylinders, then I use feeling magic to gauge how many of the glass pieces are piled haphazardly inside. I don't count them but measure their total imprecisely, like holding seeds in my palm. I start from the bottom, filling each with dove.

Soon golden light pierces the top of the bag. The sides, at least, are woven tightly enough to block most of the luminosity.

Most.

The okeanid pats my knee and then hobbles away. I try to slip from my lilith and disappear into the crowd, but multiple nymphs have noticed the exchange. They stare at me with looks of pleasant surprise.

I turn to find an oread standing in my path. He blinks his vermillion eyes as he holds up an empty cylinder. "Lady wielder, would you like to barter for light?"

A few nymphs emerge from the crowd to wait near the oread.

I growl, then hover into the air to get their attention. "Form a fucking line, then. And only ask for dove if you have booze to barter." I clap my hands as a brilliant idea forms. "Booze *or* dextro. And I'd prefer the dextro, just so we're all on the same page."

I haven't had any for weeks.

I can't believe I haven't noticed.

Two hours later I'm fucking flying.

I can't tell where the pear wine and the dextro and my

madness end. Best of all, the crowd around me is in a similar place.

We dance and shift as a few groups take the stage at the center of the packed noisy amphitheater: first a vocalist, then two bands with wild rhythms.

I'm not just partaking in desita; I'm also contributing bliss to this crowd.

Desita is like a gust of wind, and I'm swirling, swirling, like this tiny little thing that can't be hurt because it's so minute— it never crashes to the ground or gets lost. Just keeps going and going and going.

Then the ruckus stops.

I try to blink my vision straight so I can see what's happening on the stage. The okeanid to my left keeps elbowing me while the oread to my right keeps laughing at nothing. I crane my neck to see below as a languid oread steps into the light.

A robe of golden silk droops to the floor, like molten sunlight that shimmers against her deep brown skin. The heavy fabric follows her to the center of the stage. The oread has full cheeks, a shaved head, and large eyes; even from the distance, I can make out their vermillion hues as she stares across the crowd.

The oread to my right seizes my arm. "It's her—it's her— it's her—"

"Who?" I ask.

But the oread succumbs to high-pitched squealing, hands on her cheeks as she stares below.

The golden-cloaked performer raises her hands to capture the crowd's attention. Her voice echoes across the packed tiers with the help of booming magic.

She says, "The demigods are smiling. Even I can taste your desita."

It's enough to send the crowd into an expectant hush.

I look at the oread to my right. Her frenzy from a moment

before has calmed. Her hands still hold her cheeks, but now, she stares down in wordless awe.

"But the demigods didn't always smile," the orator continues. "Hundreds of years ago, Night stepped across Velm and did not leave. Snow fell and piled into mountains. Frost claimed the fields and drove deep into the land. The wolves wandered north in search of warmth, of crop-bearing fields, of spring.

"Hundreds of years ago, a strange people arrived from the place above the clouds. Demigodless and wordless, wielders descended Metamor and filled Septegeur with their magic."

I lean toward the stage, hanging on every word. Retellings of the War Years are uncommon in the west, where the fighting took place. And it's always a treat to hear stories of the War Years from a nymph; the wielder version is too full of horseshit, and the wolf version is suspiciously short.

"As the wielders wandered south, the wolves fled north. Conflict began. Wielders followed the wolves south and ransacked defenseless villages. The wolves trailed them north on the triplemoons and met their raids with gore. From Septegeur to Wrenweary, blood soaked the land. Blood poisoned the demigods."

I sense someone's gaze on me and turn to my right, expecting to see Samson. Instead, it's a warlock. He rolls his eyes as though commiserating over the oread's depiction of wielders.

I drink my pear wine and ignore his stare.

Can he not feel the capacity toward violence in himself? I can. That's the worst part about the War Years and why I *do* listen; I still watch a wolf's hands. I still think of how I'd hurt one if they lunged for me.

"The wolves sawed the horns off the wielders they felled in battle and hung them in the halls of their marble palaces. Dozens at first, and then hundreds. The wielders skinned the wolves they felled in their forms and wrapped their bodies in black-blue fur. Dozens at first, and then hundreds.

"So it went for centuries.

"Wielders died by the thousands. Wolves dwindled in population. The nymphs caught between their battles fled and languished. Driven from their homes, they became pith by distance. They were separated from their lands and their demigods; their demigods choked on blood, starved for desita.

"Life in Mieira was not life anymore.

"It was survival—

"Until, one day, the demigods convened on *these very tiers*. Hetnazzar came from the far south and listened as the demigods of Gamma, Jaws, Rhotidom, Hypnos, Septegeur, and the Deltas called for an end to the violence.

"On these very tiers, the demigods shared gifts never before seen. They gave new extracts for painting. New gums for incense burning. New spices for cooking. New metals for jewelry. New elemental powers for their kings and queens.

"These were the weapons of the nymphs. These were the tools of the new war; a battle in which pleasure vanquished violence."

My body shivers as I giggle.

How wonderful.

How blessed this land is—and how perfect that I'm a tiny thing floating in the wind, soaring on dextro and wine and all the desita that bubbles in this amphitheater.

"When Perpetua was filled with desita, the demigods walked westward with their gifts. The dryad, naiad, okeanid, hesperide, and oread kings and queens, appointed by the demigods, followed. Hetnazzar followed. They took these new weapons and went to war in the place where the Irme River became one with the Septima River."

I giggle again—I know what she's talking about. The demigods waged their war where the first Luzians later built the temple district. To this day, it's where the demigods return.

Where the hesperide demigod from Gamma said goodbye to me, to Simmy.

"The kings and queens stayed with the demigods. They convinced leaders from Septegeur and Velm to gather with them. To wage one last battle."

The oread's voice heightens again.

It shivers with the cold truth that I don't hear spoken often enough.

"And our kings and queens used pleasure to show the wielders and the wolves the fault of their ways. Not violence —joy.

"When the leaders from Velm and Septegeur sought conflict, we played music from our new instruments. We cooked from the spices given, painted from the rich colors extracted from roots, hung jewelry from their necks and wrists. We brought them burning incense they'd never smelled before.

"We gave even more when they opened their mouths to argue, when they packed their bags to leave, when they tried to arrange secret meetings.

"What was their violence compared to the superiority of extravagance? What is war compared to material glory and desita? Soon the demigods and Hetnazzar were satiated. They left the city; but the wolves, wielders, and nymphs stayed behind.

"Together.

"And so Luz was born."

I close my eyes and drink in the desita. Drink in how fucking beautiful the oread's voice is. It's all so much for my racing heart to handle and process.

Dizzy from it, I search the amphitheater for a demigod, certain one must be on its way to imbibe in the tangible desita, humming low through the air. But the city is quiet past the lights and noise of the tiered venue. I can't make out any blue-tinted limbs or snooping faces poking above the buildings.

"But before there was Luz," the oread concludes with an ecstatic tone, "there was Perpetua. There was *this* place. *Right here.*"

The crowd erupts into cheers, which double in volume when the oread bows and retreats from the stage. The okeanid to my left starts chanting a name—I can't quite tell what he's saying.

Something that starts with an L.

"Technically, the wolves went back to Velm after Luz was founded."

I jump with a loud screech as Samson's voice echoes near my left ear.

I clamp my hand on my chest and turn around. My neck bends as I stare up at him. "Moons, Samson! You're way too big to be sneaking up on people."

He looks just as shocked as I do, retreating a step. "Did you not know I was here?"

I thrust my hands up. "How would I know you were lurking behind me?"

"I wasn't *lurking.*" He folds his arms. "I figured you could at least *sort of* smell me. Can you really not smell *anything*? I've been here the whole time."

I lean toward him and make a show of sniffing with all my might. "Maybe a tiny bit of cedar." It's probably just in my fucking head at this point. "What did you say about the wolves in Velm?"

He glances around and takes a step forward to stand at my side. The okeanid, doubled over and snorting a line of dextro, leaves extra room for him. Far below, a few nymphs prep the stage. Meanwhile, the crowd shifts with chatter and anticipation.

"I said that, technically, the Velmic leaders went back to Bellator after Luz was founded." Samson shrugs. "They came back in spring, though."

"Sounds about right. I'm sure the wielders did the same." I look around with a shimmy. "Do you want any dextro?"

I glance across him. Though he still looks more prim than usual, a few strands of hair dangle at his temple. His satchel hangs loosely from one shoulder. He holds a massive goblet; I peek over its rim and realize it's half empty.

"Dextro?" He raises his eyebrows. "No. Not for me. Is that how you plan on staying up? I figured you'd be too tired from spending the night with the phoenix last—"

"I've pulled multiple all-nighters in the past, Samson."

I wish he'd stop bringing up the fucking phoenix. I'd just managed to shake it from my mind. I reach for my bag, ready to call up more dextro.

The music starts, which distracts me for a moment. I close my eyes, anticipating more desita and sensations of flying.

For a while, I dance where I stand; it's probably more like useless swaying. But I like how it feels. I like how the melodies and the drumming and the repetitive patterns lull me to peace.

(Or forgetfulness.)

I open my eyes as the oread playing below starts to speak.

He sways with the beat, vermillion hair and beard eye-catching against his rich, glowing skin and his white layers. He's engrossed in what he's doing, and it pushes me further into my own disappearing act.

"Do you ever fall in love haphazardly—like, you didn't plan it? These vibes are with you—like your thoughts were commissioned by a god, a deity, an entity, a smile."

My mind races to keep up with the performer's voice. With his words.

It's easier to get lost than it is to face myself. I know I can't see myself clearly.

I haven't since Anesot took me to bed and Oko took Milisent to Metamor.

I ran out of hope—

Ran out of wonder—

So much that my magic can't remember wholeness enough to give it back to me.

But the oread below reminds me.

He goes on, "You ever fall in love with someone you're not supposed to be in love with? Like, anagrams and epitaphs and situations of truth, but you find love in the most inconsistent of places and now, fundamentally enough, you are in love."

I remember being in love. What it did to me.

But right now, in this moment, I'm not a witch who ran out of love and trust; I have both. I know joy. I know love. The dextro and desita bring it back to me.

Tomorrow, I'll forget.

For now, I remember.

My mind is pulling things together that it can no longer fathom in the cold light of day.

I know now that the phoenix's pain was my own. I know the panic at its suffering wasn't related to its injuries, but the ongoing din of my own agony, at the witch who howls from the northwest.

Normally, she's louder than all the brandy in the world.

For now, she's at peace.

She's listening to the oread below because she doesn't trust my voice anymore.

He says, "And it makes sense to be in love at that time because love feels good and you deserve it. And sometimes, some of you... feel you do not deserve love..."

There is a witch screaming in my heart.

Sometimes, it's my voice. Mostly, it's Milisent's.

"But you do," the oread reminds the crowd. "You deserve all the love."

The next day, Samson tells me the oread's name is Lazarusman.

And we were lucky enough to attend the first concert of his tour. We follow the nymphs to his next show in Lampades, where we would have stopped anyway on our path to Ultramarine.

The short journey is like an extension of the first concert. Groups keep the party going; some even seem to be sleeping, cooking, and traveling in shifts to make sure everyone is fed and rested.

While I find comfort in the hustle, we only last one day on the dirt road to Lampades.

Samson can't stand the sounds or scents of the happy groups. Apparently, most of the nymphs haven't washed in days, and his mind keeps focusing on their alas. I trail him inland to follow the South Branch River.

The wide, muddy river almost looks to be at a stand-still. Dead leaves litter the brackish water while bubbles drift up from the riverbed.

The marshland's looming trees are bare, towering over us like skeletons. Croaking frogs, buzzing insects, and forlorn birdcalls break the deathly quiet. The dry season has left the river low; dark marks circle the surrounding trees, from last season's water levels.

I find it spooky, as though the region is parched for a flood, but Samson seems to be at peace as he steps over the flat smooth rocks at the riverside.

I drift above the water on my lilith, staring down at the feathery currents.

Lazarusman's words keep echoing in my head.

And sometimes, some of you... feel you do not deserve love...

Samson interrupts me. "Helisent, I think you should consider learning the basics of swimming. Then your magic can figure out the rest." He glances at my bare, dangling feet. "You mentioned that you'd like to move to Perpetua someday. The Deltas are prone to seasonal flooding. It's not like Septegeur and Rhotidom. You should know how to swim if you plan on moving here."

I study the expanse of leafless forest around us. The

trunks, the ground, the river are all deepening shades of uninviting brown. "So long as there aren't any caves or magical sinks, I should be fine."

"Why don't I show you the basics? The water is really warm—"

"Maybe compared to the glacial lakes in Velm." This morning when I washed my hands in the river, a chill shot up my spine and down my toes. It's still in my bones. "I'll die if I get in this."

He raises his eyebrows at me, a half-smile waiting on his lips. "It's not the cold that would kill you. It's not being able to swim."

"Who knows which would kill me first, Samson? Night doesn't come to Metamor and Jaws and Septegeur. My body didn't evolve to handle the cold."

"I've heard Metamor is freezing. I even heard there's *snow* on the plateau." He pulls a rolled cigarette from behind his ear and then holds it toward me; it's a familiar motion at this point. I light its end with ember magic, and he takes a drag. "It falls straight from the clouds and doesn't melt for months."

I snort. "When I talk about Metamor, I'm not talking about *on top of the fucking plateau.* I'm just talking about the areas around it. Barely anyone actually lives up there."

"What if you used magic to warm the water? There are plenty of coves." He squints upriver as though in search of one. "We can set up camp a bit early today or tomorrow, you can warm the cove, and then I'll show you how to paddle."

"What if I promise not to loiter around rivers and caves? Boom. Crisis averted."

I can't tell if he's offended or baffled by my staunch refusal. Maybe both. But I don't think it's a good idea for him to be stripped to his little wolf loincloth while I flail in the water.

What started with a brief interest in oiling Samson down has fragmented into a series of gushy feelings that I really shouldn't entertain.

He sucks on his cigarette, eyeing me with a bunched brow. "Why are you fighting something that might save you someday?"

I roll my eyes and fish for an appropriate excuse. "The water is freezing. It's too muddy to see under the surface, and *selkies,* Samson. *Selkies!* And it smells like fucking garbage out here. I know you think I can't smell anything, but I can smell everything that's rotting in this river."

"Helisent, explain to me how a selkie is more terrifying than a phoenix. *You went into its nest when it was in a fit of rage.*" He gestures with his hands for emphasis. "The worst a selkie will do is nitpick and ask for favors."

"They're whores and liars, Samson. With fucking hydrilla all stuck in their teeth."

He scoffs. "Really?"

Sort of—not really. The selkie talk is just rhetoric so he'll drop the swimming lesson.

Samson doesn't let it go, though. "I promise to defend you from the whims of a selkie if one approaches us. Has it happened a lot to you? Do they notice you like the demigods?"

I shrug as I study the riverbank; I don't make out any pinkish flesh cresting the murky currents. Still, I imagine dozens of half-fish beings swim along its bed. "No. I tend to avoid bodies of water, so they don't really have a chance to approach me. The only ones I met lived in Lake Deidre—and they didn't exactly win my approval.

"Once, Simmy and I were sitting by the shore and a selkie came up. He can swim, so he got into the water. And let me tell you, Samson, that selkie wanted *a lot* more than to nitpick. She was a liar because she said she didn't touch Simmy and she was a whore because... well, she did."

"Is Simmy the oread from your warren?" Samson asks.

With a sigh, I flick the volcanic beads strung to my bottomless bag. "His name is Onesimos. I call him Simmy sometimes. He's almost forty..."

Samson scratches his chin, angling his cigarette away. "Have you been warrenmates for a long time? I don't really understand how warrens work."

Not many wolves do.

"I met Onseimos when I moved to Alita six years ago. We left a warren there to start our own in Luz around four years ago. We've been with the same group since then. Zopyros, the hesperide, and Pen, the warlock, were the first to join. Then the others came. We've been the primary members, but..."

I figure he can put it together.

He stares at me from the riverside, walking without watching his steps. "But what?"

"But I left them to come on this wild goose chase with you."

Simmy knows why I want Oko. He's the only being who I ever told the truth. Anyone else who knows figured it out themselves or heard through word of mouth.

I wave a hand. "And warrens aren't that complicated. That's just what numbered wolves think since you guys are monogamous. Those who start the warren tend to be its core. They accept new members as wanted or needed.

"Everyone has a specific responsibility, and every warren has slightly different rules. I was in charge of sharing dove for general needs. Simmy handled disputes between warrenmates. Pen cleaned the apartment. Zopyros brought us food."

He exhales a plume of smoke with a thoughtful sigh. "I see."

"Did you think there were orgies all the time? It's not really like that, you know. The rumors tend to get blown out of proportion. And I'm not even attracted to women, so a full-warren orgy wouldn't really be my thing."

Samson smokes and nods.

I wait for him to ask another question, but a question pops into my head instead. It's a bit silly, but I haven't been able to ask him yet. Every time I try to, the words start to sound overly rehearsed and... awkward.

I dive in before I can second-guess myself. "Was Rex your lover? I never asked."

Samson whips his head toward me from the shore. His expression of shock fades to amusement; I wonder if he's biting back a smile. "I assumed it was kind of obvious. I had his hair tie in my satchel."

The question isn't about *Rex*, per se. "And how does that work? I mean, in terms of... your future wife."

This goads another look of shock from him. Does he rarely think about it? With each day, he's drawn closer to that future.

"I consider her more the future Female Alpha of Velm than my wife." He takes a drag and kicks a pebble out of his path. "But having former relationships isn't taboo. I'm allowed my freedom. And even after we're married, I'm allowed... happiness. So long as I provide an heir, I can have my own happiness. It will come with many limitations, but I won't be..." He gestures to nothing. "I won't be *alone* alone."

So he's allowed all the lovers he can hide from public view?

What an incredible zhuzh. Velm is just a fucking legion of barrel-chested bullshitters.

I raise my eyebrows. "I didn't mean like that. I was talking about having sex with a woman if you're attracted to men."

"Oh." His chin dips as he stares at me. "I'm interested in women. I think most wolves are interested in all genders. Same-sex marriages are common—and they're important. Many choose to raise orphaned pups.

"And wolves may be monogamous, but there's plenty of variation in coupling. We have *kofling* weddings, which are sort of... temporary marriages. If an all-male couple wants a child, they'll pair with an all-female couple who wants the same. There's a little ceremony to honor their arrangement. Eventually, both couples walk away with heirs and stronger familial bonds. Sometimes they stay in contact and even live close together. Kofling packs, we call them."

"That sounds dangerously similar to a warren, Samson."

He cracks a smile, then angles his head to look at me. "It's not, but I appreciate the thought."

It's a challenge to look away from him.

It pleases Horny Helisent to know he's attracted to women. She wants to accept his invitation to swim; she's thrilled by the idea of having something as flimsy as water between our bodies.

(The stupid little wall I've been stacking between us crumbles. I can almost hear the tiny pebbles tumble to the ground.)

We chatter on as the river hits a rocky bend, then we navigate the branching tributaries that part and rejoin like veins. As dusk approaches, Samson and I set down our supplies on a high stretch of dry land.

He claps his hands together. "I'm going to look and see if there's a cove nearby." Then he rushes away before I can tell him *no*.

I realize it might be offensive to keep turning down his offer to help me. He's mentioned before that wolves don't know spells, but passing on skills is considered the basis for lasting friendships.

He returns ten minutes later with a polite smile. I roll my eyes and follow him to the inlet.

Sure enough, the rocky cove has semi-clear water that deepens with a visible, manageable gradient. Smooth rocks dot the inlet's edges, perfect for clawing myself to safety. No conspicuous bubbles or tangled bunches of rotted debris.

Samson holds out his hands as though presenting a thrilling surprise. "There won't be a better spot. If you really hate it, we'll get out."

Horny Helisent doesn't hesitate.

She tells me, *Take off your clothes, get in the water, and see what happens.*

I take a deep breath and remind her, *The water is dirty, smelly, and selkie-infested. Also, if he catches a whiff of your snatch, he'll start seething. And don't forget you have zero time to spare on wayward affairs while you're looking for Oko.*

I stare at the cove in consideration, my distress mounting.

Horny Helisent wins.

She usually does.

With a frustrated sigh, I start to take off my mounds of jewelry. "Fine, Samson. But you'd better remember what you said about the selkies."

I tie up my hair then shrug off my robe and hang it from a branch.

As I situate my jewelry, I use ember magic to warm myself. Like smothering magic, it's all about finesse. The air warps around me, just like the extreme heat that blurs the horizon at the height of summer. It doesn't touch or get too near my skin but heats the space surrounding me.

With a splash, Samson casts himself into the cove, sending droplets over me. He crests the surface in the inlet's center and wipes his face. His hair is down, messily strewn around his face and shoulders.

I glance at his tunic and boots, set neatly atop the dry rocks. Horny Helisent is disheartened that he decided to keep his harem pants on. The rest of me is relieved.

Samson scans me, sniffing once. "You smell different without all the jewelry."

"What the fuck is that supposed to mean?" I glance down at my bare skin and beige dress. He's never seen me bathe before, so he's never seen my dark olive skin without a series of threaded jewelry and jangling metal pieces—not even in Skull. Now even my ankles are bare.

"Nothing. Just an observation." He glides toward the edge of the cove and stops with most of his torso out of the water. "Come on. It's really warm."

Water leaves fine trails of gleaming light on his bare chest and abdomen and arms. I step lightly over the smooth rocks, then leap back as my soles hit the frigid water.

"*Really warm?*" I growl. "Sometimes a zhuzh is just a lie, Samson."

I bend to touch a finger to the surface and send my ember magic through the small cove.

Water is the only element that responds physically to my magic. Its infrasound sends choppy ripples throughout the cove that create an ecstatic flurry of dancing droplets.

Samson sprints from the water. "Helisent!"

I lunge backward so he doesn't barrel into me. Water drips from his abdomen onto his waterlogged harem pants. They hang a bit lower on his hips, wet fabric clinging to his skin.

To his...

I look from the water to his face, then to his feet, and then back to the water. "What? Was there a selkie?"

"No, you did magic when I was in there." He glances down at himself as though checking for injuries. "I could *feel* it."

I roll my eyes so hard it almost brings on a migraine. "It's just infrasound. It goes away in like ten seconds. The water should be warm now. You can get back in."

He dips a foot into the water as though checking, then eases back in. I stare as his pants cling to his round butt cheeks, his sturdy thighs, his thick calves.

Horny Helisent whispers, *Get it, girl.*

Samson turns around. "Did you just hiss?"

Someone muzzle me.

"I'm petrified!" I shout. "Don't judge me."

I step into the water, holding out my arms to balance myself; even steadying magic will cause a similar ripple of infrasound, and I don't want to keep sending Samson running for the shore.

I stop when the warm water covers my knees and soaks the lower part of my dress. "Now what? Just start flailing?"

He steps forward to meet me. "No. Never flail. I can help support you—where do you want me to hold you?"

It's like he *knows* Horny Helisent is here and he's trying to coax her out of hiding.

But when she's not here, the real me is decidedly shy.

A bit afraid, too.

"I—I don't know. My arms?"

"Okay." Samson comes forward and grips me lightly around the elbows. Slowly, he draws us back toward the water. I cling to his forearms as I follow, slowly submerging my thighs and then my hips.

I stop there. "Do I kick now?"

He shakes his head. "A little farther—I'll support you. Just put your weight on your arms, and I can hold you. I know you're used to relying on magic, so take your time."

It's harder than it should be to follow him into the cove. My steps are small and timid as my feet slip on the slick rocks below. Eventually, I manage to put all my weight onto my arms.

I gasp as my feet slip from the rocks and meet with empty water.

"Start kicking," he says before I panic. "Pretend like you're running."

I clench my eyes shut and run as fast as I can.

"Not that fast. A little slower." I can hear the smile in his stupid voice. "Find a rhythm."

I find a pace that doesn't feel horrible, though I'm still too scared to open my eyes and find out if I look as dumb as I feel.

"That's good," he says. "You're kind of doing it. Let's get moving."

I squeal as he pushes off the rocks to ferry us around the rim of the cove. I bite my lip and try to keep up, feet flailing.

"Take deep, slow breaths, Helisent."

Ugh, the fucking breath talk again.

His voice is low and calm. It reminds me of our evening in the tavern west of Gamma. "You have the movements down.

Now you just need to calm yourself and get the hang of it. You're doing well."

I hate that he's right about my breathing.

As soon as I regulate my breath, I can tell what's happening with my legs more easily. I can feel how they move the water, how they propel me upward and forward. They're surprisingly reliable.

Slowly, Samson's hands lessen their grip on my elbows. They cup them from below, fingers brushing my forearms as they let go.

I strain to keep my face above, legs and arms pumping to propel me.

And then, for a split second, I'm doing it myself.

Swimming.

Or, more appropriately, surviving.

Samson smiles. "Well done." Then he takes hold of my elbows again.

I realize I'm smiling, too, as I hit a rhythm. "I can't remember the last time I learned something new. Probably back—"

Then I see it.

Three feet away from us, two sets of oily eyes peer at us above the surface. A scream peals from my lungs as I make eye contact with the selkie.

I leap toward Samson, blindly clawing at him like he's a flotation device devoid of emotion again. With a gasp, he notices the selkie then helps pull me from the water.

I perch on his arm, straddling his shoulder. One hand is on his collar, the other on top of his head in search of high ground.

We freeze.

The selkie raises its head. Its pale pinkish skin gleams like it's covered in oil—across its sharp jaw, down its thin neck, its bony collar. Silver hair clings to its scalp, flat enough that I can't see individual strands—just slick clumps.

"My cove is warm." The selkie's voice is slurred and buzzing. I've never seen inside their mouths, so I can't be sure why they're so bad at speech. I've heard of forked tongues, of sharpened teeth.

The selkie blinks its four eyes as it studies us. First the standard pair, then the additional smaller set on her upper cheeks. All four irises are bright magenta, their slitted pupils disproportionately tiny.

"Magic warmed my cove." The creature's flat nose twerks, while its wide, flat mouth opens as though drinking the air. It locks eyes with me, head tilting. "It's *your* magic, red witch."

Red witch.

I look down at Samson and he looks up at me. He doesn't look nearly as shocked or frightened as I would have thought. He almost looks... curious.

Fuck.

"My cove is *too* warm, but I'm glad you're here." The selkie glides through the water toward us. It's enough to send me floating for shore. Samson also retreats onto land.

She fixes her eyes on him next. "I'm glad you're here, too, Samson 714 Afador, son of Imperatriz 713 Afador, daughter of Sutnazzar 712 Afador, daughter of Malasuntra 711 Afador, son of Sitzi 710 Afador—"

"You know my ancestors," he says. It's the first time I've heard him interrupt another being aside from me. I'm glad he did; it sounded like the selkie would've gone all the way back to the first Afador.

With a hissing laugh, the selkie slithers through the water with only her head above the dark surface. "Two very powerful beings come to my cove—why is that? I know the answer. Do you know the answer?"

I throw my head back with a groan. Her words bring back memories of the vague statements the Jawsic selkie made to Simmy at Lake Deidre. I don't remember any of the shit she said; it wasn't worth remembering.

I prepare myself for round two.

Samson ignores my huffing. He asks, "Can I be of service to you?"

"*Both* of you will be of service to me, yes," the selkie says, lipless mouth twitching.

She hoists herself onto a flat rock with her webbed hands and lounges. She props up her head with a hand, then sets the other on her side.

I stare down at her body, starting with her magenta nipples and ending with her long fish's tail. Its iridescent scales glimmer in the pale light, starting with a few small scales below her navel. Its dual-finned end remains out of sight in the water.

She gestures at me with a webbed hand. It looks to be covered with a thicker oil than what coats her pinkish skin. "Would you like to know how you'll be of service? Sometimes wind takes the fog of Tet up into the clouds. Sometimes it's brought back to the earth through rain; the junior ghosts have much to say."

What is she talking about?

Before I can tell her to stop with the theatrics, she goes on with a buzzing tsk. "You cannot smell the fifth scent, but you will know it soon. Wolf, wielder, nymph, and selkie... but now a fifth scent comes to Mieira."

I glance at Samson, then back to the selkie. "And what's the fifth scent?"

The selkie tilts her head. "I've only heard rumors. I haven't smelled the fifth scent myself. I don't know what it is, but it does harm. You will both know it soon."

I cross my arms. "Is that a fucking threat?"

"It is no threat. What harm could the fifth scent do to you? Your magic is everywhere." She blinks again. Her eyelids are semi-clear and fleshy. I can *hear* them move over her eyes. "I can feel your magic across the world—Septegeur, Rhotidom, Jaws. It does no violence."

How the fuck does she know all of this? She can sense my dove as it powers a city?

The selkie looks back toward Samson. "The okeanids are being taken to a place where we don't swim. The fifth scent takes them there."

I pause. Samson and I glance at one another again.

"What do you mean?" I ask.

"No one can find the okeanids once they're taken from the coasts in Hypnos and Cadmium. That's where the fifth scent lingers. You could find them, Helisent Red—"

"Just Helisent is fine, thank you." I'm too nervous to glance at Samson to see how he's processing the revelation. "And what is your name?"

The selkie makes a low sound that tapers off with, "—ezzezza."

I rub my temples. I have no idea what she said.

"ImzEzzezza," Samson repeats, "have you told Clearbold 554 Leofsige about the disappearing okeanids and the fifth scent? I'm not the Male Alpha of Velm yet, so I can't send a war band to investigate. If you can find and speak with Clearbold, he can mobilize a war band to help you."

The selkie uses her hands to slide back into the water. She makes a show of twirling along the surface of the cove, letting her breasts and tail crest the water.

Eventually, her head emerges and her four eyes study us again. "Clearbold 554 Leofsige has known for years; he doesn't travel to Hypnos anymore. The Leofsige line has done nothing to stop the disappearances or investigate the fifth scent. *You* are the Afador. You will lead the wolves soon."

Samson goes still.

"I see." His words are cold and final.

The selkie smiles to reveal rows of tiny, sharp teeth. "I can feel your magic across the world, too, Samson 714 Afador. It comes north on the Irme River. It is waiting near Rouz now."

I look for a reaction, but his stony, pessimistic expression hasn't shifted.

He doesn't respond to the selkie.

Her magenta irises flash to me. "The Sennenwolf will come. Has Antigone forgotten?" Her smile deepens, eyes twinkling. "Shall I teach you to swim, Just Helisent? The Afador 714 forgot to tell you about using your hands."

"My name is *Helisent*, not *Just Helisent*." I float back toward camp, finished with her creepy stare and four eyes and hypnotic, vague words. "And I'm actually really busy for the next few months, so you should probably find another witch to harangue with your nonsense."

A fifth smell?

Disappearing okeanids?

And what the fuck is a Sennenwolf?

It's a hard no from me.

"Samson?" I nod back toward camp, atop the high ground and safe from the pink-eyed selkie. "Shall we?"

It takes him a long moment to pull himself from the selkie's lingering gaze. His dark expression doesn't shift, as though preparing an insult.

But he turns in the next moment and walks in a stunned silence back to camp. The selkie brandishes a genuine smile that sends a chill up my spine, then she slips back under the surface. With a shaky sigh, I leave the cove behind.

On the short walk back to camp, I try to figure out whether we should broach the topic of me being a red witch.

It's not a *huge* deal that I'm of the red line. The only difference between me and golden wielders is color. And magical strength, but that might come down to population.

Like I told Samson before we wandered into Tet months ago, there aren't many of us left.

Milisent was the only other red witch I'd ever met in the flesh.

As far as I know, I'm the last of my kind. And as the sole heir of the Afador line, Samson could sort of understand that.

But he's either too suspicious or upset to speak.

We make our fire, then cook our food, then eat and drink. I can't remember the last time we went so long without speaking. Our heavy silence reminds me that he and I are still mostly strangers.

The only thing we agreed on before leaving Luz was that we wouldn't pry into each other's reasons for wanting Oko.

I don't know why he's after the witch. I still have no plans to share her once I find her.

I watch him from the other side of the firepit, uncertain of what to say.

But I don't dare speak until I'm in my nest, tucked in for the night. Even then, it takes me a moment to rally my nerves.

I clear my throat. "Samson?"

"Yes?" He doesn't sound angry, just tired.

"Are you upset with me?" The idea that he might think I'm a categorical liar like the rest of the wielders bothers me.

I'm not sure why. I've lied a lot—especially in the last five years.

I *am* a wielder and a liar. I collect lies like shiny things; I keep them on a shelf in my mind. It's safer this way.

It's never bothered me until just now.

"Why would I be angry with you? You didn't say those things. The selkie did."

I can't tell which part of the selkie's wild prophecies bothered him most. "And what if she was telling the truth? What if okeanids *are* being kidnapped and taken far away? And what if there really is a fifth being that's behind the disappearances?"

"You said selkies were whores and liars. Do you think differently now?"

I blink up at the moons through the canopy's bare tangled branches. I sigh, toying with the hem of my blanket. "I'm a red witch. The selkie knew that. She also knew who you were."

"And do you think the selkie told the truth when she insinuated Clearbold knows about the disappearances and *chooses* to do nothing about it?"

Ah, that's it.

He's upset because the selkie insulted his father. He doesn't give a fuck about what color witch I am.

Now I wish it were the opposite.

Like we've avoided discussing our mutual interest in Oko, we've yet to speak of Clearbold. There are three names on my shit-list, and the reigning Male Alpha of Velm is written right behind Oko and Anesot. (I'm considering writing *Malachai* on the fourth line.) I don't doubt for a second that he might know about the disappearances and choose to ignore them.

His apathy has marked my life permanently.

Six years ago, I sat before Clearbold and told him my story of love, of betrayal, of my fallen sister and my need for justice. As Velm's representative, only Clearbold could mirror the banishments doled out in Mieira against the perpetrators.

I even cut a piece of my sister's favorite robe and presented it to the solemn Alpha; I'd heard alas helped endear wolves to strangers.

When my story was finished, my eyes teary and my voice shaking, Clearbold offered me one word, one syllable, in response.

"*Who?*"

But I didn't repeat my story for Clearbold, and I shy away from the memory now; it makes me doubt Samson, makes me hate the Kulapsi, makes me brew with wrath.

"And what about a *fifth* scent, Helisent?" he goes on from his bed mat below. "Do you believe there's another being out there that we haven't noticed yet? There are numbered wolves in Hypnos, in Jaws, in the Deltas. They would have noticed a foreign ala."

Unless the fifth-scented beings were bartering with a wielder to hide their scent, Samson.

I stare at the moons above. With Marama and Laline halved, there's barely enough spare light to navigate the darkness. I stare at the twinkling thimble of Cap and consider my words carefully before I speak. He can do with them what he will.

"Wielders lie to serve a specific purpose. We don't lie for thrills or for glory, like the nymphs and wolves think—unless thrills or glory are necessary, of course. We lie because we *need* something, and a lie happens to be the easiest way to get there. That's why we don't look down on lies. They're *useful*."

(The shelf of sparkling lies that I keep in my mind is *useful* in distracting me from the wasteland of truth that surrounds me.)

I have little trouble believing the selkie, or letting its words go. Not so long as we're zeroing in on the GhostEaters and Oko in Ultramarine and Cadmium.

Let Samson wrestle to find a higher purpose that the selkie might have had in lying to us.

He won't find one.

CHAPTER 12

BRUTATALIKA 567 SIGIVALD

SAMSON

My son,
Wolves will hand you their pain, anger, joy, confusion, sadness, hope.
This is their freedom. Give them survival so they may know passion.
Night has starved us of it too often.

After the run-in with the selkie, the journey to Lampades is just as quiet and tense as our first week traveling from Luz.

With each step, I wonder if I'm in over my head with no recourse.

Helisent's spirited drinking doesn't help soothe my unease —especially after the selkie confirmed she was a red witch, her magic palpable across Mieira.

She drinks through the afternoons then snorts enough dextro to give her a boost that lasts until dinner. What began as a string of wasted nights after her run-in with the injured phoenix has turned into an unending bender that reeks of liquor and dextro.

There's a bright side, though.

Her drunkenness gives me the time and space to sort through my own thoughts at night.

When she falls asleep, I pull a note from my satchel.

It's a transcription of the original letter I found hidden in a chest filled with my mother's effects. I discovered the wooden trunk in the Rouzen Estate last year, and I've kept a copy with me since.

Imperatriz,
I've located the witch you seek. She lives north of the Mieira River and keeps a warlock at her side. I haven't been able to ascertain whether they're gold or red wielders. Their strange habits indicate they're likely of the red line; they have few friends in Mieira.
The witch's name is Oko. As you requested, I've sent a letter to your home in Mort detailing her plans in Hypnos.
Move with haste. The warlock at her side has four horns, but she will be traveling alone to Hypnos.
May Hetnazzar run with you.

The selkie's words loop back to the letter; she mentioned okeanids being kidnapped in Hypnos along the northeastern coasts.

It's the same place where my mother was last seen seventeen years ago.

Whether this has anything to do with the supposed string of missing okeanids is beyond me. I still can't shake the instinctual rage that arose when the selkie insinuated Clearbold might know and not care about the disappearances.

If wielders were vanishing, I could understand his hesitancy, but no one balks at the chance to help a nymph. The well-being of the nymphs and their demigods ensures the well-being of all. And the bounty created between the okeanids and their demigods provides directly for wolves, in particular.

Okeanid demigods push mackerel, cod, haddock, and tilapia into okeanid nets; these fish end up on our plates. The okeanid demigods also command the tidal currents that ferry Velmic trade ships up the coasts to the Deltas and Hypnos; the bartering of these goods builds our cities.

There is no reason for Clearbold to ignore their trials.

So the conceivable conclusions are limited.

The first possibility is that the selkie was a liar. That she spoke the truth by naming Helisent a red witch and me an Afador only to make her subsequent lies more believable. That she was motivated by a whimsical desire for chaos.

The second possibility is that the selkie was misinformed. Rather than attempting to spin a web of lies around us, the selkie genuinely sensed our power and sought help without understanding the implications of the misinformation she was handing us.

And the last...

I don't like the last possibility.

That the selkie spoke the truth. That Clearbold *does* know about the disappearances and doesn't care—even though Hypnos is the same region where his own wife, the Female Alpha of Velm, disappeared seventeen years ago. Even though the well-being of Velm is tied to the okeanids.

I don't spend time considering the last possibility.

It brings to mind the marble columns of Silent City. The sound of my father's footsteps echo across the stones, which fades into the sound of the marble chipping, cracking, and shattering against the ground.

Still, I'm relieved the selkie made an appearance—especially when she did.

I'd been a happy wolf toting a happy witch around a warm cove, teaching her how to swim. And the witch had been looking at me with a trust and curiosity that made me feel like maybe I didn't actually know myself.

But I know who I am.

And I know who Helisent is.

And I know why we're here: to find Oko.

I fold the note, tuck it back into my satchel, then stare at her nest and pray for a dreamless sleep that doesn't come.

Lampades smells like moss-covered stone, fetid mud, and heavy incense.

The city developed directly on the South Branch River. Rather than expand outward like a blot of ink, it lines the roiling, muddy river. Floating platforms serve as foundations for countless structures, bound to the shoreline by anchors that adjust as the water level changes each season.

Already, the heat of the dry summer season lingers on the horizon; the days lengthen, even the nights warm. For now, sporadic torrential downpours mark the start of the growing season. The first green shoots begin to crawl from the earth, extending skyward.

The South Branch's water is muddier than ever. Debris floats on its surface, which glitters with gray light under the cloudy sky.

Dozens of bridges crisscross the river, helping locals navigate Lampades as the floodtides shift. We explore the first bridge we see, and I follow Helisent as she meanders to its center. From there, she stares toward the busy city center where naiads, okeanids, and wolves clog its largest bridges.

Here, where the rivers and tributaries snake across the land, both water-based nymphs are common. They're like extensions of the swamps: naiads with sandalwood-hued skin, tangled brown hair, and blue-green eyes that seem to stir with hidden currents, then the okeanids with rich dark skin, a backdrop like night sky against their cerulean irises, against the lapis lazuli they use to bejewel their tight black curls.

Thick drifts of incense float over the river: myrrh, sandalwood, cedar, and lavender.

Based on Helisent's gaping mouth, it's her first time here. She sets a hand on the stone railing and sets down her bottle. She's already halfway through her second brandy of the day, and dusk isn't in sight yet.

I stare toward Lampades's busy center, built around a large marble tower. "I'm going to meet with the pack leaders here, as well. I can pick up supplies. Can you think of anything we need?"

It's not *solely* for official purposes; it's also because pack leaders pick up my ala eventually. Even the most well-adjusted wolves feel a pinch in their spine when they catch an Alpha's scent in their territory. Presenting myself with a smile is a way of easing that tension.

Helisent doesn't look away from the hazy view of muddy river and bridges and clouds of incense. "I'm almost out of dextro. Don't suppose the pack leaders would have any of that lying around, would they?"

Part of me is keenly aware that she doesn't seem to be doing well.

Another part of me is certain she can handle her life. Concerning as it is, her dependence on brandy and dextro has yet to impede our journey.

"No, they won't. You have all day to find some—or maybe take a day off."

"Days off are for the dying. And what about later? I want to see Lazarusman again."

"I'll meet you there. Okay?"

She nods, and I turn away without another word.

I don't look back as I head for the streets encircling the marble tower.

Within a few blocks, the dizzying range of scents starts to give me a headache. The city's large wolf population leaves each ala layered atop another. It's almost impossible to untangle each to find a single familiar scent, then track it. Then there are the naiads and okeanids; their alas don't bother me nearly as much as the incense burning at every street corner.

I wonder if the clogging smoke is preferable to the stench of rot common in the Deltas. There's a reason Ultramarine and Cadmium were built on the coast, where the ocean winds are constant and strong. What keeps people here, I'll never know.

When I finally make it to the packhouse, situated beside the marble tower, my nose twitches. I stop mid-step when I catch the scent of a female wolf's ala.

Not just *any* female wolf.

My gut sinks when I realize Brutatalika 567 Sigivald must be inside the packhouse.

A group of gangly juveniles, male and female, loiter before the building's sliding doors. Their wide eyes flit to me before they cast them downward.

I avoid the urge to fix my hair and tunic and pants; the pups are still passively studying me, glancing up as they pretend to chat among each other. I don't want to look as caught unawares as I am.

I force myself to walk across the street and enter the packhouse, wishing I didn't smell like a witch and that I'd prepared something to say to Brutatalika. Until she and Menemone fight their last waricon later this year, I interact sparingly with either during chance run-ins like these.

It doesn't make sense to endear myself to either when I don't know who will walk into Silent City with me and become our generation's Female Alpha.

I slide open the packhouse's heavy doors and then slip through. The marble walls create a sanctuary from the maddening scents outside. As soon as I slide the door shut behind me, Lampades's brimming details quiet. Only the quaint scent of cedar smoke remains, tangled in the deep navy curtains that dangle before the arched doorways.

With a single breath, I filter through the male and female pack leaders' alas. My mind catches on Brutatalika's. Her generation count stands at 567, greater than Clearbold's; it's impossible to ignore—especially for my fangself.

Samsonfang is very aware this woman might bear the next Afador. I sort through her scent in search of any weakness, tallying her pheromones along with physical markers like hair and nails. Like my ala does, hers marks the area she walks. Its proud virile traces linger in the packhouse's entry hall.

I follow her ala, half on instinct.

Light from the packhouse's square courtyard fills the hallways with milky light, which reflects off the pale, gleaming marble. It reminds me of Velm, only a few days' journey south from here.

A few administrators poke their heads from their offices to bow to me. One female wolf wordlessly points toward the courtyard, where the trail of Brutratalika's ala guides me. I avoid the urge to groom myself again.

Brutatalika exits from a room to my left then stops suddenly, as though also tracking my ala. She glances over me with an appraising expression.

I do the same with her; her piercing deep-set eyes, plump lips, and fragile high cheekbones make me wonder how she'll survive a waricon series with Menemone. Her body is sturdy and balanced, like mine, but her facial features have always left me wondering—how does this wolf win a brutal waricon?

It might come down to personality.

In which case, Menemone doesn't stand a chance.

Like most powerful wolves born with a shot at marrying the Kulapsifang, Brutatalika's stature and words are thought out with a political purpose in mind.

She offers a curt half-smile.

I offer one back. "You look healthy, Brutatalika 567 Sigivald."

She steps forward and bends her neck toward me, inhaling a deep breath. Her blue-black eyes flash to mine, rimmed by fragile eyelashes. "And you smell like a witch, Samson 714 Afador."

Fuck.

"I've smelled worse," I counter.

She huffs, giving me the once-over again. "I don't mind the stench of the witch, so long as it's the one who insulted Malachai. I saw him south of Lampades recently. He said he attended a waricon you fought."

Fuck. Fuck. Fuck.

"Really?" I ask. "I hadn't realized the witch insulted him."

I should have, though.

She folds her arms and leans against the doorframe. The move is decidedly casual, especially considering the formal nature of our previous run-ins. She tsks. "Malachai is useless. The witch, on the other hand, might not be. Are you traveling with her with a consideration for the Northing?"

Brutatalika's head tilts; it's measured enough that I wonder if she wants me to *think* she's acting casually right now. If she's hiding the nature of what she really wants to know. As much as Helisent thinks she understands zhuzhing, the wolf before me now can spin half-truths quicker and tighter than the witch's birch-twig nest.

But her words *do* relieve me. Brutatalika has always been interested in the Northing. Like any wolf with a shot at marrying the Kulapsifang, she's always been careful to endear herself toward my mother, Velm's previous inborn Alpha. It's meant a lot in the wake of Emerel's half-symbolic leadership.

Imagining Brutatalika and Helisent interacting to promote the Northing is another subject entirely.

For now, I use my words sparingly. "Of course, I'm interested in the Northing. I'm interested in building allies across Mieira. Survive your waricon, and you'll know more."

She can read the subtext:

Don't speak to me like we're Alphas.

Don't get ahead of yourself, Brutatalika.

I bow my head and prepare to move on, but she reaches out.

She grabs my forearm with the familiar, unkind touch of wolves. Unlike Helisent's tiny bird hand, Brutatalika's almost fits around me. Her blue-black eyes twinkle with intuition, studying me.

"Come on." She nods toward the packhouse's entrance. "A naiad demigod is here. The nymphs say it's bringing gifts of spring. Watch with me. They've been talking about it for days."

I resist for a moment, glancing toward the end of the hallway where I can smell the pack leaders. My mind flits to Helisent next; I can imagine her glittering robe amid the haze of incense smoke, can hear the slosh of brandy in her bottle as she stares at the world with a ghost's expression.

Brutatalika chuckles. She tugs on my arm for emphasis. "Do you remember when we first met in Bellator? That's how you still look to me. Like you're a thousand miles away from where you stand."

I was considered a man after I killed the wooly.

After Hetnazzar stepped in to fell the beast and I was left to drag its head back to Bellator Palace.

As is custom after the slaying of a wooly, the high-numbered females of my generation came to the Palace. Dozens of families with high generational counts traveled from across Velm to present their daughters as potential Alphas. Local administrators organized meals, social outings, and other pack activities to create a foundation for the future Alphas of Velm.

I barely remember the events, being paraded and assessed

as the Kulapsi, standing next to the cleaned wooly skull and staring at a marble hall full of solemn faces. It was a blur.

But Brutatalika stands out.

The first time we met, she bared her teeth at me.

It had alarmed me; I'd looked quickly over my right shoulder where my mother had always stood. I'd expected to see guidance and security in her stare. But she'd been gone a year, and Clearbold looked down at me instead.

He'd laughed when he looked from Brutatalika to me.

He whispered, "That's her. That's how you know. She doesn't want to be your wife, Samson. She wants to be your equal, and she hates you now for thinking you're better than her. Good."

Brutatalika's eyes flash with that same cold disengagement today. "We'll miss the demigod if we don't hurry."

I turn after Brutatalika and walk down the hallway, following the jangle of her golden bangles and her alluring ala.

The rest of the wolves in the packhouse trail us onto the street. In the distance, I catch a wisp of blue-tinted limbs above the second-story buildings. Brutatalika and I head toward the marble tower's exterior staircase like dozens of others.

Juvenile nymphs sprint between us and shove each other out of the way, darting back and forth to scramble up the stairs. The adults walk with their heads tilted back, searching the horizon.

Brutatalika sticks to my side, a genuine smile hanging from her lips.

She either doesn't notice or ignores the stunned expressions of the wolves who see us together. The naiads and okeanids might only see us as two strong wolves, but our own kind can smell our alas as they tangle.

The potential future Alphas of Velm.

Their faces don't look disapproving. One female wolf even

cracks a grin as we pass, lips twitching like she might say something.

On the tower's flat roof, we stand with our shoulders near and stare westward. Goosebumps spread across my body when I catch sight of the naiad demigod. It approaches with its hands raised above the treeline—full of gifts, like Brutatalika said.

The naiad demigod's hair is poofy and tangled, far more luxurious than the brown strands of the naiads around me. A crazed smile dimples its full cheeks, its eyes wide and delirious as it approaches the city with wide steps.

In one fist, the demigod clutches what looks to be a circular ball. But it's not a ball; it's a tangle of elements and plants associated with springtime. Heavy currents of clear water whorl in the orb shape, accented by soil and seedlings. They drip from the orb like melted ice, gracing the world with fragrant clumps.

The naiad demigod's other hand grips a second orb. This one is filled with birds and bees that soar and buzz in packs, slipping out of the orb only to dive back in. I also catch blades of bright grass and more seedlings.

I stare at the blue-hued demigod's approach, wondering where it plans on depositing its mix of fertile water, soil, and seeds. Birds and bees, too.

As it nears, the scent of spring intensifies enough to drown out Lampades's stench of incense-laden rot.

I count notes of rich pollen, tangy honey, fresh grass, sweet sap, pure rainwater, saiga and sable and rabbit furs, rinds of rotted fruit, and the potent flush of marking urine from a range of mammals.

It's almost too much to fathom as the demigod reaches the northern shore of the South Branch River. Across the city, silence falls as everyone stares overhead. The great being wades into the river, its blueish legs bleeding into the water rather than parting the current.

The demigod bites its lips as though holding in laughter. Its smile grows more wicked as it beelines for the crop fields past the city's southern border.

I crane my neck back as the demigod steps through the tight streets surrounding the marble tower. Its gifts rain down on us as it holds its hands aloft, above the rooftops; first is actual rain, then a slew of drenched begonia petals and a thick layer of marigold pollen that's half-congealed into honey.

The nymphs start to bellow, rushing around in a frenzy to collect the natural delights or to gain a closer vantage of the demigod. Atop the marble tower, we're close enough to touch its abdomen as it passes.

Within three more steps, the demigod clears the busiest city streets. Its pace increases as it nears the pale dry fields that stretch across the moors toward Velm. Like a devilish toddler, it raises its hands far above its head, then bends its knees to throw the water-filled orbs across the fields.

With the sound of crashing waves, the water and seeds and bees and honey and birds soar through the air. The water and seeds fall across the dirt, while the birds and bees soar just above the ground, heading southward.

The demigod stares at all it has wrought, then it continues its path farther into the fields.

Rather than keep watching like the nymphs around us, Brutatalika politely dusts the reeking pollen from her hair, then her torcs, then her tunic.

She wipes another glob of mashed petals from her cheek with a sigh. "I miss Hetnazzar."

I also miss my demigod, but that doesn't mean I appreciate the nymph demigods any less. Their ecstatic charges often confuse wolves—especially for those who haven't seen them often.

"Samson 714 Afador," Brutatalika goes on. "I'm leaving the city in the morning. Will you eat with me?"

I turn back, endeared by her simple smile and terrified of its consequences.

Is this it?

The begonia petals left a pinkish mark on her cheek. It's the same shade as her pale lips.

Is this my future?

I clear my throat.

Until the waricon series ends, I can't show preferential treatment toward either candidate for Female Alpha of Velm.

But I hope...

I hope...

I bow my head. "If you make it to Silent City, we'll share many meals together. I hope you enjoy your stay in Lampades. I'll be gone by morning. Goodbye, Brutalika 567 Sigivald."

I take one step back. She nods then watches me backtrack from the roof, down the stairs.

I rush into the packed streets full of frenzied celebrations and waves of desita. When I glance back, Brutatalika stares after me.

With its ample floodplains, there aren't many places for Lampades to host a large concert. Soon, I find the buzzing crowd of nymphs.

The attendees are even more packed for Lazarusman's second concert.

They gather in the hundreds on granite platforms on the city's northern edge. Even so, finding Helisent doesn't take long.

I have the extravagance of her ala to thank, which my nose is now well acquainted with—her bright-peach robe also helps. This time, she's surrounded by a group of okeanids bunched too tightly for me to pierce.

Even if she wasn't, there are too many wolves present for me to justify standing by her side. It wouldn't raise any eyebrows, but it may require introductions for curious wolves who approach—even Brutatalika, if she decided to stop by. First impressions matter for wolves, and Helisent's primary impressions would be the scents of brandy and dextro.

I focus on the wolves nearby.

They bow, offer me an ale, and ask polite questions about my stay in Lampades. Close to Velm, the wolves are more comfortable. They're chattier and curious about their future Alpha.

Only a few look uneasy with my presence. In the past, I'd figured a wolf's dismay came from the potency of my ala. Now I wonder if they support the Leofsige line instead.

I tally their stares until Lazarusman takes the stage.

Then the oread steals my attention. I'm not sure *what* it is specifically that draws me to his act: his jubilant features, his entrancing music, or his words.

But as the concert goes on, it starts to feel like he's speaking to me directly.

He smiles at the crowd, stoking more desita as he sways and speaks.

"It is about what you feel. What you do. How you choose to present yourself when the situation requires you. It is about what you're looking for. What you search for."

I glance toward Helisent in the crowd. She bends her neck to snort a line of dextro then looks up at the stage with exhausted absorption.

A red witch.

"It is not about fulfillment, but it is about what is missing. How do you improve? How do you progress? Are you searching? It is about the mind. How it grows progressively. What do you feed it? How do you cultivate the mind?"

Maybe when I'm Alpha, I'll take down the red horns hung in Bellator. I'll ask her if the pink stones that linger close to them have any significance to her, Antigone, or wielders in general.

"It is about the galaxies and the stars, but not so much about the moons as much as it is about *you*. It isn't about choices as much as it is decisions, but it is about having the bravery and the strength to make those things come to fruition."

Each word drives into my mind and settles like an anchor in flurrying sand.

Part of me thinks the oread might be looking straight at me when he asks, "What is it you're searching for?"

I keep an eye on Helisent from afar.

She dances with her eyes closed during the final songs. For the last, she slides back onto her lilith and sways. I'm not certain if her eyes are just closed or if she's on the brink of a blackout state.

After a few encores, the show ends, and the crowd begins to filter away. I keep my distance and offer parting words to the wolves who spent the concert in my company. They invite me to sleep in their homes, dine with their families, and pack my bag with their supplies.

I decline, keeping an eye on the teetering witch in the velvet robe in my periphery.

When I'm alone, I cross the granite platform toward her. She yawns, wipes her eyes, and looks around as though deciding what to do next.

Her expression softens with a smile when she sees me. "I kept looking behind me. I figured you'd sneak up on me again."

My gut sinks when I realize how drenched with alcohol her ala is; I was right not to introduce her to anyone tonight. "I'd be blocking a lot of views if I stood in the middle of the crowd."

"Right." She hiccups, then she rubs her eyes again. "I'll

probably sleep where I fall tonight. Feel free to go barter for lodging somewhere."

She gestures nondescriptly behind us, where the orange lights of Lampades beckon the wayward groups.

I doubt we'll make it far in her current state, and I'm not thrilled by the idea of being seen carrying a passed-out witch through Lampades.

I glance at the trees surrounding the slab of granite; the lights from the city offer little luminosity this far away. Like the rest of the South Deltas, the trees are low-hanging and weak, unsuitable for a nest.

And it sounds like more than a few nymphs have already scurried into the shadows of the thin forest in search of privacy.

"Don't feel weird about going." She gestures toward Lampades again, then she points to her chest. "Super powerful witch, remember?"

My temper flickers.

Does she actually think I'd turn and leave her here? Wolves don't leave their pack, and we're a de facto pack since we're traveling together.

Or is that what she wants?

And, most of all, "Does your panic magic move you onto your side if you drink so much you throw up in your sleep? Or is half of you waiting to die, Helisent?"

She looks at me as though confused. "Probably more than half of me. A cool seventy-five percent. The rest is just brandy, baby."

I clench my jaw. "If you wouldn't mind accessing the twenty-five percent of you that gives a fuck, that would be great. Just until we find somewhere to sleep." I settle on a semi-lit trail that heads back toward the South Branch River at a diagonal angle. "Come on, let's go this way."

I take off toward the path but don't hear her jangling lilith follow.

I turn around. She hasn't budged. "Are you too drunk to float?"

"No," she sneers. Her nose bunches as her lips pucker in a pout. "I'm too *stubborn* to go with someone who *hates* the drunk-me."

I summon all my patience with a deep breath, then head back to the lilith. "I don't hate the drunk-you. However, the drunk-you makes me wonder why you do this to yourself."

In the hushed darkness that's filled with the happy ends of group desita, my words pick up an easy pace.

"I thought you'd be happy tonight. Didn't you see the naiad demigod walk through Lampades? I thought you loved the demigods. And what about Lazarusman? I thought the show tonight was even better than in Perpetua."

"Oh, *wow*, Samson—a demigod and a spoken word poet. Is that all in life it would take to please me?" Her indignant tone becomes crueler with each word. "What if you don't actually know me at all?"

Helisent looks up at me. Her wide, golden eyes shimmer beneath the limited moonlight.

I know they're actually red. I know the eyes she shows me are a lie.

It shouldn't hurt as much as it does to realize she's right; I don't know her that well.

I don't know if she has family. Any brothers or sisters. I don't know where she actually grew up aside from a vague description of west of Jaws. I don't know what made her happy or afraid as a child, or where she sees herself ten years from now. I don't know if the bloodred hue of her eyes that she shows me in my dreams is accurate or imagined.

She is a red witch from west of Jaws.

She lived in Antigone before she moved to Alita and then Luz.

She's a sponsor of Luz with a deep pool of magic to draw from.

She loves bitterroot brandy and dextro.

She enjoys her life in a warren and an oread named Onesimos.

That's five points I can make with certainty after almost three months of traveling with her. And I still have no clue why she's after Oko.

With a shaking voice, she whispers, "Do you ever hear screaming when you're around me? A witch screaming?"

Fuck, I can't deal with this.

"No. Let's talk about it in the morning."

She glares at me like she's going to go on. Uncertain of what to do, I offer her my arm.

She slides her hand onto the spot where she normally lets me drag her lilith, then we take off.

She sniffles, then says, "Don't be so nice to me, Samson."

I look at her, wondering if that's an apology.

She stares up at me with watering eyes; I guess it is.

It reminds me of the night after the selkie visited us in the cove. The way she'd called down from her nest in a fragile, child-like voice and asked if I was upset with her. I hadn't been, and I hadn't realized she'd thought or cared I might be.

"You're a mess right now, Helisent, but I'm going to leave you out here by yourself."

She sniffles again, then nods. "Yeah, okay."

We reach the wide path that weaves through the thin forest, heading back toward Lampades at a diagonal angle. We pass a few other groups who chatter and drink loudly, but they soon move on. It doesn't take too long to find a tree that looks sturdy and tall enough for the witch's liking.

I tap her hand then realize Helisent's head sags toward her chest.

She's snoring lightly, half-leaned toward me.

I shake her hand. "Helisent, wake up. I found us a place to sleep."

With a groan, I slip my satchel off my shoulder and let it

land on the ground with a thud. I take her hand off my arm and squeeze it between mine; it's colder than I'd thought it would be.

"Just wake up for a second so you can make your nest."

With a snort, she jolts half-awake, then slides from the lilith.

I lunge after her, knocking into the cushion to grab her before she hits the ground.

Then the permeating buzz of her infrasound rattles through my bones, setting my skin alight with goosebumps. Like in the cove, it hurts my balls; I back away from Helisent as a wave of nausea silences me.

Her magic halts her a few inches above the ground.

She slips gently into the patchy grass, half-tangled in her robe. The velvet hood covers most of her face. One arm and foot also poke out from the fabric.

The lilith hangs in the air at her side.

I take a huge breath and summon the courage to reach out and touch Helisent's leg. She'll kill me if she knows I let her sleep on the ground without attempting to move or wake her.

I meet with the same bone-shaking infrasound that courses through my body. I grab my balls with a curse as my nausea doubles.

I freeze, terrified by the idea her magic may have lessened my sperm count or altered the future generations of Afador's waiting for life between my legs.

Meanwhile, red light splinters from Helisent's form like narrow veins of lightning. It laces through the air to form a sphere that encircles her body. But the sphere takes shape only briefly before fizzling out with a buzzing sound.

Is this panic magic?

And what was it—lightning, static?

I stare at her, braced for another appearance of red light.

A satisfied laugh sounds from behind me.

I turn to find a middle-aged warlock on the path we turned

off, standing half-engulfed in shadows. Moonslight glints off his perfectly shined buttons and buckles; like most Antigonian warlocks, he wears a long cape, tailored pants, and a buttoned shirt with plenty of ornamentation.

I've never seen such a refined warlock this far south. These types don't leave Septegeur.

Is he part of the Class?

I'd rather see another fucking selkie.

Better yet, bring back Creepy Baby.

I release my nuts then set my hands on my hips. I angle my body, hoping to hide the passed-out witch strewn on the ground behind me.

"I always heard infrasound bothered the male wolves." The warlock's voice is like melting snow: cool and attention-grabbing. "I've never actually seen it for myself."

He's been watching us? Great.

The warlock takes a few steps down the path. For a second, I wonder if he'll pass us and continue on his way. Then I realize he's not actually looking at me. He's studying Helisent, his golden eyes seemingly collecting every detail of her shape beneath the velvet robe.

"Did you enjoy the show?" The warlock's eyes snap to me. "Lazarusman is a wonderful artist."

"I did, thank you. I'm Samson 714 Afador. And who are you?"

I can tell by his ala that we haven't met; I'd remember something so distinctive.

At the tips of his scent is an herb or a spice I've never smelled before, which snags my attention with each breath. I chalk it up to Septegeur's towering stone pillars and the fern-covered gulches below where no one lives anymore. I haven't traveled there, which means there are plenty of scents I've yet to log into my fangmind.

"I'm not in Velm, Samson. My name is mine to keep." The

warlock turns to me, squaring up his shoulders in line with mine.

My hair stands on end.

Squaring up is the first indicator amongst wolves that violence awaits; it's how we start our waricons and street fights alike.

I've never seen a wielder square up before.

He tilts his head and asks, "Does your father know you're working with Helisent West of Jaws?"

He knows Helisent.

And he didn't say Clearbold 554 Leofsige. He said *father*.

The moonslight and shadows shift across the warlock as the trees shift in the wind. I squint to study his features, which aren't like any other wielder I've ever met. His eyes are smaller, his jaw stronger. Rather than long white hair, he has a wild cut of short hair.

Moonslight twists across his shined buckles again.

I do not like this warlock.

He is near Velm. Near an unconscious Helisent. And he thinks his name is his to keep.

Enough, then. "Are you part of Clearbold 554 Leofsige's court?"

My father has the trust and leadership of pack leaders in every city, even Antigone. He also has personal connections to powerful nymphs and wielders; some are strategic, others are based on camaraderie.

This type of warlock doesn't seem like the friendship sort. But I wouldn't know—Clearbold hasn't introduced me to all of his connections, and I wouldn't expect or want to know each. Once I'm married, I'll start to build my own court.

The warlock looks back to Helisent. His mouth twitches.

What does he want from her? What does he know of her power?

The most likely scenario is that they slept together at some point in an exchange of clout and drunken impulse, as

Helisent does. Anything else is unknown to me and far more unpleasant to imagine.

"I was once a part of your father's court," the warlock says.

Once.

It clicks—is this a banished wielder?

Banishments are the most severe form of punishment in both Mieira and Velm. Only despicable acts like murder, rape, and critical destruction to cities or their resources warrant such action.

But banishments are also difficult to enforce. Pack leaders protect their jurisdictions from banished wolves, as do kings and queens for nymphs, and officials hired by the Class for wielders. Some beings find their way back into civilization with a few well-placed bribes, while others skate by on the fringes before slinking back into the general public.

I give the warlock the once-over. "I don't waste my time with banished beings."

He raises his eyebrows as though amused. "I never said I was *banished*. You're putting words into my mouth."

"State your name and what you want." I take one step toward him, angling to block his view of Helisent again. I'm too tired and confused for a fight, but I can't fathom what this wielder wants, and I know it's nothing good. "Or go on your way."

"I could sense the witch's power and came to suss it out. Power senses power. A wolf can understand that."

He studies me from head to toe with a growing look of disdain. I swear the golden edges of his irises fade to dark and blend with his pupils.

"I followed the trail of power and realized it was someone I knew. And do *you* know who you're traveling with? Do you know what the witch wants with you?" He tucks his hands behind his back. "Be careful, Samson. What you admire in her now you will come to hate."

He tsks, scanning me once more, then turns and continues down the path.

He must know wolves well, or, at least, much better than Helisent. Though he doesn't face me, he knows I can hear him when he speaks into the wind ten paces away from me.

He says, "One day you will need me, Samson 714 Afador. Remember my ala."

I watch until I can't see him on the path or smell him in the wind.

I turn back to Helisent. She's snoring loudly. Her visible leg retracts into the robe's folds with a twitch.

I wonder what happens to her when I'm not here.

I haven't admitted it to myself yet, but it's all shifting into focus now.

The freewheeling Helisent I've befriended these past months is a comfortable front for something way more intense than what I signed up for when she stepped into the Luzian Estate's garden.

I squat and prepare my bed mat. I take down my hair and rub the day from my face. I roll a cigarette and light it with a long sigh, then I lay down and stare over at the pile of velvet layers.

"Helisent, you have to stop making fuck to these crazy guys."

I settle in with a shuffle, staring up at the dark skeletal canopy and the moons above.

Also, why is your heart so broken?

CHAPTER 13

IT ECHOES FROM THE NORTHWEST

HELISENT

Honey Heli,
To prove my point... I stole one of papa's favorite scarves. We'll use it to track him down in Alita, then he'll see that Anesot is the best thing to happen to us. Who could have taught us so many things? Only a four-horn.
Mint Mili

Samson stands on the pier that extends into the Deltas Bay and stares into the distance.

The cloudless sky looks deceptively peaceful. Gusts of wind whip against the wooden docks and their small boats on the northernmost tip of Ultramarine. Like Samson, I stare across the saltwater inlet toward the city's twin or, depending who you ask, rival.

Cadmium.

Stacked, square dwellings with blinding white walls compose each city. Like in Cadmium, thieving long-tailed monkeys rove the rooftops and streets of Ultramarine. In fact, the only way to discern the dueling cities is the colors used to decorate shutters, curtains, pottery, tapestries, and garments.

Ultramarine is blanketed with shades of stark indigo, Cadmium with a burning red-orange.

I grab Samson's forearm before he can board the ferry to Cadmium.

He looks back at me. The wind shakes his dark hair loose from its bun.

I clear my throat then glance down at the parchment in my hands. This is already harder than I thought it'd be. "I—I have something to say."

I clear my throat again, glancing at him. He looks down at me with a patient, perplexed gaze.

"It's an apology, technically."

Gross. I hate this so much I might cry.

But this apology will make me feel better about the dark gray blur of bad things I said and did in Lampades. Each day I ignore them, the viler they become.

I don't look up at Samson as I batter through my written apology. "I'm sorry that I said I didn't want to leave with you after the concert even though you were trying to help me. I'm sorry I got so drunk I fell off my lilith. I'm sorry you had to sleep next to me and worry that I was going to throw up on my own vomit."

Moons, kill me.

How am I thirty-four years old?

"I'm sorry that my panic magic hurt your balls and that a warlock accosted you because he could sense my magic and got curious. I'm sorry I wasn't awake to deal with the snooping fucker myself."

Warlocks have done shadier things to learn about my magic, but Samson *really* hated this one.

"I'm sorry that I slept until evening the next day and made us miss Lazarusman's performance in Ultramarine."

I clear my throat a third time, fold the note, and then tuck it into my bottomless bag with all the pride I can muster. I raise my chin as the wind lifts my hair and tangles it.

Samson's smile shocks me. It's not just a content smile, but a *delighted grin*. "Did you write that yourself?"

Technically, Onesimos taught me the mechanics of an apology. "Yes, I wrote it myself. Why? Did you think I was illiterate?"

"No. But, you'd already kind of apologized to me that night. It was a lot more casual than the note... but I'm not angry with you. I didn't feel disrespected, just worried."

He'd told me as much the next day. I think his exact words were, *Helisent, I don't mean for this to sound harsh, but I think you might be really fucked up.*

I wanted to disagree, but I spent the next two hours trying to scrape any remnants of dextro from the glass container I carry it in.

"Well, I still felt the need to voice a better apology." I adjust the strap of my bottomless bag, too timid to meet his eyes. "I won't drink or do any dextro for the next week or so. Just to clear my mind."

And to give my liver a chance to breathe.

Samson glances over his shoulder. The line of beings boarding the wooden boat has dwindled. Onboard, okeanid sailors yank on thick ropes to let down the stark white sails, shouting and hustling across the decks.

Samson licks his lips as he turns back to me. "If you change your mind about the drinking, try to make it to wherever you're sleeping before you pass out."

"Fine. Fair enough." I hold out my hand. My palm tingles with the expectation to see which item he'll give me. "I'll use tracking magic to let you know what I find—you won't feel it, I promise. No harm will come to the Afador line. I'll send word to you like I did with Rex as soon as I speak with the GhostEater here."

He slings his satchel from one arm and makes quick work

of the buckles. He pulls out a brown suede bag and sets the bag in my palm; there's a small, heavy piece inside.

"Don't lose it."

He turns away and heads to the boat before I can tell him not to give me something that shouldn't be lost. I start tugging at the suede bag's cords as he boards the ship.

I pull out a cool piece that's almost as large as my palm. It's carved of white marble, but I'm not sure *what* it is. The circular piece is flat, with multiple lines that branch out from a center point, like spokes on a wheel. The lines are finely sculpted with lovely symmetrical designs.

I hold it up to the light, but that doesn't help me identify what it is.

Samson stands near the back of the boat, watching me with a smug half-smile.

"What the fuck is this?" I shout.

He holds his palm up to his ear as though he can't hear me. But now that I know more about wolves, I know he's just fucking with me. They can basically hear everything.

I hold the piece up to my face to smell it, then hold it between my teeth to bite it. All I can glean is that it's harder than gold and tasteless.

Samson buries his face in his hands, but I can't tell if he's laughing or aghast.

I stay a moment longer as the boat embarks. The okeanids line up at the railing, moving their arms in tandem as they call forth the currents that will ferry them to Cadmium. Meanwhile, wind also fills the white sails as the boat cruises with a flush of pale foam in its wake.

With a sigh, I turn back toward Ultramarine.

It should be the perfect place to be sober and healthy.

The salty air is fresh, the sunlight warm. The city's stacked white dwellings draw out the color of the piercing blue accents and the bright eyes of the local okeanids. Now and then, I catch the tang of fish in the air, but the farther I push into the

Ultramarine's narrow streets, the scent is replaced by the same sandalwood incense I noticed in Lampades.

This will be a good city to live in, too. A little heavy on the wolf population, but that doesn't necessarily frighten or deter me anymore.

Just like Perpetua, it gives me hope for a future.

Not every city needs a sponsor, but few are foolish enough to turn down a chance at an easier life and magical bounty.

Ultramarine will welcome me after Perpetua and Lampades, then comes Cadmium.

For now, Oko.

I stare down at Samson's white sculpture as I wander through the streets, but when a pair of macaque monkeys start eyeing it, I tuck it away. Since we arrived in Ultramarine last night, I've witnessed multiple incidents in which the sand-colored shaggy-headed monkeys snipe items from local nymphs and wielders.

First was a necklace, then a set of quills, and then a full bottle of wine.

On each occasion, the victims stared at the fleeing macaques and shouted a few curses. Only the warlock divested of his wine ran after the thief, but he was quickly stopped by a group of nymphs who packed around him to prevent a chase.

One of the okeanids chided, "Now, now, he stole it fair and square, didn't he?"

With Samson by my side, none of the macaques came near. Now that I'm alone, the nasty beasts don't flee to rooftops. They trail me with eyes that are upsettingly intelligent.

With Samson's ornament safe, I climb into the mazelike streets and get lost amid a similar spread of restaurants, bars, and shops. Half are outside, situated beneath taut white fabric tied overhead.

I keep moving every time my gaze settles on a refreshing glass of brandy, or wine, or even ale.

I compromise by sitting alone at a table overlooking the

bay and stuffing my face with bitterroot treats. I decide my best option for finding the GhostEater is to start with the local city council appointed by the Class.

Later, when my plate sits empty, a server comes over—but she doesn't tote away the dirty plate.

Instead, she sits in the open chair at my side, sighs like she's exhausted, and kicks up her feet onto the low barrier lining the restaurant. Without sparing a look at me, she rolls a cigarette and lights it.

I turn and study the silent stranger.

She has the pale hair of a wielder, but its ends are tinged blue. Rather than sitting flat and straight like mine, hers is a tangle of loose curls. Her eyes are a blend of golden threads and turquoise hues. Her nose's arch is slight; her skin is olive, like mine—but cooler, with richer shades.

I haven't seen many wielder-nymph offspring with such a mix of features. Typically, they tend to take after *one* parent, which would either be an okeanid or a wielder, in her case.

She notices my gaze. "Do you want a cigarette?"

I narrow my eyes. Witches don't show strangers kindness, but I'm not sure how witch-okeanids figure into that.

I play it conservatively. "No, thanks."

She reaches into the pocket of her white robe and pulls out a nub of green leaf. "Betel?"

"What's that?" *And is it like dextro?*

"It's betel nut." She takes a drag, then turns her head to exhale into the wind. "It grows in the Deltas. You chew on it. Gives you a buzz."

"Are you pith?" I blurt.

She slides her golden-turquoise eyes toward me, then puts the bundled leaf back into her pocket. "That's rude as fuck."

We eye each other for a moment. Her retort actually makes me trust her more. "What's wrong with being pith?"

"Are you *straight* from Antigone?" She gives me the once-over just like I once did to Little Esteban. "Well, maybe not. You seem to be fine with ground-walking."

I try and fail not to be offended. "I'm from west of Jaws. I live in Luz now. I've been ground-walking all my life, *thank you*."

"Then haven't you met plenty of pith nymphs in Luz? The okeanids and oreads who live there won't have much, if any, power from their demigods. It's too far from Jaws and the coasts.

"Have people not noticed there are pith nymphs all over the city? I mean, I know the west is conservative, but everyone always talks about how Luz is a city of the future. And the future is pith for many."

I fold my arms. "There are pith nymphs all over Mieira. One of my lovers in Luz is an oread—and he didn't lose his magic when he left Jaws to go west. Are you sure *you* know what you're talking about? And Luz *is* the city of the future. We don't have any of these stupid fucking monkeys, either."

To my great surprise, this delights the okeanid-witch. She reels back with a loud laugh, clapping her hands together. "I'll be the first to admit they're problematic. Tell me how this works—the nymphs punish hoarding with bloody severity, but they'd let these fucking monkeys build a city of gold."

I nod. "There's a sable issue in Rhotidom that sounds simi-lar. Little fuckers have formed packs. It's basically organized crime, but the Rhotidic Kings and Queens dote on them. I saw one with a little vest once, and another one with a hat. Separate incidents."

"Oh, see, well that's cute." She chuckles. "The monkeys don't let us dress them."

The stranger swivels in her chair and nods discreetly toward a couple in the corner of the restaurant. Like us, they face the bay with a spread of food between them. One is large enough to be a wolf, though her hair is a flat black and her skin is too dark to be from the land of Night. The other is a dryad with cropped, emerald hair; she bounces one of her legs as though nervous.

"The larger one is fully pith," she says. "And the dryad is her girlfriend—she's pith by distance. She was born west of Rhotidom, so her demigod is too far away for her to call on elemental powers. It's a full-on *pith couple*."

Nymphs who wander far from their demigods and the land they roam lose control of their elemental powers. Any being without magical power to call on is labeled pith; many nymphs become pith by distance, like the witch mentioned.

However, as more wolves and nymphs and wielders inter-mingle, there's a growing number of beings who are *born* pith. The coupling of wolves and wielders, for example, always yields pith offspring. They can't wield magic nor phase into a wolf under the triplemoon.

Or so I've heard.

The pairings are so rare that I've yet to meet a pith wolf-wielder in the flesh.

I try not to stare and fail. My eyes keep drifting to her hair. Without its blue undertones, it looks distinct from Samson's tinted locks.

The okeanid-witch snorts as she studies my expression. "It's hard for us to imagine what it's like because we use our magic for everything."

She's right. Without my magic, I'm punishably useless.

As though sensing my curiosity, she goes on, "Her dad's a warlock. Actually, he just became a sponsor of Ultramarine. And her mom's a wolf from north of Mort."

The witch sends another plume of smoke into the air, then pulls out the leaf bundle again. "You should try betel. It's cultural, you know."

I pluck the little bundle from her palm. I don't trust her, but I don't think she's attempting a dastardly trick. She's prob-ably attempting some sort of mid-range deception to run off with a bit of extra dove.

And I still need to find the GhostEater.

I pinch the leaves, testing their contents. "So do I eat it?"

She waves a hand at me, eyes widening with alarm. "No. Tuck it between your teeth and your gums. Spit out the saliva —don't swallow it. Your stomach will hurt."

I look from her to the prim white tiles at my feet. "Spit it out where?"

"On the floor. Get wild, girl. Don't they use cleaning magic in Luz? That's the only reason everything looks so pristine here. We're not actually that clean."

"We do." I roll my eyes and tuck the leaf into my mouth as instructed. I move the bundle around, glancing at the witch as she watches me. It tastes like a generic spice with a bitter twang at the end.

"So what do you want?" I ask.

She flinches. "What?"

I repeat myself, slower this time so she knows I'm not a fucking dolt.

She makes a long nervous sound. "Me and my friend saw you and wondered if you'd moved here or were just passing through. He said you looked like someone looking to get lost —a lot of beings come here just to fuck off for a few months. It's kind of like Hypnos. Then I said you were just passing through. I could tell you'd never dealt with a monkey before."

Flavorful saliva fills my mouth faster than I thought it would.

"So I just..." I motion to the ground so she knows I'm really going to spit out the betel nut juice.

Before I can, a long string of dark red saliva leaks through my opened lips. I lean forward just in time to spit onto the beige tile.

I look down at the splatter of saliva then glance at the witch.

She looks just as unimpressed as I feel.

I pull a handkerchief from my bottomless bag and dab at

my mouth. Already, I can feel my face flushing and my heart rate increasing from the stimulant.

When I open my mouth to speak, saliva rushes to my lips again.

I bend forward and empty my mouth of saliva and the folded leaf.

I even dry-heave.

What the fuck is betel? Am I being poisoned?

I use washing magic to clean my face, robe, and the floor of the goopy, reddish saliva. The spell is tied to the handkerchief in my hand, which absorbs my mess. Rather than save it for another day, I use fire magic to gobble up the material. With a *whoosh* of disgusting smoke and sizzling, the handkerchief dissolves into ash.

Only the half-crushed betel leaf remains on the tile at my feet.

"Maybe warn someone next time you offer them betel," I say. "It's fucking disgusting."

I cross my arms and stare back into the bay. I wait for the stranger to leave.

The witch sits up in her chair. She looks from me, back toward the restaurant's kitchen, then across the glittering water.

"I didn't mean to offend you." The witch takes a long drag of her cigarette and shrugs. "I forget how touchy wielders from the west are."

"Tell me what the fuck you want, or I'm leaving without bartering for my food."

With each second, the witch looks less comfortable with our interaction. Good. "What do you mean? I already told you—"

"What do you think it means? You came over here, offered me a cigarette, then the betel nut. You even gossiped about the other couple in the corner. The only place I've ever met truly friendly strangers is in a tavern at highmoons. And *very* few of them had wielder blood."

She exhales quickly, dropping her cigarette and stamping it out with her sandal. She lowers her voice, speaking quickly. "The GhostEater wants to see you. A strange witch went to see her last week about a haunting."

There was a reason I wanted to part ways with Samson.

Assuming Oko was ahead of us and had already sought out Ultramarine's GhostEater, I knew it was possible the Ghost-Eater would be expecting me.

That the GhostEater would have figured out my plan to drive Oko out of hiding with a haunting. Six years ago, Oko betrayed me; word spread quickly throughout Septegeur, and not all wielders forgot.

I study the street behind us, as though I might find a powerful GhostEater spying on us. "If she knew I was coming, why didn't she come to find me herself?"

"Because she's old as dirt. I've been running errands for her for years. She said to keep an eye out for a powerful witch who'd never been here before." With a sigh, she starts to roll another cigarette. Her thin fingers work quickly. "I'm Butter, by the way. I'm her granddaughter. Hope you're ready to barter your soul for whatever you seek. She's a real bitch."

I stand up and give the witch a flat look. "Let's go."

With a weighted glance, she stands and leads me from the restaurant.

From there, Butter walks three steps ahead of me and doesn't look back to ensure I keep up. She hustles quickly, a qualified ground-walker after all. She slides between chatting groups and leads me up the smooth wooden ladders to take shortcuts across rooftops. The wind catches and tangles her spiraling curls. Twisted together, they look like strands of sky and clouds.

The city is a maze of white walls, deep indigo accents, spying monkeys, and luxurious, drooping plants. I'm convinced we've looped back to where we started when Butter pulls aside a thin curtain and gestures me into a cramped vestibule.

Metal charms and amulets hang from the ceiling, immediately putting me at ease.

I wander beneath them, feeling at home by the number of copper and bronze and brass and iron ornaments. They're Antigonian, either crafted in the city or wrought by a wielder born there.

I tap one of the bronze ornaments, sending it spinning.

Butter doesn't enter the room. She watches me from the doorway with her arms folded.

I blink, surprised by how suddenly attractive I find her. It hits me in a rush, accented by the betel's stimulants—her blazing eyes, her secret cunning, the plum color of her curved lips against the burnt caramel of her skin.

I'll deal with that later.

"And where's grandmama?" I ask.

Butter gestures to a dark threshold at the room's end.

A foreboding croak echoes from the back room. Then a gnarled olive-skinned hand pierces the shadows to grip the wall.

An ancient, crooked witch pulls herself into the foyer. She looks at Butter. "Calypso. What took you so long? She arrived last night, did she not?"

I study the GhostEater, her mashed features entirely separate from Butter's smooth skin and plump features.

Butter yawns as though bored. "It took me less than a day. You're welcome."

The witch's wrinkled face twitches as she walks toward me. She hobbles with a cane, swinging one leg as she approaches.

Her cloudy eyes fix on me. "Helisent West Jaws. Go on, then. Into the back room."

I guess she made the connection to Oko quickly.

I shuffle toward the back room. I glance back and find

Butter studying me from the doorway. She raises her eyebrows. "Goodbye, Helisent West of Jaws."

Is that why she stayed? She wanted to know my name?

I stare back. "Goodbye, Calypso."

She turns with a bright smile, indigo curtain fluttering in her wake.

I commit the okeanid-witch to memory.

She'll be useful to me someday—either as a friend or an ally.

The GhostEater bumps into my hip as she hobbles past me toward her private room. Her bulging eyes switch back to me often, as though making sure I'm following. She's got to be at least one hundred and ten years old; I wonder why she doesn't hover. I've seen a few wielders around her age drifting through the streets on indigo liliths.

She stops before we cross the threshold.

She reaches out and seizes a handful of my velvet garment. "I know the warlock who made this garment. They don't make textiles like this anymore. He wove the robe in Alita. It was the rainy season. He was depressed. Many moons ago."

Finally, the witch floats. Her crooked back straightens for a moment as she raises herself into the air to meet my eyes.

She grunts. "Hiding your real irises, then? I'll try not to be offended."

I can't sense her magic, but she must have two *large* horns. Only long-lived and powerful wielders can pinpoint specifically where another funnels their magic. I wonder if she can sense my magic as it toils in the western cities, my dove compounded in the processors to clean the streets, light the lamps, and store the rainwater in Mieira's greatest cities.

"I met a red witch once," she says.

I freeze. Very few beings say that anymore.

Her head tilts, eyes widening. "Strange that I'd meet a *second* red witch shortly after Oko came here bitching about a full-blown haunting."

I was right—if the GhostEater connected Oko's arrival with mine, then she knows why I'm after the witch.

She floats back to the ground then slams her walking stick on the tile as she leads us toward the shadowy room. "Come on, then."

I follow at her heels, mind racing. "When did Oko come here? Do you know where she's going now? Look, it's—"

"I'm too old to walk and think at the same time. Pipe down."

I follow the GhostEater into the room. It's occupied by a narrow table with a series of amulets that look similar to the pieces in the foyer. Dripping candles affixed to the walls light the windowless room. Only shreds of cool light float in from the entrance.

The GhostEater drifts onto a wooden chair piled with cushions, then gestures for me to take a seat on the opposite bench.

I shift into position, tallying my questions with budding apprehension. "Did you end the haunting? If Oko already left the city, I—"

"Quiet, witchling." The GhostEater slams her ragged hands flat on the table, causing the metal pieces to jangle. "Collect yourself."

"I'm not trying to rush you, but this is a big deal. Very sensitive."

And if she *knows* a story about Oko and a red witch, then she should understand why I'm here. How important this is.

"And what are you willing to barter for information on Oko?" she asks.

I snort. "I'm a red witch. I think we can stop with the niceties. You tell me what I want to know, and then I fork over whatever something as old as you still has the capacity to desire."

She laughs, a crooked smile lifting her sagging cheeks.

"Excellent. Let's get down to business. Oko came in last week with two ghosts harassing her."

Two?

...Creepy Baby?

"She offered me magnificent things to end the haunting. Oh, you would have liked to see it. Yes, you would have. Her begging like that..."

I nod. Someday soon, I'll see it for myself.

The GhostEater doesn't go on, shifting in her seat as she studies me.

"And what did you tell Oko?" I push.

"I told her to fuck right off. I was in Antigone when word spread about what she and Anesot did to your—"

"I get it." I try to use the breathing techniques that Samson taught me, but I can hear wayward screaming in the back of my mind already.

I need a drink. Several drinks.

"Do you know if Oko went to Cadmium to find the other GhostEater?"

The old witch shakes her head. "The other GhostEater left Cadmium years ago. I don't know where she went—probably back to Antigone. She once lived in Red Pier. Her son lives in Luz. His name is Itzifone. I think he trades information with bounty hunters."

I blink at her; I've only met one warlock with the uncommon name.

For fuck's sake.

The GhostEater goes on, "Your best bet is finding him and bartering for an item of hers so you can track her. Don't worry —I didn't tell Oko any of this. She's probably still combing Cadmium looking for the other GhostEater. Strong witch— not very smart, though."

"How far ahead is she, then? Butter mentioned she came here last week."

The GhostEater nods. "Something like that."

It's a manageable timeframe, at least. My optimism rekindles as I eye the GhostEater's ravenous expression. "Do you mind if I ask you a few other questions?"

"It was your sister, Milisent. That was the other red witch I met. Not your mother."

I flinch, body locking.

The screaming witch gets louder, echoing through my mind as though it's coming from hundreds of miles away.

I clear my throat. "That's not what I was going to ask. I heard from a selkie that okeanids are disappearing. Do you know anything about this?"

She nods gravely. "Each year, we lose more. Most of the disappearances are in Jaws and Hypnos, but okeanids in the Deltas have started to go missing in larger numbers. The city councils have used bounty hunters to try to track down the perpetrators, but there's been little progress. Do you think Oko might be related to the disappearances?"

At least the GhostEater seems to be aware of how dangerous Oko is.

I shake my head. "I don't know. First, I need to find her, then I can ask questions."

Her golden eyes twinkle in the candlelight. "I wouldn't bother asking questions if I were you. And what about Anesot? Do you have plans to—"

"I have it figured out." His name sends a flash of anger through my blood. It doesn't pass, but boils and intensifies. I need that drink—several drinks. All in a row. "Thank you. What about a fifth scent? Have you heard about a fifth scent?"

"A fifth *scent*? No. Ask a wolf."

"And what about a Sennenwolf? Do you know what that is?"

For the first time, the GhostEater looks surprised. Her fingers drum against the tabletop as though excited or nervous. "A *Sennenwolf*. Of course. I haven't heard the stories since I was a child... and even then, the Sennenwolf was just a scary story told to keep the littlelings in line."

"What was it? I lived in Antigone for years and never heard of it."

"Because you're young. There was no need for wielders to fear the Sennenwolf by the time Andromeda birthed you."

My mother's name hurts least of all.

Still, it's like having a wound ripped open.

"Stop staying their names." But there's no force in my voice. No gumption. Sober me is so fucking pitiful. "I don't... I don't even think their names anymore, okay? It's a little jarring."

"Have it your way, but such habits won't heal a broken heart, Helisent."

"Riveting. And the Sennenwolf?"

"The Sennenwolf was how Velm almost won the war. Bloody Betty was child's play compared to the Sennenwolf."

My mind tries and fails to comprehend her words.

"Child's play compared to Bloody Betty? Betty was a four-horned witch who killed thousands under Velm's control. You're saying there was something *more dangerous* than her?"

What did it look like? Was it a wolf? Where is the Sennenwolf now?

The GhostEater's gnarled hand finds mine. It squeezes, catching my fingers against her fleshy palm. "The tales I heard said the Sennenwolf came long before Betty. Before the War Years, even. Before the harsh grip of winter forced the wolves north and the curiosity for more drove wielders south.

"All I ever knew of the Sennenwolf was that it was a weapon.

"And only when it died, and the War Years began, could the wielders fight back against Velm. With the Sennenwolf alive, Velm was too powerful."

For a long time, I chew on her words.

The revelation is too big for this tiny room. Fear and panic bubble in my blood. Even though there's no inkling of another war, I fear the possibility of it starting. I fear the sacrifices I would be asked to make to win that war—to take down something like a Sennenwolf.

I take a deep breath. "Do you believe it existed?" I ask.

She raises her eyebrows. Her voice is gentle. "I'm glad I don't have to think of it at all, Helisent."

"Right. Fair enough." I shove away my apprehension. I hold up a finger as another question pops into my head. "You know about ghosts—do you know what Skull is? I heard it's not actually a city. Oh, and junior ghosts. What are those?"

Her loud cackle turns into a series of coughing. "A *city*? Is that what they say now? Witchling, I can't tell you what Skull is or what a junior ghost is. I bartered too dearly to give such things away for free. But if you can figure it out, then you can command the ghosts."

I narrow my eyes. "I see."

I mull over her words in silence once again. She's offered more than most witches I've met before. So long as she handles this next part well, I'll trust all the knowledge she imparted.

"And what do you want to barter for this information? Feel free to include something extra for telling Oko to fuck off." I glance up at her. "It's appreciated."

Based on the high value of the information she offered me, the GhostEater should be aggressive with her bartering demands.

She watches me with a hungry smile; good.

"What do you want, then?"

"Don't be offended."

"Out with it."

"Your horns. Just a peep." The GhostEater glances toward the bright entryway that leads back to the foyer.

My gut steels. It's a demanding barter, all right. Aside from my brothers and father, no one has seen me in my form. And they only saw me in my form because I would reveal myself if I got too worked up emotionally. Which happened almost daily as a child.

"Can't you think of something more useful?"

"I'm a dying witch. Utility has little relevance for me anymore. Just your tail, then?"

I roll my eyes. "No. Never."

With a curse, I glance toward the opened doorway. I lean back on the bench to make sure no one waits in the foyer or spies on us from its square windows.

Then I turn back to the wielder. "Do your eyes work well enough for this? I won't do it twice."

She shakes her head in preparation, then opens her eyes as wide as they'll go. "Ready."

I shift into my form, careful to slow the infrasound that rolls off my body, from my toenails to the tips of my hairs. Still, my form gives off enough undiluted infrasound to send shivering bass through the room. The metal amulets clatter atop the wooden table while their dangling counterparts in the foyer shiver.

I stare at the GhostEater to avoid looking at my own hands.

My skin has turned from a clean olive to a maddening blood-red. My nails are longer, sharper, curved. They're basically talons.

I avoid looking at the walls, too. These candles will cast my six-horned shadow somewhere. It's bad enough I can catch the red-hued glow that leaks from my eyes and horns. They're like festival lanterns whose light I can't escape.

I also ignore the sensation of my long tail, which instinctually wraps around my abdomen so it doesn't get in my way. My seventh horn is technically the flat, central bone of my spade tail. It rests against my belly beneath my dress and robe, twitching as though eager to be put to use.

The GhostEater's mouth falls open.

I sigh. "You have five seconds, four, three, two... and one."

I hide my form again, relieved by the silence that follows the clattering amulets.

I stand up. "Thank you for your help."

I duck between the dangling ornaments and beeline for the entryway, wondering when the next ferry to Cadmium takes off.

The GhostEater hobbles in my wake with her walking stick. She says, "Many of us spoke directly to Clearbold and every city leader we could find. We wanted justice for Milisent in Velm, too. The banishings in Mieiran cities weren't sufficient for the wrongs committed against you and your sister."

I turn back and look down at her. Though once likely my height, her back hunches her into a smaller stature. "I *still* want justice, GhostEater."

She assesses me with narrowed eyes. "As powerful wielders, we spend much of our lives attempting to fit in. To share our power out of a sense of joy rather than obligation and manipulation. But sometimes... sometimes it's wrong to pretend to be something we're not. I hope you are cruel when you find Oko and Anesot. I hope your punishment reminds the wolves and nymphs of our greatness and our honor."

I feel like a schoolgirl again, nervously standing before a teacher. "Okay."

She nods again. "It wasn't your fault, Helisent West of Jaws."

I've never felt closer to believing someone.

I *don't*, because this GhostEater doesn't know exactly what happened six years ago when Oko slaughtered my sister in cold blood. When I shared the bed of the warlock who ordered her death.

I slip away with a quick wave then hustle back toward the pier, trying to forget the ongoing drone of screaming.

It always echoes from the northwest where she was struck down.

By the time I reach the pier, the sun has set. I consider floating across the bay, but the gulf of dark water looks more intimidating beneath the glittering night sky. It almost looks like a writhing living thing, as though monsters twist below its surface and spew rushing waves.

I wait for the last ferry then take shelter with the other seasick wielders at the far corner of the deck. By the time we reach Cadmium's docks, I've thrown up everything I ate in Ultramarine.

I stagger onto the docks in Cadmium, too reeling to call on my magic until I've caught my breath.

When I'm well, I barter for lodging at one of the hostels lining the pier.

I write a note to Samson telling him to meet me tomorrow in the city's central plaza. I don't know where it is or what it looks like, but all cities have one. I pull out the white marble piece and try to figure out what it is before sending my note skipping through the air with tracking magic.

I nestle into the comfortable bed in my private room, then glance around at the walls that confine me. It feels strange to sleep in a room after months of nest-dwelling. Though I feel safe, it takes me a long time to fall asleep, the marble carving warm in my palm.

The next day, I wake and head to the central plaza.

Like Ultramarine, the macaques in Cadmium are rampant thieves. But the first robbery I see here is quickly ended by a wolf who manages to lunge after the fleeing monkey and snatch the necklace it grabbed.

The male wolf hands it back to a naiad with a smile, and the pair go on with their day.

It's one of several incidents I witness while sitting on the central plaza's highest wall and searching the passing wolves for a sign of Samson. I squint at each, certain the next hulking blue-black-haired male will be him.

The sun tilts across the sky.

Hours pass.

No Samson.

Thankfully, there's plenty to watch. Aside from the thieving monkeys, there's also a scuffle between nymphs. Though rare, they're unforgettable. A group of okeanids chase a screaming nymphling and catch him in the center of the plaza; from there, a swift and violent beating leaves the nymph in an unmoving heap on the pale stones.

The brawny nymph leading the beating yells, "Hoarder! Disgrace!"

Blood speckles the nymphling's vibrant orange layers as the group departs.

The rest of Cadmium's civilians carry on as though normal, stepping around the fallen nymph like he's a piece of furniture.

The nymphling doesn't move for a long while, though I can see his ribcage rising and falling at a normal pace. Eventually, he lifts his head, tears staining his bruised face, then he picks himself up and hobbles away.

Though not as calculated as the wielders or as balanced as the wolves in their justice, the nymphs are equally violent.

The only difference is that the okeanid below will be forgiven quickly if he manages to share his resources better. Then he'll be welcomed back by family and friends. Along with crimes like physical violence, hoarding is considered a travesty; greed is treated like a trait that must be weeded out with a swift, unforgiving hand by nymph leadership.

It disgraces the demigods and the abundance they provide. Just like the demigod's bounty is indiscriminate, its collection should also be.

For a moment, the beating makes me hopeful I'll see Samson.

Maybe he'll smell the blood and think I had something to do with it.

But there's no sign of him. Oko, neither.

By nightfall, I wonder if he might've picked up on Oko's trail. If that's the case, it's possible he already learned what he wanted from her and moved on. We never discussed what would come *after* finding the witch...

And Samson, rigid as he is in standing by his word, never promised he'd share her once she was found. I know because I was also careful not to promise the same.

As the marigold and magenta streaks of dusk fade to deep blue, I stand and clean my robe. I glance back toward the pier then study the twinkling lights of Ultramarine across the bay. They shimmer in the distance like a mirage that's half-sunken into the sea.

I make it halfway down a sloping lane that leads to the pier when a massive shape barrels toward me from a side street.

I scream and raise my hands, prepared to slap the intruder.

The figure stops, then glances at the passersby who stare at us. "Helisent. Sorry, I didn't mean to scare you."

I smooth my hair and take a deep breath. "I'm sober, Samson. My nerves are shot. And where the fuck have you been? Didn't you get my note? I waited for you in the plaza. My face was in the sun all day." I feel at my cheeks. "I think it's burned."

Once again, he glances at the beings who pass us. "I was meeting with Cadmium's pack leaders. Everything took a bit longer than I'd expected. Do you want to go by the water? Have you eaten?"

"Fine. I'm starving." I try not to dwell on his cedar scent or study his features, searching for a difference born in the last two days. "You lead the way."

He takes off down the slope. I practically gallop at his side to keep up.

I glance up at his face, wishing I could use my lilith so our height disparity wouldn't make me feel like a child.

He seems relaxed; for once, he's not toting his satchel. His bun is loose, strands of hair framing his face. As in Perpetua, his torcs look freshly shined.

As we head toward the docks, wolves bow to him and offer smiles. A few even offer low hoots; I'm told it's something akin to their howling, but it doesn't sound the same at all.

I don't think they notice me at his side. It could be that I'm too busy dodging other pedestrians or because I'm too short to be noticed.

At the piers near my hostel, Samson ducks into a restaurant. Its wooden panels stick out compared to the smooth buildings around us. The arched roof reminds me of Luz and Gamma, where most constructions are at least partially built of fir and pinewood.

Inside, the restaurant's mismatching tables and chairs also bring to mind eclectic Luzian tastes. The low rafters give the space a cozy feel, though Samson has to duck a few times as he leads us to a table in the corner.

He sits down, then gestures to the bench across from him. "I thought you might be missing Luzian specialties. The cook just moved here a few months ago. The pack leader recommended the food."

I glance around. Sure enough, the hesperides and dryads common to Gamma and Rhotidom dot the tables, chatting happily.

Beyond their pleasant conversation, I can hear the wayward echo of a witch screaming from far away. It's been chasing me all day.

Samson rubs his hands together. "Your note mentioned we're a week or so behind Oko and that a warlock named Itzifone can lead us to the other. Any idea if it's the same Itzifone we bartered with for information on Oko?"

I snort. "I've only met one warlock named Itzifone, so I

think we're in luck. He'll hand over his mother's location. All we need to worry about now is getting back to Luz before Oko finds a way to get to the other GhostEater. Shouldn't be too hard—if we leave tomorrow, we'll be back in Luz in a month."

"Let's eat well tonight, then. We can leave at dawn."

"Sounds good. I've had enough of the monkeys."

Rather than commiserate, Samson takes a quick breath. I notice because he usually breathes with a pace that would make someone think he's sleeping. His eyes dart from my hair to my lips to where my bottomless bag is strung across the back of my chair.

"Helisent..."

I fall still, suspicious about the shift in mood.

About how he says my name.

A waiter comes over with a wide smile. The okeanid, who has a halo of tight curls, batters through a list of specials, then she starts on the drink menu.

"Water!" I bark at her. "Just water."

She glances from me to Samson with raised eyebrows. "No food?"

Samson orders, then he waits for me to decide what I'd like.

I order, and then we sit in silence.

I wait for him to broach the topic he just brought up, but he looks shy. His shoulders hunch, hand holding his opposite arm.

"What did you want to say before?" I ask.

He sucks down another quick breath. Again, it's uncharacteristic enough to send my mind reeling. I'm too sober for this—

For whatever horrible thing he's about to tell me.

And with all the names the GhostEater spoke yesterday still so close to me... so much more *alive* than usual...

"Samson, *just say it*," I push, desperate for him to get it out.

He shakes his head, staring at the table. "You figured it out then?"

Figured out what? Am I not the only one here with a horrible secret?

My mind assembles a worst-case scenario: he knows I'm a centerheart, incapable of using my magic against those I love, and Clearbold sent him to turn me into Velm's next Bloody Betty.

Just like Anesot once tried to.

My hands start to shake, but I try not to lean into that— not until I'm sure.

Samson sets his hands against his chest "I didn't *mean* for it to happen, Helisent. I really, really didn't."

I shake my head as my temper fires. "Samson, *I don't know what you're talking about*. Just say it."

"Then why did you get so mad right now? What did you *think* we were talking about?" His brow bunches. He glances at the restaurant's entrance. He whispers, "Is this not about the seething?"

The seething?

The restaurant falls silent, and I realize I shouted the words. Luckily, the patrons go back to their meals after sparing a few glances.

I bow my head and rub my temples as my hands continue to shake. I try and fail to calm myself. "When did it start?"

Holy shit.

Samson has seen me naked.

"Skull. The flood."

Correction: Samson has seen me naked *for months*.

He goes on in a rush, "I didn't say anything to you because—"

"Because you didn't feel like telling me you've been playing with my titties in your fucking dreams?" I stare at him with a clenched jaw. My robe lifts around me, reacting to my emotions.

My hands clench into fists beneath the table—I *can't believe* this—

Out of everything he could have said, this was *not* what I was expecting.

He bares both of his palms at me. "I have *never* seen you naked. The dreams aren't sexual in nature."

"Oh, whatever, you fucking pussy-sniffer!" I hiss. "How did it happen?"

He lowers his voice so it's barely audible. *"Pussy-sniffer? Don't call me that. I said I didn't do it on purpose, Helisent. I was saving you from drowning* and then you started *clawing at me. I came up for air because I'm a mammal* and I *need air*, and then you..."

As though too scared to look at me, Samson looks at the table, then at the wall. His hands move and gesture at nothing. "You were trying to climb onto my head, all fucking akimbo, and then I just..."

I cross my arms. "This is why you weren't surprised by what the fucking selkie said about me being a red witch." I close my eyes and take a deep breath. "Tell me if you've seen me in my form, Samson. Yes or no."

"No. Never." I open my eyes to find Samson looking at me with a lowered chin and a tense jaw. He goes on, "I need you to listen to me carefully, Helisent. Can you *please* do that?"

"I need you to take *me* seriously, Samson. You have no idea how close I am to leaving right now. Wolves don't lie—so why does this feel dangerously close to being a full-on fucking *manipulation?*"

He exhales as though frustrated. "I'm terrified of magic. I would *never* do this to myself on purpose."

At least that checks out.

"It happened when I saved you in Skull, and the dreams started that night. I promise, Helisent, they aren't sexual. I thought they would be but..." Rouge flushes his cheeks. "I'm a child in the dreams."

I slap the table with my palms. "That's fucking *worse*! What the—"

"Listen to me," he says in a low baritone.

I lower my voice, too. It's not nearly as intimidating, but I hope it scares him. "Don't use your fucking Alpha tone with me. I will gore you with these horns like it's the War Years, little boy."

"*Then let me finish*. I'm twelve years old in the dreams, and you're you. You're this age. And you're... I don't know. You're comforting. You're really nice to me in the dreams. The exact opposite of how you're acting now. You ask me questions and tell me stories."

His words trip me up; I wasn't expecting that. My bristling anger settles into something manageable. I take a deep breath and close my eyes.

I'm comforting?

He goes on at a breakneck pace, "You aren't in your form— only your irises are red. And they only changed after the waricon. The rest of you looks the exact same. You're fully clothed in your robe. I didn't tell you at first because I thought it would only last a few weeks or a month. I thought we'd find Oko and it wouldn't matter."

He rubs his face as though trying to shake the tension between us. "But they haven't faded. It's almost every night. Sometimes I remember what we talk about. Other times, it's just the normal nonsense of dreams. Most of the time we're just hanging out doing something."

It sounds surprisingly innocent.

I'd also been led to believe that seethings were always sexual in nature.

I clear my throat, picking at the table's warped grains. "And what did you dream about last night?"

He sighs. "We were swimming. I've been teaching you in the dreams."

"Child Samson is teaching adult Helisent how to swim?"

"Yeah." He offers a short, nervous laugh. "It's going horribly."

In a way, it's worse that the seethings *aren't* sexual. That they don't give me a perfect reason right now to excuse myself from his life.

Samson was supposed to be a pawn. That's been changing rapidly.

I roll my eyes. "You shouldn't have told me about the seething."

He should keep his secrets; I won't give up mine.

I won't tell him that once we find Oko, I'll torture her for information on Anesot. And once she's given me the information I want, I'll kill her.

And when I find Anesot, I'll kill him, too.

Then I'll plead my case to the Class to be spared banishment from Mieira's cities. I'll have a roster of sponsorships to point to and say, 'Though dangerous, I am useful. I will be quiet now. Just don't make me go.'

By that point, Samson will be in Silent City with a Female Alpha at his side—assuming his collusion with me hasn't tarnished his reputation and legacy.

He eyes me now, head tilted like he can sense a hidden depth in my words.

Meanwhile, a witch's scream drifts over his left shoulder, echoing from the northwest.

He asks, "Is that... what you really think?"

I shrug. "I'm a wielder. I don't *pine* for the truth like you do."

I can't even stand my own truth.

That I fell in love with a warlock named Anesot while a witchling in Antigone. That he conspired with Oko to kill my sister to consolidate the magic my mother gave us at birth. That he did it thinking I'd never connect him to the murder or realize that he planned on using me and my new unmatched power for his own goals.

Samson's voice is soft. "But I'm a wolf, Helisent, and I *do* want to be honest with you. We've become friends over the last month. I've been thinking that I'd like to... I'd like *for us* to..."

For a split second, I question my decision.

For a split second, I wonder what I'd do if presented with the opportunity to be with Samson—not just as a travel partner or flirtatious cohort, but as a lover.

"For us to be allies in the future," he finishes. "Officially, I mean. I'll need your help with the Northing and similar topics when I'm Alpha."

I swallow. His words should be a relief.

And they do honor me—especially the idea that he might *need* me.

But it's not *me* he needs.

It's my power.

"Is the honesty too shocking?" he asks. "You look very shocked."

I wipe my face and shove everything I've thought in the last five minutes into the back of my mind. "Welcome to sober Helisent. She's a nightmare."

His smile is a relief. I offer one back, then I sit through the meal.

I pretend to enjoy the food. I even drink the water.

Samson tells me about his meeting with Cadmium's pack. It turns out Clearbold *is* aware of the disappearing okeanids, and local pack leaders assigned two war bands to look into the vanishings. Though they've uncovered little, their notes are meticulous.

This turns into a diatribe about the possibility of a fifth scent.

"What if there's... if there's another land beyond what we know?" Samson asks, full of wonder.

I barely keep up. I smile and laugh like someone bartered

with me to do it. All the while, the thoughts about Samson I
shoved into the abyss of my mind creep back to the surface.

Are his cheeks coarse because of his thick facial hair?
What if he rolls over on me while we sleep at night and
crushes me? And would he expect me to hang out with him on
the triplemoon?

When we finish our meal, I tell him I'm tired.

He walks me back to my hostel then points into Cadmium's mazelike streets. "I'm staying at the local estate. I'm sorry
I can't invite you to sleep there, too."

I shrug. "It's okay. I'll meet you in the plaza in the morning." He turns, but I grab his arm. "Wait—this thing—" I pull
the suede pouch with the white carving from my bag. "What
is it?"

Samson smiles in a way that makes me wonder how I ever
found him cold and unfeeling. "It's a snowflake, little bird.
Hold onto it for a while. Who knows when you'll get to see
the real thing."

He turns and leaves. When he's out of sight, I pull the
snowflake from the pouch and run my fingers along its carved
edges.

And when I can't stand what I feel for Samson or that the
GhostEater said my sister's name, and my mother's, and Oko's,
and Anesot's, I take off for the noisy tavern at the edge of the
street.

I sit alone at the bar and drink a bitterroot brandy. I
pretend I can't hear Milisent's screaming echo in the back of
my mind.

And then I drink another.

And then one more, until they all start to bleed together
into a never-ending goblet of tart liquid.

I flirt with the weird-looking hesperide who sits on the
stool next to me. We laugh and shout a conversation back and
forth, and when I put my hand on his leg, he smiles with a
drunken glory that I find familiar and easy and safe. And when

I forget about the snowflake and the wolf it belongs to, I drag the nymph back to my hostel.

And once I've peeled his clothes off and slipped my top down, I revel in a familiar and dizzying sort of bliss that I know will last until I careen back in a dead sleep.

The hesperide kisses my neck, licking and nibbling. He pulls back and asks, "Can I bite you?"

I snort a laugh. "Sure."

"Cool." And then he kisses my neck, and runs his tongue along my jugular, and when he presses his teeth against my skin, I like it.

Until he actually bites down, breaking the skin with a quick and painful rush.

I scream and push him off me, but his teeth are lodged into my flesh. In the split-second before my panic magic takes over, it feels like he *sucks* with all his might.

Past the fiery agony, I'm certain about what I feel.

His mouth pinches as though collecting my blood.

And then his teeth shift where they're wedged into my skin, as though he's gulping it down.

CHAPTER 14

FRAGRANT COAGULATED GOO

SAMSON

My son,
You will have two inner circles. The first is based on generational count
and clout. The second is based on safety and comfort. No one should
know about the second group—not even those in it. They will not be
those you call on when Night comes.

I try to ignore Helisent's hangover the next day, but it grates on my mind. Her ala tells me she's dehydrated with low blood sugar, and her pace is slow.

She doesn't slow us down as we leave Cadmium and follow the North Branch River back toward Luz. Still, I wonder what happened between me leaving her at her hostel last night and her arrival at the central plaza this morning.

Things had gone reasonably well at dinner.

I confessed the truth about the seething, she freaked out then calmed down, and we hashed out a tentative plan for the future. Not a *plan*, per se, just an acknowledgment of the truth: as two of Mieira's most powerful beings, we'll need to maintain contact even after we find Oko.

Forever, probably.

And now that we know Itzifone can lead us to the next GhostEater, and that Oko is only a week or so ahead of us, there should be little reason for Helisent to stress out.

I glance at her throughout the morning. She toys with the ends of her hair as she floats on her lilith. As with the South Branch, she floats above the river while I stick to the flat rocks on the shoreline.

Rain showers come and go, spurred on by the arrival of spring.

I barely notice the drizzling. I keep sliding my eyes toward Helisent, wanting to ask why she drank last night after we parted. Then I criticize myself for caring, and then I hate myself for *wanting* to know why she's always drinking, and then I remind myself that these aren't normal feelings.

A heavy silence hangs between us.

It continues even after we set up our camp after dusk.

I prepare the fire, then Helisent starts it with a snap of her fingers. She sets out her food to cook, then I do the same. Instead of reaching into her bag for a bottle of brandy, as expected, she looks at me with her eyebrows raised.

"It's the doublemoon, right?"

Overhead, the full faces of Vicente and Abdecalas glimmer behind the clouds. They burn my mind with a heat that's impossible to ignore, relieved only by the thin clouds that lessen their light.

I nod. "It is."

I've been hoping the doublemoon is to blame for my heightened anxiety about her state. Like the triplemoon calls wolves to phase, the doublemoon calls those with higher generational counts to turn skin, too.

The doublemoon tends to offer more of a choice when it comes to phasing. Depending on my stress level, Samsonfang appears and reappears.

He's close by tonight; I can feel his instincts compelling me to mark our campsite, to sniff Helisent's hair to check her ala more thoroughly, to separate Helisent's food from mine as it cooks near the fire.

"Are you..." She wags her head back and forth. "How are you feeling?"

This time, I raise my eyebrows. "Fine, thank you. How are *you* feeling?"

She clears her throat then reaches to adjust her vegetables near the fire. "Fine. I was talking about the doublemoon. Are you going to phase tonight?"

"I wasn't planning on it. Did you want some privacy?"

And what the fuck happened last night?

"No. I just wanted to know if you're... in control of phasing on the doublemoon."

I backtrack all my assumptions about her current state, wondering if she might be nervous about the moons and my self-control. I straighten my back, then try to lower my voice to a gentler tone. "I'm in control of my phasing at all times, Helisent. My fangself can sense that it's the doublemoon, but I won't shift randomly or without consent."

At least, not in theory.

"Right. But I heard that sometimes wolves aren't as aware that they're going to phase on the doublemoon. Once, a wolf told me even a little surprise can make them turn skin. Just if they're not prepared for it."

I bend my neck to look at her. I wait until she meets my eyes to tell her, "That isn't the case with me. It's not that I'm any better than other wolves—my instincts are just as strong. But I've... trained a bit harder. I can't have any lapses in control, Helisent. An Alpha can't show that type of weakness. I've been meditating since I was a toddler. I like to think I'm *very* practiced at containing Samsonfang."

Just like that, he pads through my psyche; I can almost feel the weight of his presence condensed into four paws.

Oh? Samsonfang asks.

I shrug off his sudden appearance.

Helisent nods. She glances over me, then reaches for her bottomless bag with a sigh. "Right, well... I hope you mean that."

My gut steels.

Did you mean it, Samson?

I shove Samsonfang into the back of my mind.

I focus on Helisent as she raises her hands to her neckline. Like when we swam near Lampades, her necklaces rise from her skin under a magical touch. Their backs untie at the nape of her neck, then float around to settle in her waiting hands.

She fishes inside her bottomless bag next. She bites her lip with her hand sunken inside. "Some crazy shit went down last night. I need your help cleaning my neck."

Did you mean it, Samson? Samsonfang is insistent now. *Did you?*

I suck down a huge breath as I realize Helisent must be injured. Adrenaline fires into my system, sending my thoughts reeling. Each is darker than the last.

I suddenly know how she must have felt last night when she could tell I was about to broach a serious topic but didn't know what it was.

"Cleaning your neck?" I struggle to keep my voice light. "What happened last night?"

Who hurt the witch, Samson?

She pulls a bundle of pale gauze and a container of salve from the bottomless bag.

"It happened in Cadmium?" I go on.

Testosterone and dopamine join my adrenaline. They flood into my saliva and leave a bitter taste in my mouth.

Who hurt the witch, Samson?
Find them. Make them—

"Be quiet."

Helisent freezes. She grips the medical supplies, brow bunching as she stares at me. "What? I didn't say anything."

"It's—I'm fine." I clear my throat. "Will you please tell me what happened?"

I'm too worked up to be embarrassed by the slip-up. Half of me is grappling with Samsonfang as he tries to tear through my self-control; he doesn't like this surprise, doesn't like that someone hurt Helisent, doesn't like that she's so small.

The other half of me is staring calmly at Helisent and controlling my facial expression, painfully aware that I just claimed to be fully in control of my fangself.

She glances across me. She may not be able to smell or hear as well as a wolf, but I wonder if she can sense Samsonfang is close.

She licks her lips and explains, "It happened in Cadmium. I went to a healer who said she'd tell the authorities what..."

I stand up.

Let me smell the wound.

"Let me smell it, Helisent."

Her features bunch. "Smell what?"

Smell the wound. Find the ala of the one who injured her. Track it back to Cadmium. Then kill it.

"Smell the wound. Find the ala of the one..."

I clear my throat.

She leans back and stares up at me, then she looks at the towering birch tree beside our campfire. "You said you wouldn't freak out. You seem like you're freaking out—*who are you talking to?*"

"Samsonfang."

Yes?

As the food cooks and the fire crackles, I take a long series of deep breaths to prevent the testosterone and dopamine from spreading. To slow down Samsonfang's escalating urges.

Helisent mirrors my long breaths; I can't tell if she's doing it for her sake or mine.

She says, "I'm going to tell you now. If you feel like you're going to phase, just run away so I don't get scared."

Scared? Of me?

"Yes, of you."

How ridiculous. I will give her vengeance. Give me form.

"No."

You haven't seen the injury yet.

"Because you're scaring her—"

"Stop talking to yourself!" Helisent screeches. Her look of unease has changed to conviction. The firelight lashes over her stilled features. "Sit down, right now. You and Samsonfang."

She points to the place at my feet.

Do not sit down. Phase. Run. Give her vengeance.

"Sit down," the witch repeats.

Do not sit down. Phase. Run. Now, Samson.

I haven't been this confused and distressed in years.

I squat on my haunches in an attempt not to bow to either. The lights of Vicente and Abdecalas that leak through the thin clouds burn where it touches my skin, setting off an instinct to run.

Tart foam starts to fizzle in my mouth. I swallow it, ignoring the disgusting taste.

Helisent starts a speeding explanation. "I took a stupid fucking hesperide back to my hostel last night. I know I said things went well with the GhostEater in Ultramarine, but she... fuck, this is hard to explain.

"The GhostEater knew me. Sort of. And she brought up a lot of uncomfortable truths about my life. I don't like to look at those truths, okay? That's the reason the phoenix fucked me up. It reminded me of... of things I don't like to think about."

Things she doesn't like to think about?

And what are those things?

Part of me is afraid of the answer.

Helisent rubs her face with her hands. "Whatever. I got

drunk and then I took a hesperide back to my place and he asked if he could bite me, and—"

"A *hesperide* asked if he could bite you?" I stand back up.

As though clubbed with shock, Samsonfang recedes.

His emotional domain doesn't include lesser feelings that arise from insecurity, like jealousy.

And what I'm feeling right now isn't only anger or indignation at wrongdoing.

It's a twang of envy.

I can't believe she lets men bite her. I know it's not the same for nymphs and wielders, but... it doesn't sound very respectful. And I like the idea that her partners, at least, *respect* her.

"I thought he meant like a cute little nibble." Helisent rolls her head back, staring up at the canopy. With a frustrated sigh, she looks at me. "It was *not* a cute little nibble."

Part of me is relieved that Samsonfang shied from my jealousy. But the rest of me is on-edge, prepared for a fight. "Let me smell your clothes. I need to make sure this wasn't a wolf biting."

She scoffs. "I know a wolf when I see one."

In my mind, adult Helisent and young Samson are climbing in the yew tree together. Samson is twelve, like in all the seething dreams. This time, he stops mindlessly following Helisent through the canopy as soon as he notices me.

He stares through the crossing branches and meets my eyes. His widen, as though dumbfounded.

"You let them?" he asks.

"Will you show me where he bit you?" I'll be able to tell if it's a wolf bite by the nature of the teeth marks, their angle, and their size. "If it's a wolf bite, we're going back to Cadmium, and I'm going to handle it."

"I was *going* to show you, then you started freaking out." She gestures to me. "You're still not sitting down. Like I said, I need help cleaning it. The healer gave me stuff, but... just see for yourself."

Helisent turns her head away. One moment, I'm staring at the soft flesh of her neck and the fine tendons that run between her collar and her jaw. The next, I'm staring at four puncture wounds.

The deep, swollen marks look like they're from upper and lower incisors. A few other shallow marks frame the main four.

Her throat shifts as she takes down a huge breath. "It doesn't hurt as bad as it looks."

With a long sigh, I sink onto my butt and sit next to her. "Helisent, I know what neck bites feel like, and mine always ached for days."

She gasps. "Who bit *you?*"

I raise my eyebrows. "My Alpha."

"Why would Clearbold bite you?"

The memories are loaded and painful enough that Samson-fang peeks through my mind again, just making sure.

He will not bite me again.

I shrug a shoulder. "Normal wolf stuff."

Helisent makes a long sound.

I hold out my hand and she sets the supplies in my palm.

Rather than turn away from me so I can assess the wound, she watches me with a pout.

This time, I recognize the expression. It's not sadness or nervousness, but a gentle hint that Helisent needs comfort. She shuffles a bit closer to where I sit with my legs crossed.

"Would you like a hug?" I ask.

She nods before shifting into my lap. Unlike our first embrace, I'm less nervous about why she's wrapping her arms around me, and slightly less focused on where her breasts push against me. Where her legs fold between mine.

I even stroke her back. I vaguely remember my mother doing the same when I was young.

She sniffles, head near the crook of my neck. I smell a few salty tears.

"It's okay, Helisent." It's not *really* okay, but I don't want to admit that. "It's okay."

She sniffles again. "Don't worry. This hug is for you, not me. You've been bitten, too, after all."

I roll my eyes. "It's *very* different. But thank you for being so selfless with me."

Her arms tighten before she pulls back. "Who were you talking to before? Samsonfang?"

I nod, hoping the night hides my blush. "That must have been weird. Sorry. A fangself is very loyal. Since we've been traveling together, he's... aware of you. He sees you as a tempo-rary pack member. I do, too. So knowing you were in danger set off an instinct to defend." I clear my throat. "And sorry again."

"That makes sense. He's sweet to worry about me." She wipes her eyes as she extracts herself from my lap. "And my magic is the same. It has its own instincts, sometimes. Are you sure wolves aren't magical—even a little bit?"

I sort through the sanitizing supplies she handed over. "I don't think we're *magicless,* if that makes sense."

"Sort of." She finally looks away from me, toward the chug-ging fire, to let me see the wounds closer.

I get to work and try to push away the thought that I might not know what Helisent looks like at all—if she hid this wound from me all day, she could be hiding other scars. I hadn't sensed a thing.

The punctures on her neck are deeper than I'd originally thought. She squirms and hisses while I work the solutions into each and then dry them.

We stop each time she accuses me of being too rough, or using too much solution, or focusing on the scrapes more than the puncture wounds.

I say, "If it hurts too much, we can take a break."

Each time, she responds with some variation of, "It doesn't *hurt*, Samson, you're just doing it wrong."

When I'm finished, we eat a silent dinner. After, she pulls out honeycakes that she brought from Cadmium. She splits one of the bun-sized cakes and hands it to me.

"So," she chirps, licking her fingers, "now that you've confirmed it's not a wolf who bit me, I was wondering if you'd do me a favor."

I finish the honeycake, wishing she'd brought a proportionate serving to share with me. Wielders have a bitter tooth; wolves have a sweet one. "What's that?"

"I want you to smell this guy's ala so that if you ever find him again, you can send word to me. Then I can take my vengeance."

I stack our dirty plates, then pick up the scraps on the ground. I try to find an appropriate response that won't make her feel like I'm shrugging off the incident.

"Wolves don't deal in vengeance, Helisent. If you told a healer what happened, then they're responsible for telling local authorities. They'll hand off all the information you provided so that nymph bounty hunters can track down the perpetrator and punish him. He's a nymph, after all."

Whatever they do when they catch him, it won't be sufficient.

Not given the sexual angle, the depth of the bite marks, or the fact that this witch means a lot to me personally.

But I have no jurisdiction over the actions of a hesperide.

Helisent asks, "What if we pretend I hadn't brought up vengeance?"

The Alpha in me says no; if I *do* happen to catch the nymph's scent in the future, it will be extremely difficult not to treat him like he's my subject and dole out punishment as I see fit.

Samsonfang says yes; someone needs to punish this hesperide for what he did to Helisent.

I shake my head at my own stupidity. "Fine. Hand it over."

To my surprise, she doesn't reach into her bottomless bag for an item of clothing. Instead, she hands me her bundled necklace. Though almost too numerous to count, the individual threads tie together at the ends to form a single necklace.

They're heavier than I thought they'd be.

Helisent taps one of the thick, beaded straps. I brace myself for the infrasound of her magic, but there's nothing more than a barely palpable buzz.

In the next second, dark bloodstains appear on the necklaces. Almost the entire bundle is coated in a fragrant coagulated goo.

I clear my throat to try to avoid my discomfort.

My distress.

That's *a lot* of blood.

When I was cleaning her wounds, I felt she was overly sensitive. Now I realize just how much blood she must've lost, and at what a quick pace, and all without healing magic to call on.

She must have been very afraid.

I exhale as deeply as I can, then lift the necklace to my nose.

I suck in until my lungs are full, sorting through the scents as I go: Helisent's nutrient-rich blood, her pheromones, ancient thread and metallic pieces, several nauseating perfumes, and multiple traces of male ala.

Not just general male ala, but complex notes; sweat, oil from their skin, semen, hair.

I tsk.

"What?" she asks. "What do you smell?"

All the men you've slept with in the past year.

"Your perfumes. They're very heavy." I suck down another

deep breath; there are three primary male alas my mind clings to.

The first two I recognize from her warren: Onesimos and the warlock.

The last is...

My body freezes.

I push the fabric against my nose and suck in a quick series of breaths.

I close my eyes to eliminate all other sensory stimulation.

"Please don't lick the blood, Samson. I really can't handle that."

I ignore Helisent's comment and repeat the process just to be sure.

I hand the heavy necklace back to her. As soon as it settles in her palm, the traces of dark blood disappear in lieu of bright colors and shined metallic pieces.

"What happened?" she asks. "Do you know him or something?"

"The exact opposite." I rub my face. "I don't know that scent."

She doesn't understand. "I'd never seen him before, either."

I shake my head. "No, Helisent. It's not that I don't recognize the nymph—it wasn't a nymph."

My head reels, world tilting.

"It's a fifth fucking scent," I say. "What the selkie told us before Lampades... about there being a fifth scent. This must be what she was talking about."

She shakes her head and shoves the necklace back toward me. "Smell it again."

I don't spare a look at the necklace. "I know what I smelled."

A shrill, wordless cry peels from her lips. "So there *is* a fifth being out there and it was *fucking drinking my blood?*"

"What do you mean *drinking* your blood? You said it bit you."

"I could feel it like sucking on my neck, like this—"

She lunges toward me and angles her head near my neck, as though preparing to demonstrate.

No—no—no—no—no—

I panic and raise my hand, palming her face before she can get close to my neck.

She thrashes her head to free herself.

I let go and she sits back, both of us startled.

"Well, *damn,* Samson. I wasn't actually going to bite you." She rolls her eyes. "Whatever. You probably remember what a hickey is. It felt like that, except he'd already bitten me so there was a *lot* of blood."

I stare at her, torn between my suspicion about the selkie's revelation and the fact that she just tried to bite me. Or demonstrate a bite on me. She doesn't seem to be too fixated on the latter, though it would be enough to warrant a waricon in Velm.

She takes another bite of her honeycake. "So do you think this means the selkie was right about *everything*? She said the fifth scent is kidnapping the okeanids, which means these filthy blood-suckers must be doing it."

My mind slowly switches gears away from Helisent and her wound to the selkie's words about Clearbold.

In the meantime, Helisent keeps drawing conclusions. "What else did the selkie say? The okeanids are taken to a place they don't swim? I guess that means the ocean. I heard selkies shrivel up if they get too close to the saltwater. I met an okeanid who swore they turn into seals as soon as they cross over.

"And then she said that Clearbold knows about the missing okeanids, which you confirmed in Cadmium. He's been sending war bands to investigate—that fits, too. He's not going to do it *personally*, but he's sending wolves on behalf of Velm."

That's not what the selkie said.

I remember her words perfectly.

She said, *"The Leofsige line has done nothing to stop the disappearances or investigate the fifth scent."*

Doing *nothing* is a lot different than what Helisent suggests: that Clearbold isn't going *personally*.

The selkie intimated my father hasn't been pushing for an investigation at all. Technically, the pack leaders in Cadmium didn't mention Clearbold, either. They said they'd been handling the disappearances by sending out war bands to investigate reports from Cadmium up to the northernmost coasts in Jaws.

I'd assumed that meant my father knew, since packs don't keep secrets.

What else could it mean?

Helisent continues at breakneck speed. "You know, the selkie also mentioned your magic, Samson. Maybe Samsonfang *is* magical, like we talked about earlier. We should ask a selkie if we see another one..."

She starts making wild and fantastical conclusions. But she doesn't mention my father or the selkie's words about the Afador line. Given how open she is with her opinions, it's a noticeable omission.

Does she think Clearbold might know and choose not to pursue justice for the okeanids?

Though the facts might auger suspicion, we're not working with all the available information. All I have are the creepy musings of a selkie, my mother's last letter, and a series of notes from Itzifone on Oko.

The warlock from Lampades comes to mind.

"One day you will need me, Samson 714 Afador. Remember my ala."

I wonder if my father has bitten off more than he can chew in the years he's spent ruling Velm alone. Typically, leaders have the wisdom and support of their fellow Alpha, but he's navigated seventeen years without Imperatriz.

Emerel's role as a Female Alpha has been more symbolic

than anything; she attends meetings and manages female war bands as needed. I doubt her advice offers much help.

How could it? She's not the Female Alpha; she's a stand-in.

Combined with a second heir, Clearbold has had to deal with more unforeseen circumstances than any other Alpha since the War Years.

And cunning wielders know it.

My gaze snaps back to Helisent's bright clean necklaces, as though I'd see or sense the blood-soaked threads that lie beyond her magic. I don't.

I do it throughout the day.

Then the next.

And the one after that, too.

Three and a half months into our search for Oko, Helisent and I hit a rhythm as we return to Luz as quickly as possible.

We wake at dawn. Helisent prepares the fire while I prepare food. Then we take down our hair and brush it as our food cooks. One morning, we even feel the other's locks. She's stunned by how thick my hair is, while I'm surprised by how thin and soft each of her strands is. They're like spiderwebs compared to mine.

Then we set off. Though Helisent attempts to goad me onto her lilith multiple days, I still fear the hum of her ultrasound. She assures me it won't bother me since it's a minimal spell, but I'm happy to walk at her side.

Most days, she holds my forearm while we venture.

I come to expect and enjoy it.

We stop for lunch; she lights the fire and I prepare the food. We rest while it cooks, then eat and keep journeying. Though I've spent similar stretches on the road from the early days with my war band in Mort, and again in Wrenweary, I was still young. My body didn't pack on the same muscle mass as it does now, which I notice more with every day.

I wouldn't mind except that my appetite is almost insatiable.

We usually look for villages and outposts as dusk nears. Rather than lodging, we search for a large meal for me and a bitterroot brandy for Helisent. To my great surprise, and strong disbelief, she claims not to carry a spare bottle in her bottomless bag.

Most days, we find a tavern that offers both. When we're full, we return to the tree line to make camp. We pass lodging often, but neither of us seems keen on them. I prefer to sleep beneath Helisent's nest to know where she is, listen to her snoring, and smell her ala.

I'm not sure why she's also unenthused by the lodging houses. I like to think she also likes being close to me, but that's the other thing about the warm, gentle, glowing camaraderie that blossoms between us: I have no idea if it's reciprocated.

Or to what degree.

Helisent is so loud and vibrant with everyone that I can't tell what's offered to me alone.

Part of me wishes this was my life; waking up with Helisent and walking toward a distant goal that feels like it will never be real and then falling asleep beneath her nest at night.

It isn't.

I keep reminding myself.

One day from Luz, reality looms like an ax waiting to fall.

In the early morning, beams of marigold sunlight crack across the plains south of Rhotidom, unspoiled by trees. Tiny flowers and green buds litter the fields, fed by the ongoing rain showers. The flat expanse ends with a hazy tangle of low buildings.

Luz.

Helisent climbs onto her lilith with a long sigh, staring westward.

I offer my arm to her, and she takes it with another long-winded exhalation.

We find the wide dirt path that runs parallel to the Mieira River. Marshy bushes and muddy patches dot the riverside, tangled with the narrow tributaries that flow from Rhotidom's wild forest.

A few other nymphs travel along the road: a hesperide with a toddler on her shoulders, a group of middle-aged naiads, a lone oread. Like us, they wander toward the faint outline of Luz.

Helisent stifles a yawn. "So what did me and baby Samson do last night?"

It's become a common question in the last weeks; she wants to know if I remember my seething dreams. The more I recount the dreams, the more detailed and memorable they've become.

It blurs reality for me. I can't remember my twelve-year-old self without thinking of Helisent and feeling like she may have known me as a child. Recollections of the dreams slip into my mind and take root, supplanting real memories. Supplanting truth.

"Well, now that you're comfortable in the water, you're very interested in the beach. Last night, you tried to convince me to go to Hypnos with you."

She throws her head back with a laugh. I study the clean planes of her neck beneath her heavy jewelry. She has scars from the bite in Cadmium that I wonder if I'll ever see again.

"Go to Hypnos, Samson! Missing okeanids aside, it's a fantastic place."

"I didn't know you'd gone to Hypnos. Me and my war band went to have fun there once. We snuck north when we had a week off."

She pinches me as a conspiratorial smile spreads onto my

face. "You *snuck* north? Please tell me about your war band years. All I know is that you partied in Hypnos and tracked a murderer near Tet."

"That was in Wrenweary. That was my second tour, not the first."

"What's the difference?"

"A wolf's first tour is less strict. I was seventeen when I joined my first war band near Mort. I served with a few other wolves my age—Rex, Riordon, Pietrangelo, and Berevald. That's where we learned the basics of Velmic justice: how to track, how to judge, how to punish.

"We were working with older wolves. Senior wolves nearing retirement take on juveniles like us. Like everything else in Velm, it's gendered. Women do the same, but with female veterans. So our first tour in Mort was more about learning. And having fun. A little trip to Hypnos wasn't too scandalous given our age and responsibility level."

She snickers, low and devilish. "Maybe I've thought you're more ascetic than you are."

But she doesn't ask any more questions about my war band years.

Instead, she refocuses on the western horizon. "Speaking of scandalous, should we figure out what to do with Itzifone? Maybe if you offer him a week in the Luzian Estate, he'll hand over his mother's location."

My mind flashes back to my first meeting with Itzifone. I'd asked what Helisent could offer that I couldn't; he'd looked directly at her bosom and said something about her personality.

The envy that flickered outside Cadmium rekindles. I shove it away quickly, keeping my eyes on the path before us.

"I still can't offer him a week in the Luzian Estate alone, so it might be best if you think of a better offer."

Helisent waves a hand. "Don't worry about it. I'll handle it. We go way back."

I have no words to articulate my thoughts, but they're revolving around the idea of Helisent luring the informant into a dark room with a bottle of liquor and giggle-filled whispers. I slide a look toward Helisent, eyebrows raised.

She throws her hair over her shoulder with a tsk. "What, Samson? Did you think you were the only being with a waiting list of potential suitors?"

The pit of envy in my stomach deepens. Wielders like Itzifone, who spend their lives hawking half-truths in places like Soulless, shouldn't be in the running.

"I see," I manage. "So what's the wielder version of a waricon?"

She shrugs with a chuckle. "Whatever I fucking say it is. Warlocks like Itzifone and Absalom only bother with me because they can sense my power, like the warlock outside of Lampades. They don't know I'm a red witch, necessarily. They just want the notoriety and free dove that comes with a powerful littleling."

"Is it—is it like with me?"

She chews her lip. "Is it like what with you?"

"I'm the last Afador, so I'm responsible for bearing the next Alpha. My child will carry on the Afador line. And you're a red witch, which I'm led to believe are rare... so...?"

Rare is probably an understatement.

Before we went to Skull, she asked if red horns were still hung in Bellator. Even before I realized she was a red witch, the mention sent my stomach into knots. Now it's enough to make my palms sweat.

Bellator Palace is full of horns.

They're hidden in the deepest hall in the palace, far from public eye and wandering visitors. The final room has no windows, no furniture—not even a cubic marble throne.

Two cushions sit on the ground, surrounded by light-pink stones whose function I've never learned. The marble walls go up and up and up, the tallest room in the palace, which ends with a glass skylight.

And hung from the floor to the ceiling are sets of horns, curled and jagged and blood-red. I never bothered to count; there were hundreds, maybe close to a thousand. Most have only two developed horns with needle-sharp tips, but some sets near the ceiling have four.

As a child, they meant nothing to me. Like Helisent touched a wolf's hide, I touched the horns hung within reaching distance. As a young adult, the room disgusted me; some horns still smell like blood, like hair, like entrails. But as a man, my curiosity renewed.

I've only seen horns on the warlocks foolish enough to showboat in front of me.

Only one had two well-developed, gold-hued horns reminiscent of the red sets hung in Bellator. They jutted from his forehead before curving back along his scalp.

Helisent likely has four red horns. But when I imagine what they look like, I don't have a clear image. I imagine one of the sets hung in Bellator, sawed off at their thick bases.

I slide my eyes toward Helisent. *Where do her horns grow?*

She stares ahead with a withdrawn expression. "It's not just a one-and-done deal like with you and the Female Alpha. I need daughters, not sons, to pass down my power. And even if I was sure I could have a daughter, same-sex births are risky for wielders. Not physically speaking, just magically. Passing down my magic to a daughter would split my store in half."

Her hand slips away from my arm. "I don't have to decide anything soon. I have a few names on the shortlist. But... I guess..."

Is that why she sleeps around?

Is it like try-outs?

"But what?" I ask.

"But I don't trust wielders. That's why it's easy to string along the Itzifone types. They're too fickle and self-centered to manipulate me. You might see him as a bit... unsavory because he exchanges information with bounty hunters. But he's simple beneath it all. That's comforting to me."

I pull my morning cigarette from behind my ear. Helisent lights it for me with a quick snap of her fingers.

She goes on, "He works with the unnumbered wolves in Luz, too. The pack leaders obviously don't do anything if something happens to an unnumbered wolf, but Itzifone keeps track of who does what. It's basically a blacklist for wolves who hurt unnumbered wolves. He does it for Gautselin—that's another one of my friends. He's unnumbered."

The name rings a bell...

The unnumbered wolf with the hesperide on his arm flashes through my mind; the couple that led me to Soulless. I almost roll my eyes. "Of course, you know Gautselin."

She chuckles. "He told me he knew you. He likes you, you know."

I nod and nurse my cigarette, uncertain how I feel to have the support of an unnumbered wolf. It certainly doesn't bolster my image as a leader with conviction. Velm has offered no leniency for unnumbered wolves—not even under Imperatriz's optimistic Northing plans.

"When did he tell you that?" I ask. "I met him the day I met you."

"Oh, he came to the waricon. Malachai attacked him—and one of his little fuckboys attacked Elvira. She's an unnumbered wolf, too."

I stop walking as her words settle in. Her lilith comes to a halt at my side.

Aside from a quick catch-up post-waricon, I never discussed the incident in more detail with Helisent. "Malachai *attacked* someone at the waricon? I had assumed this was a *minor* run-in."

Unnumbered wolves aren't invited to waricons... but *attacking* an unnumbered wolf, no matter how warranted, is below a wolf who claims to have a shot at becoming Alpha. It's hitting below the belt.

"Well, Gautselin is unnumbered," Helisent explains. "Attacks like that happen a handful of times a year—I think he's used to it. Didn't even bat a lash. Elvira didn't like it, though. She was about to punch one of them back before I stepped in."

"A female wolf was attacked by a male wolf? Was she unnumbered, as well? Was it one of Malachai's friends who attacked her?" I turn and glance behind us, as though I'd see Invidio's village or the thin forest surrounding the waricon grounds. Instinct compels me to go back, to search for Malachai, to somehow right this retroactively.

Helisent's amused tone becomes curt. "I'm not sure—I don't know any of his friends. It was definitely a male, though. And yes, she's unnumbered."

I remember Brutatalika's comment in Lampades about a witch insulting Malachai. Panic flushes through me at the idea of Helisent confronting him. "And... how did you handle things?"

She tsks. "Let's not have this conversation. It was in Mieira —far beyond the bounds of your authority, Samson."

"Not if we're going to be allies someday." Just like having an unnumbered wolf in my corner may cause some wolves to raise their eyebrows, so would having a vigilante witch. "In the future, please notify me if Malachai acts up. He's *my* problem, Helisent. He must be punished—*by a wolf.*"

She whips her head toward me. Her brow is bunched, her nose curled. "And let him beat my friends in the meantime? How long and brutal is a standard beating? How much blood is enough, Samson? I'm sorry—I've never bitten necks or punched people. I may need a little reminder."

I take a deep breath and continue walking down the road. She follows a moment later.

For a few minutes, we don't say anything.

I work off my bitterness toward feckless warlocks like Itzi-fone, my resentment toward my own people for being so quick to violence, and my uneasiness at the idea of Helisent choosing to do something that would make it difficult to be her friend as a representative of Velm.

Maybe I'm saying it more for my own sake. "I'm going to address the lives of unnumbered wolves once I'm Alpha. It's going to be one of my focuses with the Northing—a greater understanding between numbered and unnumbered wolves.

"In the least, a formal agreement between pack leaders and influential unnumbered wolves like Gautselin. So the cities are safe. Please let me do that, Helisent. As I need to. As my people need me to."

I stare at Helisent until she turns her head to look at me.

She raises her eyebrows with a look of contempt. "Words mean little to wielders."

I look ahead, frustrated that she doesn't seem to see my point. "And trust? What does trust mean to wielders?"

"Trust is what the weak cling to when their shaking hands can't hold more, dear wolf. I have little use for it."

"Fine, Helisent. That's just fine." I roll my shoulders and finish my cigarette in a single drag.

I stare across the Mieira River and chew on multiple responses.

The weak have nothing else to cling to, Helisent.

It's too condescending. And I don't know if I understand weakness well enough to back up the statement.

Trust is all that binds our world together, Helisent.

I'm not sure it's true anymore. Maybe in the fragile decades after the War Years, but not in a city like Luz. Beyond trust is desita, possibility, and all that's been wrought between wolves, wielders, and nymphs in the last centuries.

Trust is not lost on the world, Helisent, just on you.

That's it.

Almost—

I sneak a glance at the witch. She folds her arms as she stares in the opposite direction as me, chin raised with a defiant stance. Even her lilith's dangling ornaments have stopped jingling, as though rescinding their metallic song from the world.

Trust is not lost on the world Helisent, just on you.

But I will find a way to remind you that it matters.

CHAPTER 15

CENTERHEART

HELISENT

Honey Heli,
Just come home. Are you scared of what I'll say? I can't think of why
else you'd avoid me. I'm always on your side, remember? Even when
you're acting like a piece-of-shit brat. Come home now. You're my
piece-of-shit brat.
Mint Mili

I return to Luz how I left it: with a grumpy wolf at my side.

I stick to my lilith as we pass the wooden watermills on the city's outskirts. The groaning mills are followed by the scent of foxglove and damp stone, then the vibrant noise of the seedier streets that house Coil and Solace. The sun sinks at our backs and gilds the city with blazing marigold, which catches on the metallic spires craning from wielder-built roofs.

Since our disagreement yesterday morning, Samson and I have stuck to minimal interactions. As we pierce the first wide streets that lead into the crooked labyrinth of markets, I slide from my lilith and walk at his side.

I glance northward where my warren lives, where fluffy canopies peek above the stone buildings. I'm not sure how to feel about my return. I glance southward where the Luzian Estate sits near the temple district's empty plaza of columns.

For the last few days, I've tried to figure out what I'm going to say to Onesimos. How I'll explain the last four months and how they changed me.

I'm suddenly ravenous for life after Oko and Anesot's deaths; I'm also suspicious of how my plans will pan out.

I hear Milisent's screaming less and less, and the echoes of her pain are shifting my desire for...

For what, Helisent?

"Helisent."

I turn and realize Samson has stopped walking. He clasps his hands behind his back in the center of Luz's busiest cross-road. I hadn't noticed how far into the city we'd wandered. Nymphs and wielders hustle around him, while a few passing wolves offer smiles and nods.

I stare at his chest. I don't want to look at his face anymore. Until our disagreement yesterday, I'd seen him as entirely separate from his father.

"He's my problem, Helisent. He must be punished—by a wolf."

His critique, no matter how well-placed or deserved, changed how I see his face.

Now I see Clearbold's clone. Clearbold's heir. Clearbold's *son*.

"I'll deal with Itzifone tonight. I'll come to the estate in the morning, then we'll leave when you're ready." I raise my eyebrows in case he wants to object..

He studies the city at my back with narrowed eyes. Eventually, he slides them toward me. "Tell your warren I'm sorry for keeping you so long. Goodbye, Helisent West of Jaws."

Before our disagreement yesterday morning, we'd drifted close.

A closeness that involved every routine: meals, washing,

sleeping, resting, planning. Every morning, I woke to birdsong and his voice. Every night, there were three moons and the fire and Samson sitting beside me. Rain showers and the scent of his cigarette smoke and his leather articles each day.

I don't know why, but a handful of insults flood my mind.

Don't say my name, Samson. I hate how it sounds.

Or something like, *You're not sorry for anything. Don't pretend to be.*

Maybe just, *fuck off, wolf.*

Instead, I nod.

I turn away and beeline for Luz's northern district. I stick to the side of the road and offer half-hearted waves to the beings who recognize me: a hesperide looking to barter dove for jewelry, a warlock whose name I can't remember asking for directions to Coil, a naiad who asks me to tell Zopyros she's looking for her.

When I reach my stone building dotted with canary poop, I stare up at our peach-painted terrace. The dangling plants shift in the wind, beckoning. But returning feels less familiar and less comforting than I thought it would.

Like putting on an article of clothing that doesn't fit anymore.

I go inside with a sigh and walk up each stair, hoping it will endear me.

At the landing, I stare at the door for a long time.

When I finally push it open, I almost run into a witch with a red cloak. She laughs and pulls the door toward her, as though about to leave.

I gasp when I see Esclamonde's narrow face and large eyes.

"Bitch!" I shout.

She gasps, too, then tries to pull the door shut.

I shoulder past it while she screams and flees inside.

I raise my hand to cast a halting spell, but she slips behind Pen just in time for cover. Pen reacts by also raising his hands, opening his mouth as though prepared to intervene. In the next second, he recognizes me with a tick of his head and a flashing smile.

He lowers his hands. "Helisent West of Jaws. Hello, dear witch!"

I stay focused on the slivers of red cloak visible behind his cerulean tunic and pants. I keep my hands raised. Part of me is secretly relieved to have an outlet for my brewing discontent from the past two days.

"*Move*, Pen. Didn't Absalom tell you to get rid of the mentee? Get out of the way so I can teach the witchling a lesson. She wanted to learn something here, didn't she?"

Pen's features bunch with confusion. "Wait, what? What did Absalom say?"

Behind him, Esclamonde starts shouting an explanation. "My mother stole the earring from me to track you! Onesimos gave it to me—"

"Where is he?" I finally look around the apartment and realize we aren't alone.

Aleixo, Melita, and Zopyros watch me from the kitchen. They stand at the counters and stove. Aleixo has stopped cutting a spread of green vegetables, while Melita and Zopyros also stand stupefied before their steaming pots.

"Oh, look, it's Helisent."

"Hi, Helisent."

"Demigods aren't smiling upon you today, huh, Helisent?"

I offer them a wave, then turn back to the wielders. Pen crosses his arms with sheepish amusement as he stands resolutely before Esclamonde. The witchling hunkers behind his skinny frame, hands raised to cover her head as though expecting an explosion.

She goes on, "Simmy went back—"

"No, no, no," I bellow. "You call him Onesimos. *I* call him Simmy. First the earring, then the nymph? Good fucking moons, Esteban!"

The witchling keens with distress. "Just chill out, Helisent! I can't think when you're freaking out—"

"This is not even me freaking out!"

Pen raises his eyebrows with the silent suggestion that I might be freaking out.

I smooth my hair and take a huge breath like Samson taught me. It barely helps settle my fizzing thoughts.

I manage to lower my voice to a normal tone. "Fine, then. Speak in a coherent fucking fashion and tell me how I'm somehow mistaken thinking *your whore mother* tracked me down to accost me *in a public tavern* for abandoning you. I was perfectly clear! I never wanted you!"

Pen winces. "Aw, Heli. She's not that bad."

Esclamonde goes on, "My mother came here and tried to take me home when she found out you'd left. We went out to eat, and she stole one of the earrings from me. I told you, Onesimos *gave them* to me."

The nymphs in the kitchen offer a few confirmatory grunts, which Pen backs up with a nod.

"I didn't realize they were yours," the witchling goes on. "My mother must have figured it out, took them, and then tracked you down. She's just angry with me because I won't go back to Antigone."

I narrow my eyes as my stubborn anger cools. "And why don't you want to go home? You'd never have to ground-walk again in Antigone."

"Because you were right. Luz is the greatest city in Mieira."

With a sigh, I glance around. It looks like Pen was sitting at the desk, and Aleixo, Melita, and Zopyros were cooking dinner. A few spare articles of clothing lay on the ground, forgotten, while the bed mats and blankets sit neatly before the largest arched window. It's all so hopelessly familiar and comforting that it reminds me I'm exhausted and hungry more than I am enraged.

I strive for a neutral statement. "Actually, my opinion may

have changed now that I'm well-traveled. Ultramarine is pretty cool. Fucking zero out of ten for Cadmium, though."

Esclamonde stands at her full height behind Pen. She peaks over his shoulder with wide eyes, studying my hands. "Onesimos has the other earring. He took it back once he heard my mom stole the other one. He was really upset with her. Oh— he's visiting home. He'll be back soon. He said to tell you that he wasn't *moving* back to Lake Deidre."

My stomach coils; I wish Simmy was here.

I need his advice. Need to figure out precisely which mess I've made is more deserving of my attention right now—the useless mentee, or Samson's stupid face, or Milisent's vengeance. It's always fallen to the latter, much to the detriment of all else.

"I would never disrespect you, Helisent West of Jaws," Esclamonde goes on.

I roll my eyes. "I guess it's fine. I was once just as incompetent and naive as you." I open my arms, once again finding myself too tired and hungry for any more confrontation. My warren wouldn't lie for her benefit, and if Simmy approves, then she must be trustworthy. "Do you do hugs yet?"

With a nervous smile, Esclamonde slinks around Pen. "Yeah." She scans me once, as though uncertain about my offer, then rushes into the embrace.

After touching and hugging Samson last, she feels like a bony little creature.

When she pulls back, I stare at her wide eyes and her arched nose and finally see it.

Holy shit, we are like birds.

She straightens to stand at her full height and clears her throat. "I'd like to take you out to make up for the wrongdoing my mother committed against you."

Before I can correct her on the direct offer, Pen meanders to her side. "To a wielder, that sounds *suspiciously* nice. Try to be more casual."

Esclamonde nods. "Right." She turns back to me. "Helisent, want to get fucked up? I'll barter for everything. This lady wolf named Elvira Ultramarine owes me a favor—a *huge* one."

I raise my eyebrows. "Oh, you're bartering now—and with wolves? By the way, be careful around Elvira." I can still see the wolf cocking her fist, ready to take down one of Malachai's cronies. "I might have made an enemy of her."

"Oh, really? Well, we don't have to go to Coil." She shrugs. "I know all of the best party houses now. Did you know there's a thing called *after hours*? It's a party that starts *after* the other parties."

I raise my eyebrows higher, too stunned by the changes in the Black Rock Antigonian's to respond.

As though sensing my disbelief, Pen offers me a wide smile.

"The mentee has become a bit of a passion project of mine. I think it's the age difference and the fact that she can't party for shit. Always throwing up and getting lost. Very innocent and helpless, like that little canary last year whose mother abandoned it. Remember?" He elbows Esclamonde. "We taught it to fly. Well, almost."

I ignore the witchling's confused response and Pen's wayward explanation to head toward the cooking nymphs. Zopyros's hug lingers longest. She holds onto my wrist until I've sampled the broth she stews, which includes a sweet flavor from Hypnos.

When dinner is ready, the group batters me with a series of predictable questions.

They ask for details about the underlying character of Velm's next Male Alpha, about my next departure in the morning. About macaques, Skull, and spending a triplemoon with a wolf. I glance at the washroom door, eager for privacy and a chance to decompress.

When dinner ends, I warm the water and indulge in a long bath. I sort through the bottles of perfume and soaps and oils.

In the last month, I've barely worn any since becoming aware of how acutely Samson smells everything.

When I'm clean, dinner concludes with a bitter tart.

The questions from earlier intensify, especially after Makarios and Evgenia return home. I nurse a bottle of bitter-root brandy and pick at the colorful tart until their interest in my journey wanes.

Before Eslcamonde can gorge herself into a deep slumber, I tug at her red cloak. "You and I need to speak before I leave again. So long as you stay here, you're my problem, after all."

Only Pen narrows his eyes, glancing from the red-cloaked witchling to me.

"And where are you going?" he asks. I know what he really means. *And where can I inquire about Esclamonde in case this is the last time I see her?*

I tsk. "To see Boonma. Did you want to come?"

At the mention of the stalwart old witch, the nymphs recoil. Even Pen looks a bit turned off, though I've seen warlocks in the establishment before.

I stand and clap my hands clean. "I'll take that as a no. We'll be back tonight. Does anyone need any dove or spells before I go?"

Esclamonde also stands, then heads for her bottomless bag at the far side of the room.

Zopyros raises a hand. "Warm the bathwater, please. Escla-monde's warming magic doesn't last." She hunches her shoulders and glances at the witchling. "But it's gotten *much* better recently."

Makarios leans forward and grabs the end of my peach robe. "I'd love extra dove for washing. We're running low, so we've been doing things the old-fashioned way." She smiles guiltily, highlighting the gap between her wide front teeth. Her brown eyes twinkle like amber beneath her thick, turquoise eyelashes and eyebrows. "I'm starting to get blisters. *Blisters*, Helisent."

I hand out dove, warm the bathwater, then help Aleixo send a message to a friend in Lampades.

Esclamonde scurries after me as I head to the door, waving back at the happy warren that sits with empty plates between them. With a rush of footsteps, she runs down the stairs. I try to keep up, holding my breasts and wondering why the mentee is sprinting.

She bursts past the entrance and then throws her arms out. "I love Luz," she shouts into the muggy night air.

One passing warlock leans to whisper to his companion with a sly smile, while a grizzled old dryad looks around as though expecting to see something incredible.

I glare at her as I guide us toward the market district. "Are you on fucking dextro?"

"No. It makes me throw up. And then I get confused and lost and Pen has to find me." She sighs happily. "So what's Boonma? No one has mentioned it—and they've taken me just about everywhere.

"Well, at first it was just Onesimos and Zopyros. Then everyone else started to get used to me. Pen showed me where all the good food is, and the nymphs started taking me to taverns and concerts and trade shows. I don't think Makarios likes me very much, but neither did you, at first."

She even talks like a nymph now. And for all her fear four months ago, she ambles comfortably through the streets. Her chin is raised, her mouth set in a happy line.

"Right. Great. Well, Boonma isn't a place. She's a witch. Boonmasent Luz."

"Oh. I see. I haven't made any witch friends yet."

I nod with knowing. "I'm glad you aren't stupid enough to think you might have."

I turn into a crooked alley in the center of the market district. We pass a luxury textiles shop with furs, velvets, and cotton straight from Rhotidom. Then comes the bookstore dressed like a plain library that only offers erotica. Last is a windowless single-story stone building.

The wooden door is thick and spotless. I knock with all my might.

"*What?*" someone shouts from within.

Esclamonde flinches and withdraws, but I lean closer. "It's Helisent West of Jaws. I'm with a witchling. We want to get our nails done."

"Come back later. We're full."

"Are you fucking serious, Boonmasent? I'm going to knock the door down in ten seconds if you..."

The door rips open to reveal a livid witch. Though in her early seventies, Boonmasent's plump lips and curved eyebrows retain their animation. Only her settling smile lines and crow's feet hint that she passed her prime.

Boonmasent sets one hand on her hip and bears her weight onto a single foot to account for her pregnant belly. Though I'm not familiar with pregnancy or children, she can't be far from delivery; she's uncomfortably round.

A sound of disgust peels from me.

I take a step back like Esclamonde. "Why didn't you say you were pregnant? I would have left immediately."

Esclamonde leans to whisper in my ear, "We should go. There's nothing unluckier than a pregnant witch. At least, that's what we say in Antigone."

I lean away from her warm breath. "They say that everywhere. Chill out."

Boonmasent glares at the witchling. "You're not supposed to say it out loud, either. Bad luck has ears."

She reaches into her black robe and pulls out a letter. With another seething look at Esclamonde, she hands it to me. "The witchling's uncle left this here for you a few months back. He came straight from Septegeur. Looked like he was in the Class, too, so I couldn't exactly tell him to fuck off."

Fuck.

I quickly review my tantrum in the village in Gamma.

I don't remember threatening the Class—only Absalom and Eslcamonde's mother. Still, the letter could be entirely personal if Esclamonde has an *uncle* in the highest order of wielders. The Class isn't supposed to expect favors or ask for them, but the private group notoriously runs without a rulebook.

For a second, I wonder if her uncle might have sent Esclamonde here to spy on me.

I snatch the note and turn to glare at the mentee. "My fucking moons, Esteban. I hope you're worth all this trouble someday."

She hangs her head and follows me as Boonma opens the door to let us in.

Though the old witch stands aside to let me by, she bares her bulbous stomach toward the witchling. Esclamonde has to graze her belly as she passes. She lets out a forlorn squeal as her abdomen slides against Boonma's.

I step to the side in the cramped vestibule and tuck the letter into my bottomless bag. Esclamonde presses herself against the wall so Boonma can pass toward the next door.

She waddles a few steps, then she works the locks with a grunt. Her white hair is strewn into a messy bun rather than its usual pin-straight glossiness. Her robe is dark and loose, not tight and detailed. She looks half-ready for the grave.

I lick my lips. "Not to sound rude, but aren't you too old to be pregnant?"

"That's what I thought." She pulls the door open. "I've been letting men shoot in me for three years. That's what they always told us growing up—a witch isn't fertile past sixty-seven."

No one has ever told me that. Based on the perplexed look Esclamonde slides my way, it's her first time hearing the rumor, too.

Bonnma shoulders open the next door then gives us a large berth to pass her.

The cold vestibule leads to a large hall. Massive candle chandeliers and firelit sconces cast honey light and warmth across the vast room, which lessens the severity and chill of the cobbled walls.

On one side of the room, clear pools of water are inlaid into the stone floor. Naked witches float in the pools with their heads lolled back and their eyes closed. In the center of the room, Boonma's silent witchlings work oils and conditioners into the white hair of seated witches. Others kneel on the ground to scrub at their bare feet, propped up on velvet stools.

A series of tables and chairs sit to the left where employees work on hands and faces, squinting at their relaxed subjects to smooth wrinkles and cover dark spots.

No one bats a lash at our entrance. I can feel the hum of Boonma's magic as it works to silence and contain the room's noise, from the trickling water in the pools to the low conversation shared between a few witches.

"Where are we?" Esclamonde whispers in my ear.

"It's called a *spa*," I whisper back.

"I thought only wolves did *spas*," she murmurs.

Boonma crosses her arms. "They invented them, but we perfected them. Now what do you want? Did you say nails before?"

I nod. "Hands and feet. I've been traveling for months. And Esclamonde needs to learn a few things."

With a click of her tongue, Boonma turns and looks around to survey the full, silent room. Though I've never seen the witch smile, I've also never seen her lose her temper or lose a customer. What she lacks in joy she makes up for with unbeatable service and the absolute guarantee of privacy.

Luz is littered with nail salons.

But this is the only place that was built by witches, for witches.

"This way." Without looking back, Boonma waves us forward toward the farthest inlaid pool.

I follow her around tables and pools, careful not to stare too long at any of the witches we pass.

"You're responsible for casting your own smothering spells on top of mine if you want total security, Helisent. My magic is out of whack with this little fucker. It must be a daughter. The other day, I woke up and everything in my bedroom was floating right below the ceiling. Took me an hour to get everything back in place."

I stare at the black fabric covering her belly. "I thought those were just rumors. Why is it wielding now? Can't you tell it not to?" The more I think about it, the less secure I feel. "And should you... be here... if that thing is casting spells already?"

"Oh, I told it a lot of things. Didn't listen to its dear mother, though. I can sense when it's gearing up to use magic now. You're safe here, Helisent West of Jaws. Have no fear." She looks back with a pessimistic cackle. "Who do you want working on you? Any preference?"

I lead Esclamonde to the wire rack hanging from the wall then shrug off my robe. I glance at Boonma's belly a few more times. "Doesn't matter. Give me a minute to set up."

Boonma waddles away without another word.

I cast smothering magic around our square pool as Esclamonde undresses. Though not all witches come here to exchange secrets, no one bats an eye when I raise my hands to cast the spell.

When I'm done, Esclamonde stands next to her discarded robe as though suddenly shy. She glances at the neighboring pools where naked witches float in the water, their hair and breasts buoying on the surface.

I ignore her discomfort and slip off my dress and boots.

With a happy sigh, I step into the shallow pool. The water only reaches my thighs, so I hunker down for full coverage. I've never felt more comfortable in the water thanks to Samson's brief swimming lesson near Lampades. I paddle with my hands a few times, testing my skills in the shallow water.

I think about boy Samson and adult Helisent. I didn't ask Samson if he dreamed of us last night before we parted. I wonder if we argued like we did in real life.

Esclamonde follows with a few extra splashes. She flounders as she settles onto her knees, short hair half-wetted.

"So what did you want to tell me?" Her wide eyes trail me as I settle against the pool's wall.

"Well, you're still my mentee. And judging by your mother's stupid fucking attitude, I'm guessing you're still realizing how different life is outside of Antigone and Septegeur. For wielders, at least. So listen up."

Esclamonde nods with a tense jaw. Part of me wonders which lessons she's already learned the hard way.

"First, don't trust a warlock until you've known him for ten years. That doesn't mean you can't enjoy his company or want to spend more time with him. Trust is... ill-advised. For example, I've known Pen for almost four years. I don't trust him, but that hasn't stopped us from being close."

Her round eyes narrow. "But why don't you trust Pen?"

"Because I haven't known him for ten years. No one can hide their true self that long. I'll trust him soon."

"But you live together."

"Sharing a bed means nothing. And the comment about warlocks was just a lead-up to the important shit, which is actually about witches." I glance at the rack on the wall where our bottomless bags hang. "Did you want to write this down?"

She shakes her head. "I got rid of the notebook. Onesimos said it made me look stupid. I'll remember what you're saying. No trusting warlocks for ten years. And what about a witch?"

"Easy. You never trust a witch. If a witch smiles at you,

check your pockets and your bag. Know what I mean? The only time I'd say you're in the clear is if she insults you a bunch first. Then she's probably reasonable. Boonmasent, for example, probably likes you a fair amount based on all the glaring."

Esclamonde buoys away from me. Her eyes cut back to me multiple times, but her lips remain pinched in a line. "So I guess that means you like me, too. But..."

I raise my eyebrows. "But what?"

"Nothing." She huffs, then uses touching magic to tuck the wild hairs at her temple behind her ears. "I just think it's dumb we don't trust each other, especially considering how nervous we make the other beings. Why do we make enemies of each other?"

With another sigh, she moves around the pool's perimeter. She floats over my legs, using her hands to push off the pool's smooth bottom.

She shakes her head with a sigh. "And *I am* very trustworthy. I'm not just saying that either. I'm kinder than the others. I've always been soft. That's how my mother describes me. But I'd never hurt another being for pleasure. I mean it—I'm a center—"

I cast smothering magic on her before she can get the word out.

She jolts to a stop, glaring at me.

I close my eyes, drag down a huge breath, then open them again.

She's a centerheart?

Fuck.

I hadn't realized.

I return to her glare and raise a finger to emphasize my point. "I'm going to let you speak, but only after you understand *how fucking idiotic it is to tell anyone you're a centerheart.*"

My heart reels as I shift onto my knees and lean toward her.

I should've put it together before.

I abandoned a *centerheart* witch in Luz.

I go on with a deepening sense of guilt, "I'm guessing your mother is the only one who knows? And your father, if he's around?"

Her mother's anger comes into perspective. Her uncle's letter, too.

I replay her mother's grimace as she rushed toward me in the tavern in Gamma and Absalom's desperation as he followed her.

She wasn't angry because I didn't volunteer to take care of her daughter.

She was afraid for Esclamonde.

Afraid that Esclamonde might run into a dangerous warlock like I once did with Anesot.

That Esclamonde would fall in love with him, and then be barred from using her magic against him—no matter how deeply, or violently, or cruelly he betrayed her.

I release my smothering magic.

Esclamonde takes a deep breath. "My parents know. And Onesimos. I told him after my mother came."

I rub my temples to calm my racing thoughts. "You can trust Simmy. But no one else, Esclamonde. I mean it. You could be manipulated in the worst way possible if someone figures out you're a centerheart and you can't wield magic against those you love."

For a long time, her eyes switch across my features. "Like what happened to you."

I don't spare a second for the witch who starts screaming somewhere northwest of here. "Just like me. Even after I learned Anesot had convinced Oko to kill my sister, I couldn't... my magic wouldn't..."

Though my mind understood Anesot had manipulated me, and my heart was shattered, my magic refused to believe.

Refused to punish Anesot when I had the chance for vengeance right after Milisent's death.

It kills me to wonder if part of me did still love Anesot.

Kills me to remember raising my hands and casting killing magic only to realize my magic wouldn't give itself, and Anesot would slink away unpunished.

Some beings, like the children of wolves and wielders, are born pith. Some, like the nymphs who wander far from the domain of their demigods, are made pith by distance. Centerhearts are made pith by love.

Esclamonde's white eyelashes flutter as she blinks at me. "But... not all warlocks are like Anesot. I've never met anyone who would do something like that... not even the cruelest and most pompous warlocks in Antigone."

Not because those warlocks *wouldn't* but because they *couldn't*; what Anesot lacked in power he made up for in cunning, in tenacity, in patience.

The witchling runs her finger along the surface of the calming water. "And Anesot is banished from Antigone and most of the northern cities. Other warlocks planning to do something similar to a centerheart have learned their lesson through him."

I raise my eyebrows. "I wouldn't hold out for that. There are plenty of wielders who are still in cahoots with him and Oko. He's a four-horn, Esclamonde. He can barter for anything with dove—especially now that he's banished from larger cities. Once, he sponsored them—and now that that's over, he has plenty of magic to spare.

"How else would he and Oko survive all this time? They don't live off the land. They're used to luxury. They have allies from Jaws to Velm. I'd bet anything on it."

"Is that what you've been doing? Tracking him down?"

"What did I just tell you about witches? Just like you shouldn't trust another witch, you shouldn't expect one to trust *you*."

She exhales sharply, then kicks off the bottom to float around the shallow pool. "It's not fair, Helisent. We're both centerhearts. Let's trust each other, at least. And what have—"

"I'm not giving you a fucking lecture on trust. I'm saying that you're wasting your energy trying to convince others you're trustworthy. Let that go. They'll never trust you, whether you're a centerheart or secretly as evil as Anesot.

"That's the second point we need to cover tonight. How to handle the anger you will receive for things you never did. And also for the things you *have* done."

Esclamonde lowers her chin, features tightening with frustration. "That would be useful. On my way to Luz, a dryad denied me lodging in Rhotidom. The tavern-owner was drunk. He said wielders had cleared out his storehouse the week before, so he wasn't bartering with our kind anymore."

"Unfortunately, that's not so uncommon in the north. Did you offer to help restore what was lost?"

She shakes her head. "No. He was so angry…"

"Don't take it personally. Next time, offer help. That's usually enough to put any nymph in a better mood. Nymphs want you to be happy and useful to them. Wolves just want to know you're being fair—no smiles needed."

She shrugs a thin shoulder. "But I don't know tracking magic. Or returning magic. I couldn't help the nymph."

"Sure, but you could have done something else for him. They hate doing laundry, as I'm sure you've already learned from my warren. That's always a solid barter." I count with my fingers as I list off spells. "Cleaning is also a reliable go-to. Not all nymphs bother with reading and writing since they're short-lived, so transcribing notes and records is another good option. There's also fortifying magic for older buildings, collecting and storing magic for harvests, or even something like stitching magic for clothes repair."

She chews her lip, then glances at her bottomless bag. "Right. Good. I'll have to remember this."

I gasp with realization. "And if you *ever* see a weird-looking hesperide in the Deltas or Hypnos, *do not take him home*. And *do not let him bite your neck*. It's not a kink thing. It's a blood thing."

"A *blood thing*? What does that mean?"

I sigh. "I don't know yet. Ask me in a year."

Over Esclamonde's shoulder, I catch Boonmasent holding up her hand in our direction. Her five raised fingers let me know we have five minutes before witches come over to start cleaning and cutting our nails.

I study the witches floating in the pools around us, as well as the attendants that scrub their hands and hair.

Then I look back at Esclamonde, feeling the words build on my lips.

"Look, witchling, I need you to protect your heart. I imagine wielders everywhere struggle with the expectations of nymphs and wolves, but there's another layer for witches like you. Like *us*."

The last time I felt any sense of camaraderie with a witch was when Milisent and I lived in Antigone. Though I have plenty of cordial relationships like those with Boonmasent, and possibly Ninigone and Butter Ultramarine, there hasn't been a thread of tenderness like what exists in this pool right now. The tenderness of needing.

Esclamonde clears her throat. "My mother isn't centerheart. That's why she wanted me to be with you."

"I understand. And I'm sorry to say... but I don't have anything more to offer." I take her hands beneath the surface, and we hold each other. With each word, my heart pounds. I push myself toward truth; toward what must be said to Esclamonde, what must be said to myself. "Everything I've learned has been the hard way. I had to lose Milisent West of Jaws to understand what it is to be centerheart. And now, I..."

Now I've done it all over again.

Fell in love with a powerful being even though it's highly ill-advised.

Fell in love knowing I won't be able to use magic against him now that I...

Now that I...

"Now you what?" Esclamonde asks.

Though I was raised on a peaceful, rocky plot of land west of Jaws with a jovial father and two untamed brothers, a deeper thread connected me and Mili as sisters: knowing we were centerhearts.

It puts wielders in great danger—but only if we're alone.

If we find another centerheart who's just as bound to our protection and well-being through love, we form an alliance and friendship that transcends all bounds. We don't need to bother with trust because we couldn't hurt the other even if we tried.

I never thought I'd have another chance at that again. Never thought I'd want one if presented with the opportunity.

"Now I'll do anything I can to help you and guide you." I clear my throat and squeeze her bony hands. "Just after I find Oko and Anesot, okay?"

Esclamonde nods. "A witch's death must be avenged."

When we leave Boonma's, Esclamonde stares down at her nails, flaring her fingers to gain a new vantage of her clean cuticles.

I clutch the letter from her uncle, desperate for a bottle of brandy and a dark corner to read it in.

I glance at the columns of the temple district. They poke above the crooked rooftops and canopy, catching the moonslight like glowing obelisks. Someplace just beyond is the shining marble of the Luzian Estate.

I've been wrong to hide the reason I'm after Oko.

I don't necessarily mind Samson keeping his own motive a secret... but I need him to know how serious the search is for me. That I'm going to turn into someone he doesn't recognize as soon as we find Oko, and especially if we manage to locate Anesot.

I elbow Esclamonde. "I'll meet you at the warren later, okay?"

She looks away from her hand with a start. "Okay. Are you feeling all right?"

"Yeah." I shrug. "I just realized I needed to tell Samson something. I'll be home soon."

"Okay." She bites her lip, glancing toward the road that cuts straight to the temple district, then back in the direction of our warren. Before I can ask if she knows the way, she raises her arms. "Hug?"

I roll my eyes and sink into the embrace. "You don't have to ask anymore. Okay?"

She squeezes me with a happy sigh. "Okay. Thanks for taking me to Boonma's."

I watch her bright-red cloak fade amid the passing groups, then disappears. I head south toward the temple district, glancing back to make sure she isn't following.

I head into the nearest tavern and sit beneath its dimmest string of lights.

I order a bitterroot brandy just to have something sat next to me at the bar.

I unfold the letter with shaking hands.

Helisent West of Jaws,
I regret that my sister tracked you down in Gamma. I ask you to separate Esclamonde from her mother's foolishness. They are not the same.
When I visited the village to make amends for your tantrum, I learned you were traveling with Samson 714 Afador. It made me curious about your goals. I contacted Class representatives around Mieira and discovered you're now the sponsor of many cities.
I send this letter to remind you that all sponsorship titles should be

submitted to the Class for approval. Your power does not give you free
rein. It certainly will not excuse any acts of vengeance taken against
Anesot Hypnos or Oko Hypnos. Remember that the Class holds the
exclusive right to punish wielders for their wrongdoing; they must be
turned over to our authority.
Any attempt to skirt the rules set by the Class damages the
reputation of wielders across Mieira. Any attempt at vigilante
revenge divests the Class of its inherent power. I send this letter to
remind you that banishments will be the only answer for your
disobedience.
Ethsevere Black Rock Antigone, Fourth Member of The Class

I burn the paper immediately, then fold my arms over the bar
and set my head on them. I let out a long cry, then stare at the
pile of ash near my hands and wish I'd kept the note. I'm not
sure what for, just that maybe it could make me rethink my
current path.

I take a few calming breaths.

They don't help shake the pit in my stomach.

I have no choice but to avenge Milisent. I have had no
peace, no sanity, no stability since she was taken from this
world. I don't *want* it, either. Not until I know that Oko and
Anesot are blue-tinged corpses rotting in the earth. That
centerhearts like Esclamonde are somewhat safer.

I stand and leave the rest of my brandy at the bar.

Without thinking, my feet lead me to the Luzian Estate.

I take a deep breath with every other step. It does little to
calm my nerves.

I stop once the smokey-white marble walls come into view.
Even from my place down the street, I can smell a faint hint of
cedar smoke. I flare my nostrils to try to smell more like
Samson does, but I'm met with the same sweet and earthy
scents of Luz.

I pop onto my toes and see slivers of firelight reflecting off the walls that encircle the interior garden.

For a long time, I watch the light flicker across the marble. I should be bartering with Itzifone right now to prevent delaying our journey. Instead, I'm staring at the dead, shimmering rock and trying to figure out which truths Samson needs to know before we leave again tomorrow.

A figure stops in the middle of the street to my left.

The large wolf turns toward me and says, "Helisent West of Jaws."

I turn and bend my neck to stare up at Rex. I smooth out my grimace with a prim smile. "You're Rex... Rex... Rex Kane-something." The fucked-up part is that I'm not trying to be snide. I can't remember and my nerves aren't helping. "Rex 500-something Kane-something."

"If you're going to butcher my name, then don't say it at all."

"Fine." I give him the once-over, starting with his tight bun and ending with his boots. "I won't say your name at all."

He doesn't move on like I expect him to. He studies me with such disdain that I start to look at him with the same. Though he's remarkably handsome, from his chiseled jaw to his deep-set eyes, his beauty looks empty.

Empty like the Velmic Palaces carved from pure marble, then polished.

"You're here to see Samson," he says.

I raise my eyebrows. "What are you, his errand boy?"

"Does my Alpha know what you're doing with Samson?" he asks.

My Alpha. Clearbold 554 Leofsige.

My gut steels at the implication that Clearbold might know about our journey. I've known from the start that Clearbold wouldn't like my mission—or the fact that I brought his son along for the journey.

Unlike Samson, Clearbold knows why I'm after Oko.

I glance at the warm light emanating from the estate.

Rex follows my stare. "I'm sure Clearbould would love to speak with you again. He's here now, if you'd like to meet with him."

Is Clearbold in there telling Samson a story about two red witches? Fuck.

I've lost my chance to get ahead of this.

To tell Samson myself what happened.

With a casual tone, Rex goes on, "I like to think I know Samson well. I like to think I knew him before I joined his war band south of Mort. Like him, I grew up in Bellator. The Velmic code is part of who I am. It's not just a way of life, Helisent. Our codes, our way of being, is a part of our blood and our instinct. It isn't something we move away from or forget."

"Are you giving lessons about Velmic culture now?" I raise my eyebrows. "Last I saw, you were gnawing on a wolfling's neck."

"Samson is different from the rest of the wolves. I love him because he will be my Alpha someday. He is just, visionary, and steadfast. He will be a leader who wolves remember for generations."

He lowers his voice, but I can't fathom why Rex changes his volume. This late at night, we're almost alone on the street.

He says, "Samson is out of time for affairs with a drunken witch or a childhood sweetheart. And you are selfish for pursuing something that hurts him."

I either drank one too many brandies to hear this or not enough.

A keening rage starts in my toes and spirals toward my head.

"Each involvement you have with him, private or public, gives the wolves of Velm the impression that Samson might not be a worthy leader. That every rumor Malachai spreads might have more truth than anyone cared to admit before."

I open my mouth and prepare a response, but Rex doesn't give me time for one.

He goes on, "I need you to understand that Malachai isn't just a *spare*. He is *the end* of the Afador line. And if Samson doesn't make it to that throne, do you think Clearbold or Malachai will let him live?

"He will spend his youth and health running from the only life he's ever known and being shunned, driven out, and disrespected as a threat to the Alphas. And the wolves eager to take his place won't bother with the Northing or with any of the projects Imperatriz started. Our people will be set back centuries under a conservative Alpha like Malachai wants to be."

Rex takes a step closer to me.

It takes all my nerve not to back up. Not to yield to him.

"He will *never* let another woman take the space in his heart that he left for Imperatriz. And he will *hate you* for compromising her legacy."

Though I'm certain I can't grasp the gravity of that statement because I'm not a wolf and I've never respected an Alpha, I understand that Samson adores his mother and wants to emulate her version of leadership. I understand why, too.

He's right.

I *know* Rex is right.

But I'm too stubborn to accept that I'm wrong.

That I *am* selfish. Even though I *am*.

"Did you have anything else you wanted to add?" I smooth my hair, then my robe. I look at Rex and hope he dies. "I doubt we'll be speaking for many, *many* years to come."

He turns away swiftly. "Nothing."

I watch him go, expecting him to open the gate and turn into the estate's courtyard.

He continues straight, passing the marble walls without so much as a glance. I wonder if Clearbold sent him out here to intercept me.

If so, how did Clearbold know I'd come tonight?

If so, how did Clearbold find out that I partnered with Samson in the first place?

Was it Malachai? Or was it Rex?

With a curse, I stick my hand into my bottomless bag and summon the spare bottle of brandy that I swore to Samson I'd tossed away. I tilt my head back to guzzle the tart liquid then stare at the estate.

Shadows and light warp on the interior wall, barely in view.

If I were a smart witch, I'd walk away.

That's always been my problem, though.

I'm wicked and foolish, and I won't ever change.

CHAPTER 16

A FLIMSY THING LIKE FRIENDSHIP

SAMSON

My son,
You will live in two worlds. One will be that of the wolves and Velm.
The other will be one of your own creation. I look forward to knowing
this second world someday. You've seen me paint, Samson. You
remember the songs from my kalimba.

When we finish dinner, I stare across the table at my father and wait for him to bring up Helisent.

Since I arrived at the Luzian Estate shortly after dusk, he's ignored the potent ala that clings to my satchel and belongings. Helisent's scent saturated multiple items during our trip back from Cadmium, and I only made the barest efforts to lessen it before returning to the estate.

I hadn't been expecting Clearbold—nor an invitation to dine with him before he leaves for Wrenweary later tonight.

We sit on the floor in the dining room before the low marble table. Crumbs and bones litter the empty plates between us. Only the drinks remain, the orange firelight reflecting off the liquid in the wide goblets.

Clearbold stretches with a long sigh. Like I've done multiple times, I rehearse my explanation about my journey in the past months; the letter from Imperatriz, the search for Oko, my partnership with Helisent West of Jaws.

Already, we've hashed out the waricon. I'll send gifts to Invidio's village to lessen the shame of his defeat. I also brought up the rumors floating around southeast Velm, perpetuated by Malachai in Mort.

Clearbold questions whether they're rumors or opinions; I have little authority to challenge an opinion, and wolves will always have them.

Now he studies me from the other side of the table. We sit in mirrored forms, our legs crossed and our backs straight. Watching him is like watching my future play out; what my face will look like when I'm in my late seventies, how my body will change to account for my age and increase in power, and what types of issues will matter most when I'm an established Alpha.

Our voices mark the strongest physical difference.

His is coarse and low. Those who didn't grow up at his beck and call struggle to untangle his syllables and words. My voice is louder and clear; at least, for now. I wonder if it will change, too.

The longer I stare back at Clearbold, the more amused his expression becomes.

Finally, his face breaks with a smile. It puts me on edge; Clearbold doesn't joke.

"I wondered when you'd put a wall between us, Samson. It's high time you did. No worthy Alpha slinks around in his father's shadow forever... but..." He rubs his cheeks with a humorless laugh. "Helisent West of Jaws?"

Part of me is relieved I won't have to explain who she is.

The rest of me is highly suspicious about his opinion of the witch. Worse than his negative opinion of her will be my inability to react.

I can't pick a fight with Clearbold. The Alpha's rule is total and final. I really can't even disagree, except for carefully chosen words and a plan of retreat at the ready.

Then Clearbold's features deaden into grim lines. "I hope you know what you're doing."

I dive into my prepared explanation. "Last year, I was going through the Rouzen Estate. I hadn't spent time in my room there in years. I found a chest sitting in the back of my closet —but it wasn't mine. It was Imperatriz's."

As always, the mention of her name causes Clearbold's nostrils to flare, as though searching for her ala close by. As though he might find it.

I go on, "There was a letter hidden inside, which described a meeting in Hypnos. The letter hinted she was looking for a witch named Oko around the time she disappeared. I've been following up the lead."

Clearbold's eyes narrow. He takes a long breath, as though deep in thought. "I see. A witch named Oko..."

I nod. "Have you heard of her? I would have sent word to you, but it seemed... sensitive to discuss in a letter. I was in Luz when I was able to learn more about Oko and where she might be found. I left immediately after. That was four months ago."

"I've heard of many wielders in my day, Samson." Clearbold reaches for his glass of water then downs it with quick gulps. He reaches next for the clear bottle of moonshine sat at the table's farthest ledge. "And what have you learned about Oko?"

I stick to the rudimentary details. If Clearbold wants to know more, he'll keep asking me questions. For now, I'd rather leave out the more dangerous elements of my journey, like the trip to Skull and the collection of phoenix ash.

"Halfway to Ultramarine, a selkie mentioned that okeanids have been disappearing along the coast." I ignore Clearbold's dumbfounded expression. "From Jaws to as far south as Mort, they vanish without a trace. The selkie hinted they're being taken elsewhere by a *fifth* scent and—"

"*Lekeli Kelnazzar*, Samson..." Clearbold rubs his face again, expression sliding back toward amusement. "A fifth *scent*? Did it smell like the selkie's lies? And what does this have to do with Oko?"

I set my hands in my lap and clench them so Clearbold won't see. But for a long moment, I can't find my voice. My mind shifts between the idea that Clearbold isn't taking the disappearances seriously, that he might think I've been misled... and my partnership with Helisent.

A witch who doesn't believe in trust.

"Oko, the vanishing okeanids, and Imperatriz's disappearance could be connected. I've verified the existence of the fifth scent, too. It bites. It drinks blood. And if the selkie was right, and the okeanids are being *taken* somewhere, then maybe Imperatriz met a similar fate."

Clearbold stares at me with smug disbelief while I fight to hold his stare. I find it just as improbable that Imperatriz, one of Mieira's most powerful beings, could be *taken* against her will. But the other conclusions, like death or *choosing* to leave, are just as unfathomable.

"I don't expect it to make sense now, but I'm getting closer to answers," I insist. "I can feel it."

I ignore the rut in my stomach that deepens with each thought of Helisent.

She didn't even look me in my eyes when we parted earlier.

She turned away like she was bored with my existence.

Clearbold looks just as tired now. He sighs again and pours another serving of moonshine.

"I'll find Oko." I lean toward him, jaw clenching. "I'll figure out if she had anything to do with my mother's—"

"What makes you think Helisent will give you that chance?" Clearbold's question is direct and rushed. "She's just *leading* you to Oko?"

I sit back. "We're working together. She's also interested in finding the witch."

Clearbold laughs, cold and humorless. "Obviously, Samson. She's thought of little else for the last six years. And what will you do when you find Oko? Helisent has no control. She'll kill Oko the second she lays eyes on her. And then what will you do?"

Kill her?

Helisent wants Oko dead?

Based on how thorough her description of Oko was in Skull, I figured she had a personal vendetta but... *killing* someone?

Clearbold goes on in my silence. "Samson, tell me you actually know who Helisent West of Jaws is, and you haven't been traipsing around Mieira with a red witch blindly."

In my defense, I at least figured out she's a red witch.

I lick my lips as I think of a neutral response. Based on his reaction so far, he's not a fan of Helisent. While it doesn't surprise me, I'm not keen on my Alpha realizing how close we've become.

Especially when he just revealed that she's keeping secrets from me.

Killing-sized secrets.

Trust is what the weak cling to when their shaking hands can't hold more.

I clear my throat and push away her awful words. "I know enough of Helisent to trust in her character."

A disgusted sigh peels from Clearbold's lips. "This is why southeast Velm questions your right to the throne, Samson. For *fuck's sake*. You *trust* the character of a witch? Are you being serious or is this some romantic Northing notion?"

All beings want safety, love, and possibility. The rest are details.

I hear my mother's words spoken in Helisent's voice.

Please don't make me regret this, little bird.

I repeat, "I trust Helisent's character."

"*No*, Samson, you trust a witch to want something from you, and you trust that she wants it enough to listen to the rules you set out, and then you give a witch *no space to deviate*. This is what I've taught you since you were a pup. A few months in Luz and you're already as soft as an unnumbered."

There are times when I've seen my father as a subject. When I've been painfully aware that a waricon series landed him in his position; not being born from the Afador line. Growing up, it helped me excuse the aspects of his rule that I found abhorrent.

It's becoming less palatable—and quickly.

"She's motivated to find Oko, just like me."

"And *why*, Samson?"

I fold my arms. "I didn't ask. She doesn't know why I'm after Oko, either."

With a sigh, he clears the table between us then moves the bottle of moonshine to its center. He pours himself another serving then half-fills the empty glass before me.

"I suppose you've made at least one sound decision in keeping that to yourself," he admits. "The rest of your plans are fucked."

He knocks his drink back then waits for me to do the same.

He pours another as the liquid burns my throat, my stomach.

I think of a way to disagree, but I have little proof that demonstrates Helisent's reliability.

Clearbold says, "Twenty years ago, I met a powerful warlock with four horns. He was the strongest being north of Velm aside from the demigods. I took him to Velm. I showed him our lands and made sure we became allies. Some of his dove was used to lay roads in Rouz. Even more was used to fortify Mort's levees.

"I didn't fear him—he was ambitious with his plans to lead Antigone and wanted nothing from Velm but a clean reputation. Though I guess I shouldn't say that he had plans to *lead* Antigone. Wielders aren't capable of true leadership, are they?

"He had plans to *rule*.

"And all worthy leaders need followers. This warlock had one witch, in particular, who supported his vision. Oko. She'd do anything to help the warlock leverage his magic into more power.

"When the warlock left Velm, I sent word to the local pack leaders in Mieira to keep an eye on him. While I trusted him to respect Velm, his plans in Mieira seemed... grand. If he left Antigone, the pack leaders sent word to the places he traveled so that the wolves could anticipate his arrival.

"Just in case...

"But his plans to lead Septegeur and Antigone slowed. Maybe not for lack of wanting, but for lack of vision. The Class saw he was making power grabs, trading dove for clout, and unified against him.

"Twelve years ago, he found his way into Antigone's upper echelon. The warlock, named Anesot, had found himself two witchlings more powerful than anything Mieira had ever seen. Two sisters from a shitty little outpost in the volcanic cones east of Metamor. Anesot quickly made himself relevant to the sisters.

"But having access to the sisters wasn't enough. Power spreads evenly for wielders of the same gender. So long as both sisters lived, their power would be *split* between them. But if one sister died..."

I reach for my glass and pour another serving.

My fingers clench around the cup.

Please don't be Helisent.

Twelve years ago, she would've been twenty-two. A witchling.

Clearbold also pours another glass. The corners of his lips tremble, as though he's holding back a smile. "And what would a warlock hellbent on ruling Antigone need? A powerful, malleable witch. The younger, the better. The dumber, the better."

The moonshine sours in my stomach.

I'm not sure where to look.

I don't want to hear this story from Clearbold.

I don't want to hear it at all.

"They called the older sister Mint. She was cooler. Complex. They called the youngest Honey. She was sweet. Compliant. Would you like to guess which one he took his chances with? I know which once I'd pick if I had to craft a Bloody Betty." He takes his shot with a grunt. "So that's what Anesot did. He took the younger sister's heart before it grew fully and bent it into the shape he most needed. Within a few years, he possessed the witch in every way.

"And when he was sure of their bond, Anesot sent Oko to where the red witch's sister slept near Metamor. Oko killed Milisent West of Jaws, and all of her power flooded to Helisent West of Jaws, making her the most powerful witch Mieira has ever known."

I see Helisent in Lampades, too drunk to hold herself straight on her lilith.

"Do you ever hear screaming when you're around me? A witch screaming?"

I pour a third serving of moonshine.

Clearbold's hesitant grin wavers again. "Unfortunately for Anesot, his plan fell apart—rather quickly. He went on the run before Helisent could destroy him. Then he and Oko were banished from Mieira's largest cities.

"Six years later, Helisent still hasn't been able to find them. If you've traveled with her for months, then you understand why. She's a drunk, Samson. A whoring drunk. And she's using you to find Oko because she's too useless to do it herself."

Six years? Helisent told me she'd been searching for Oko for one.

I untangle my hands where they're clenched together, fingernails digging into my palms, and set them on my knees.

For a long moment, I'm numb and wordless. My thoughts slow down.

One sister named Mint. Another named Honey.

All I can think to ask is, "Why aren't Anesot and Oko banned from Velm? You said they were banished from a the largest Mieiran cities, but not all of them."

Clearbold raises his eyebrows. "Velm doesn't take sides in these types of affairs. The crime didn't involve our people or our land."

"A warlock like Anesot is a threat to all, isn't he? And you took him to Velm. He knows Velm." I can't imagine any amount of dove or urban infrastructure that would make Clearbold tolerate a dangerous warlock like Anesot. He barely tolerates the soft ones.

"I'm more concerned about Helisent."

I sit back. Indignation whirls in my gut, twining with rage and bitterness. "And why does Helisent concern you more than Anesot? She never sought power like he did. She was born with it."

"I can see that. But compared to Anesot's magic, Helisent's power is unchecked. All the power from her mother's line belongs solely to her. No sisters. No aunts. Anesot's magic is a fucking thimble compared to hers. Do you know how many cities she sponsors?"

And what is wrong with taking power from a mother's line?

I shove the thought away and focus on Helisent. "I never asked how many cities she sponsors. I know she sponsors Luz. That's it."

Clearbold shakes his head, features bunching. "And why not? Why *wouldn't* you do everything you could to gauge her power? These things matter to the Alphas of Velm, Samson. Her power could threaten our people someday.

"As you aged, I told you stories of the War Years. What did

our ancestors do to destabilize wielder populations? What worked best—or have you forgotten?"

Clearbold watches me, waiting for me to recite the words.

The words lodge in my throat. In my mind, Helisent blinks her golden eyes at me in the yew tree's canopy, waiting for me to grit them out. "Wielder magic moves down an ancestral line, not back up. When we kill the children, we forsake their parents' magic. And we forsake their souls."

Clearbold nods. "A grown wielder is a threat. A grown wielder is full of festering emotions. They rot, Samson. They are not whole. And Helisent is no exception."

He doesn't know her at all. Behind her drunken bravado and laughter is a despondent witch who can still hear her sister screaming.

"Then it's good that I've befriended her," I reason. "As an ally, she won't find a reason to use her power to hurt Velm or the wolves."

"Look beyond the obvious. She's the sponsor of Luz, Antigone, Alita, Eupheme, Lake Deidre, and other villages across Metamor, Jaws, and Rhotidom."

I reach for my drink, but it's empty. My fingers pinch the glass as disbelief floods me.

She sponsors *five* cities—and that doesn't count the villages that litter the forests and volcanic cones.

Holy shit. That's a lot of extra dove.

Clearbold goes on, "And you think a flimsy thing like *friend-ship* will protect Velm if she has a bad day and turns on you? She has no self-control. No discipline."

"As far as I can tell, she wants Oko—and Anesot. Nothing more."

"What starts with a vengeance killing will easily turn into other power grabs. What starts with Oko and Anesot can spiral into something far darker and more dangerous. Have you considered the possibility that she's using *you* to gain a foothold in Velm? She knows better than to approach me again."

Again?

How well does she know Clearbold?

Though we had a rocky start to our journey, she didn't give me the impression she loathed me—and most beings who dislike either me or my father bundle us together.

"She knows that you'll need her, too." Clearbold lowers his voice to make his final point. "That Malachai will look to overturn your throne even after you've taken it."

His words send adrenaline into my veins.

I hadn't realized Malachai had plans to pursue power even after I'm married in Silent City. What sort of advantage could he hope for with the Female Alpha at my side?

"So, Samson, are you still certain that you trust this witch's character? That you're in a true partnership with her and not being moved around the board like a pawn?"

My head reels as I try to string together every implication in Clearbold's words. My heart clings to Helisent in the meantime, refusing to believe that she might be using me for a power grab.

I remind myself she doesn't want political power. She wants beautiful jewelry, a crisp bitterroot brandy, and reassuring hugs.

All beings want safety, love, and possibility. The rest are details.

Most of all, Helisent believes in Imperatriz.

"I trust in our partnership," I say. "I'll be careful to keep my wits."

"That's all you have to say?" Clearbold's nostrils flare slightly.

"It is."

"Tell her to show you what her eyes really look like. Then you can tell me you trust in your partnership with her. And the next time you're in Bellator, go into the deepest room of the palace. Study the walls, Samson, and how many red horns are hung. Then ask yourself how many she has. Once you know, you can tell me you trust your partnership with her."

Clearbold raises his eyebrows, inviting me to more doubt.

I nod. "I will."

I'm not sure if he scoffs or sighs as he reaches to pour one last shot of moonshine. Coupled with the dark ales we drank for dinner, I'm approaching sturdy drunkenness; I'm glad. It helps me balance every new insight Clearbold has handed me tonight.

I hope he leaves soon so I can meditate alone beneath the fir tree.

So I can stare at the place where Helisent first entered the garden and wonder whether she's manipulating me.

We clear the rest of the burning moonshine, then we stand. Clearbold heads toward the foyer where he left his packed satchel. Though close to highmoons, he's long preferred to travel by night. With so many responsibilities to handle in the light, the night is an Alpha's only guarantee of privacy. Of peace.

He pauses in the foyer near the entrance, then he turns back toward the large salon that opens into the garden. Helisent's ala hits me a second later.

Clearbold's nostrils flare as his attention levels on the open threshold where the warm wind ferries in her ala.

I take a steadying breath to calm my racing heart. The last thing I want is for Clearbold to understand how I actually feel about the witch. That I fear for her safety in his presence, and that I'm not sure *why* that is.

Clearbold stares at me.

I stare back at him.

He takes off toward the salon and the garden. "Stay here." His footsteps are heavy and loud against the marble.

He doesn't define *here*. I wait until he turns into the salon out of view, then listen for his footsteps to stop echoing. Once I'm certain he's in the garden, I walk to the end of the hallway.

I can't see the courtyard or my father from the angle, but I can hear and smell the pair much better.

I suck in deep breaths to process Helisent's ala. She's not very drunk; her skin and hair are clean; she's been with the witchling she mentors.

"Helisent West of Jaws," Clearbold says. "We meet again."

She doesn't respond—*why not?*

After a long beat of silence, Clearbold goes on, "Samson tells me you're on the hunt for Oko. I hope you remember our last conversation. If you raise a finger to Anesot or Oko rather than turn them over to the Class for punishment, you'll be banished from Velm. And I'll stop at nothing to see that you're banished from Mieira. Vigilantes threaten order across our world. Local councils decide the means of justice, not powerful wielders."

Helisent's silence is louder and more terrifying than anything she's ever shouted.

"Nothing to say tonight?" Clearbold goes on. His voice shifts, as though he's distancing himself from me.

Is he approaching her? And how close is she?

"And why not, red witch?" he goes on.

"I'll do a lot of things, Clearbold, but wasting my breath isn't one of them." Her sumptuous laugh is bored. "Now where's the boy-wolf? I hope you realize I'm not here for you."

Though neither speaks again, I don't smell a shift in their positions.

My entire body tenses. I've never heard anyone speak to Clearbold with such a direct and disrespectful tone. Even in my own fantasies when I tell my Alpha to fuck off, I take a cooler and more measured tone than Helisent just did.

Now where's the boy-wolf?

It's basically a command.

I wait at the room's edge and wonder what I should do if the pair's meeting escalates.

Then my father's sigh echoes back to me. I retreat a few

steps so he won't know I was at the edge of the hallway. When he rounds from the salon, his jaw is tense, his footsteps even heavier than before. He grabs the back of my neck, fitting his palm and fingers around me.

It takes every ounce of self-control not to rip away from his touch. To let his thick fingers settle around my neck with a firm grip, then guide me back toward the front door under his momentum.

It's the closest he's come to pinning or biting me in years.

My right hand twitches with the urge to mirror the hold on him.

Samsonfang wants to grapple with Clearbold; he knows he won't win, but he doesn't want to accept this touch, this domination, without a fight.

But I do. It's his way of reminding me of the pecking order. Reminding me that he'll decide what happens to Helisent in Velm, not me.

Twenty more years, then it ends. Then he won't touch me again.

He'll be too afraid. Too physically weak from age to hope to wrangle me into submission.

Clearbold stops at the entrance and strengthens his grip around the back of my neck. I try not to let my rage show. I keep my eyelids and jaw relaxed, as though tired.

He pulls me toward him and whispers into my ear, "If you would have played this right, she could have been Velm's next Bloody Betty. Who knows when we'll need another wielder like that? Who knows what dangers lie beyond our little vision of life? But you don't have the backbone for that. You never have, Samson. You always learn the hard way."

He releases me with a shove, causing me to stagger forward. He slings his heavy black cape over his back, straightens the satchel looped over his arm, and rips the door to the side. He heads to the gate with large strides.

And what about Oko?

Ten seconds with Helisent and *he's* the one who forgot the goal at the end of this wayward journey.

Which is finding Imperatriz, not taming a witch.

And what dangers is he talking about? Why would Velm need another Bloody Betty?

Clearbold glances back once from the street. He gives me the same look that he has since I brought the wooly's head back to Bellator at age twelve. It's a blend of expectation, curiosity, and the slightest edge of fear that I've never been able to quantify.

I watch him go, hoping Helisent sticks around.

Still, I wait until I can't smell Clearbold's ala in the air. The latter takes a long time given the still night, but he walks with a quick pace.

When I'm sure he's gone, I step back inside and shut the door. I turn into the hallway to find Helisent standing at its far end where the salon leads to the garden.

Her velvet robe pools on the ground, its peach hue glittering in the firelight. Her chin is lowered, highlighting the vibrant glare on her face. Her eyes are pink, as though she's been crying.

I freeze.

We left off on bad terms earlier today, but my heart bleeds for her now.

Honey.

She wipes one of her cheeks and sniffles. "The bracelet I gave you so you could track me if you needed—I'm taking it back. We're done. Where's your room?"

I freeze, body chilling.

"What? Why?" I don't move, afraid she means what she's saying. "We had an agreement to find Oko. We need to see it through, Helisent."

Please don't leave.

"Because I'm done!" she screams. The echo of her words shatters any illusion that I know what I'm doing. Her shrill tone reverberates through the walls; I doubt there's ever been such a loud sound made inside the estate. "I'm fucking *done.* The deal is over. Find Oko yourself. Where is my bracelet?"

"Why are you angry? I know we had a disagreement, but we can talk about it. Let's talk about it."

Please don't leave.

"Because I can't stand all of this *wolf shit.*" Her fingers ball into fists. She looks around as though crazed, the scent of her salty tears filling my lungs. "Fuck you, and fuck Rex, and fuck Clearbold—fuck *all of you.*"

My heart sinks into my gut. "Rex?"

I caught his ala earlier, but Clearbold mentioned he'd sent him on an errand. I wonder what the chances are that errand had to do with Helisent. Terror grips my heart as I realize the gravity of everything that's transpired in the last hour.

We stare at each other from opposite ends of the hallway.

"What did he say to you?" I ask.

"Give me your bag." She takes off toward me. "I want my bracelet, and then I'm leaving."

I don't move, and she twists to get around me. Rather than head down the narrow hallway toward the bedrooms, she stomps into the dining room.

I trail at her heels. "Helisent, just tell me what happened."

She quickly turns and heads back into the hallway. This time, she beelines for the kitchen.

All the while, she rants angrily. "Don't fucking play dumb. Rex knows who I am. I'm sure Clearbold sat here and had a ton of wonderful shit to say about me—me and my..."

She starts panting as she realizes my satchel isn't in the kitchen. She sidesteps me when I try to get in her way, then rushes down the hallway that leads to the bedrooms.

"I don't give a fuck, Samson. Think what you want about me. This is done."

I rush ahead of her to block the first door. "Use your words, little bird. I know you're—"

"Don't call me that!" Her hands ball into fists again. Her lips pull back from her teeth while her wild eyes stare up at me. They're bulging with fear, with panic, with wild emotion. "Fuck you, Samson. Fuck *all of you*."

Why are you hurting me?

I take a deep breath.

I remind myself that she was betrayed by the last person she loved. That his actions probably took away her ability to trust in others. That my father's decision not to support her search for Anesot and Oko has compromised her ability to trust me, trust the world.

That Rex probably found a way to hammer the nail into the coffin with whatever he said to her.

I follow her into each empty room until she finds mine. I beg her to slow down and let me explain, and she screams that she doesn't care, and she never did, and she never will.

Please don't leave.

She finds my satchel at the edge of the bed and claws through it. My chest pumps, panic flushing into my system. She's actually going to leave and abandon our partnership. Our friendship. And she's been through enough in life that no matter of pleading will change her mind.

She rips out spare leather, spare clothes, my notebook, my toiletries and throws them across the floor. Her body shakes, her jewelry trembles.

Then she pulls out the green bracelet she handed me north of Cadmium.

She's leaving you, Samson.

I step in front of the door again. I know it's wrong to block her exit and force her to stay, but if she'll just give me a second, I can find the right words to make this right—to convince her that I'm in love with her, and I don't care what Clearbold thinks about her character—to show her that I value justice for her sister, and won't stop her pursuit for it—

But she doesn't give me time.

She rushes toward me, stopping with a tense jaw and staring straight into my abdomen rather than meeting my eye. It's just like our parting earlier.

"Move," she growls.

Think of something to say, Samson.

Anything.

"Not until you show me your eyes. Your real eyes."

I expect her to balk—to scream or scoff at me. Instead, she hovers into the air so we're at eye level. She blinks once and the façade of her golden pupils vanishes.

It's not replaced with a vibrant red like in the seething dreams.

It's her *entire* eye. Even the whites are deep pink, while her irises are just as blood-red as Sennen. And they *glow*. A vibrant rouge light emanates from each with such luminosity that I wonder if she can see in the dark.

My lips part, and my mouth falls open.

Every part of my being, Samsonfang included, focuses on that red hue and all the danger it promises.

As though satisfied by my reaction, Helisent tilts her head and drifts closer.

"What now?" she seethes.

Think of something to say, Samson.

Anything.

"Kiss me."

She pulls back immediately. She blinks and her eyes return to their normal hue.

Her shock fades quickly.

Rather than freeze, she reaches for my face. Her fingers skate over my cheekbones, my temples, then follow my jawline to my chin. I can't tell if she's irate, or baffled, or intrigued.

Maybe all three.

Her eyebrows bunch. "Kiss you?"

I nod, jaw clenching. "Kiss me."

Her hands sweep beneath my ears and her fingers weave

into my hair. But her face keeps breaking, increasingly suspicious.

I inch closer to her, desperate to close the distance between our lips. I'm too close now—too near a chance I never thought I'd have—

Her head tilts as her eyes work across my features. "This is *stupid*, Samson."

I do the same, studying every single detail. "I know."

How the fuck is Helisent the one with self-control right now?

I'm too focused on keeping her here with me, on knowing that she reciprocates the wild feelings that have been building in me since Skull, on convincing her that I don't judge or mistrust her.

I lean into one of her hands as it opens across my cheek. I close my eyes and savor its warmth.

She tangles her hands in my hair, tugging it free of my bun. I press forward slowly, so slowly, and wait for her to slap me or use magic to fling me out of her way.

I clear my throat to keep my own tears at bay.

Fuck, the marble walls always make me cry.

I open my eyes. "I'm sorry, Helisent."

I'm sorry that you were hurt in Antigone then.

I'm sorry that I don't have the strength to bow out now.

I'm sorry it seems like you love me back.

She blinks, eyelids fluttering. "I'm sorry, too."

I don't know what she's sorry about, but I don't care.

I inhale her ala as deeply as I can while I raise my hands to touch her, hoping she doesn't move away. She closes her eyes and relaxes as my fingers stroke her cheeks. Her fragile white eyelashes graze my thumb.

I lean forward and kiss her. My lips melt into hers as, after four months of smelling and seeing and hearing and touching, I finally *taste* Helisent.

I pull back and take another breath to gauge how her scent has changed now that I know her taste, too.

But Helisent's lips follow mine and lengthen the kiss, deepening it as she floats toward me. Our bodies meet; her full breasts and belly push into my chest, and my hands sweep around her hips to caress her ass.

We groan at the same time when I grab a handful and squeeze.

Lekeli Kelnazzar—

I want to bite her ass.

The thought is forceful enough that I pull back. "Helisent."

She looks at me with dazed eyes. "What?"

"Will you—I mean, I'll be very careful—but will you tell me if I touch you too hard..." *How do I say this without sounding threatening?* "If I'm hurting you, I mean."

She tilts her head. "Grab my ass."

I mimic the same grab from before. This time, I manage to suppress my groan.

She stares at my lips. "Harder."

Like that, I'm fully hard, cock pressing against the fabric of my pants. I emulate the hold a third time, grabbing more of her ass. I shake my hand to feel her jiggle, maddened by the sensation of her full body in my grip.

"I like that," she purrs into my lips. "That's a good amount of strength to use."

I think that's what she said.

My mind shifts as I kiss her again, instincts grating to be closer to her, to be inside of her, to be covered with her ala.

"Take off my robe," she says into my lips.

I sweep the fabric down over her shoulder, tugging lightly where the velvet is trapped between our bodies.

She wraps her legs around me as the robe falls onto the marble. Given our height disparity, her legs grip me just below my solar plexus.

Part of me wishes I would have taken Gautselin up on the offer to visit Coil. She's a little bird, I'm a big wolf. I've never been with a partner who might feel like my sex is too large to be enjoyable and a crash course from an experienced wolf would come in handy right now.

It's also been years since I was with a woman.

But Helisent seems to be content to guide me through the experience.

With her robe gone, she starts tugging on my tunic, pinching the fabric to pull it up and over my head. Her lips crash into mine once the piece is discarded, then she presses her body against my bare skin.

She runs a hand across my chest before twining her fingers into my chest hair. What starts with a tickle ends with a rough grab, then a soothing stroke. Meanwhile, she grinds against me, tightening her thighs so she can rub herself against my belly.

I tug her closer; I want her to rub herself all over me.

I want our alas layered atop each other, indiscernible.

Her intimate scent drifts up to me; like her glowing, red eyes a moment before, it's impossible to ignore. My hands sweep over her thighs, her hips, her ass again, before slipping under her dress and running upward. I hook my thumbs around her soft skin to hold her waist.

She's small, but she's not frail.

A low hum starts to echo from my chest. While I'm surprised it took this long for my body to respond with the growl of comfort, Helisent freezes.

Her hand lifts from my chest as she pulls back. She stares down where our panting bodies collide. "What is that?"

She doesn't know what tadmazzar is?

Joy flushes through me. "You've never been with a wolf before?"

She lifts her chin. "Maybe. Maybe not."

That's a no.

She glances once more to my chest, though the sound has stopped. "What's with the growling?"

"It's called tadmazzar. It's something wolves do when we

feel... happy and comfortable." I'm just now realizing that the sound and buzz of tadmazzar probably seems frighteningly close to the actual snarling of wolves. "I can't control it... I hope it doesn't bother you."

"I'll let you know." Then she leans forward to kiss me again.

When the tadmazzar restarts, she doesn't flinch or pause. She keeps running her hands through my hair, then over my chest and across my shoulders and down my arms. With every flushed breath, our bodies loosen and meld closer. My hands return to her ass.

"So," she asks between feverish kisses, "where do wolves normally...?"

This time, I pull back. "How different do you think we actually are?"

In reality, I'm delighted she doesn't seem to have any experience with wolves. I like that this is Helisent's first intimate moment with a wolf; it's my first encounter with a witch, too.

I've only been with Maia, a wolf from south of Mort, and Rex. Unlike female nymphs and witches, Maia wasn't born with extra fat. Her breasts were wide and small, and her belly was flat. Her ass and legs only had a touch of softness and dimpling. Rex had just as little as I do.

Helisent is a handful of curves that I want to *squeeze*, that I want to see jiggle. Her breasts, her tummy, her butt, her thighs, her calves—all of it.

I look around from where we stand near the door. The estate is minimal; my bedroom consists of a rectangular chest of drawers, a basin of water for washing, a series of sconces and candles, and a wide bed laid flat on the ground. Then the articles Helisent ripped from my satchel.

She stares at me expectantly, cheeks rouged and limps plump.

I glance to my right. "Can I interest you in a bed?"

With a giggle, she pulls away from me and lowers herself to

the ground. I clamp a hand over my erection; I'd like to present my cock to her in as refined a way as possible. Rex and Maia liked my size and shape, but I keep getting flashes of Absalom's boyish face and Itzifone's lanky frame.

What if she prefers men like that?

Helisent notices my hesitance. She sits down on the bed and raises her eyebrows, glancing at my crotch and then my expression. She leans back onto her hands and watches me with a lazy grin as I slide the bedroom door shut.

But she keeps her silence, and I'm thankful, as I sink onto my knees on the thin mattress and wait for her to meet me. Once again, she floats to wrap herself around me. I sit back so that when she grinds herself against me, I feel the warmth of her sex press against my throbbing cock.

My ongoing tadmazzar fades as our kisses turn into desperate exploration. With the door shut, the room starts to fill with her ala—mine, too. Without breaking our kiss, she uses magic to take off her necklaces and earrings.

"Take off my dress," she whispers.

She leans forward to help me shimmy the fabric over her hips, then her round breasts. They fall as the fabric sweeps upward. I barely remember to keep tugging the pale dress over her head and arms as my attention settles on her bare chest. I wait a polite second before arching my neck to run my lips over her skin, to kiss and cradle them.

There's so much more to work with than ever before. I nuzzle her breasts, run my hands beneath them, squeeze them, surprised by their weight and softness.

She arches her back with a moan as I run my tongue over her nipples. They're mauve like her lips and sized well for her large breasts, begging my attention each time I try to pull back and kiss her neck.

Her hands tangle in my hair as her breaths quicken. Her sexual ala intensifies, clogging my nose and filling my brain. My cock twitches at the ready—but I know what I want first.

"Helisent, can I kiss you?"

She bites her lip. She looks out of it, like she didn't hear or understand the question. "What?"

"I want to kiss you." I run a hand on her thigh, sweeping my thumb toward her vulva so she knows I'm not talking about her mouth. "Do you like that?"

She raises her eyebrows. "Oh... *really*? See, I knew there was a wolf thing at play here."

Good. I don't want anyone else doing this.

This is mine.

No, Samson. Bad, Samson. No possessing the witch, Samson.

My whole body is fizzing; even Samsonfang seems keenly aware that Helisent is now naked in my bed, her wetness seeping into my sheets and soaking my brain.

"Okay," she says with a quick smile.

I lean in for another kiss. Again, she giggles as though thrilled. Her laughter spurs on more tadmazzar as I start to feel more comfortable; she's enjoying this experience, and I'm giving her pleasure, and making her feel safe.

I rub her thighs, kissing her breasts as I make my way down her waist. I kiss her stomach, which sets off a fit of laughter at my light touches. I like her squirming, I like her breasts as they sway with her quick jerks, and the soft fat that lines her tummy. She's so... whole and deserving.

I kiss her thighs and make my way toward her vulva. Helisent doesn't lay back but stays propped on her hands. As though eager to watch, she looks down as she moans and moves.

I glance at her sex, mind and body focused solely on the thin patch of curly white hair and the mauve folds beneath. Her lips are wet, her clit large enough that I can see it exactly at the crest.

I love how it smells, I love how it looks—soft, just like the rest of her. I rub her clit with my thumb and wait for a sigh before bending down and kissing her. She whines at this, too, until I run my tongue over her lips, her clit, her warm wet center.

My hands grip her hips, pulling her closer as I slide my tongue into her.

She jerks back. "Holy shit, Samson."

I raise my head. "I'm sorry, did I—"

"You just put your whole fucking tongue in there?"

I glance around and wonder if I'm missing something. "You don't like it?"

Her laughter fills the room. "Do it again." Then she falls back.

I spread my hand on the back of her thigh to push one of her legs slightly back. I glance up at her foot when I lick her vulva again. It twitches twice, then her toes curl in time with a moan as I slip my tongue inside of her again.

She does like it; it's just new.

Good. I don't want anyone else doing this.

This is mine.

No, Samson. Bad, Samson. No possessing the witch, Samson.

I start to feel the rhythm her body craves: deep strokes, light circles, a slow pace. I hold her and kiss her vulva until I can feel her muscles contract, and I hear the one noise I've never heard Helisent make in these last months.

A bleating sort of panting that tapers off into a high-pitched, almost surprised keen.

It's *very* loud. I'm not surprised.

I wait for its echoes in the marble room, closing my eyes to hear every note.

And then she's kissing me, small hands holding my cheeks. "Take your pants off." I oblige her as well as I can while she hovers close. "Make me cum again." She's still out of breath, planting kisses all over my face while I try not to rip my pants in the frenzy to be naked with her. "Is this what my pussy tastes like?"

I set my pants to the side. Now that I'm naked with her, I sit back with my legs folded beneath me.

"Yeah."

Her eyes widen. "And you like that?"

She has no idea. The seething was just a taste, just a tease, for months. "Yeah."

"I see." She presses herself against me, then reaches down to grab my sex.

I shiver at her grip. She kisses me as she leans to stroke my head. I sit up, hungry for more of her warm touch, for more of her scent.

One second, I'm holding her waist and wondering how much to move, and then she's fitting herself around me. I take a deep, steadying breath that turns into a low groan as Helisent winds her hips to engulf me.

Her moans deepen, and her grip on my face tightens as she slides up and down.

I try not to move so she can find her pace and comfort zone. She studies my face as she moves, breath catching as her legs start to shake and her breathing picks up another urgent pace.

I throb inside of her as instinct tells me to thrust and meet her. Slowly, I start to drive my hips, once again glancing at Helisent's feet to make sure her toes are curling as we move.

Pressure mounts in my gut, sending me over the edge as her bouncing breasts and smothering ala and keening moans drive me insane.

I bury my head in her hair as I breathe through my orgasm. I seize the blankets near our legs just to grip something with all my might.

As my breaths slow, I realize she didn't cum a second time.

But, undeterred by the softening of my dick, she keeps riding me. She grips my cheeks, then my jaw as she sweeps deep and quick over me. A second later, she peels herself off me and lays back. Her eyes clench as she rubs her groin, as though teasing out the last of her pleasure. Her white hair catches on her sweaty face, breasts pushed together as her hands reach below.

Panting, I stare down at Helisent.

Helisent West of Jaws.

She looks up at me, wipes the hair from her face, and asks, "So can I sleep here or what?"

CHAPTER 17

ITZI
HELISENT

Honey Heli,
I'm not sure when you'll find this note since my hiding magic is getting
really fucking good. Anyway, I wanted to congratulate us on becoming
Antigone's youngest sponsors. Younger than mom was. Congratulations
to us. We deserve it—and more. Let's have it all together. Forever.
Mint Mili

I wake up with no idea where I am.

For the first time in my life, I'm pleasantly surprised by what I find.

The *Luzian Estate.*

I sit up with a yawn and wrap the beige sheet around me; the marble walls are just as frigid as they look. I stare across the plain room and let last night's memories float through my mind.

I check the sheets for stains just to make sure I'm not imagining sex with Samson.

It would make sense if it was a dream, a blur of candlelight and ecstasy.

But these are real memories; those are really his torcs at the bedside. I think of his little facial expressions, and knowing what his moaning sounds like, and having his tongue inside of me.

I press the sheets to my nose and inhale. My nose isn't nearly as functional as his, but I can smell Samson. Cedar, leather, musk. With a sigh, I fall back and bury my head in his pillow.

A few minutes later, footsteps echo from the hallway.

I fix my hair to look messy in an attractive way, then pose myself on the bed.

Samson grips the doorframe and leans into the room. His loose waves dangle to his collar, his harem pants hung low on his hips.

His eyes lower before meeting mine. "Good morning, Helisent."

"Helisent?" I sit up. "I thought you'd call me little bird."

He glances at the floor again, a slight blush on his cheeks. "Good morning, little bird."

"Good morning, sweet wolf."

I don't think he'd like to be called *big* wolf. He spent the first half of our encounter last night hiding his dick like he was afraid it would scare me. It may have been my first experience with a wolf, and I wasn't sure exactly how things would play out, but it wasn't my first time seeing one naked. Bless his heart.

I reach for my robe, set neatly at the edge of the bed. "Should I leave?"

"No." His eyebrows bunch as he comes forward to kneel on the bed.

I leave my robe half-strung on my shoulders, then shift to wrap my arms around his abdomen and rest my head against his chest. His hair scratches my cheek while he strokes my back.

"Are you hungry?" he asks.

"Yeah. Should I start the fire?" But I don't move. My empty stomach and slight hangover don't feel nearly as important as our newfound intimacy. I crane my neck to stare up at him. "You always look different with your hair down. Will you keep it like this when we're together? At least some of the time?"

He glances at a dark blue lock with a crooked smile. "Sure."

He bends toward me, and I think he's going to kiss me. Instead, he inhales a deep breath of my hair.

Samson pulls back, features soft. "You can take your time. I'll start the fire and cook us something. Come out when you're ready. The washroom is next to this one."

He extracts himself and leaves without another glance back.

I stare around the empty, cold room and wonder how someone as kind as Samson grew up between walls like these.

I wash in the room next door, then pick up the items I tore from his satchel and threw around the room last night. I repack them carefully, though I lack the precision Samson always manages.

Afterward, I even make the bed. I have no idea how it should look or why I bother when he'll have to change the sheets. But I leave the room cleaner than when I woke up, then walk toward the sound of sizzling in the kitchen.

Samson stands in the corner of the cramped room, which only has basic tools like a wood-burning oven and a massive sink and a few huge pots. I help him work through the raw ingredients laid out on the table: cassava, egg, a series of colorful peppers, and small vials of spices.

Though my hands twitch with the urge to use cooking magic, I'm not sure if it would be considered disrespectful; this is a Velmic estate, after all. And anyway, Samson usually cooks his breakfasts the old-fashioned way.

I mostly hover and cling to his back with my chin set on his shoulder. I watch him move the pans around the flat stove to prepare the food.

When it's done, we walk to the salon. Rather than clean up the remnants from Clearbold's dinner the night before, we leave the dining room as it is and head farther into the estate. I'm happy to sit beneath the natural light from the garden, which floods the salon with a hopeful hue.

Samson eats like he's half-starved, and I watch while I pick at my meal, trying to decide if it's sexier now that we've been intimate. I think it is. Especially now that I'm more familiar with his tongue. With his lips.

When our plates are empty, he totes them away. He comes back with steaming tea, and then I watch him sip. I watch how his lips move, how they frame the mug's top, how his throat shifts to swallow the tea.

I try to focus.

Delightful as last night was, it comes with a slew of consequences.

"So last night..."

I wish I had grimoire so I could force him to tell me the truth.

Does he really find me interesting and attractive? Is there an ulterior motive to this affair? Does he know I'm a center-heart? What the fuck do we do when winter comes and Silent City calls?

"What did Rex say to you?" he asks. "And how many times have you met Clearbold?"

I look up with a start. "Oh... *that*. I was thinking about the rules. I mean, wolves have a thousand rules for everything, and especially *you*. So... if there's anything I should know, I'd like to know now."

This time, Samson looks taken aback. He clears his throat and sets his mug down. "Oh. Rules. I figured you'd want to start with... other stuff."

Like what?

He looks past me, toward the garden. Then he looks back

at me, blue-black eyes shifting across my face for a long moment. "The rules aren't going to sound very nice."

I raise my eyebrows and ignore the fear that takes root in me. "Then make it fast."

"I'm bound to the Female Alpha of Velm, whoever she ends up being. We already covered this at some point, but... in case you forgot, I *am* allowed to be with other people aside from her—just not publicly."

I clench my gut and pretend I'm fine with that.

That I'll exist in his shadows just like I exist to the rest of the world.

Samson studies me with a bland expression. "So if we leave a place where we've been intimate, I have to ask you to clear our scents. From the place, from me, from you. It looks really bad for any Alpha to have an affair exposed... and for me that's even more important."

I run a nail across the sparkling marble table near my mug. "Rex told me how our affair would be taken in Velm."

Suddenly, Samson looks like he's staring at me from a great distance away. Like he's looking at me but can't quite make out who I am.

He rubs his chin. "It wouldn't be good. Not with Malachai prepared to leverage any mistakes of mine—not that you're a mistake. You aren't, but—"

"I get it. You don't need to explain it, Samson. I know the position you're in. I'm also well aware of what Clearbold thinks of me. I don't want to compromise your future in Velm. I hope you trust that.

"The first rule seems easy enough. I need to get rid of our scents—clear a place, then clear you, then clear me. That's fine. You'll have to remind me a few times, but once my magic realizes it's a habit, a regular spell should pick up."

He nods. "Thank you. The other topic we should discuss is pregnancy. Worse than an affair going public would be a pregnancy... that's the whole point of the Alphas' marrying. The

Afador line has to continue, and it has to continue with the Female Alpha. With Brutatalika 567 Sigivald or Menemone 571 Erenel."

I cut off the pain of that statement before it can settle. I tell myself that I face a similar future. I need to bear a red witch, and I need to do so with a warlock. Any child conceived with a wolf would be born pith.

Samson stares at the table, shifting his mug. "I'm taking pitroot. It will lessen the chance you would get pregnant, but... I haven't really had to think about that in a while. Since I've mostly been with Rex the last few years. It's best if you also take something."

Before I can respond, he shakes his head, scratching at an arm arrantly. "The only story I've heard of an Alpha impregnating a woman aside from his Female Alpha didn't end well."

Rex's words flash through my mind from last night.

And if Samson doesn't make it to that throne, do you think Clearbold or Malachai will let him live?

"They killed the Alpha for getting her pregnant?" I ask.

Samson's eyes shoot to mine. "No, not him. Her. Their child."

I sit back. Unsure of what to do, I glance at the courtyard like he did a moment before. I study the towering fir tree and its lazy needles, letting my mind consume its endless details while the reality of what he said sinks in.

I clarify, "Because you'd be the Alpha, right? Not just because I'm a witch."

I need to understand what specific type of evil his last statement was.

"Exactly. I will have one child and it will be the Kulapsifang. He or she will lead Velm someday." He takes a long drink of his tea, head hung. "If I wasn't the Afador, we'd have freedom."

Already, my gut is sinking.

All the optimism from last night's orgasms fades to black.

I clear my throat. "I'll take vagueroot. It's an anti-contraceptive for witches. What other rules do I need to know?"

Samson shakes his head. "That's all from me, unless you'd like to tell me what Rex said."

I smooth my hair with a sigh. "That I'm the most selfish person to ever love you. That you'd never forgive me if I compromised Imperatriz's legacy."

His eyes widen. "He's always been a little possessive."

I take a long sip of tea. "You don't say."

"I love you, too, Helisent."

I look up, shocked by his words. I wasn't exactly confessing my love for him, though I'm relieved he feels the same. "Good. And I'm guessing... Clearbold had a lot to say about me."

I stare at the steam curling from the sweet tea. Though I hate that it was the growling Alpha who told my story, I'm relieved I won't have to recount it myself. I'm sure Clearbold added a few flourishes I would have left out, but the bare facts are simple enough.

Samson's voice is soft. "He told me why you're after Oko. That you're also after a warlock named Anesot."

Hearing Samson say Anesot's name pleases me.

I think Samson could destroy a warlock like him.

He'd have to get those hands on him first, but I'd love to watch that.

I run my fingertip over my mug's lip. "I don't expect you to tell me why you're looking for Oko. Keep your secret, Samson."

He doesn't say anything for a long time, and I start to wonder if he'll tell me the truth.

Instead, he asks, "Do you have any family?"

I fall still, surprised by the question.

"I do." I adjust the sleeves of my robe, wondering how much to tell him. "My brothers live in Antigone. They're twins, Yngvi and Yves. They're around ten years older than me. My father still lives west of Jaws where he raised us, but he likes to travel around Rhotidom and Septegeur. He stays with my brothers in Antigone a lot. They also spend a lot of time in Rhotidom. His name is Parsifal. He's kind of famous. Big belly, bigger heart."

Samson tilts his head. "You don't speak of them."

Each word is fragile, gentle.

I shrug. "I'd hate for something I do to hurt them."

Like with Milisent. Like with Andromeda.

I try to push myself into memories of them, into the warmth they've left·in my heart.

"My brothers work with metal. They're builders in the top lanes of Antigone. They're fearless in a stupid, endearing kind of way. Yves found a witch he likes. I think they might have a littleling someday—but another part of me thinks Yngvi might get in the way of it just to keep Yves all to himself.

"Me and my father are a lot alike."

We never moved on. He from Andromeda, me from Milisent.

"So they're..." Samson bites his lip as he searches for words. "They're not red wielders, are they? That was your mother's line."

Andromeda North of Skull.

"No, they're gold like the rest of the wielders in Mieira. And... I know I don't speak of them, Samson, but I love them. I love them with my whole heart. I'm just—I need to get rid of Oko and Anesot before I can let myself..."

Be happy again.

Be part of my family again.

I shake my head, frustrated that I'm not explaining myself well.

"It's different than what you feel," Samson murmurs, "but I understand being fixated on a goal. Most of Velm thinks Imperatriz died or abandoned her post. Sometimes it feels like I'm the only one who thinks there could be another possibility."

I look up.

I realize that we might be more alike in our power, in our convictions, than I'd ever realized before. That we might both be tethered to the ghosts of the women we no longer have.

I nod. "That's all I want to say about it for now."

"And... everything else?" Samson asks. "About what happens in winter..."

I reach across the table and take his hand between mine. I stroke his knuckles with my thumb. "What if we leave that until after we find Oko?"

Neither of us have the backbone to say what we're thinking.

That, as much as we desire the other, we both want Oko more.

Samson nods. His fingers shift to hold mine. "I agree. But after that, we talk about it, Helisent. About all of it."

I return his nod. "And... speaking of finding Oko—you can go first when we track her down. You can take all the time you need to speak with her."

"I'm not sure how long it will take to get what I need, but thank you."

I shrug. "I'll stay close by. I'm not opposed to torture, in case she doesn't come forward with the information you need."

Samson's mouth falls open. He glances at the garden again, as though searching for a distraction.

I shift to block his view. "Don't look so innocent, boy-wolf. She's a murderer; she'll play on every honorable instinct you have to manipulate you."

I can tell by his discomfort that he either doesn't believe me or doesn't want to. He doesn't even mention the words *boy-wolf*, which I specifically crafted to torture him.

"So..." I gulp down the rest of my tea. "I need to find Itzifone and make our barter. Do you want to come with me?"

Samson crosses his arms.

I pinch my lips to keep from smiling; I love it when the

men get jealous. Like I'm a shiny little thing that has to be held with a tight grip lest someone steals me. Like I'm a rare treasure worth hoarding.

"Relax, Samson. I've never even slept with Itzifone. It's like I told you on the way back to Luz—he's just after a place in the running for a powerful littleling."

"*Wonderful*." He raises his eyebrows. "I still don't think it's a good idea for me to go. He'll be more willing to barter wth you."

A second ago, I thought he was disheartened by my past with Itzifone. Now he seems fine using my female charm as a bargaining chip.

"It might be better for you to come in case he knows we're working together now," I reason. "If he thinks we're competing for information like last time, he'll pit us against each other to leverage our offers."

Samson wags his head. "Good point. I'll pack my things so we can leave right after. Do you need to go back to the warren before we set out?"

"I should probably stop by." I stand and leave my mug, heading toward the bedroom. Samson stands and follows me. "Most of my stuff is there. And the mentee."

"She *stayed?*" he asks. "Even after you threatened her mother?"

"Some things have come to light. She's still in Luz, and it seems like she's found her place in the warren. Blessed little witchling."

I head into the bedroom, disheartened that I can't smell Samson's scent anymore. It's all just a bland mix of clothes and bedding and the leftover scent of breakfast.

I pause when I realize Samson stares at me with bald disbelief.

I set my hands on my hips. "What, Samson? Am I not allowed to change my mind about the mentee?"

A smile edges onto his lips. "I'm not thinking about the

witchling. I was thinking about the room—who taught you how to make a bed? And did you *fold* all of my things and *set them nicely* back into my satchel?"

He pinches his lips as he tries and fails to hide his laughter.

Past his mirth is genuine surprise, which I find offensive.

In response, I use tossing magic to send the pillows, sheets, and duvet around the room. The satchel is close behind, articles soaring in the air while Samson lets a long sound of disappointment and tries to dodge the flying items.

I rush into the hallway then call back, "Meet me at Solace. I'll be there in an hour."

I move my hands as I backtrack toward the garden, summoning cleaning magic to wash everything of our scents— even the items tucked inside my bottomless bag.

"Helisent!" he yells from deep inside the marble walls. "Helisent, please come clean this up!"

My smile reaches toward my soul as I listen to his distress, as sweet as a lullaby.

The warren is empty aside from chirping canaries.

I write a note to tell the group goodbye then fill the empty cylinders stacked neatly under the kitchen counter with gleaming dove. I stand in the doorframe and bid farewell to the rectangular room and its arched windows.

The pastel canaries flit onto the twining plants along the windowsill. They shift their heads to study me with bulging eyes.

I tell the birds, "I don't think I'll be back for a long time. And if I am, I won't be the same. Just look after Esclamonde in the meantime. Simmy, too. That's the witch and the oread. Got it?"

One of the yellow canaries shits. The rest of the reddish birds stare at me, anticipating a meal.

With a sigh, I turn and leave.

I keep a lookout for my warrenmates as I head east toward Solace. I even make sure my peach robe flares with extra sass in case one of them glimpses me, but no one emerges from a side street or building to greet me.

With each step, I feel like I've passed a new frontier.

It's not just what happened with Samson last night but also what lies ahead with Oko, too. After years of brandy-addled stupor, my search for Oko is nearing a conclusion.

I find Samson waiting outside Solace, leaning against the tavern's dark wood and watching people pass by. He kicks off the wall when he sees me, stopping in front of Solace's door-less entrance.

We meet each other with polite smiles; for whatever reason, it already sets me off.

There's nothing sexier than a forbidden secret.

For now, at least.

I step into the tavern, and he follows.

On the cusp of morning and afternoon, the dingy wooden tavern is as empty as it ever gets. Nymphs and wielders line the bar, hunched over and speaking in loud voices meant to be whispers. A few groups occupy the square tables, but the second floor sits vacant. Half-drunk ales from the night before litter the tables whose chairs sit scattered.

I squint toward the bar and look for Itzifone's dark-green cloaks. If he's not trading what information he has, he's usually coaxing it from the drunkards sipping their drinks.

"There's no trace of his ala," Samson says. "Do you know anyone who could point us to him?"

I chew my lip, squinting again at the bar. "Yeah. Stay here a minute."

I round the wooden bar to study its patrons; aside from an old witch who I recognize from Boonma's spa, it's an anonymous stretch of half-drunk, half-bored Luzians.

The bartender rounds from a back room and raises her eyebrows at me. "Can I help you, witch?" The naiad's brown hair is pulled back tight against her scalp. Her light-blue tunic pulls the sapphire from her river water eyes.

I keep my tone curt. "Where's Itzifone?"

She takes her time pouring a mug of wine. "And who's asking?"

I set my hand on my hip. "Helisent West of..."

Before I can finish, the naiad rushes toward me, nearly dropping the bottle of wine. She wraps her hand around my wrist and drags me away from the bar. The row of seated patrons swivels their heads to watch us go.

I glance from the naiad's hand to her panicked expression.

She guides me onto the street. She barely spares a look at Samson. "I'll be with you in a minute, wolf."

He follows us away from Solace. The naiad stops a safe distance from the entrance, then she glances back as though afraid of eavesdroppers. Compared to her ruddy brown hair and the dark wooden buildings around us, her blue-green eyes pop like pockets of pure sky.

"Itzifone's in trouble..." She stops speaking when she realizes Samson followed us.

I wave the wolf forward then turn to the naiad. "He's with me. We both need to speak with Itzifone—what happened?"

Though she spares one last nervous glance at Samson, she doesn't move away. Her grip tightens on my arm as she explains, "He told me a while ago that his mom is a Ghost-Eater—one of only two left in Mieira. She moved back to Alita a few years ago. She left us enough dove to keep Solace going for a year—bless her heart."

She sighs, nostrils flaring. Once again, she glances around the wide street. "Two days ago, a terrifying witch stormed in here with two ghosts on her heels."

Oko.

Like me, Samson leans closer to the naiad.

"She wanted to barter with Itzifone for information about his mother, but he refused. I know he'd usually barter for anything, but he was right to deny this witch what she sought. She was from the depths of Septegeur in the worst way possible."

I nod, happy to hear that Itzifone has *some* backbone.

The naiad's features pinch. She wipes her eyes as though on the verge of tears. "And then she left like it was *nothing*. I *told* him to stay at my place or the tavern that night, but he went home like an idiot.

"When I went to check on him last night, he wouldn't come to the door. He wouldn't say if he was injured or not, but he always comes to the door—and he sounded *nervous*. He never sounds nervous. All he would say was that Helisent West of Jaws is the only person I could trust with this information." She shakes her head, setting a few tears loose. "Do you know who it was? What should I do?"

I rub my temples while I figure out what to tell the nymph.

If Oko couldn't get what she wanted out of Itzifone, then she would have punished him. Even if he'd just made her wait for the information, she would have punished him for his tardiness.

"I have an idea who it is. Where does Itzifone live?" I ask. "Can you take us there?"

The naiad nods as she dabs at her eyes. She glances at Samson again. "Itzi didn't say anything about a wolf."

I roll my eyes.

Itzi.

I glance at Samson, then the naiad. "Well, you just told the wolf everything, so he might as well come, too."

The naiad's fingers readjust on my wrist as she studies Samson, neck bending. I've already forgotten how intimidating his presence can be. He wears a purposefully blank expression, hands uncrossed and at his sides.

I pat the naiad's white knuckles. "He's trustworthy, dear nymph. I take responsibility for him."

She turns away the next second, dragging me along.

Luckily for me and my wrist, Itzifone lives nearby. We turn down one dark crooked street, which funnels into a narrow sidewalk. From there, she turns onto a colonnade where canaries flit between nests tucked into stone archways.

We hustle up the stairs onto the colonnade's terrace. The naiad beelines for the short lane's last door then releases my wrist.

She knocks, leaning forward to whisper against the door. "It's me, Itzi. I found Helisent West of Jaws. She's here—and there's a wolf with her."

As though he's been waiting by the door, Iztifone starts working the lock from the other side. "What kind of wolf? Samson?"

For the first time since meeting the nymph, Samson speaks. "Hello, Itzifone."

"Where were you two days ago when I needed you, you big scary fuck?" the warlock replies.

Only two days ago?

With a metal crank and a wooden groan, the door lurches open a centimeter. A single golden eye comes into view, along with Itzifone's white eyebrow.

"Wait outside," he tells the nymph. "Just Helisent will do for now."

"Why?" The naiad sets her hand flat against the door. I can tell by her hushed question that she's more worried than upset. "Itzi, you have to—"

"No. Just the witch." Iztifone doesn't leave any room for compromise. "Everyone else back up. I'm not in my best form."

I wait until the nymph and Samson back up a healthy distance, heart sinking to my feet.

I'm not in my best form. For a warlock with as much pride as Itzifone, it's a confession: he's been injured and, like most wielders, he's not open about licking his wounds.

I put my lips to the door's opened crevice to clarify, "I

don't know healing magic." Though the naiad can't hear me, I know Samson can. "If she hurt you, I need to get another wielder to come and help you."

"*Fuck*." His low voice sounds close to trembling. "Why not? Strong witch, no skills. This never pans out—"

"Itzifone, do you want help or not?"

He sighs. "Come in."

I slide into the widened gap, then he shoulders the door shut behind me. Though I've been to his cramped apartment before, it takes me a moment to recognize it. Torn cushions and broken glass fill the square salon, droplets of blood splattered. Debris fills the hallway that branches from the room—a fragmented shelf, more broken glass, torn books.

Then there's Itzifone, who watches me with his back leaned against the shut door.

He holds his bare hands to his chest. They're warped and swollen and purple. His broken fingers at least remain curled in the right direction, but I can tell that his wrists have also been sprained.

Tears rim his golden eyes. His white hair is frayed around his face, the uncombed shoulder-length mane a knotted mess. Even his emerald robe is askew, as though he's been unable to take it off.

Though wielders can speak a spell or lend it momentum with just a movement of our body, we tend to rely on our hands. Wielding a spell with injured hands is nearly impossible. As such, breaking them is a common punishment from the Class, and a common form of revenge taken by enemies.

Itzifone whines once, as though the madness of the last day is finally bubbling to the surface.

I stroke his cheek. "I know, I know. It's okay, Itzifone."

He parts his deformed hands so I can offer him a hug. He cries once into my collar, then when I pull back, he wipes his eyes on his shoulder.

I study his warped fingers and ignore my nausea. "They

don't look like serious breaks, okay? Should I go get the healer, or—"

"No. You need to get moving." He gulps down a breath to calm himself, then he heads to the shredded couch. "They're going after my mother. They fucking raided my place, as you can see, and—"

"*They?* The naiad said it was just a witch. I'm guessing it was Oko. Or are you counting the ghosts, too?"

He falls back onto the couch's single intact cushion, keeping his hands raised before him. I wish he'd put a cloth over them. As he moves into the milky light from the tall window, I can see every grotesque bruise and swollen joint.

"I'm not talking about the ghosts. Who travels with Oko, Helisent?" He almost sounds annoyed, but his words make me pause.

Anesot.

I fold my arms where I stand near the door. "What the *fuck*, Itzifone? I didn't know you knew."

At some point, all wielders in Mieira likely heard the story about the red sisters in Antigone and the warlock who conspired to consolidate their power. I just figured most would have forgotten about his crimes after the Class doled out its banishments and started their inane hunt for Anesot and Oko.

Based on how Itzifone watches me now, he hasn't forgotten. He says, "There was a reason I always collected information on Oko."

I hope Samson hears this. I hope he starts to understand how warlocks work.

Itzifone isn't saying he did it for the sake of justice or for the sake of my revenge. He did it to put himself in better standing with me, for the possibility of being in the right place at the right time when I'm ready for a littleling.

"Aren't you such a fucking sweetheart, Itzifone. Now get to the point. Your hands are going to make me throw up."

"Oko came to Solace looking for a GhostEater. She wants my

mother. I think the only other GhostEater lives in Ultramarine, and she refused to work with Oko, so she only has one option left. I obviously pretended not to know where my mother was.

"Oko asked a few other indirect questions that I didn't particularly feel obliged to answer. I think she was trying to gauge whether or not I was refusing to work with her out of respect for you. I tried to stay vague, but...

"I left work and came home. Anesot was sitting on my couch with his fucking horns out and then..." Itzifone looks up at me, lowering his chin. "I hope you've been working on your spells, Helisent. You might not need to know healing magic, but you'll need to know killing magic of all stripes if you want to get him. He's not going to—"

"Stick to the relevant details. He came in here and broke your hands, and then what?"

He rolls his eyes. "Anesot came in here, trashed my fucking place looking for something he could use to track my mother, broke my wielding hand for sport, then asked me about you."

Fuck.

If Anesot isn't blindly fleeing me anymore, I can't imagine what he's planning.

"What did he ask?"

"How long you've been a sponsor here." Itzifone adjusts on the couch with a twitch of his hips. "How long you've been working with Samson 714 Afador. Whether you two were after him or Oko."

How did Anesot learn me and Samson are working together?

"What'd you say?"

"I told him to ask you himself. Then he broke my other hand."

Though he's no bolder than the average warlock, Itzifone is cheekier and, oftentimes, more useful. I clear my throat, mind raging. "Thank you, Itzifone. For standing up to them."

He waves his hands with a crazed look in his wide eyes.

"Who gives a fuck about that? I need you to find my mother before they do."

"I need something of your mother's. And do you know if they found anything of hers? How quickly do we need to move?"

"They took a bunch of shit—probably around ten little things they could sense weren't mine. There was a chain from my mother in the pile, but I'm not sure when and how they'll figure out that it's hers. You guys aren't far behind, but you need to go after them *now*."

He scoots to the edge of the couch, then rocks back before lunging forward to stand up. It's an awkward moment that he grunts through, but quickly forgets about. He takes off down the hall, sidestepping the mess.

"You can take her scarf," he calls back to me. "You have to bring it back after, though. I wear it all the time."

I hover after him into the washroom. He jerks his chin toward a bundled silk scarf near the empty basin.

I pick up the orange scarf, then I immediately drop it. "Why is it all oily?"

"Oily? It's not oily."

"It's oily. Tell me why it's oily."

"Who knows? Crazy world. Lots of textures."

For a long time, he stares at me with his broken hands cradled against his chest; it's almost like he's baring them at me in the hopes of auguring pity.

I stare back, blinking into his wide eyes until he finally says, "It's for hair treatments, Helisent. Nobody likes a balding warlock."

I pluck the scarf from the counter, happy to hear it's only hair product. I don't think anyone actually minds a balding warlock, but I don't tell him that.

I turn back toward the salon. "Fine."

He hobbles after me, knocking into a stool. I head to the

door, and he sinks back onto the couch with another series of undignified sounds.

"Did you tell Ninigone and Absalom that banished wielders entered the city?" I ask.

He snorts. "No—and don't you tell them, either. The last thing I want is the Class showing up at Solace."

"I'm telling them. This city is their problem. If they want to pretend to be in charge, they should act like they're in charge sometimes. I'll send a healer back before we leave, too —any preferences?"

He rolls his head back to stare up at the ceiling. He lets out a fussy sigh. "The one with the big tits and the curly hair. Please."

I roll my eyes. "Which one is that?"

"I don't know. Starts with a 'T.'"

"Fine."

He rolls his head forward to stare at me again. "Don't tell Absalom. I mean it. Tell Ninigone, *if you must*. She can handle it. And tell her I'm reporting her back to Antigone as soon as I can write again. Those two claim to have wards set up to prevent banished wielders from coming into Luz. What a joke. Anesot must've wiped his ass with them and had a good laugh. I mean, seriously, those two—"

"Anything else?" Given the chance, Itzifone will whine until dawn.

He tsks. "I wasn't finished on that last point, but yeah. And don't tell Sergia about my hands. She's a fragile soul. Tell her I'll be back at work in three days."

"Should I be writing this down?" I ask.

I reach for the door handle so he knows he's running out of time. He wags his head in consideration, then shakes it. "No."

I tuck the orange scarf into my bottomless bag. "I'll make sure a healer comes today. And I'll look after your mother. I promise."

Itzifone watches me with a serious bend to his brow.

His set mouth opens like he may speak, but he doesn't.

At last, he says, "Good luck."

I slip back onto the landing and shut the door behind me. Samson and Sergia wait at the top of the staircase at the end of the terrace. Sergia dabs at the corners of her eyes. Samson looks calm as ever.

We take off back toward Solace.

First, I calm Sergia and assure her that Itzifone will be back to work in a few days. Then I find the healers where they're stationed near the processors and send the biggest-titted nymph for Itzifone. Last, I head back north with Samson to begin our journey to Alita. Unlike our other destinations, this trip won't take longer than a week.

Within a few hours, the towering canopy of Rhotidom comes into view.

Most of the trees are primary and ageless, taller than the even the highest columns in Luz—and their branches are just as thick as trunks. The region's humid heat feeds an endless range of lush green plants. They blanket the floor and the canopy, drooping back toward the dirt roads and wide ferns and trickling streams.

We keep walking until dusk falls. Beneath Rhotidom's thick canopy, daylight recedes earlier than on the plains of Gamma. The forest is so thick with plants and shadows, great and tiny, that some emerald-haired dryads who never leave don't develop long-distance sight.

Based on Samson's flitting eyes and craning neck, he's enamored by the endless range of details. He follows me off the road that leads north from Luz, choosing each step so he doesn't crush saplings and bushels as we search for a minor clearing.

It's a bit pointless; I use stomping magic to flatten the flat ground between three mid-sized trees to make camp. Though Samson looks nervous about erasing the life of a plant with a misplaced step, most of the forest floor is already dead, fallen from the canopy.

Soon, our dinners cook above a chugging fire.

I reach for my bottomless bag and summon the oily scarf into my hand. With confirmation from Itzifone that his mother is in Alita, there wasn't a need to refine our path before now.

I look from the scarf to Samson. "Do you want to talk about Itzifone? I know you must have overheard what he said."

He takes a deep breath, shoulders lifting. "I'm guessing his hands were broken?"

I nod. "He should be back to normal in a few days if he listens to the healer. They're usually pretty good at fixing broken hands."

He rubs his cheeks. "I see. Anesot did it, correct?"

I nod again. "Oko was with him. They must be traveling together now. Did you not hear? I figured you were listening."

He sighs. "No, I did. I just wanted to make sure I understood everything... I caught a familiar scent from the opened door. An ala."

He stares into the fire. His jaw works and his expression darkens. "It was the warlock's scent from Lampades, Helisent. The warlock who followed us from the concert and spoke to me after you'd passed out. If it was Anesot's ala in that apartment, then it was Anesot who I spoke with that night."

The scarf slips from my fingers.

Has Anesot been following us, or was it a chance run-in?

I comb through everything Samson told me about the warlock. He'd sensed my power and come to see who I was; he wore the finest trappings from Septegeur; he'd refused to give his name; he brought up working with Clearbold at some point; he'd stared at me.

Well, that checks out.

Still, it takes me a moment to calm my rage.

The idea that I was *so close* to Anesot...

That I could have *killed* Anesot...

"Helisent, your eyes..." Samson murmurs.

I squeeze them shut until I can rein in my temper. Much like the wolves fear accidentally turning skin on a double or triplemoon due to emotional reactions, wielders can also lose control of the instinctual magic that hides our forms.

It's much rarer, but so are the circumstances of my life. And at least Samson has already seen my real eyes.

I smooth my hair and then open my eyes, relieved not to see any more red glowing. "They know we're after them, Samson. Oko must have realized we were after her, then she must have found Anesot and warned him."

For a long time, he doesn't respond.

While I cast my tracking magic, he stares into the fire. Eventually, he says, "When Anesot was walking away, he said that I'd need him someday. Any idea what that's about?"

Panic seizes me, quickly curdling into a sense of doom.

I wish I would have pushed Samson to reveal his reason for looking for Oko—it would give me some clue at what we're going to face in the coming weeks.

I just hope he believes me when I say, "It's about keeping you bound to him. It's about manipulating you, Samson. If you think he's significant, you might try to stop me from killing him."

I study his profile, lashed with firelight, but I can't tell if he's taking my words seriously.

I go on, "He speaks in half-truths as a rule. I know you have your misgivings about wielders—but I need you to know that none of them are misplaced when it comes to Anesot."

I want to trust Samson. I want to trust whatever motivation he has in searching for Oko.

And I know that begins with my own honesty.

"Samson, if we find Anesot and Oko together..." I clear my throat. "What I told you earlier about letting you have Oko—

I'll stand by that. But nothing like that exists with Anesot. I won't think twice when I see him, and there's nothing that matters more to me in this world than killing him myself."

He turns away from the fire to face me. "I understand."

His words and expression don't give me any reason to doubt him. And I don't want that to change, so I remind him, "Don't get in my way."

Being a centerheart, I wouldn't be able to stop Samson if he did.

Which is why he doesn't know.

Which is why he never will.

Samson nods.

But I can tell by how he stares ahead that he's chewing on the memory from Lampades. He's going over every little detail from his run-in with Anesot and attempting to figure out which details he missed and what they meant.

Six long years.

Me, too.

CHAPTER 18

THE TRIPLEMOON, SAMSONFANG PART II

SAMSON

My son,
The Afadors became the inborn line of Alphas not because of generosity,
nor brute strength. When winter came, we shared our grains, our peat,
our furs. Hetnazzar made offerings to us, which our ancestors shared
with other wolves. So it went, on and on. Give, Samson. Keep giving.
This is the secret of our power; you will never run out.

Each day that takes us closer to Alita brings equal notions of bliss and fate.

Bliss, because the road to Alita isn't well-traveled and we spend our days in relative solitude and peace. Fate, because the road to Alita is also the road to Oko. To Anesot.

Scarier than my future in Silent City is the verdict the Class will eventually level against Helisent.

Bliss again, because Rhotidom is the most fertile place I've ever stepped foot. The evergreen forests of Velm that fill the steep mountainsides are almost incomprehensible memories compared to Rhotidom.

I stare around in wonder at the towering trees, their

tangled canopies, and the busy forest floor. It's filled with ferns taller than Helisent and enough flitting birds and insects that I cover my mouth when I yawn.

And after the heat-filled, phantasmagoric days come the cool evenings.

Every night I spend beneath Helisent's nest, the more obsessed I become with her ala, with her voice, with her laughter. And every intimate moment we spend together, I start to fear the inevitable future without her.

But it's not really *fear* that I feel.

It's wrath.

It's fury that I'll have these memories with limited chances to make more in the coming years.

This evening, I stare into the canopy of a tree with sturdy roots. Its trunk is thick enough that my arms wouldn't wrap around one-third of its breadth. I move to the other side of our firepit so the tree's flaky bark and clinging moss don't rain down on me as Helisent prepares her nest.

As the birch twigs weave together, she gathers her robe and squats on an adjacent branch. She notices my stare and raises her chin. "You're coming up here tonight, motherfucker."

I knew it was coming. "Helisent, I can't—"

"No, no, no." She shakes her head in frustration while the nest weaves itself. "I go *all* day without touching you in public, just like you asked. And then I'm supposed to go all night without touching you either? Meet me halfway, sweet wolf."

The birch twigs rustle as they intertwine, accenting the blaring insect and bird songs. The twigs loop around distant branches to create a monstrosity of woven twigs, twice as large as the nest normally is.

I realize what she's doing. "Helisent, I said no. I can't climb the tree, and your magic will—"

"I say *no*, too. You won't feel my magic this time." She tsks loudly. "You can only feel infrasound in the water or if I'm using a really powerful spell. You won't even *notice* floating magic."

"What about Lampades?" I avoid the memory of Anesot. Of that leering, posturing, evil warlock. It's like he lives in my head, like he knew what to say to make me wonder, and stew, and rage. "You zapped me *twice* with panic magic."

"I don't have any plans to blackout tonight, so there should be no panic magic. I'll float you up here and that's that. There's plenty of room—the tree is sturdy enough for both of us. Nest-living is very refined. I'm sure you'll approve."

I set my hands on my hips. With night overtaking dusk, there's barely any light on the forest floor aside from the dim fire. Though the moons are nearly full, they're hidden by the thick canopy. Only the barest residual light bleeds down to Helisent's nest. There's hardly any where I stand farther below.

"And what about the rain? There have been light showers on and off all day."

The skies tend to clear in the late afternoon, but spring rains have kicked off across northern Mieira; they come and go at any hour, only loosely respecting a pattern.

"I'll use covering magic to protect us." The nest falls quiet, no longer snaking into a larger form. She scurries across a narrow branch to settle in. Her head pops into view from the ledge a moment later. "What else, Samson? What else are you afraid of?"

I rack my brain for excuses to avoid getting in the nest. Aside from fearing her infrasound, I also fear the height. I won't feel comfortable that high up. These feet belong on the steady earth.

I snap my fingers as an idea comes. "What if I roll over on you while we sleep? You've brought it up on multiple occasions. It could happen in a tiny nest—I probably wouldn't even notice your kicking and screaming."

"I never should've told you that." She rolls her eyes. "There's enough room for both of us up here. *Next.*"

"What do I do if I have to pee at night?"

"Just point your dick past the nest's ledge, and we'll make it. *Next.*"

I narrow my eyes and opt for distraction. "Is that what you do at night when you have to pee? Just hang your butt over the edge?"

"I hate to ruin the mystique, but I don't pee out of my butt, Samson. And I think you would've noticed that a while ago." With a sigh, she disappears. Out of sight, she calls down, "You know, I didn't want to do this, but..."

She sidles back into view with her breasts bared, then she leans over the nest and lets her long, white hair fall loose. The tresses curl around her breasts as she pushes her shoulders back.

"Wow, where did these come from?" She looks down and strokes herself. "They're so soft and heavy..."

She glances down at me as though gauging whether it's working.

I keep my hands on my hips and try to ignore my growing erection.

She disappears from view then comes back with oil. She starts rubbing the oil across her breasts with long, yearning sighs. "So much oil up here, Samson..."

I like to think I have a strong sense of self-control.

I like to think a lot things.

I study the massive trunk in search of knots I can use to scale the tree. The moss will be the problem, along with its weak lower limbs. Some look as old as the Afador line, way too crooked and ancient to support my weight as I climb to the nest.

"Are you really going to try to climb the tree? You'll fall and break your neck."

Helisent shrieks, loud and wordless, then leaves the nest to fly down to me. She's naked under the velvet peach robe, which gathers around her like wings. I glance past the fabric toward her breasts, which don't fall toward me but stay suspended, like the rest of her body.

When she lands, the robe covers most of her chest, but her sex and the small patch of white hair aren't covered. She stands on the other side of the firepit with her hands on her hips, looking from my face to where my dick presses urgently against my pants.

She points to the nest. "I'm taking you up there."

I try to frame my words, but all I get out is, "Infrasound..."

She wanders over to me. Now, Helisent is close enough that I can sense her warmth. That I can almost taste the oil on her breasts.

She hisses, then says, "Fine."

She starts hovering to return to the nest, but I grab her robe and tug her toward me. To my surprise, she lets me kiss her lips, then her cheek, then her neck. Half-caught in her massive robe, I'm tucked into a cocoon of her warmth and ala.

I close my eyes as she kisses me, tongue slipping past my lips.

Then my foot knocks into something.

I pull back and realize I'm not standing next to the firepit.

A shocked yelp peels from my lips as my body curls as though weightless, as though I'm floating on the surface of the water. Then my butt rests on soft bedding.

I whip my head around, but only see the dark folds of Helisent's robe from the inside, along with her patient, amused expression.

The velvet layer sweeps back, and Helisent stares at me from the other side of a hulking nest.

She bears a smile at me, lifting a shoulder as though feeling a bit guilty. "Super nice up here, right?"

It *is* really nice.

Though the nest looks lopsided from the outside, the

inner floor is perfectly flat. Lush bedding sits piled to one side; more pillows and blankets than I'd ever think to use. On the other side sits a tray with tidy stacks of what look to be beauty products: liquids, oils, creams, and small trinkets. Another tray has a glass jug of water and a wooden cup, along with woven bowls of snacks—nuts, berries, and dried berries.

Combined with the rich notes of Helisent's ala, it feels like a piece of heaven.

But I don't tell her that.

"Little bird, I'd prefer if you didn't trick me."

"Even though I was right about my magic not hurting you?"

I nod. "I'm a wolf. We like to figure things out ourselves."

"You'll never figure out magic by yourself. And you never considered how it made me feel every time you've shied away from my magic." She raises her eyebrows, then flicks away a piece of bark on her knee. "It makes me feel *bad*, by the way."

My stomach drops. I hadn't thought of it like that.

"My magic isn't dangerous, Samson," she goes on, picking at things nearby and tossing them from the nest's ledge. "I know how to control it. And now that I know that infrasound hurts your precious nuts, I'll be careful.

"I mean... not just *me*, either. Remember when I told you magic is like a twin? Well, my magic knows about you now. It knows what you like and don't like. It pays attention, Samson. And *I'm* paying attention, too."

I extend my hand toward her, palm up. "I'm sorry, Helisent. I didn't want to make you feel like I didn't trust you, or that I feared you. I don't—I just..."

I don't want to say this next part, but it would be dishonest not to share.

I clear my throat. "I grew up hearing a lot of horror stories about wielders. I don't know why they've stayed in my head like they have—especially when I *know* you're different."

I keep seeing the deepest and tallest room in Bellator Palace.

The gray light from the glass ceiling falls across the endless rows of red horns mounted to the marble walls. The spread of pale pinkish stones set on the floor in the center of the room.

This is where Clearbold taught me the strategies our ancestors used to survive the War Years.

Like he mentioned up in the Luzian Estate, child-killing was the primary method of protecting the future of wolves. But it was only one of three tactics developed in Velm.

The second was to *avoid* killing elders. Magical power flows down a wielder's ancestral line—not up. When the elders learned they were protected from our wrath, they began to kill themselves.

This led to the development of the third tactic. Velm's cruelest act of war was the killing of vanity. This was the true nature of Bloody Betty's wartime escapades—not just to destabilize and slaughter wielders, but to insult.

And sometimes, when I look at Helisent...

I remember these lessons my Alpha taught me. The memories spark adrenaline in my veins, a panic at the idea of having to figure out how to kill something as powerful as Helisent.

And unending shame of knowing I think these thoughts around her when she has shown me more kindness and care than most other beings in my life.

Helisent sets her hand in mine. "It's okay. I get it. I'm still scared of wolves, sometimes. Go on, then. Get comfortable."

I hope she means that; it would make me feel better.

She releases me and I adjust to cross my legs, leaning back and forth to test the strength and dexterity of the nest. It doesn't budge, doesn't groan, doesn't sink.

I nod again to reassure myself.

"And, now that you're in the nest, you'll be rewarded greatly." She wiggles her eyebrows.

My eyes shoot to her chest. My erection rekindles as I

search for her shape beneath the velvet robe. Now that she's seated cross-legged like me, she's mostly hidden.

She tsks. "*No,* not that. I meant grooming. I've noticed you spend as much time with your hair as I do with mine, so..." She leans over to grab one of the clear bottles on the flat tray and shakes it. "Take down your hair. I'll brush it."

It makes me feel even worse about how I've treated her magic. There are few things a wolf likes more than co-grooming, especially related to hair. Some married couples exclusively care for their partner's hair, from cutting to washing to combing to conditioning.

And Helisent noticed.

I take down my hair and turn around. She guides me to lay down with my head in her lap, then she tangles her nails along my scalp to separate the strands. Within a few breaths, I'm fully relaxed in the nest, staring up into the canopy with a sense of childlike wonder.

I've never been this high up before. Never seen so many leaves tangled like this.

It makes me think of young Samson, climbing through the yew with Helisent in a dream.

"This is oil from one of those weird-ass fruits in Hypnos. You know, the big brown things. What's that called?"

A warm liquid spreads along my scalp, then a comb starts tugging.

"A coconut?"

"Yeah. Those things. Did you ever go back when you weren't with your war band? You said wolves like to swim."

"No, but I swim in the ocean in Velm. East of Mort. It's a lot colder, but less salty."

"*Salty?* Sounds gross. Does Samsonfang like to swim as much as you?"

"He does. Maybe more than me." I watch her work for a moment, calming more with each breath. "And speaking of Samsonfang... the triplemoon is two nights from now. We can't

really spare any time to take a day off, so I might be a little...
feisty."

This goads a delighted smile from Helisent. She smooths
the baby hairs near my temples as though unconcerned by my
announcement.

I go on, "I'll try to tone it down—but at night, I'm not sure
what will happen."

I study her understated smile. She looks absorbed in her
work, eyebrows slightly pinched as she sorts through my hair,
combing then setting the strands aside.

I clarify, "It's possible Samsonfang might... be curious."

She raises her eyebrows. "I'd imagine he has a few questions about where you've been putting your dick lately."

"Don't say it like that. Look, there's not often hesitation
for a wolf in its form. I'll either come directly to see you, or I
won't come at all. There aren't many wolves in Rhotidom, so
my scent around camp should be enough to deter any other
phasing wolves." I clear my throat. "I know I said that last
time. This time, I mean it."

"Fair enough." She runs a fingernail along my hairline near
my ear. Then her golden eyes study mine. "And what do I do if
Samsonfang comes to see me? I've never seen a wolf in its form
before... and I know I just made a point of saying that my
magic isn't dangerous, but—"

"You should always fear a wolf in its form, Helisent. No
matter what happens between us."

I have a lot of misgivings about what wielders and nymphs
think of wolves, but there's no compromising on this aspect of
Velmic culture: an untrained wolf in its form is at best a threat
and at worst a killer.

And an ala as powerful as Helisent's is difficult to ignore for
wolves who wander close on a triplemoon. What begins with
curiosity can easily end in fear—and most phased wolves will
lose a fight before they'll back down from one.

She pauses. "Even you?"

"No, not me. I'm—it's like with your magical twin. Samsonfang is a lot like my magical twin. He wouldn't harm you because I wouldn't."

She makes a long sound as her fingers start to work again. "Then I hope you come to see me."

I've been terrified of the same since we left Luz and I realized we'd be on the road together for the next triplemoon. Around other wolves, I feel nothing but pride in Samsonfang. With Helisent, I'm terrified of what my most unbridled self might do.

"So... if I *do* come to visit in my form..."

Her eyes widen with delight. "I'll be on my best behavior, I promise."

"It's not that—I wanted to tell you what *I* might do. I'll be running on instinct, which might compel me to... encourage you to do things I think you might need to do."

I'm not sure if it will happen like this. The only time Rex and I dared to meet in our forms, there was growling and chasing and dominative nipping, and it didn't make us feel closer the next morning. I was ashamed, Rex was furious.

Her eyes narrow, and I follow up quickly with, "Like eating or sleeping."

"What? How would you make me eat something if you're a big wolf?"

"I'd... herd you toward the food."

"What's that? *Herding*? Like a shepherd?"

"Yeah. I'd nudge you toward the food. I'd... probably not want you to leave the food until you've eaten."

"Bossy fucking wolf, aren't you?"

"No, I'm just..." *In love with you.* "I'll be interested in your physical health. Aside from herding, I'll probably just hang around. There might be some growling, but it wouldn't be at you. It would be at things I hear or smell, okay?"

She keeps working the oil into my hair, massaging my scalp

so that I'm half in a state of ecstasy while trying to describe Samsonfang.

Eventually, she asks, "I thought you said that wolves only want to claim territory and hunt and dominate things in their forms. How do I fit into that? If you're going to stomp over to camp and try to dominate me, then—"

"That's only with other male wolves, Helisent." I shake my head, staring up at her. "I don't feel that way toward female wolves or women in general."

She makes a high-pitched sound. "I see. Very good answer."

Her words nag at me. "Do I make you feel that way? That I'm trying to control you?"

That's not what a male wolf should ever do to a female, wolf or not. It's morally reprehensible, but, in the case of female wolves, dangerous.

They're more aggressive than the males, more demanding when it comes to their partners. They're the ones who carry children through winter and birth them when the brief summer returns. They're the ones with bodies like Velm: rich and unyielding and capable of great beauty, great bounty, swift death.

Helisent bends down to kiss me. "No. I don't get the feeling you're trying to dominate me." She lingers a moment, reassuring me with her soft lips. "So what about me? Am I allowed to touch Samsonfang?"

"I'm not... I'm not positive. I've never gotten close to another being while in my form—only other phased wolves. If I don't like something you do, you'll know."

I lean to one side as she gathers my hair and wraps a towel around it. She taps me on the back and I sit up, taking hold of the towel and my wet hair within.

I wait for her to ask for clarification, but all she says is, "Okay, scoot back. My turn."

Without skipping a beat, Helisent floats in front of me, then shoos me back toward where she sat. Then she lays herself down and shimmies to get comfortable. As she arranges her head and hair in my lap, I prepare the oil and brush.

I get to work on her silky hair, tangling it a few times before my fingers get used to handling the fragile strands.

She lays with her eyes closed, a smile on her lips as though supremely pleased.

I take my time, drawing out the process.

I've been doing it more and more often.

Fate looms like a hammer about to fall—then bliss.

I pace in a circle as the full light of Vicente, Abdecalas, and Sennen worm into my psyche.

It's the first time I've phased beyond open plains and clearings fit to race across. Even the thick evergreen forests surrounding Rouz and Bellator are interspersed with treeless valleys perfect for sprinting, marking, and howling.

With the heavy cover of Rhotidom's canopy and the spread of wide ferns beneath, this triplemoon will differ greatly.

Then, of course, there's Helisent's presence. Though I've traveled far enough away from her to let Samsonfang choose freedom or the witch, my mind keeps switching back to her ala.

My head tilts as I search the wind for a trace.

Each strained inhalation that carries less of her ala grates at me.

Even as I start panting and gripping at a tree trunk in preparation of turning skin, my mind snaps to our camp. To the nest she wove across the primary branches of a mature kapok tree.

My body curls toward the ground, dry leaves and twigs snapping under my weight. I grip the tree's bark and spit out the thick foam in my mouth. It's laden with dopamine, testosterone, adrenaline. I try to inhale her ala each time my airways clear. Now I'm not checking that Helisent is okay; I'm making sure I don't smell her approach.

This isn't the Kulapsifang of Velm.

This is just a naked man curled on the ground, clothes folded neatly on a rotting log at his side. First comes blistering apprehension, then my vision turns black, and then unforgiving pain strings a threshold only Samsonfang can pass through.

The last thing I feel is my skin cracking, then tearing to make way for thick tufts of blue-black fur.

"Don't hurt the witch," I breathe into the dirt.

I will never hurt the witch.

"Good."

Goodbye, Samson.

This is a new place.

I'm interested in this place; I mark it with urine. It's mine now.

The soil is heavy and wet. It smells like iron, clay, and sand. It's filled with traces of nitrogen, magnesium, and phosphorous. This is a fertile place.

I sniff under logs—fertile. I claw at the logs until they fall apart like dust—fertile.

There are new animals here. I've never smelled these small mammals; their alas meet beneath the ferns and fan across the ground like tree roots. Not all are small. There is one large enough to eat, but its ala is too faint to track.

I'm hungry.

I search for a clearing.

I circle the forest for a long time.

There is no clearing; there is no sky. Where are the moons? I howl for the moons I cannot see. I like this forest less now. It hides the moons. Hides Vicente, Abdecalas, Sennen; their light gives me power, they want to see that I use this power.

I search for a clearing. I find an ala in the wind instead.

It belongs to a very powerful witch.

My hairs stand on end until I smell more of her ala. I have smelled this ala before. Many times.

The powerful witch is not a threat; she is my witch. I am the strongest male in all of Velm, and she is the strongest female in all of Mieira.

I rush toward her ala.

I move faster as her scent comes into focus. She is fertile. She will menstruate soon. She is healthy; her hair is long, her nails are strong. I can smell all the places she's peed around the campsite. Her nest smells like birch twigs and coconut oil.

I stop at the edge of camp.

The witch is in the tree. The witch stares at me from the nest.

I'm now displeased; my ala is faint compared to hers.

I am the strongest wolf in all of Velm, and my ala should cover hers. When someone smells her, they should smell me, too. Together, we are the strongest. (This is my witch.)

I mark the campsite.

This pleases the witch. She laughs from the nest. "Samson-fang! Not on the orchids!"

I circle the firepit. I stop under her tree. I sit down.

This is a tiny witch.

I lay down; I will make myself smaller like her.

Then she will come down.

And I will make her smell like me.

She doesn't smell enough like me. (How will the other males know to stay away?)

The witch watches me. She's not laughing anymore. "Should I come down? Samsonfang, you're fucking huge. Way, way, way bigger than I thought wolves got. I'm not scared. Just a little nervous..."

She will feel comforted by words. I can't speak. I make a

sound. I move my jaw. These aren't words, but she will understand.

She doesn't understand. "What the fuck does that mean?"

She needs to come down. She needs to smell like me. I move my head, then paw at the ground.

"What are you all worked up about? Do you want me to come down?"

I howl. What does Samson say to her? What does she not understand right now? Will she stay in the tree all night?

"Okay, okay. Stop fussing."

The witch floats down the tree trunk. She stops halfway. She doesn't let go of the tree.

I back up. I lay on the ground again. I try to make myself small; she is very tiny.

I set my head on the ground, too. She understands that I am safe now. She floats to the ground and stands. She presses her back against the tree. She wears a large robe. I will put my scent on that first, then her body.

She watches me; I watch her.

She curls up on the ground. I smell more estrogen now. She's fertile like this forest.

"I'm feeling more comfortable now." She pats the ground at her side.

I go to her side. I smell adrenaline; I lay back down. I lay my head flat. Is she scared of me? Does she not trust me?

The witch tilts her head. "You're very beautiful. And very big. I thought you'd be the size of a saiga, dear wolf."

This is good; she should think I'm beautiful and know that I'm bigger than a saiga. Saigas are tiny. Saigas are food.

I move my head closer. Does she realize she doesn't smell like me? That I don't smell like her?

I want the witch to touch me.

She raises her hand. It's very small.

She pats my nose; she should touch my fur. It will keep her

scent better. When someone smells me, they should smell her, too. Our scents should be smelled together.

Eventually, they will mix.

Two alas will become one.

The witch's hand is warm. She smiles. She comes closer. Her robe brushes against my whiskers. I like how she smells.

I don't move so she can put her scent on me. She isn't very good at it.

I put my scent on her instead. I sniff her robe. This makes the witch laugh. She falls to the side. I use my snout to keep her upright. The witch is powerful and fertile, but maybe she isn't very strong.

She runs her hands into the fur between my eyes. Her body presses against my snout.

She's getting too close to my neck.

Too close to my neck—too close to my neck—too close to my neck—

She backs up. Good. She was too close to my neck. She sits down.

Now I can put my scent on her. I rub my snout against her left side, then switch to the right side. She keeps laughing. I try to rub my scruff and then my flanks on her robe. She's too small. She doesn't understand. She tries to move out of my way instead of leaning into me and leaving her ala in my fur.

"What the fuck is this, Samsonfang? Is this herding? I already ate dinner."

I move my mouth. She doesn't understand.

I lean forward and inhale a large breath from her robe.

She puts her hands on her hips. "My ala?"

I scoot closer and inhale her robe again.

She smiles. "Oh! You want us to smell the same? Because we're a pack when we travel together?"

She takes down her hair. Her ala is stronger in her robe, but she doesn't understand. I don't mind. The witch can do whatever she likes. I will not leave. There is nothing more interesting in this forest.

She shakes her head so her hair flares out. She runs down my side and tangles her hair in my fur. Her hair catches on my fur; she doesn't nuzzle into my fur to mix our scents properly.

But I smell no more adrenaline. I smell oxytocin in her ala now, and estrogen. This is good; she is bonding with me. I am bonding with her.

She sits down again. I sit behind her; she should stay close to the fire. She needs warmth. She leans against my side; this will work better to mix our alas.

She is quiet. She yawns.

I wait for her to sleep.

She doesn't. She speaks. "Samsonfang... I hope you can understand me like this. The other morning when you asked about my family, I didn't tell you about my mother or my sister. I've been... feeling kind of bad about it. It's just hard for me to talk about them. Maybe like this... maybe like this, I can be more honest with you. With Samsonfang."

She leans forward. She looks at me. I look at her. I blink; does she know I'm listening?

"I hope that's okay with you." She sits back. "My mother's name was Andromeda North of Skull. Her mother took her to Antigone to develop her spellwork. She was the city's sponsor for a while in her 30s and 40s, but she didn't like Septegeur. My father told me she wanted to live like a nymph.

"So she left Septegeur and lived in Jaws and Rhotidom. She met my father, Parsifal South of Jaws. They fell in love and they stayed in love... not like most wielders. My father said her love was quicksand. He just kept sinking.

"So they built a little homestead west of Jaws.

"They had my brothers, and then my sister. Yves, Yngvi, and Milisent West of Jaws. It's a big family for wielders, Samsonfang.

"Transferring magical power takes a toll... and four children... well, it's a lot. And Andromeda didn't survive when it was my time to come to Mieira.

"So I know what it's like to grow up without a mother.

"But I wasn't alone as a witch, either.

"I always had Milisent.

"I didn't really feel alone growing up, even if I always felt guilty about Andromeda. I don't usually call her my mother. She feels like... she feels like...

"Never mind. It's stupid."

She stops talking. I smell salty tears. I turn my head and set it close to her. Does my scent comfort her? She touches me. She sniffles.

"Me and Milisent always wanted to go to Antigone. We wanted to be city sponsors like Andromeda. And we had to learn to control our magic. There's no better place for wielders to develop intricate magical skills. My father and brothers didn't want us to go..."

She cries again. She buries her face into my fur; my scent does comfort her, then.

She looks at me again. Her cheeks are red and damp.

"Anesot was a city sponsor. He was the one who taught Milisent and I to package our dove so it could be used at the processors. Our dove was wilder, given our power...

"I was twenty. I thought... Anesot was so refined. I wanted to impress him and prove that I could be... cool, I guess. Two years later, I spent half my days with him.

"My father hated him. My brothers hated him."

She turns to sob into my fur. She needs to breathe. She tries to speak. I can't understand her. She needs to breathe. Her heart is racing. My scent isn't helping.

"The—the stupidest part—she was the only one who liked him. Milisent—she stood up for him—for Anesot—and that's why—"

She sobs. I wait.

I know the warlock she speaks of.

Anesot.

I raise my head to search the wind for his ala; nothing. I search the wind for his descendants, his ancestors, his extended family; nothing. I will keep looking.

She doesn't pull her face from my fur. Her breath is warm against me.

"We were supposed to meet Milisent and Oko on Metamor. I couldn't sleep... I couldn't sleep... and when I did, I woke up. I could feel her magic rush into me. Her twin saw my twin before they become one. Her twin told my twin. I could feel it... could feel that it was Oko who had killed her... and that it had been Anesot's plan for years. To make sure only one could wield the red line's power."

Her hands tighten on my tufts of fur. Snot and tears mix against my fur; this will work better to mix our alas. Still, I do not like her sadness.

My witch is very upset; she doesn't smell like oxytocin anymore.

She has no more words.

Her heart rate slows. She is calm; now she is also sleepy. The witch looks up at her nest. I don't want her to go.

She looks around, then she turns back into my fur. I stay close to the fire. She will stay warm.

I listen for the sounds of intruders.

I tilt my head to smell for intruders.

I stare into the trees to watch for intruders.

I look at my witch.

She is safe.

Maybe not then, but now.

I stand before my head stops reeling.

I take a deep breath to get rid of the fog that clouds my mind.

The witch is mine, Samsonfang tells me.

I stand up and dust myself clean. I don't bother checking for spies in the dense forest, still dark as dawn breaks beyond the canopy. I tug on my clothes and review what happened last night.

Helisent's story comes first. I'm glad she told me about Milisent in her own words. I never doubted what Clearbold shared at the Luzian Estate, but I knew it failed to convey *her* deeper truths.

I remember the story of her mother next, Andromeda North of Skull. About the little homestead where two wielders, deeply in love, built a happy life together.

Then I remember rubbing my scent on her and wishing she understood how to cloak herself in my ala.

Samsonfang was *obsessed* with her ala.

Our scents should be smelled together.

Eventually, they will mix.

Two alas will become one.

I head back toward camp as the reality of those thoughts settles in. I swat aside the craning fern blades and crush twigs under my boots, each step quicker as the implications fill me with dread.

There's only one way for two alas to become one: mixing.

It's an informal term for two bonded wolves whose alas eventually blend together into a unique third scent. The mixed ala contains elements of both originals as well as more information about the pair, like how long they've been together and whether they're still fertile. Mixing is rare and tends to happen in a married couple's latest years—if at all.

Most importantly, mixing *only* occurs between wolves.

The composition of nymph and wielder alas isn't malleable like ours. Even the most devoted wielder and nymph couples don't mix.

Why does Samsonfang think our alas will mix?

The only explanation trickles back to Helisent's magic.

Once a month since we met, I've found myself stunned to learn how powerful she is... once again.

I think I'd like a definite answer now.

A moment ago, my steps gained momentum with each stride. Now, I halt. I gather my thoughts and try to figure out which topic to broach first—what Helisent shared with me about her sister and mother or Samsonfang's fixated scent-rubbing?

Right as the hulking kapok tree comes back into view, Helisent rushes toward me from the firepit. Her hair and breasts bounce as she jumps to meet me, then she latches her legs around my abdomen. Before I can return her embrace or warn her that I'm covered in dirt, she starts sobbing into my neck.

I run my hands down her back; I'm not sure if something specific happened or if it grates on her to recount her most difficult memories like she did last night. "It's okay, little bird. It's okay."

She stutters for breath. "I know. I'll be okay soon."

When she pulls back, I use the edge of my tunic to wipe her cheeks clean. I kiss her then pinch her chin. "Thank you for sharing so much with Samsonfang."

She sniffles, eyes twinkling with fresh tears. "You were just so big and cuddly."

My stomach locks, as though someone just hit me in the gut. "Big and *cuddly*?"

I remind myself that she was also unafraid of an irate, injured phoenix. And that she's been scooped up by passing demigods presumably for most of her life. What should she think when she looks at Samsonfang? I should be relieved she didn't respond with fear.

Still...

Cuddly?

She smiles briefly and wipes her cheeks. "I'm kidding. But

you *did* seem interested in cuddling. Or was that just about alas? I couldn't tell."

I clear my throat. "You didn't smell very strongly of me, and I found that problematic."

She raises her eyebrows. "Oh?"

I shrug as she remains clinging to my abdomen. "It's a wolf thing."

Although, it's not *really* a wolf thing. I didn't care how much Maia or Rex smelled like me, and vice versa. Even during the most intimate portions of our relationships, I wasn't concerned with whether their ala carried traces of mine. Not even on the triplemoon when Rex and I met in our forms.

Samsonfang's fixation on Helisent's ala and insistence on mixing isn't just novel.

It's worrying.

I'd assumed that sort of impulse would be reserved for the Female Alpha, not a powerful witch.

But like most of my life's mounting problems, I shove that topic away for another day. For when the search for Oko has concluded.

I lean forward to kiss Helisent's cheek, then I smell her hair and kiss her neck. "Did it bother you?"

She smells more like me than ever before; it's difficult not to linger, not to try to imagine what our alas would smell like mixed into a single scent.

"No." Her lips pinch, a slight blush filling her olive cheeks. "I liked it. Getting to see you like that. It makes me feel bad that I won't be offering the same to you anytime soon."

Though desperate to learn more about her form and how many horns she has, I try to keep my voice light. "And why is that?"

She stares across my features. Though I support her butt with my hands, she's using hovering magic to cling to my abdomen and remain at eye level. I'm relieved it's become a

habit for us; I'm too tired to support her full weight indefi-
nitely right now.

In her ongoing silence, I guess, "Does your magic do its
own thing, like Samsonfang? Are you worried you wouldn't be
able to control it?"

She rolls her eyes. "No, it's not like that. I'm a wielder—it's
about vanity. You looked beautiful, Samson. And the more
comfortable I got, the more beautiful I thought you were. But
that's not what I look like in my form. I'm more..." She traces
my nose with her fingertip, then moves on to my lips. "I'm...
not very pretty."

I stare across her features. When we first met, I didn't
think much of her lips or eyes. Now, they're the baseline I
compare every other being's features to. Worried saying that
might sound too infatuated or indulgent, I go a different route.

"But you're still *you*, right?" I ask.

"What do you mean?"

"I know that wielders start hiding their forms when they're
children on instinct. I guess part of me wonders what you
looked like... before that."

How she was born into this world.

That's the Helisent I want to see.

"I don't change my features, you know. Not my face and my
body—they're the same in my form as they are right now." She
opens one of her hands between us and studies her fingers. "I
change my hands, though. This isn't what they look like. And...
obviously, my horns are hidden. Also, my skin. It's... bright."

Bright? What does that mean?

She sighs, shoulders slumping. "Then there's the fucking
tail. I *hate* the tail."

I try and fail to hide my smile. "I also have a tail."

She smashes her palms against my cheeks. "Stop smiling.
It's not funny."

"Fine. No smiling. But can I eat? I'm starving." I shuffle

past a fern with Helisent still clinging to me, then step onto
the flattened dirt surrounding our firepit.

She lifts her hands, but her legs stay wrapped around me.
"But you'll wonder, won't you?"

I crane around her shoulder to try to find my satchel.
Delightful as I find her body pressing against mine, she's
currently in the way of me and my breakfast, and I don't like
having to choose between the witch and food.

I say, "That's not necessarily a bad thing."

With a frustrated sigh, she pulls away from me. Her boots
touch down near the dead firepit where kindling sits stacked.
Her eyes stay fixed on me as she snaps her fingers, and a flame
catches on one of the dry leaves in the kindling pile. Her hair
is messy, her robe littered with flaky debris from the heavy
forest.

"You can just feel them." She says it like a threat, tossing
her hair over her shoulder. "My horns, I mean. Not the last
one. Only the main ones. And you have to wear a blindfold."

I drop my satchel as thoughts of breakfast disappear.

What does she mean by the last horn? All the horns I've ever
seen, in-person and hung in Bellator, came in even sets of two
or four—not prime numbers.

*What do they feel like? And why would a blindfold change the
experience that much?*

Too scared a pause or a question might deter her, I say,
"Whatever you're comfortable with."

She stoops to pick up her bottomless bag, set on the
ground at the base of the kapok tree. She pulls out a piece of
fabric, then she points to a spot near the firepit. "Sit there and
put this over your eyes."

I obey and keep my distance from the growing flames.
Already, the morning hints at a hot day. I prepare the blindfold
and glance at her as she paces with her hands on her hips. Part
of me wants to reassure her that we don't have to do this now,

but I don't want to get in her head. There looks to be a lot going on in there right now.

I sit back, tie the blindfold, and then blink into the dark fabric. Aside from a seam of light above and below, I can't see anything.

"If you take it off, I'll blind you. Do you understand?" she says.

"I won't take it off. No need for threats."

Like a falling tree that bludgeons the ground, a deep thrum of infrasound starts to my right; I almost rip the blindfold off just to be sure it's Helisent and not some other deadly force. Within a few seconds, I recognize the infrasound, as though it's humming a familiar pitch of bass. At least the roiling, humming magic is out of range so as not to cause me physical discomfort.

Still, my hands flex at the ready, prepared to shelter my nuts.

The infrasound beats at my psyche. It sets my mind on fire.

I can't concentrate on anything but that palpable humming.

And, once again, Helisent's ala.

Every single element of her scent intensifies as her magic unleashes into its form; she smells bitter and... ancient.

It's almost like a separate ala settles on top of hers.

"Remember when I told you that magic is like having a twin?"

"Well, my magic knows about you now."

I get it now. This isn't *just* Helisent.

She says, "I need a second to figure out how to dampen my infrasound... I'm never in my form."

I clear my throat and hope her magic can't sense how unnerved I am. I remind myself she was also nervous around Samsonfang; I don't think she'd be offended to know this is a little overwhelming.

"Take your time," I say.

The infrasound lessens incrementally. With a whoosh of wind, it almost disappears.

"There. Can you still sense it?" she asks.

"Move around so I can tell."

I inhale to follow her ala as she crosses the camp. Though I can hear her boots shuffling against the leaves, I can't sense her infrasound anymore.

"I think it's okay." I lean forward to pat the ground in front of me in invitation; I'll feel less on edge when she's stationary.

My heart rate increases as I anticipate her movement. Though her infrasound is gone, I can *sense* that it's being hidden. It's like draping a sheet over a huge object and pretending it's not there just because the details are hidden.

"Can I request to start with the tail?" I ask.

She tsks from close in front of me. Her jewelry jangles as she situates herself on the ground. "No, Samson. I said you couldn't touch the last horn."

"You have a *tail horn?*"

"Samson!"

"What? I didn't ask how many you had."

"Just... *sh.*" She takes one of my hands and drags it toward her. She sighs, then curses, then groans loudly. "Okay, just be gentle. *No grabbing.* If you grab my horns, I'll blind you."

I roll my eyes under the blindfold. "May I remind you that I touch you gently all the time?"

"Yeah, but everything inside of me right now is saying '*don't let the wolf grab your horns, or he'll kill you then head for the village.*' Sorry, I'm not trying to offend you. It' just..."

Though I hate to admit it, I'm also painfully aware that the roiling infrasound gently placed beyond the bounds of my senses could level Bellator. Probably several times over. "I understand."

She sighs, then guides my hand upward.

My pointer finger knocks into something hard and... coarse.

This isn't like the rest of Helisent—at all. The horn is a fibrous jagged bone. It's thick enough that my finger doesn't round it with a quick touch.

She guides my finger to trace the outline of the horn. It curves back then arches around toward her ear, like a looser, jagged ram's horn.

A full-grown, *huge* ram.

I don't know what I expected, but it wasn't *this*.

"So that's the middle one," she whispers.

She doesn't let me feel its twin on the other side of her head.

Instead, she guides my hand back to her forehead. It knocks into a second horn, which feels only slightly narrower than the first. Rather than curve back, it follows the top of her head and then curls upward before tapering at the end.

"That's the center one," she goes on.

I pull back, but she doesn't let go of my hand.

She takes it to a third horn on the same side of her head.

And if she isn't letting me feel the horns' twins, then that puts her total count at six.

Seven, if I'm counting the tail.

While I was growing up, Clearbold mentioned the threat that four-horned wielders pose; it's why he would have kept tabs on a warlock like Anesot. Most wielders only have two, and even those horns can be as small as a thumb.

My heart ratchets at an uneven beat.

I feel like a child.

Like I've grown up thinking I understand and wield power only to realize I've been given a drop of it to harness—and only under the light of three full moons. But Helisent's power...

This is... forever.

This is... unending.

"This is the baby horn," she sighs.

I follow the path of the third horn. It's not a *baby* horn at all.

It juts from her forehead rather than her scalp and hairline, like the first and second. The third horn pokes outward and upward like the other wielder horns I've seen. Still, hers are thicker and coarse, like the husk of a wooly tusk.

I inhale deeply; her horns smell like dry fiber, minerals, and bone.

She takes my hand to her lap, then runs something across my palm. It's coarse and thick like her horns, only much smaller. "That's my thumbnail. My fingers weren't always like this. All of me got a little... wilder after Mili died. I didn't have a tail horn back then, either."

I realize this wasn't how she was born, either—her horns must have been smaller until Milisent's power became hers.

I run my fingertip over her thumb to feel at the sharpened edge of her nail.

It's thicker than a normal nail, and dense, like bone. Like a talon, almost.

"Samson, why haven't you said anything yet?"

I clamp onto her hand when she tries to pull away. "I'm waiting for the seventh horn."

"I said you couldn't feel that one."

"Why not? Is it bigger than the other ones?"

"No. But I'm not very good at using my tail. I have to get it out if you want to feel..."

A laugh peels from my lips. "Get it out? Where do you keep it?"

I can't tell if it's the novelty of everything I've learned in the last few days, exhaustion from Samsonfang keeping me up all night, or the hysteria of realizing just how powerful Helisent is at last, but I'm giddy with mania right now.

I jump back a second later as something hard and flat whips my bare triceps. "Fuck!"

"Oh, there it is." She giggles. "Oops."

I feel at my arm; I can already feel a welt swelling. "That was your *tail?*"

Then something knocks against my knuckles, dragging along each. I raise my fingers and feel a spade-shaped tail. Its skin is smooth and soft, like the rest of her, but the cartilage beneath is rigid. At its center is a flat bone that sharpens into a rounded tip from the tail's tapered top.

The seventh horn.

My smile returns. "This is my favorite horn."

It slips from my fingers. "Really? Are you sure, Samson?"

Something drives into my ribs, wheedling and tickling. It switches quickly to my other side when I reach for my right.

Is it her tail?

She seems comfortable now.

Exceedingly comfortable—especially when she sticks the tip of the horn into my mouth. It hits my teeth, scratches my tongue.

I reel back with a cough. "Helisent! *None of that!*"

Her booming satisfied laughter puts me at ease. Talk of her form and horns makes her uncomfortable, and I'm still not sure how to cheer her up without a huge bottle of brandy. Letting her toy with me seems to be a solid bet.

Still, I don't part my lips far to ask, "And where do you usually keep the tail?"

"It wraps around my belly on instinct. I have to use magic to make a hole in my clothes if I want to get it out. That's why I never understood why you guys call us birds. If anything, we're more like monkeys. Like the ones in the Deltas."

"Should I call you my little monkey, then?"

She tsks. "No. I'm obviously your little bird, Samson."

My smile renews. "Good. I hated the monkeys."

Her lips press against mine for a quick second. "Me, too."

Before I can react, she tears away the bitter ancient ala of her form. It disappears into a void far more convincing than her previous veiling of infrasound.

Then she tears the fabric from my eyes, blinding me like she threatened a moment before.

I stare up at Helisent, her skin a warm olive and her ala simmered to a basic series of notes. I glance to my right and realize she already set out my food. A pot bubbles as rice cooks; eggs fry on another flat pan above the mounting flames.

She sets her hands on her hips. "Eat your breakfast before I get any ideas about this blindfold or we'll never make it to Alita."

CHAPTER 19

I ONLY HAVE ONE LEFT

HELISENT

Honey Heli,
I wish we were traveling together. Oko is a fucking weirdo sometimes.
And she always takes forever to get ready in the mornings. I guess I
should get used to it. See you on Metamor!
Mint Mili

S amson looks around at Alita's city center with loathing
in his eyes.

I set my hands on my hips and wonder what his
problem is. His thick eyebrows pull together, then his nose
scrunches. I glance around at the bustling, unpaved plaza filled
with wooden carts and merchants hawking colorful textiles
and fruits; I don't find anything worth hating.

Alita is just as busy as the deepest depths of Rhotidom's
jungle.

Crawling vines and vibrant flowers blanket the city's
untouched surfaces—the sides of paneled buildings, the
unused sidewalks, the shingled rooftops.

Dryads fill the streets. Their emerald hair is like an extension of the canopy, their glowing, tawny skin like polished teak
and cherrywood. Though also numerous, the white-haired
wielders, along with oreads and naiads and few dark-haired
wolves, almost disappear amid their numbers. Beneath the
cloudy sky, every color in Alita seems richer, brighter.

A golden saiga with spiraling horns passes us. Its sagging
nostrils shuffle against my robe, sucking the fabric as it
inhales.

I reach out to scratch its forehead, which reaches past my
shoulders. "Fuzzy bunny."

Its dark wet eyes shift to my bottomless bag as it follows
its nose to the faded leather.

"You're letting it touch you?" Samson glares at the saiga,
then at the dryad who guides it. The nymph chatters with
another passerby, unaware of its curious saiga.

"Is that why you're pouting?" I keep scratching the antelope's forehead as it investigates my bottomless bag. "You don't
like saigas?"

Samson looks away to study the milling crowd. In the
center of Alita, home to a few thousand residents like Luz,
groups tangle and part. The city's main roads branch out from
the massive plaza where temporary stalls are unloaded and
repacked each day.

Gamma is known for producing enough food to keep
Mieira fat, Septegeur for maintaining the guilds of craftspeo-
ple, Jaws for mining jewels and precious minerals, and the
Deltas for building urban utopias for all beings—selkies
included.

Rhotidom is Mieira's wild playground of fertility.

Its thick forests produce roots for incense and various
dyes, herbs and extracts for medicine, fibers for textiles, and
enough wood to build a sturdy house into the clouds.

I guess I shouldn't be surprised that a challenging scent
hangs in the air.

Samson looks pointedly at the saiga as it unleashes a heavy stream of piss onto the dirt.

I gather my robe with a gasp, floating to avoid the mess.

Samson shifts his gaze to me. "That's what the *whole* city smells like. We should stop by the city processors to make sure they're applying your dove appropriately. No place should smell like this."

I try not to gape at his expression of displeasure.

Based on the experience I once had with his mother in this very plaza, I thought he'd adore the city.

Thirty feet from us, an ancient jacaranda tree stands in honor of the nymphs. On opposite sides stand a bronze spire to represent wielders and a marble column to represent wolves.

Imperatriz 713 Afador once gave a speech to the city standing before the white marble column. She asked Alita to welcome the Northing. She acknowledged the power and legacy of wielders and nymphs.

She brought gifts from Velm: furs, peat, marble trinkets, and a bounty of sweets. The small treasures filled the trunks that sat near her feet, and the Female Alpha greeted all those who came to choose an offering from Velm.

She didn't say anything about Alita's scent.

At least, not that I remember. My recollections consist of the tiny purple flags the people waved to welcome her, the buzzing croon of Alita bells, which are actually thin brass horns, and the Female Alpha's hair.

It was so long, and dark light like the night sky, and shimmering like a star.

She didn't scale a platform to speak to the crowd. Like Samson does now, she stood a full head taller than most of the city's inhabitants. Resolute like the marble column.

She didn't linger after the nymphs and wielders had emptied her trunks. She just started walking, and the beings who stood packed in the plaza parted in immediate response.

I sat on my father's shoulders, watching. Milisent sat on Yves's.

Time slowed as everyone in the plaza turned to watch her go, as though we'd never seen anyone walk before.

She didn't turn to meet the awestruck eyes that followed her; she stared straight ahead like nothing existed aside from the path before her. Her boots pounded against the dirt as the crowd fell absolutely silent.

She walked right in front of me and my father.

An abundant mane of blue-black hair flowed in her wake, just as heavy as her black cape.

Samson has a long way to go before an entire city stops just to watch him walk, especially with his current pout.

But he'll get there.

I have no doubt.

"What?" He tucks a cigarette between his lips. The saiga has moved on, but in its wake wobbles a cart of incense piles. Even I flinch from the strong mix of aromas. "I can't believe you don't smell what I'm smelling. Or can you turn off your sense of smell? Will you light my cigarette? And how long until your magic summons the GhostEater?"

"You're increasingly fussy, Samson." I light the cigarette with a snap of my fingers, studying his distress with mounting curiosity. "Lucky for you, wielders love a helpless thing."

"I'm smelling things no man should smell. What about the GhostEater's arrival?"

"It depends. My magic alerted her that you and I are waiting for her here, but if she's even half as old as the Ghost-Eater from Ultramarine, we'll be waiting a while. Well, maybe not if Itzifone's mother uses a lilith. The other GhostEater didn't. Also, she might not come if she doesn't want to help us. I gave her both of our names."

He takes a long drag of the cigarette. "Give me her scarf. I'll track her the old-fashioned way. The city is small enough that I'm sure I'll pick up her ala somewhere."

"It was *originally* hers, but not anymore. Itzifone uses it for hair treatments. I doubt you'll be able to smell her at all."

"*Lekeli Kelnazzar,*" he curses.

He leans away from a shouting witch with a pack of parrots seated in a line on her shoulders. One clicks its dark beak at us, then it shifts its bright wings and squawks with all its might.

He nurses his cigarette, twisting now and then as though he'd be able to pick the GhostEater out of the crowd. I scan the passersby, too, both terrified and desperate to catch sight of Oko or Anesot.

Nothing.

"Breathe through your mouth," I suggest.

"Helisent, that's what I do if I want to get a *better* smell of something."

"Oh, relax," croaks someone behind us.

Samson and I whirl around to find a toothless witch perched on a lilac lilith.

If I thought the Ultramarine GhostEater was old, then Itzifone's mother is ancient. A thick purple cloak shrouds her in an abstract shape, leaving only her hands and face visible. Deep wrinkles cover her olive skin, heaviest around her bursting golden eyes and warped knuckles.

To compensate for her age, shimmering silver jewelry dangles from her ears and around her neck. Circular accents also dot her robe.

In her right hand, she clutches a stick of burning incense.

She shoves it toward Samson. "Smell this and shut up." She looks at me and juts out her other hand. "Where's my scarf?"

I dig inside my bottomless bag for the silk piece while Samson takes the incense.

Though he looks suspicious at first, he quickly leans toward the lacing smoke that rises from the brown stick. His features soften with relief. "It smells like... it smells like..."

The GhostEater leans toward him with a wicked smile.
"Go on."

Samson's features fall as he looks at me. "It smells like
nothing." He inhales deeply, shoulders rising as his eyes close.

"That's why the wolves see me first when they come to
Alita. I'm surprised no one told you, Samson 714 Afador." The
GhostEater turns toward me as I set the scarf in her hand.
"You didn't bring Itzifone Bugs Alita, Helisent West of Jaws.
And why not?"

"Well, his hands were..." I backtrack on my explanation
immediately. There's nothing more dangerous than a witch
whose little warlockling has been hurt, and I want Anesot to
myself. "His hands were full at Solace. That's where he works.
All the other employees are new hires. He had to stay behind
to take care of the tavern."

The GhostEater growls, undistracted by my attempt at a
lie. "Who broke my warlock's hands?"

"Who can be sure?" I add in a maniacal smile to throw the
GhostEater off. As much as I'd love to trust her, I still don't
know her name. "Your son has many enemies."

"He's too fickle for enemies. I raised him to be useless. It's
the only way to be truly safe as the child of a powerful wielder." With a sigh, the GhostEater looks over her shoulder.

I follow her gaze; all I see are more busy streets half-eaten
with vines and curling incense smoke that reaches toward the
gray clouds.

"Did you at least heal his broken hands?"

"No, but I sent him a healer."

"I see." She swivels on her lilith, which starts to float
through the plaza.

I follow close behind so the bustling nymphs don't separate
us; Samson also stays close at my back.

The GhostEater turns back to us with an arched eyebrow.
"I figured you would have learned healing magic by now. Why

aren't you taking your spell-work more seriously? Itzifone is a fine warlock, isn't he? I would have great feats of magic to share with you. With your littleling, too. I would start with the ghosts, Helisent West of Jaws. I would teach you to command Skull. To command its ghosts. That alone would be worth a littleling."

I wait until she faces forward again to roll my eyes.

Then I explain, "He's not at the bottom of the list, if that makes you feel any better. But it's too bad he's fickle and useless, just like you raised him to be."

"Don't cajole with me." She cranes to look at me again. I can't tell if her brittle smile is a threat or genuine. "We aren't friends."

She turns back around and resettles on the lilac cushion.

I sigh as I smooth my hair; Rhotidom's humid air always leaves me with a puffy white mane. "I was hoping you'd be more like the other GhostEater. She was a real sweetheart."

Something pokes me in the shoulder. I turn to find Samson's features tense. His eyes widen for a second, but I'm not sure which brand of panic he's experiencing.

I scan the crowd, body tensing as I expect to see either Oko or Anesot.

But Samson pokes me again, this time jerking his chin toward the GhostEater on her lilith. He shakes his head as though confused or disappointed.

Does he think I'm being rude?

I roll my eyes and mouth the words, *"This is how witches talk to each other—chill out."*

He shelters his nothing-scented incense as he leans down and mouths back, *"What?"*

I wave him off, then continue wordlessly. We follow the GhostEater from the bustling city center back toward the road we traveled from Luz. The streets grow wider the farther we backtrack, but they also start to loop and twist into a labyrinth. I stare around and pick out a few landmarks from my years in the city.

I lived on the other side of town, aptly nicknamed Afters for its never-ending festivities. Iztifone's mother lives in the center of Bugs, nicknamed for a peaceful silence that's interrupted at dawn and dusk by the raging grasshoppers, cicadas, and mosquitoes that call the jungle home.

Trees, four times the height of Alita's single-story structures, crane along the forest's edge. It makes the city easy to find by flying overhead; it looks like a dark mahogany bowl carved into the endless stretch of fluffy green canopy.

With marigold dusk beginning behind the gray clouds, the insects' visceral buzz begins to emanate from the trees lining Bugs's outermost streets.

Now and then, the GhostEater cranes her head as though searching for someone or something. But the streets are mostly empty in Bugs. Wildflowers grow along the dirt roads while mundane conversations drift out from the opened windows of squat homes and shops.

Samson stays close to my side. He throws a glance in my direction each time the GhostEater scans her surroundings, but I convince him with a series of gestures to let me handle the witch.

She stops outside a dark-paneled, windowless home. Aside from the door, painted bright lilac, the building looks like a forgotten storage shed.

With a long groan, the GhostEater slides onto the dirt from her lilith. She straightens her robe with a few brusque pats, then looks at me.

"You should ask for a witch's name before following her somewhere, Helisent. You should already know her name before you meet her, then ask her name to verify if she's willing to tell you the truth. You didn't know my name before, so now you have no way of telling whether I'm being honest."

She worms her arms into her purple sleeves, then crosses them. "I'm Draginine West of Jaws, by the way."

I was wondering when she planned on sizing me up.

"You aren't west of Jaws," I reply, crossing my arms. "Which makes you a liar."

She reels back with a scoff. "What makes you think I'm not west of Jaws?"

"You're Alita-born. I can tell by your home and by the way you dress. They'd never give someone born outside of Alita jacaranda wood to build a home. And you'd never wear the lilac color of its flowers unless you knew the tree. It's important in Alita, if I remember correctly. And you raised your warlockling right here in Bugs."

"Alita-*born*, yes. Alita-*living*, most certainly. But not Alita-raised."

She adjusts her arms again with a shuffle. I return her plaintive gaze as she studies me; she breathes deeply as though taking some kind of magical measurement. Unlike the last GhostEater, I have no idea if she knows why I'm after Oko, or that Oko is after her, or where her allegiance falls in my war against Oko and Anesot.

My tracking letter gave only our names.

"Great GhostEater," Samson begins. "We—"

"I can feel two ghosts in Alita." The witch ignores the wolf; she hasn't taken her eyes off me. "Whoever they haunt hasn't yet sought my services. So which are you after? The ghosts or the witch they're haunting? There's another wielder involved, too. The ghosts like him even less than the witch."

And does she know who that witch and wielder are?

"Is that what you were looking for on the way here?" I ask. "The ghosts?"

"Ghosts don't frighten me, red witch. The ones you seek, though..."

The ones you seek...

I nod with relief; she knows that I'm after Anesot and Oko. I'm guessing she also knows why.

I glance at the lilac door, grains warped and peeling. If she hasn't invited us in yet, she either doesn't trust us or she's not interested in helping us find Anesot and Oko.

The witch raises her chin as she waits for my response. Milky light pools along her silver ornaments. They sit in contrast to her white hair, balanced atop her head in a fragile heap.

The GhostEater doesn't *look* threatening, but that's half the charm of a wielder: it's exceedingly casual until someone starts bleeding out. She might not have more power than me, but she has more experience. She probably knows fighting spells. She can probably concentrate enough to cast powerful spells even when injured and in pain.

I'm reckless enough to fall back on panic magic, trusting my magical twin to hash things out on my behalf—or, at least, I am when I don't have a defenseless wolf at my side.

Should this interaction with the GhostEater go awry, I prepare an externalized form of halting magic for Samson's sake. It will prevent anything from touching us, either magical or physical.

With my spell at the ready, I cross my arms and give the GhostEater the one-over. "If you want Itzifone to stay on my list of potential suitors, then you'd better start talking. *Fast.* Especially if you know why I'm here."

"I do," she confirms.

"Where are the wielders I seek?"

"With the ghosts. Somewhere in the city—I can't be *too* precise."

"And have you seen them since they arrived in Alita?"

She tsks. "No. They know better. Like Kierkeline Ultramarine, I sought heavier punishments against Oko and Anesot. I may be Alita-born, but I was raised west of Jaws. Andromeda North of Skull was a patron to those lands. She gave dove blindly. I'd say you also give it blindly, but I assume that's changed since Metamor ran red with Milisent West of Jaws's blood."

We stare at one another for a long moment.

Draginine West of Jaws.

I take a step closer to the wielder. "Give them to me, then. Where are the ghosts? Where are the wielders they haunt?"

The GhostEater slides her golden eyes to Samson. "And what's this one got to do with it? The Alpha of Velm was uninterested in justice for your family six years ago. What has changed? What promises has the son of Imperatriz 713 Afador made to you?"

"The wolf is with me. That's all you need to know."

She sighs as though unconvinced, but her gaze softens the longer she stares at Samson. "There is a candle that never stops burning. We put it in the place where she spoke about the Northing, near the marble tower. The city's dove feeds the flame. But if Imperatriz 713 Afador really *is* gone, the candle now burns for you. I hope that you are worthy of it, Samson 714 Afador."

As though suddenly exhausted, Draginine points to the city's northwestern edge. "The ghosts are someplace in Afters. They haven't moved since they got here. If you want my guess, Helisent, they're waiting for you there. Make a plan before you go. For all your power, you still can't heal a wound, witchling. Let's hope you can make them, at least."

With a sigh, Draginine gathers her robe above her ankles. She takes the three stairs to her lilac door, swinging her legs one at a time. Her lilith drifts at her side, as though prepared to catch her fall.

She looks back at us as the cicadas start their roaring.

The door creaks open and the lilith floats inside.

"I will listen for their screaming. I won't sleep until I hear it," the GhostEater says. "Send word to my Itzi that I miss him. He doesn't visit nearly as often as he should."

For the first time since meeting us, Draginine smiles. Her wrinkles twist her face into an unrecognizable shape, a broad smile at its center. A spooky cackle echoes out to us just before she seizes the door and slams it shut.

I set my hands on my hips and let out a long sigh.

It went better than I'd hoped; Draginine seems to be amenable to the Afador line and promised to teach me great feats of magic in exchange for a littleling with Itzifone.

But it also went worse than I'd wished; she can't point us to the ghosts or wielders precisely, and she didn't seem convinced by my ability to destroy Oko and Anesot.

I look up at Samson.

He grips the incense stick's shortening nub. His knuckles are white, and his jaw is tense. He stares toward the end of Draginine's street where an unceremonious spread of vines crawls up toward the canopy. Shadows twist as wind shakes the leaves.

"What?" I whisper. "What do you smell?"

My magic rolls my sleeves to my elbows. My hands raise in preparation.

I search for a trace of Anesot's dark robe or Oko's moonstone jewelry. I face the dead-end and pivot my hips, lowering my stance. My fingers flex as my magic pools in my core, coiling like a snake prepared to lash out.

I glance once at Samson.

His nostrils flex and his chest rises as he fills his lungs.

"Where are they?" I whisper.

He looks down at me as though snapping out of a trance. "No—it's not that."

I drop my hands with a curse. "What the *fuck*, Samson? My heart's in my ass." I study the street just in case, tallying the windows and corners in search of quick movement.

"What? Why?" His confusion doubles as his nose shifts again. "I smell *your* scent."

I crane my neck to smell my shoulder. My robe's velvet

smells the same as always—if not a bit muskier from the passing saigas. "What do you mean? What's wrong with me?"

"Not *yours* specifically. It's your family." His jaw clenches and his eyes widen. He faces me as his look of alarm intensifies. "I smell your father. Is he here? I thought he lived West of Jaws. What do I do if we..."

At the end of the street, a commotion starts.

The shutters covering a large window burst open, clapping back against the house's paneled sides. A dirty, bare foot juts out, followed by a flush of pale green fabric. As though fleeing, a short warlock rushes out of the window and falls onto his shoulder on the dirt street.

His magic quickly picks him up and sets him on his feet. He reaches up to grapple with his wild tangle of white hair and long beard as he hustles away from the window.

I sprint toward the wayward warlock who's led by a round belly.

"*Papa!*" I screech.

I haven't seen my father in over a year—haven't told him that I'm closer than ever to giving us vengeance...

The warlock flinches and thrusts his hands up when I reach him, as though prepared to defend himself. The next second, his look of indignant confusion melts to delight.

"*Honey Baby!*" His eyes glitter as he spreads his arms to welcome me into a hug.

I hunch down to squeeze my father with all my might. Though I'm the shortest of his children, Parsifal only stands to my shoulders. His magic lifts him into a more comfortable embrace so I can set my head on his shoulder.

A perfect golden warmth washes over me.

Tears rush into my eyes as I smell my father's cloak and he pats my back with the same tempo that reminds me of childhood. Of safety.

"Honey Baby." He huffs a few breaths and starts sniffling. He pulls me closer as he starts to cry, shoulders bobbing as he hiccups. "Is this really you? You were running remarkably fast just now. I haven't seen you move that quickly since Yngvi stole the rubies that dryad demigod gave you. Do you remember that?"

I nod into his shoulder as my own tears come. "It was Yves, not Yngvi. And I was running because I didn't think you'd be here. I was surprised. What are you *doing* here?"

"Trying to convince Kiki Red Tier to take your brother back. No luck finding her so far, though." He sniffles, holding me close. "And don't run too much. You'll lose weight. No one likes a skinny witch."

It's not his mindless drunken sobbing, just a surprised sort of weeping. Like with me, there's a great range in his crying, which is largely dependent on how many drinks he's had.

Now he's mostly drunk and a little sad and happy; it's a safe ratio.

"I know, Papa. I don't run often, trust me."

I try to pull back, but his arms tighten. He goes on, "And it's bad to rush around all the time. It upsets the body and the mind. If you want to live forever, Helisent, you should *dream* a lot. Dreaming while sleeping, dreaming while awake. It's the secret to longevity."

"I know."

"And cherries, Honey. They're very tart. Something about the juice keeps you young. Have you tried a cherry yet?"

"No. They only grow in Velm, you know."

"Well, of course. I thought maybe you'd gone. And why haven't you gone to Velm yet? I thought you would have seen the world by now. Instead, you're back in Alita. Are you living in Afters again? Me and your brothers just walked by your old warren. They repainted the door red. Only makes me think of you more."

He finally pulls back. He floats before me, pudgy hands wiping my cheeks to push the hair out of my face, just like they did when I was little. His thumbs sweep beneath my eyes to dry my tears.

I do the same for him, setting his thinning hair back into order and tidying his unruly beard. I straighten the hem of his tunic, his string of crystal necklaces, the collar of his crooked peridot cloak.

Meanwhile, I catch him up. "I didn't move back here. I'm still living in... well, it's a long story. I guess I still live in Luz. Ninigone gave me a fucking mentor—can you believe it? Oh!" I seize my father's cloak with both hands then pivot us toward Samson. "Speaking of Velm..."

Samson stands in the center of the street with his hands tucked behind his back. His formal appearance shocks me; his features are locked, his gaze set on me and my father. He doesn't look like my shy lover but rather a stalwart extension of Velm's cold Male Alpha.

My father curses loudly. He grabs my arm, then sidesteps to put me between him and Samson.

"*What are you doing with Clearbold?*" he hisses.

I drag my father out from my shadow. "Chill the fuck out! It's Samson, not Clearbold. And he's my—"

"Parsifal!" A burly dryad with a shaved head leans out the opened window to our right.

My father sidesteps again to put me between him and the angry nymph.

He whispers into my back, forgetting all about the wolf. "Helisent, my dear Honey, you know how I told you people never change? Well, I meant it. Your papa really dug himself a hole earlier today trying to find sweet little Kiki Red Tier. If you wouldn't mind offering a little boon to the big scary dryad..."

I set my hands on my hips and stare at the nymph. His face is red and sweaty, contrasted against his emerald eyebrows and amber eyes. A wrinkled tunic hangs loosely around him.

"Hello, dear dryad." I clear my throat. "The warlock is

coming with me. I'll trade for any outstanding debts on behalf of Parsifal South of Jaws, so state your needs or hold your peace."

The dryad leans over the window's wooden frame as he pants. His narrow eyes settle on the sliver of green cloak that's visible past my velvet layers. "Then it's too bad I want the warlock. I'll settle for nothing less."

My father whispers, "Tell him that's what the naiad told me."

Moons, I've missed my papa.

I fail to repress my giggle. "He says that's what the naiad told him."

The dryad bellows in wordless anger, then he braces his hands on the window frame and raises one foot. Before he can launch himself from the house, a skinny warlock rushes past him, throwing the nymph off-balance. A second brushes past his other side, sending the dryad to the ground.

It gives both warlocks time to leap from the opened window.

One lands on his knees with a grunt. The other lands on his feet and grabs a fistful of his companion's cloak, hauling him upward. They barrel forward blindly and almost run into me and my father.

I gasp as I catch sight of the first warlock's features.

Milisent and I took after our father: round faces, soft curves, chubby cheeks. Yngvi and Yves have sturdier features, starting with their sharp chins and pointed noses. Both are tall and thin like Andromeda, who I've heard towered above Parsifal. Only their eyes are the same bulbous size as mine, flitting wildly around the world.

I grab the closest one and crush him with a hug. This time, I hover off the ground to cover the height difference, squealing wordlessly as I clutch my brother. I pivot and see Yngvi and my father; I must be hugging Yves.

My father tells Yngvi, "Dear moons, shut the window so

the nymph can't follow us. I think he was telling the truth. He doesn't know where Kiki is. Neither did the naiad."

Yngvi tsks as wooden shutters clack shut. "Yeah, I know. What is it with you and naiads? When did this obsession start?"

My father mumbles an unintelligible response.

Meanwhile, Yves teeters back and forth as he hugs me, just as drunk as our father. "Honey Baby, Honey Baby! Where the fuck did you come from? I thought I'd have to go to Luz if I ever wanted to see you again."

As soon as Yves' arms loosen, Yngvi bodies his way toward me. I barely have time to study their faces and make sure they haven't aged too much before I'm crushed by the next twin. Only their hair looks different, swept into tight ponytails rather than hanging loose.

Yngvi takes a deep breath as he holds me. "Honey Baby, guess what? I was—*holy shit, it's Clearbold.*"

All three warlocks turn away from me to fixate on Samson. I flail to break loose from Yngvi, then float to the ground.

The wolf stands in the same position as before. This time, I realize he's not serious as much as he is tense. He clears his throat, then presses his lips together as though unsure whether to smile.

"Wait," Yngvi whispers, "it might be the boy-wolf instead."

"Why does he look like that?" Yves asks.

"It's Samson," my father barks. "Not Clearbold."

Yngvi holds up a hand. "We pieced that together, old man. We're trying to figure out what's wrong with him. Look at his face. Is he angry? Helisent, did you piss him off?"

"No, no," Yves whispers. "I think he's *deep in thought.*"

"Nothing's *wrong* with him," I hiss. "That's just what his face looks like. Stop ogling. Also, I'm here for something really important, so try to be less drunk."

Before they can reply, the dryad beats at the shutters

behind us. I cast blocking magic against the window to fortify Yngvi's original spell.

Yngvi and Yves whip their heads toward Samson.

In a split-second, both forget about the irate dryad.

Yvngi shouts in his direction, "No fucking way—here for something *really important*? Dear wolf, my dear Kulapsi-boy—" he leaves our side to head toward the wolf, "—she must be tricking you. Hello, nice to meet you. My name is Yngvi West of Jaws. I'm the eldest—"

"No, he's not." Yves takes off in his wake, gray cloak flaring at his heels. "Samson, *my great Afador*, he's not the oldest. Parsifal can't remember which one of us came out first."

I look down at my father, who stares at the window. It's silent, the wooden frame unmoving.

"He probably remembered the door," my father says. "Shall we?"

"Good idea." I cast blocking magic against the house's front door just before the dryad starts to beat against it. It's a loose spell that will break soon, giving us enough time for a head start; it's not good form to use magic against a nymph's home.

My father and I hustle after Yngvi and Yves. The pair don't stop when they reach Samson. Yves grabs his forearm to get him moving away from the dryad's house while Yngvi glances behind us to make sure the nymph doesn't follow.

Samson follows their swift pace. He looks over his shoulder, blue-black eyes scanning me once before turning back.

"Boy-wolf, you're a long way from Velm." Yngvi straightens his cloak, then runs his hands against his scalp, checking for stray hairs. "How do you know Helisent?"

"If she stole something from you," Yves cuts in, "your belongings are probably in her bottomless bag. You'll never get them back now. That thing is murkier than Tet. I could *probably* get your things back—for the right offer, of course."

They're being half-serious. They bear undecipherable expressions at Samson, their golden irises laced with chaos.

"I imagine her bag is full of stolen goods," Samson says in a neutral tone, "but I don't think any of them are mine."

"Listen to how he talks." Yngvi flashes a wide, fascinated smile. "Wow. What a wordsmith."

"It's called zhuzhing, Yngvi. I read about it in a book." Yves drifts closer to Samson, craning his neck to meet his eyes. "Samson, did you know there's a candle that never stops burning for your mother? It sits by the marble tower in the central plaza. We can take you there. I pretend it's for my mother all the time."

"I only learned about the candle today. It's very thoughtful," Samson says. "I don't mind if it also burns for Andromeda North of Skull."

Well, that didn't take long.

My brothers and father fall silent as the cicadas and grasshoppers blanket the city with their spirited buzzing. They turn their heads to glance at me, and I offer them a wide, guilty smile.

Samson, wordsmith of Velm, doesn't realize that he just offered my mother a great compliment. And for wielders, there aren't many reasons to offer praise to another being's parents. Especially a being they never met personally.

In fact, there's really only *one* reason someone would offer such deference to a mother or father, alive or dead...

And that's if they were *very* close to their child.

Sharing sheets-kind of close.

My father pats my shoulder. "Well, Honey, you were born on the triplemoon. I can't say I'm surprised."

My brothers take longer to process the information. Yves skips away a few steps for a better vantage of Samson from the roadside. He studies the wolf from head to toe, sidestepping as a couple passes by.

Samson shifts his gaze to each of us, as though attempting

to follow our logic. His steps are jumbled, confused by our off-kilter trajectory. Wolves walk in straight lines, but we move like an amorphous blob, separating and coming back together as Alitians pass.

Yngvi tilts his head and looks at me. "What if he rolls over on you while you sleep at night?"

Yves tsks. "Panic magic would save her. Obviously. What *I'm* more curious about is ala stuff. Samson, can't you smell a rat in the Deltas from here? How do you deal with Helisent? She's had horrible taste in perfume since she was a child. She came home with a skunk when she was twelve and said she never wanted to take a bath again. Kept the fucker tied up outside and—"

"Yves," I shout, "remember the time you shit your pants at the tiproot festival?"

"What?" He scoffs. "No. That was Yngvi."

Yngvi levels a hateful gaze at me. "I only shit my pants because I was *sick*. I had a *stomach virus* and my tummy *couldn't handle it*. Helisent, you got an animal fart confused with perfume. Let's not get off track here."

"Yngvi," my father cuts in, "you shit your pants because you spent the first day of the festival eating the oiliest food you could find and then the second shooting liquor. No need to be ashamed, my boy. There was no other possible outcome."

Yngvi ignores us and stares at Samson. "Wielders are *liars*."

The twins chatter on as we re-enter Alita's center. Samson listens and responds as requested, but most of Yngvi and Yves's nonsense loops back to where it started.

They begin with a story about Yves meeting a witch named Kiki Red Tier while laying new bridges in Antigone's top level. Then they jump ahead to last week when Yngvi "accidentally" thought he saw Kiki kissing another warlock in what was a case of mistaken identity—or, more likely, sabotage.

Parsifal came from west of Jaws to help the twins search

for Kiki in Alita. It's not the first time the witch has fled to the jungle to escape her woes with warlocks.

I did the exact same six years ago.

The recounting of Kiki and Yves's sordid affair ends in time for us to stop at the single candle burning before the marble tower. My brothers tell Samson the story about seeing his mother speak in the plaza as children, and then again as young adults.

Samson listens closely but says nothing. Sometimes, he glances at me, as though wondering what we're doing. I let him wonder. Ambiguity builds character.

My father sticks to my side as we head back to the city center, and his hiccups dissolve into loud yawns. He hooks his arm through mine as the cloudy sky fades to black and the bulbs strung above the streets blink to life one by one. After a long argument about where to eat, we end up in a vast restaurant where the waitstaff look pleasantly surprised to see a wolf.

Like they've been eating here all week, my brothers and father lead us quickly to one of the long tables cut from dark wood. Samson and I sit on one of the benches, while my father and brothers take the opposite side.

Before we order, a cook comes out to greet our table, dressed in the lilac of Alita-born beings. The female wolf wears shimmering neck and arm torcs. She offers Samson a wide smile. "I've been asking Yves and Yngvi to bring a wolf to my restaurant for years. Some dishes aren't popular among wielders and nymphs, but I like to cook them all the same. It will be a pleasure to serve the Kulapsifang and his guests."

Samson bows his head. Once again, his mouth presses into a line as though he doesn't know whether to smile.

The cook bows in return, then she disappears into the kitchen.

After we order, Samson looks just as uncomfortable as he did when catching my family's scent in Bugs. With my brothers and father close by, I haven't been able to give any context about their wild behavior, how they figured out we're lovers, or which details of our mission we should share with them.

Lovely as it is to be in their company again, I didn't come to Alita to see them. And I keep looking over my shoulder in search of Anesot and Oko, along with the green glow of ghosts.

Before my brothers can derail us with another diatribe about Kiki and my father can fall asleep with his head in his hands, I cut in. "As I mentioned before, Samson and I are here on *business*. Ten minutes before Papa escaped the dryad, we were meeting with a GhostEater."

I glance around. The restaurant is packed, bodies heating the large room as happy conversation drowns out the buzzing insects outside. No one noticed our entrance, even with Samson in our ranks.

Still, I lower my voice and keep my words vague. "It's kind of a long story, but we went to Skull and hired a ghost to haunt a *certain nameless enemy*—and it worked. All that's left to do is make a plan. One *last* plan."

I glance at Samson, sat to my left.

He nods in agreement.

For the first time, my family falls silent. The sweet glint in their eyes gutters to black.

Yngvi narrows his eyes. "Which nameless enemy? I don't want to get my hopes up."

"We were originally tracking Oko," I explain, "but it's turned into a two-for-one deal."

Yves nods. "And who kills who?" He points at Samson. "And how are you planning to kill them? The triplemoon just passed, my dear Kulapsi-boy, and you won't stand a chance against wielders like Oko and Anesot if you can't turn skin."

"My goals are different." Samson folds his hands in his lap. "I need to speak with Oko before Helisent deals with her. I have no reason to speak with Anesot. Helisent can do with him as she pleases."

Unlike Yves and Yngvi, my father doesn't look satisfied. His jovial features are set in stone, his chin raised with defiant anger. "And how does Clearbold feel about your participation in this little mission?"

"He knows my goals with Oko. He has no issue with my plans. Helisent and I have worked together for months to track Oko. Our agreement stands."

"And what agreement did you make with Helisent West of Jaws, daughter of Andromeda North of Skull?" My father weaves his fingers together, then leans over them toward Samson.

Two minutes ago, he looked prepared to pass out on the wooden table. Now he looks prepared to threaten the wolf. At his side, my brothers also lower their chins to leer at Samson.

Quietly, my father goes on, "I only have one left, and I have less reason with each I lose, Samson."

I clench my stomach at his words.

But Samson doesn't hesitate. He nods. "Our agreement was to find Oko. I get her first, alive. Helisent gets her after."

Like a flame snapping to life on a wick, I realize Samson's search for Oko has to do with his mother.

There is nothing the wolf wants more than to find Imperatriz 713 Afador—not his marble throne, not my warm body, not the adoration of wolves.

My father's words were harsh and disgusting.

I only have one left, and I have less reason with each I lose.

But Samson didn't hesitate.

I get her first, alive.

I shut my gaping mouth; I can't believe I didn't realize it before.

I stare at his profile as the implications bubble in my mind.

Anesot said that Samson would need him someday.

What if it wasn't a blind attempt to manipulate Samson?

What if he meant it?

I try not to remember Anesot at all. Not the way his fingers tapped against mine when he held them at night. Not the soft tenor of his happy laughter. Not the scent of the blazing copper he wrought. Not the stories he told about a world where he was born across the ocean.

But I've never let go of one grandiose claim he made to me on a stormy night.

Once, he told me no wielder had ever stepped foot in Bellator Palace—except for him. Anesot claimed to have dined inside its halls with the Male Alpha of Velm, Clearbold 554 Leofsige. He said the palace's white marble walls were colder than the frost of Metamor and brighter than the sun.

That I'd run my hands along them someday.

I sit back.

Did Anesot do it again? Is he five steps ahead of me right now?

Yves waves a hand from the other side of the table to get my attention. He raises his eyebrows. "I guess you haven't thought about how you'll do it, then?"

He must be talking about killing Oko and Anesot.

But my mind is far away.

My heart pumps as I consider the possibility that Oko and Anesot might know something significant about Imperatriz's disappearance.

Yves stares at me, waiting for an answer.

I shrug. "I'll break their hands. Then I guess I'll see how I feel."

But what if they *are* the key to Samson finding the Female Alpha of Velm?

What will you do then, Helisent?

I stare at the table.

I draw in a huge breath—

As my blood begins to boil.

Yves is still watching me. His fine lips turn down. "For Mint."

I wipe my face and try to focus on the restaurant's mundane activity. But each breath sends more heat into my body; it rattles my mind, shakes my vision with a single impulse.

To kill.

"For Mint," my father and Yngvi chime.

I stare at the three of them.

I nod. "For Mint."

Who meant more to me than Imperatriz 713 Afador ever could.

CHAPTER 20

BECAUSE SHE CAN'T

SAMSON

Samson,
My wisdom has been built on a foundation of mistakes.
My love for you has been the only exception.
For you, I would end Night. For you, my sweet wolf, I could.
Your mother,
Imperatriz 713 Afador

I lay sleepless on a soft mattress in a hostel on the outskirts of the city.

There's too much in my head to sort through for sleep. Instead, I wait for dawn.

Helisent sighs and tosses at my side, sounding just as unrested. The squat room we rented feels claustrophobic. Dim light filters in from the street where the insects roar through the night. The wooden walls smell like musk and mites, while the bedding retains the alas of all the beings who have slept here in the last year.

Humid air hangs still in the room.

I don't speak with Helisent.

I stare at the uneven ceiling planks.

Her father's words replay in my head over and over.

I have less reason with each I lose.

Helisent West of Jaws, daughter of Andromeda North of Skull.

Near the marble column in the city center, a finger-nail-sized flame churns atop a white candle. I can see it in my mind, flickering with every breeze.

Unease doesn't keep me from sleep, just a pervasive awareness that clings to me like the anticipation of a waricon.

Today, my four-month journey to find Oko ends—along with the seventeen-year uncertainty about my mother's disappearance.

I have a list of questions for Oko organized in my head, etched into my mind like the names carved into the columns of Silent City.

I wonder if it's the same for Helisent.

Will she have anything to say to Anesot?

After dinner last night, she sent her brothers and father away from Alita on the road to Antigone. Fearful they might be in danger with Anesot and Oko nearby, she filled their bottomless bags with dove and convinced them to leave the chase for Kiki for another week; then we walked them to the city's western road.

Parsifal followed Yves and Yngvi, but looked back often.

Helisent stood in the middle of the dirt road until they were no longer visible. Cast against the black and emerald depths of the jungle, amid the unfathomable buzz of the living forest, her peach robe glittered like light on water.

She'd looked at me and asked, "Can we stay until you can't smell them anymore? Just to make sure?"

It was the most she'd said to me since we left the GhostEater.

The longest she'd returned my eye contact since we ate dinner.

I sit up in the stuffy room with a groan.

The pale blush of dawn seeps between the shutters and the doorframe.

Helisent rolls over. She stares at me with exhausted eyes that are rimmed with dark circles. Her white hair sits in flat messy braids.

"Samson." She clears her throat. "About the plan..."

I stand up and go to the window. I open the shutters to let fresh air sweep into the room; it's lighter outside than I thought. Carts groan as they pass, while a few roosters caw in the distance.

"What are you thinking?" I ask.

I'm not surprised she wants to review our plan; they never pan out as expected.

My years in a war band taught me the importance of bonding more than planning. Tactics are always tied to shifting variables; what's most important is that pack members have the same basic understanding and goals. It allows for improvisation.

What Helisent and I have is a loosely tethered mutual goal. So far, it's been enough.

I lean back and stretch. Though my body feels heavy, I'm wide awake. Ready.

Helisent doesn't rise. She clears her throat again. "What do you think Oko knows about your mother?"

I lower my arms, body stilling.

Helisent stares at me. Her features strain, eyes flitting around the room.

How did she figure out what I want from Oko?

And when?

Even my most polished zhuzh won't deflect the direct question. I opt for the truth instead, reminding myself that I'd once promised to teach Helisent that trust matters.

"That's what I need to find out. Did Rex tell you?" I can't fathom how else she would have pieced it together.

"No. I realized it last night."

I take a few steps, then start pacing in the small room. I run my hands through my hair and give my thoughts time to assemble.

Helisent's support of Imperatriz has meant a lot to me.

But...

I don't want her anywhere near Oko when I go through my list of questions.

Her goals are too different—and I need *time, sanity,* and *cunning* to get the answers I need from Oko. Not Helisent's fixated wrath, no matter how justified.

But I don't know how to phrase that.

"What, Samson?" she starts. "You don't trust me? Look, you don't need to trust me right now. But you need to tell me what you know about Oko. I don't want to pry into your personal life or Velm's torrid affairs, but I'm worried you don't understand who we're dealing with."

She scoots to the edge of the bed. Her eyes are dead, their golden hue flat and smeared with pink, as though her red irises are peeking through.

She says, "I know you have endured great pain, but that doesn't mean you understand danger. *Real* danger, Samson. The kind that put a copper blade through my sister's heart."

The hairs on the back of my neck stand up.

Something is wrong, but I'm not sure what, precisely, is falling apart in this room right now.

Long ago, my mother wrote me a letter that read, *In the privacy of your heart, all feelings are safe, Samson. Forever.*

In the privacy of my heart, I know that Helisent will deceive me. Either right now or in the coming hours.

In the privacy of my heart, I know that I fear secrets more than her betrayal.

In life, I have lost many times. But I have never been the one to walk away.

I take a deep breath. "I know that I don't understand danger like you do, Helisent. Not yet. But I will—and I'm not afraid of that. Seventeen years ago, my father sent me into the dark forest past Bellator. It was deep Night, when the sun rises for a single hour.

"It was weeks after my mother's disappearance. I was twelve, not fifteen—too early for the wooly-killing. But I wasn't afraid. Neither was Clearbold. He wanted to prove to all those who doubted my claim as Kulapsifang that Imperatriz's disappearance didn't indicate that I was weak.

"Killing the wooly would be proof that I was a man. That I would rule Bellator one day. And I wasn't afraid. Even when I found the wooly, and made a fucking mess trying to kill it. Even when I dropped my ax and it backed me against a rockface.

"You say I don't know danger... have you ever prepared for death, Helisent? Personally? I thought the strangest things. One was a yew tree—I couldn't get it out of my head.

"Before the woolly could gore me, a wolf stepped out of the shadows. A wolf I'd never seen before. It was Hetnazzar. My demigod killed the woolly, then sat with me until dawn. My demigod stayed as I cut the wooly's head from its body and made a sleigh to drag it back to Bellator."

She sighs as she sits on the edge of the bed. She looks up at me, eyebrows pinched together.

I hope she can understand.

"Helisent, I am Samson 714 Afador, son of Hetnazzar, son of Velm, son of Imperatriz 713 Afador.

"If I cannot find my mother alive or bring home her bones *with answers*, my people will not rest. My people will doubt my claim as the inborn Alpha. I will doubt it, too. I have twenty years before I sit on the throne. I won't wait any longer to find her."

Helisent looks away.

She wipes her face and stares at the wall.

When she finally turns back to me, her irises are red. Not

her whole eye, just a band of blood-red that traces her black pupil.

"Anesot knew your father, Samson." She rubs her face again. When her hands drop, tears rim her eyes. She shakes her head and turns back to stare at the wall. "I'm *begging* you to put this together."

Put this together?

I know she hates my father, but I can't tell what connection she's drawing.

I set my hands on my hips. "Anesot admitted as much when I saw him in Lampades. He said he was once part of Clearbold's court. I know it sounds suspicious to you, but an Alpha has to keep many connections. I'm sure Anesot left his—"

"Tell me what you think Oko knows about your mother. You still haven't told me."

I start pacing again. The hairs on my neck remain standing on end; instinct tells me to cut my losses, pack my things, and leave. I have a solid goal in finding Oko, but it's being muddled more with each of Helisent's statements.

And yet—breaking our partnership now would be unwise, if not dangerous.

I admit, "I found a letter that implicated Oko and my mother. My mother was going to Hypnos to seek out the witch before she disappeared. I need to know how they knew each other and what Oko remembers about their meeting."

Helisent shakes her head. She stands up, then sits back down.

"Oko is Anesot's devotee," she says, gesturing with sharp movements. "She would and *already has* done anything for him. If Oko is connected to your mother's disappearance, then so is Anesot."

I shake my head. "I find it hard to believe the witch does *everything* with Anesot at her side. I can appreciate what you're saying, and I'll definitely keep—"

"Do you remember what Anesot said after claiming to be in your father's court? He *fucking told you* that you'd need him someday. Do you get it now, Samson? Or should I spell it out?"

I let out a long breath.

Just so I know how offended, how irate, how distressed to feel right now, I clarify, "You're telling me that you think Oko *and* Anesot had something to do with my mother's disappearance—and that Clearbold 554 Leofsige, my father and my Alpha, *knew* about their plans?"

She scoffs with a humorless laugh, then floats to meet me at eye level. Livid tears rim her eyes, slipping down her cheeks. She's not upset or sorrowful—she's overwhelmed, crazed. "Why else would Clearbold make you go into that forest to *kill a wooly* three years too early? He thought he'd get rid of you right then, just like he'd gotten rid of your—"

"*Don't.*"

My chest pumps faster with each breath.

Is this what she really thinks about me? About my father? About my people?

"*Never* insinuate such a thing to me, Helisent West of Jaws."

Rage shivers through my body, through my mind. I can't tell who it's directed at, but I can feel the moons where they hide behind dawn. Their waning faces are full of power; it descends, it pools, it waits within me.

The witch smiles, more tears falling away from her red irises. "It *hurts*. Doesn't it, Samson?" She laughs again, low and crooning, as she lowers herself back to the floor. "Dawn is always pain."

She bends to pick up her bottomless bag, then rips her robe from the hook on the wall. The witch pulls the door open, then steps into the morning light.

She looks back at me, nose curled. "You'll remember this moment the day you realize I was right. Until then, stay the fuck out of my way."

For a while, I stand there and wait for my nausea to send me hurling.

It doesn't.

I waver on my feet and try to remember what I was doing before the last ten minutes shook my deepest-held convictions. Every thought loops back to the possibility that Helisent was right—that my father conspired to get rid of the Afador line, starting with my mother and ending with me.

Malachai's existence doesn't bode well for Clearbold's innocence.

But that thought takes me straight back to Velm, to the land of emerald forests and snowcapped mountains and burning peat.

Outside the marble walls of our cities, Night freezes bodies in threadbare cottages. Blood feuds lead to carnage on the triplemoons. No measure of summer light ever satisfies a wolf's desire for warmth. All order is held on a tightrope that leaves little room for deviation.

But inside the marble walls is safety.

Dead or alive, it's where my mother belongs.

Once I find her, I'll deal with Clearbold.

With Helisent.

I turn to grab my satchel, then I head in the same direction as Helisent.

As though she'd never stepped foot in Alita, Helisent's ala disappears from the city.

It only reminds me how outmatched I am in this conflict against wielders.

I wander until I find a restaurant to barter for food, then ask for directions to Afters. I don't have a plan to find Oko—only her ala from Itzifone's apartment. My list of questions starts to shift the more I consider Helisent's proposal.

Instead of asking Oko whether she met my mother, I want

to demand to know the last place the witch saw her. Each question sharpens into a direct question, a passive accusation.

The stench and heat of Alita do little to calm me.

Especially when I reach Afters and realize it makes the rest of the city look sterile. Saigas and goats and sheep fill the open plots between wooden homes, undeterred by the shouting and music emanating from the residences. Even with shut doors and shutters, the numbing racket of drunken and dextro-ridden conversations fills the streets.

Rain showers leave puddles in the dirt, which quickly turn into mud pits.

I walk slowly, filling my lungs to comb Alita's rancid scents for a trace of Oko's ala.

I trace each street on one side, then loop back on the opposite side so I don't miss a single alleyway. The rainclouds thicken and darken; heavy raindrops slap against the mud.

Afters extends far from the city center, its alleyways growing smaller with each turn. Soon I'm surrounded on all sides by dark wooden buildings and colorful, waterlogged clothes dangling from laundry lines. A gaggle of chickens flits around my feet while a peat fire burns past an open window nearby.

Then I smell an ala laced amid the scents of smoke, mud, and fowl.

I draw in a huge breath and turn toward a wider alley where a naiad sets out buckets to collect the rain.

The strange twist, the foreign spice in the ala doesn't belong to Oko.

It's Anesot.

I stare into the alleyway.

Rain patters against the buckets as they start to fill. The naiad picks up the hem of her orange skirt to protect it from the mud, then hustles back indoors. Bright blades of grass pop up from seams near the door, stark against the dark wood.

I wanted Oko, but I'll settle for the warlock.

Finding him is better than wandering aimlessly around Afters until I find Oko—especially considering time is already running out. I wonder if Helisent has found the witch. If she has, it means Oko is dead, and Anesot is my only hope for uncovering more information about Imperatriz's letter.

I walk toward the ala.

My steps are slow, my breaths lengthening.

Without Helisent at my side, I'll be defenseless against Anesot's magic. I'd have to get my hands on him and clobber him into submission—which he's well aware of. Without the triplemoon or the doublemoon, Samsonfang can offer me no help.

I walk between the wooden homes. Streams of rain fall loudly from their steep roofs.

His ala leads to an empty hall with a wide, doorless entrance. The large room sits empty aside from a table whose end I can't see. Two candelabras sit atop the broad table, their flames casting warm light up to the angled rafters.

I stop at the precipice of the dim, quiet room.

Anesot's ala pools like poison between its walls.

"What are you afraid of?" the warlock asks, hidden inside.

My body locks at his voice. It brings to mind the words he spoke outside of Lampades. This time, I don't recall his mention of my father's court or needing him someday.

What you admire in her now you will come to hate.

I stare into the room. My shadow stands in the center of gray light cast from the street.

I take one step inside; I leave Helisent outside.

Outside of my head, outside of my heart.

I can't carry her and Imperatriz in this moment.

As soon I step forward and find the warlock with tidy layers, shimmering buckles, and short white hair, I push Helisent even further away.

This isn't the warlock who murdered your lover's sister.

This is your chance to find Imperatriz 713 Afador.

Anesot sits back in his chair, hands folded atop the table. A single glass sits at his side, filled with rich wine. The only other chair sits opposite the warlock at the table's other head. He doesn't take his eyes from me as I study the room. Past the table, two short sets of stairs lead onto a modest stage.

Anesot gestures to the empty chair. "You look tired, Samson."

I take my seat. The grand table is long—far too large for me to clear with a jump and grab him.

He's been expecting me, then. Or, in the least, has prepared for this meeting just in case.

I study his ala with a few quick breaths—first his clothes, then his metal jewelry, then his hair, then his skin, then his wine. Like in Lampades, a strange note hangs amid it all, foreign and unforgettable. Like a smoked spice.

"I know you wanted Oko. My apologies." He keeps his hands on the table, square fingers unmoving and visible. Though his tone is cynical, his gaze is solemn. "But you should know it was me who lured her onto the boat. Imperatriz."

Lured her onto the boat.

If I hadn't left Helisent outside of this hall, I would mourn my own stupidity for not listening to her this morning.

For turning my back on a witch to whom I'd sworn to prove the value of trust. Especially when she'd predicted this exact moment. When I'd misinterpreted that prediction as her imminent betrayal.

I throw out the script I wrote for Oko. I focus solely on the warlock in front of me.

My only option now is to study each of his words to make sure I don't miss anything.

I set my feet flat on the floor and take a steadying breath.

"If you know where my mother is," I say, "then I'm more interested in speaking with you."

"Wonderful. My name is Anesot. No neighborhood, no place, no number. Just Anesot." He reaches for his glass and takes a long drink. He stares at me as he swallows the dark wine. "I see you're uninterested in formalities. I'll keep it simple, then—you're going to save my life today, Samson. And I'm going to make it worth your while."

I wish I had a glass of wine.

Or a bottle.

I set my hands on the table. "And why is that?"

"I already told you. I was the one who lured your mother onto the boat. And then, as boats do, it *sailed* someplace. Someplace far away. Someplace very hard to find."

She's alive—she's alive—she's alive—she's alive—

I move my hands into my lap as they start to shake. Though my body fills with chaotic energy at the idea that Imperatriz is alive, that I could go and find her *right now*, my mind empties.

It waits.

"Where is your proof?" I ask.

Anesot reaches into a pocket inside his cloak and pulls out two hair ties; one is small and marigold, the other is large and white.

The warlock holds them up. In a split-second, potent alas waft from their fabric.

The marigold tie was mine; I can smell my ala from seventeen years ago clinging to the cotton fabric. It smells of a juvenile, not a man—

The white tie was Imperatriz's.

But her ala doesn't smell like it did when she disappeared seventeen years ago. Though it's unmistakably Imperatriz's scent, this isn't the ala I remember. I stare at the white hair tie, sucking in quick breaths; she was between the ages of seventy and seventy-four, she was lacking vitamins and minerals, her fertile years were coming to an end.

"You'll be happy to hear it was a clean affair. A wielder doesn't even need to use magic to command a wolf. Your scent alone brought her onboard."

My eyes flash to the marigold hair tie.

The alas clinging to the hair ties disappear, as though burned to nothingness.

I stare at the white fabric as Anesot tucks it back into his pocket.

I stare at the oval-shaped imprint it leaves against his cloak.

Anesot pats the spot twice.

He clears his throat, angling his head as he stares at me with golden eyes. "So here's how this is going to go. Honey is going to find Oko, break her hands, then bring her here. If she's feeling generous, she'll offer you the witch in exchange for me."

Anesot smiles without humor; it's more like a friendly wince. Like he regrets this. "And then you'll stand in front of me. I know, I know—warlocks are shameless. But I saw how you two interacted in Lampades. She won't be able to touch you, and you could hide two of me in your shadow. We'll—"

"What makes you certain she wouldn't touch me?" I ask.

Somewhere, far below my memories of Imperatriz and Hetnazzar, a sentiment of self-loathing brews. I ignore it— shove it past the doorless entrance where I left Helisent.

"The witch would level a city if it meant getting to you," I go on.

"Because she can't." He narrows his eyes. "I was wondering if this was all a ruse from your Alpha—if he'd put you up to this with Honey or not. He was the one who told me about Bloody Betty to begin with. He was the one who gave me the idea to search out the red wielders. Centerhearts are common in their line. And if he hooked me on the idea of creating my own Bloody Betty, why not convince you of it, too?"

He shrugs ruefully. "We don't have centerhearts where I come from. Life is too difficult. Do you know what's more important than love in Zarzynn? Breath."

I clench my hands to stop their shaking, but it worsens with each of Anesot's words.

That's why Anesot went unpunished all those years ago.

Not because Helisent lacked the conviction for murder, but because a centerheart's magic can't be used against those they love.

Anesot points to the space before the entrance. "I'm going to stand there, and you right there. But don't let your guard down. Just because she can't use magic against you doesn't mean she won't find a way to get to me. Stay close, Samson."

He takes another gulp of his wine. "All I need is time to explain myself. I can calm Honey down, but it will take a few minutes.

"Once that's sorted out, I'll take you to Hypnos. I left your mother in a place called Stretch, on an island called Pit. It's a chain of islands between this world and mine—and before you consider killing me, know that Stretch and Pit can only be reached by phoenix light. Aside from yours truly, no one knows how to use phoenix light to navigate the ocean there. Not even Oko.

"Imperatriz is doing well for herself, by the way. Or she was the last time I visited. I wish I had another hair tie to share with you, but she's quite careful with her belongings these days."

I shove away my wrath, my pain, my self-hatred, my doubt, my pride. It's all waiting for me outside this room, and I'm certain each feeling will bury me the second I'm alone, but I don't let my focus shift away from the warlock.

Not just from what he says, but all he doesn't say.

"If you're wrong about Helisent being a centerheart, then I have a lot to lose in helping you right now. And I still think you're a fool to think the witch will hear you out. Even if you could bring Milisent West of Jaws back from the dead, she'd kill you."

Anesot sits back in his chair, face alight with optimism. "Good thing that's exactly what I'm planning to do."

For a long moment, we stare at each other.

Bring someone back from the dead? Anesot is wilder than I'd ever anticipated.

Outside, rain patters against the mud. Clucking chickens shuffle past the doorway, pecking at the ground.

"Really?" I can't think of any other response.

He smiles genuinely for the first time. "Oh, yes. In my world, we have something called a vampire. The nasty little fuckers survive on blood alone. Hot blood, if you know what I mean. But they can do *extraordinary* things—especially with an okeanid at their disposal.

"A few little bites, a few little rituals, and Mieira's nymphs turn from okeanids into something called a necromancer. I wouldn't have believed what they could do if I hadn't seen it for myself. They pull the dead from a mirror. It has something to do with sand."

The fifth scent: a vampire.

The disappearing okeanids: necromancers.

The selkie was right.

Clearbold knows of the disappearances.

I reach into my pocket and pull out my packet of tobacco. I fish around for dry shreds then a sliver of usable rolling paper. With a long sigh, I roll the cigarette and then lean toward a candelabra to light it.

I take a long drag. "If you want me to protect you from the witch, then tell me what Clearbold knows about Imperatriz's disappearance. Tell me everything."

Anesot grabs his glass, swirling his wine while he stares at me. "Your father has been a great friend to me, Samson. I don't take betraying him lightly... but you're now more useful to me than he could ever hope to be.

"What did he know about her disappearance? Well, where do you think I got your hair tie? Why do you think you were deep in Velm when Imperatriz traveled to Hypnos? Who do you think fed her information about a dangerous witch named Oko?

"And most importantly, Samson, why the fuck would I bother with your mother unless I was being rewarded handsomely? She can't cast a spell, but I've never taken her power lightly."

Clearbold—Clearbold—Clearbold—

My father, my Alpha, my enemy.

"Why did he want her gone?"

"Because he was too much of a chicken shit to ask me to kill her. Because he needed an extra bargaining chip down the line. I didn't ask too many questions. But looking back, I think he wanted to test the waters—to see if Velm would be amenable to a new dynasty of Alphas. To the Leofsiges."

I don't let myself imagine what my mother has endured. What it must be like to live on Pit in Stretch, between Anesot's world and ours. I don't let myself dwell on what the white hair tie hinted at in terms of her physical health.

I smoke my cigarette and stare at the warlock.

"Helisent will be a while longer," Anesot says, glancing at the gray light cast from the entrance. "I suppose she wouldn't have told you much about me. Maybe nothing at all. But I was the one who taught her spellcasting, Samson. How to make dove, how to store it. She'll find Oko first, break her hands, then bring her here. I hope you aren't squeamish."

I suck on my cigarette and stare across the table.

The truth is that I've never felt more powerful in my life.

After seventeen years of ignorance, I have all the pieces.

There's only one other time I felt this way.

When I was backed against the frosty boulder in the forest outside Bellator. When Night's cold drove deep into my bones as my breaths came quick and hard. When the wooly mammoth roared and lowered its head, preparing to charge forward.

I was breathing like a bleating goat, but in my head, all was still.

I saw a yew tree, standing on a mountainside.

I see the same yew tree now, standing on the same mountainside.

Hetnazzar won't come this time; I'm far from Velm.

"Remember," Anesot says, pointing to the space near the entrance. "I stand here, and you stand there. Stay close, Samson, and we'll leave for Stretch tomorrow."

CHAPTER 21

ARE YOU WATCHING?

HELISENT

Honey Heli,
I keep having nightmares. Someone is screaming in them. It's a witch.
Sometimes, it kind of sounds like mom. Don't get freaked out—I'm just
writing this down so I'll stop worrying.
Mint Mili

I clap my hands when I finish my third brandy.

"I fucking mean it—stop serving me."

The dryad behind the bar looks down at the full glass in her hand, then she glances around as though searching for someone else to hand the brandy to.

A few groups toast and laugh loudly from the booths behind me, but it's too early for the lone drinkers like me to fill the bar stools. Even in Alita.

The dryad blinks her brown eyes at me. She sets the drink on the far side of the bar, slides me an uncertain and pessimistic gaze, then heads to the booths.

I stare at the tiny bubbles gathering around the glass's rim. They pop and fizzle.

It would be wrong not to drink the brandy; I *did* order it before berating the bartender for serving me. And though she seems accustomed to semi-irate witches, she'll decide to *actually* stop serving me if I keep it up.

With a sigh, I slide off my stool and loop to the bar's far side to pick up the drink.

I bring the full glass to my lips and gulp down the cool brandy. I tell myself that this is the last one before I head into Afters.

What happens then is still a bit of a wash.

I want nothing more than to find and kill Oko, then Anesot. Samson can learn the hard way that Clearbold is somehow involved in Imperatriz's disappearance. That Oko and Anesot likely were, too.

But I can't shake the fear that Samson might find the pair on his own, without me. Though it would give him time to interrogate Oko, she would have little reason to offer him any information unless under the threat of my magic. And without my magic, he'll be at the mercy of theirs.

My hand twitches now and again, as though eager to call up the snowflake I still carry in my bottomless bag and track the wolf.

"Just this last one."

With another sigh, I float back onto the stool.

I raise my drink to my lips, then catch movement in my periphery.

I look over to find a green-hued, semi-transparent ghost standing atop the bar's polished wood. The toddler's face is crossed with age lines, its chin dotted with stubble.

I shriek with all my might. My glass of brandy slips to the floor and shatters.

I lock eyes with the smug-looking ghost. "*Creepy Baby*."

The ghost wiggles its shoulders and hips, as though delighted by my fear.

Behind me, a few angry nymphs shout threats. One tells me to be quiet, another tells me to clean up the mess.

I ignore them as I stare at the ghost, heart rate ratcheting. I stare into the toddler's gleaming, too-large eyes. "Take me to Oko right now, my dear Creepy Baby, and I will give you *anything* you want."

The ghost smiles, then it turns and gallops across the bar; his bare feet make no sound as they batter against the wood. With a leap, he soars into the air and lands on the ground; his jump arcs as though he's weightless.

I grab my bottomless bag, then leap over the mess of broken glass and brandy to follow the ghost.

If I can get to Oko before Samson, I can still deliver the witch to him—can still honor our arrangement and have my vengeance—

And my *vengeance.*

My vengeance.

I lick my lips as I prepare my magic and mind for meeting Oko.

I throw away everything from the last six years to soar back to the misty morning when I woke up to the sound of Milisent's screaming.

The carnal rage I felt last night at dinner starts to shake like boiling water. It pushes away the panic and anxiety of my argument with Samson. Magic brews, heaving against my mind, my psyche, my will.

The dryad catches me by the arm before I leave the tavern. Her nose curls, and her chin rises. "Where the fuck do you think you're going? You owe me for four brandies and a glass."

I look at her hand, clenching my robe.

Red light from my eyes bursts free and falls across the dryad's face, tinting her brown skin and her emerald curls. Her eyes meet mine and she flinches, releasing me to stagger back inside the bar.

I turn and follow Creepy Baby, who cuts across the narrow

street and speeds into an alleyway. I ignore the nymphs and wielders who stare at us with wide eyes and gaping mouths.

I smile.

There's nothing in my way now.

The memories of Milisent that I've buried for years whirl through my head. I remember the smell of the lavender oil she used in her hair. I remember how we held hands; whose fingers fit where, how long it took before our palms sweat. I remember how much she hated rain but loved lightning.

How much honey she liked in her mint tea.

I rush after Creepy Baby as he turns again and again, breaths ragged as my boots slip in the mud.

He speeds into a square window, passing through the closed shutters. I take the open door beside the window and careen to a stop in a small kitchen. I raise my hands and look around, prepared to find Oko and start a bloodbath two feet from the peaceful street.

But she's not here.

A ghost sits at the lone table, weeping with his face in his hands. His glowing form casts peridot light against the wooden furnishings.

Creepy Baby lands on the ghost's head and seizes his hair—I recognize the nymph-ghost's long locks from Skull. He raises his head and hands to shoo the toddler ghost, then he notices me with a gasp.

He sits up and sets his palms against the table. "Helisent West of Jaws—*how could you?*"

Creepy Baby stands on the kitchen table, looking from me to the nymph ghost.

I look down at my hands to check for blood. "Do what? I haven't done anything yet."

"The witch is *pure evil.*" The ghost wails and sets his head back in his hands. He speaks into them loudly, "Do you have *any idea* what it's been like to haunt her? I almost *begged* Kierkeline Ultramarine to send me back to Skull. The witch—

she's—she's—she's..."

I throw my hands into the air. "You tried to *drown* me! What the *fuck* are you blathering about? *Where is Oko?*"

The ghost looks up with a bent mouth. He sniffles, then glances at the half-open door at my back. "She'll be back soon. She went to look for bergamot incense. She knows I hate it. She burns it *constantly*, and—"

"I put the phoenix ash where you asked." I ignore the ghost and shut the front door. "Red sack on the riverside, right as the lights of Perpetua come into view."

I move further into the cramped kitchen. Tall cabinets cover one wall near the table and chairs. Two doors on the other side of the room lead into a salon and a bedroom, both filled with gray light from their windows.

It'll work for an ambush.

I head toward the bedroom then look back at the ghost. He remains seated, shoulders bobbing as he cries.

"You can leave. The witch is out of hiding. We're squared."

"Right. Well." He wipes his cheeks, then straightens his tunic. He pushes back from the chair, which doesn't actually move, then stands up. "This has been a nightmare. I hope I never see you again."

Without another look in my direction, the ghost turns toward the wall and then passes through it with a blur of green-hued light. I catch a wisp of his green form from the square window, then he disappears entirely.

Creepy Baby rubs his belly as he watches me from the tabletop.

I wait for the ghost to say something, but he just ogles.

I shake my head, frustrated and baffled by the silent being. "I don't have time for you right now. Stay out of my way or I'll figure out how to make you die again."

But part of me is glad for the sniveling little creep.

Without him, I'm standing in a dim, quiet kitchen waiting

to break the hands of my enemies and then unleash slow death on them.

Without him, I'm utterly alone as I prepare to leave behind a half-fascinating, half-atrocious existence that's been life without Mint.

I can feel my rage, my magic, my fate fizzle inside me like bubbles in a freshly poured brandy.

It's been waiting for years just below the facade of wild amusement that I wear each day.

I retreat into the bedroom. I slide into the narrow space between the door and the wall, staring through the seam of its frame. Outside, beings chatter as they pass. Birds caw over-head and rain patters against the roof.

I breathe loudly and unevenly. Creepy Baby stays put on the table, glancing from my hiding spot to the front door.

The doorhandle rattles.

And in walks Oko.

She sighs and turns toward the table. She pulls her bottom-less bag from across her body, ignoring Creepy Baby's presence and the nymph-ghost's absence.

She doesn't notice me as I stare from behind the door.

Her lilac cloak flows to the floor without a wrinkle. Her moonstone necklace and earrings catch the faded light and shimmer like moonslight on water. She was always beautiful. Refined.

But she's aged greatly since I last saw her. Her thin lips are framed by lines, her eyes are sunken, and her golden irises dull. The scars on her neck have deepened and warped in the last years.

She shuts the door behind her then sets her bag on the table.

I wait until she raises her hands toward her face.

Then I cast smothering magic around the apartment's walls; it moves inward to silence the noise inside. Then I cast halting magic onto everything in the apartment.

A foolish witch would just halt the wielder they seek to immobilize, but I make sure every surface, from the nails in the floorboards to the spiderwebs in the rafters, stops under my magic.

Though breaking a wielder's hands is a solid way to disarm them, a skilled wielder can still cast a spell with their minds alone.

And I'll never underestimate a witch again.

I step from behind the door.

I can feel Oko shivering under my magic. Her eyes, frozen to stare ahead at the table, strain as they attempt to look up. Her hands twitch, and her magic flounders, unable to take shape as mine surrounds her, buries her.

A smile tugs at my lips.

I walk toward her. With each step, my form unleashes, unwilling to hide as my rage surfaces. My eyes cast red light across her face as I study her fragile, symmetrical features.

Her body is taut, posed in a half-step under my magic. Her hands are frozen in front of her chest, as though rising to brush away the strands of white hair that fall across her face.

I study her small hands, her graceful fingers, her sheltered palms. I run my hands over hers. My fingertips slide across her soft skin, her veins, her knuckles. For a wielder, her skin is pale, the veins below dark and visible.

I can feel her magic struggle and panic as I touch her hands.

I take a deep breath. "These are the hands that killed Milisent West of Jaws, daughter of Andromeda North of Skull."

A smile blooms on my face, quiet laughter clenching my stomach.

Six years.

I did it.

Tears fill my eyes.

I close my eyes and suck in a huge breath.

I appreciate this moment.

I don't even care that Creepy Baby is still staring from the tabletop.

I did it.

"Mint, are you watching?"

I cast breaking magic next.

I learned it just for this.

It takes me forever to leave for Anesot because I almost kill Oko several times.

Never on purpose.

First, she throws up from the pain. I have to shift my halting magic and reposition her to keep her from choking on it. It's *a lot* of vomit, which spreads across the floorboards and seeps into the wood and fills the room with an acidic scent. It soaks her lilac cloak, along with blood from her shattered hands.

Then she passes out. With the witch unconscious, her panic magic takes over and launches an assault. First, it sends enough force magic to level all of Afters, which shakes the apartment before I can contain her force spell with sinking magic.

Then comes an attempt at fire magic, but that fizzles out under my water spell. Last is shining magic. Amorphous light flares around Oko, bright as the sun and quick-moving as lightning.

It's not an active defense, but it gives me a headache and makes it difficult to concentrate. I can't see the witch beneath the shifting light, can't figure out how to get rid of the flares.

All the while, I maintain my smothering magic so Alitians won't hear us. Maintain my halting magic over her form in case Oko is only pretending to be passed out. I lift the halting magic now and then so she can suck in deeper breaths. I also release her eyes so she can blink and look around.

Eventually, she slumps forward, limp and subdued, but conscious.

Her lips shake as he drags in wild breaths.

I meet her eyes; they aren't golden. They're green now, just as bright as the grass lining Alita's streets.

A *green* witch?

I'll deal with that later.

"Tell me where Anesot is," I say. "He's the one I want. Samson 714 Afador wants to speak with you. Tell me where Anesot is, and I'll make the trade."

I have no plans of letting her live when Samson is done with her, but Oko would be an idiot not to take her chance.

She doesn't mull it over for long. Her voice shakes. "Afters. The old theatre. The empty one."

"Let's see if you're still a liar, Oko."

She's covered in vomit and shaking; I doubt she has the capacity to lie.

But I'll never underestimate a witch again.

I take out my lilith. I layer lifting magic onto the halting magic cast across Oko, then situate her on the floating cushion. I drape a scarf over her hands; it's the only time I look at her misshapen fingers.

Joy flushes through me, maddening and addictive.

Then I lean to the side and dry heave.

I savor Oko's pain—

But seeing it is different. Inflicting it is even harder. I know these memories will bother me someday... but for now, I've never felt more powerful. More vindicated.

I force her eyes shut with halting magic then turn her chin down. I slump her shoulders and pose her hands in her lap, under her robe and the scarf. I cast more smothering magic to prevent her from talking.

Then I walk around the lilith to make sure the witch looks like nothing more than a drunken friend being toted home after a long bender. The vomit on her robe actually adds perfectly to the illusion, so long as the blood stays hidden.

I double-check the spells binding Oko, then coax my form back into hiding.

Then we set off.

My smile comes and goes.

I never imagined it would have been so easy to capture the witch.

Even her wildest panic magic felt like butterflies trapped beneath my hands. Just the whisper of fragile wings against my palms. Like Oko, Anesot has four horns—I doubt his magic, panicked and wild as it might become, would be much more difficult to handle.

Especially so long as I have the element of surprise on my side.

The walk to Afters makes me less certain; I feel like an alien to the world as I drag along the witch in the lilac robe covered in vomit.

I feel like an enemy of the demigods, of desita, as I take the suffering witch to Samson.

The old theater isn't far. I slow down when we turn onto its street. I suck in a breath through my nose to check for Anesot, as though I'd be able to smell his ala. All I register is wet wood and mud and Alita's fertile rotting.

I set my magic at the ready; halting, smothering, and breaking spells linger on my fingertips. A burning spell, too.

I walk slowly, then stop before the doorless entrance. After a breath, I drag the witch with me inside, then stop to let my eyes adjust to the dim hall. There aren't seats lined up or costumes hanging in preparation for a show later tonight.

Instead, there's a long table to my right with two chairs at either end. And there, straight ahead, stands Samson. He faces me with his hands clasped behind his back. His torcs are shined, his navy-blue tunic and pants neatly situated.

And there, just behind his dark boots, stands a shrouded figure.

Anesot's dark cloak piles on the ground.

At the table to my right, a glass of dark wine sits near a candelabra.

My indignant wrath halts suddenly.

If Samson is standing here protecting Anesot, then he must know I'm a centerheart. And he's using that knowledge, and my love for him, to protect Anesot.

My anger freezes for just a moment; then it starts to double and coil and *twist*.

Samson stares at me with his jaw clenched. His head angles as his nostrils work, tallying my ala and Oko's. I see fear in his eyes, as well as an edge that I've never felt in him before.

How long has he known I'm centerheart?

How did he find out?

How long have he and Anesot been working together?

Samson speaks in a direct, loud voice. "He says he's the only being who can take me to a place called Stretch. Imperatriz is alive—she's there. On an island called Pit. *Right now.*"

I study the black cloak behind Samson's boots.

Is Anesot tricking Samson to protect himself? Or is it the truth, like I'd suspected last night?

How long has Anesot planned this?

Did he put it together in Lampades, then string us along to this very point?

Samson shakes his head, as though attempting to break through the wild noise of my thoughts. "Helisent, I need you to *please* let me go to Stretch before you take your vengeance. He says he can bring back Milisent. There's something called a necromancer—the missing okeanids, that's what they become in another world. And..."

He trails off when I look away from his eyes to stare at his chest.

I can't stand his features.

All the love I find keeps somehow turning into evil.

Just like it did with the warlock behind him.

All the memories from the past months with Samson, which once made me happy, now spoil into a fetid mess.

All of these things I thought were real *aren't* real.

"Honey, it's true."

I close my eyes when Anesot speaks.

His voice is molten copper; my heart is my sister's.

I send my magic through the empty theatre. I don't cast halting, smothering, or breaking spells. I cast burning magic and send it toward Anesot.

Adorable as his plans with Samson were, I've become intimately aware of the limitations of my centerheart magic.

My magic won't be able to surpass the bounds of Samson's will. My love for him means my magical twin won't carry out a spell that doesn't serve his higher will.

As such, my magic could never move him to let me have a clear shot at Anesot.

But I don't need a clear shot.

A burning spell speeds toward Anesot, skating around Samson to leave him untouched. In response, Anesot casts halting and freezing magic. The collision of our spells sends enough infrasound pumping through the theater that Samson staggers out of the way. He rushes out of view, cursing.

He leaves Anesot exposed.

The warlock's hands are raised near his chest. They're positioned with his palms outward as he forces halting and freezing magic around his body, attempting to stop the torrential push of my magical heat.

My burning magic cranes for Anesot's body; it targets his eyes and his testicles.

Anesot stares at me with empty eyes as his spells form a thin shield around him. His lips part, then his jaw clenches. He's aged just as quickly and poorly as Oko.

The lines of his face come into focus as he concentrates.

He's flailing.

What the fuck made this idiotic man think he could best me?

If Oko's panic magic was like butterflies trapped beneath my hands, Anesot's magic is like a salamander. It attempts to slip free. It bites. It nudges and pushes and slithers.

From the outside, it probably doesn't look like anything of consequence is happening. Magic doesn't take a form of its own; it only becomes apparent when it meets matter. We're just two quiet wielders staring at each other from ten feet apart, hands raised absentmindedly.

A silent witch sits on a floating lilith nearby.

A wolf cowers on the floor just past her.

Feature by feature, Anesot's façade of calm focus breaks. His narrow eyebrows bunch, then his small eyes clench as he winces. His lips pull back from his teeth.

I want him to speak again; I want his voice to be the impetus for my magic to strike through his feeble barriers and *scald* him.

My smile returns.

The theater's wooden walls and roof shake as infrasound flares around our magic.

"Mint—Mint, are you watching?"

I straighten one of my hands toward Anesot. I cast smothering magic around the theatre walls so Afters will be sheltered from the noise of his suffering.

His eyes widen on my raised hand. "Honey—"

I close my hand and clench it, summoning every thread of magic that Andromeda North of Skull and Milisent West of Jaws gave me. Like burning copper sinking through soft skin, my magic pushes through Anesot's halting and freezing spells.

The warlock crumbles to the ground and screams.

One hand goes to his face as I burn his eyes, another to his crotch as I incinerate his testicles.

Someone grabs my arm, but I don't look away from Anesot.

Anesot's suffering, his bellowing, his writhing body, which jerks and tangles in his robe, closes one chapter of my life. Unless I bear witness, it will all be empty. Nonexistent.

"Helisent, *I am begging you to spare him...*"

Samson's fingers tighten on my forearm.

I don't look at him.

I was a fool to ever wander into the Luzian Estate.

I keep my focus on Anesot. The scent of charred skin fills the theater. Like Oko's hands, it disgusts me, but I hold it with all my attention just like I have Milisent's absence in these last years.

Samson turns away from me.

Some sort of struggle begins to my left, but I don't care.

I lower my hand; the warlock isn't dead yet.

Anesot's magic has stopped struggling. His breaths are ragged; I wait for him to pass out. For his panic magic to attempt something like Oko's did. But he lays crooked, facing the ground and half-hidden in his cloak.

I can't see his face.

He shakes, hands fumbling under his dark layers.

I sigh.

It's almost done now. Six years of suffering.

I raise my hand again and send burning magic over his entire body.

There's only one broken scream, followed by more nauseating scents and a burst of flame that engulfs him. I stare as Anesot burns. A smile twitches at my lips, but I now feel more exhaustion than rapture.

Normal thoughts wheedle back into my head—

I wait until the flames have satiated their hunger, then end the spell.

All that remains of Anesot is a pile of charred bone and goop.

Each second I stare ahead, the more tired I become.

I clear the room of the horrible scent, then turn toward Oko and Samson.

The witch has fallen to the ground. She lays on her side in a heap. Her destroyed hands are splayed in front of her, as though attempting to cast magic. Her head lolls to the side, her eyes closed.

And there, a few feet away from her outstretched hands, lays Samson.

He's curled on his side facing the witch. His hands clutch his chest where a metallic ornament from my lilith juts from his chest. Bright red blood pumps from the wound, coating his hands and pooling on the floor.

I scream and rush toward him.

I forget about Anesot, about Milisent, about the world beyond his bleeding chest.

I throw a wild breaking spell toward Oko; I hear her body jerk with a wet crunch, hear her last breath leave her like a ragged cough. But I don't look away from Samson. I slide onto my knees and touch his shoulder, then the bronze piece sunken into the center of his chest, then the large fingers that clutch the metal.

"*Samson.*"

Behind my dumb shock is unfathomable panic. It stirs and gathers like a storm.

I touch his face, which is strained and taut. The blood from my fingers coats his cheeks, his brow, his lips. His eyelids flutter as he tries to open them.

"*Samson—stay with me—please don't go—please don't go—*"

His eyelids open a sliver, and his blue-black eyes roll up to me.

His lips move, but I can't hear him.

He's dying.

The last Afador is dying.

And it's your fault, Helisent.

I push my hands against his chest. I don't know healing magic, but I am the last red witch in Mieira.

I am the daughter of Andromeda North of Skull. Sister of Milisent West of Jaws.

I bend my head toward my hands, concentrating my magic against the wound. I tell my magical twin, "*Save him. Save him. Save him.*"

Panic magic never feels any different.

But it does this time.

Infrasound starts in my palms, then careens across my form swiftly.

"*Mother—Andromeda North of Skull—please. Please save him. Do whatever you have to do. Do not let him die.*"

Infrasound takes over Samson next. A low sound of anguish peels from his lips, but, as though my body is no longer my own, I can't move. Red light flashes around me, pooling in my hands like a candle's flame, then spiraling into a wildfire.

Samson slackens against the floorboards, unconscious.

It must be my panic magic—

Because it definitely isn't me—

I seize the metal ornament, then rip it from his chest.

Blood spurts across my face, my chest, my arms.

My hands rush forward to block the wound; red light shivers and flares and intensifies.

I stare ahead with relief.

It seems to be working—

And then I get tired.

As though all my lifeforce concentrates in my hands, pressed against Samson's chest, my toes and legs go cold. They start to tingle. Then my hips, then my stomach, then my chest. Cold, tingling, forgotten.

My eyes slip shut, and my mouth falls open.

It sort of feels like falling asleep.

CHAPTER 22

DEEP IN VELM

SAMSON

I adjust the pillow at my back, then shuffle into a more comfortable position.

Rex notices. "Should I stop?"

He glances down at the book in his lap, then at the candelabra at my bedside. Pale wax drips from the disappearing candles, piling dop by drop on the marble floor.

"It's getting late," he goes on.

"It's just my back. It's from the cold." A snowstorm rages beyond the marble walls of Bellator Palace. I can hear the raging wind whistle from down the hall.

I'd thought returning home would spur my recovery. Two months ago, a red witch named Helisent West of Jaws attacked me in Alita. What started with a chest wound has spiraled into back pain, chest pain, and feverish nightmares.

I don't remember the witch from memory; the past four years are a blur of murky recollections. The half-real bank of alas that my fangself remembers is just as incomplete. I can feel my memories displacing my thoughts like a splinter; still, the last I remember, Rex and I were finishing our second tour in a war band near Wrenweary.

The only hint that the past four years are real is the scar on my chest and my backaches... and the dreams that hound me of a witch with red eyes.

Rex stares at me with a neutral expression. Since arriving in Alita to help take me home, he's been reserved. He says the past years haven't changed much between us, but he'd never watched me from the corner of his eye before

He must think I'm weak.

Like the rest of Velm, he must wonder what I was doing in Alita with a volatile witch.

What I would do to answer that question, too.

"Keep reading."

Rex licks his lips, glancing from the book about Velmic myths to me. "The next one's about Bloody Betty."

I raise my eyebrows. "Are you afraid of red witches now? I'm not."

With a sigh, Rex looks down at the text. "In the sixth decade of the War Years, Aloysius 311 Vendeven led his war band north of Gamma on the triplemoon. Like his other raids, Aloysius was successful in his endeavor to level the village. The wielders were killed. Their homes were trampled. Their food supplies were obliterated. Their livestock was eaten.

"The next day, Aloysius 311 Vendeven went on foot with his pack. They collected valuables, remaining supplies, and searched for survivors. His pack found a single wielder: a red witchling. The infant had been protected by panic magic on the triplemoon.

"Aloysius picked up the child. He walked to the river and threw the infant into the rushing currents. Panic magic brought the infant back to the surface. He spent the day attempting to kill the witchling. Aloysius was unsuccessful each time.

"Ilona 344 Leklein took responsibility for killing the infant the next day.

"Her attempts were met with equal strife.

"The red witchling was powerful, her magic tripled overnight from the massacre against her village and family.

"Ilona was struck with a great idea. She fed the infant. Within days, the witching's panic magic no longer unleashed wayward spells and infrasound. She raised the child; each day, she prepared to kill the red witchling. But the witchling didn't understand what she was. She remembered nothing of her life before the massacre. Of her people.

"Food was love to the witchling. Shelter was love to witchling. Survival was love to the witchling.

"Ilona took the child further into Velm and raised the witchling in Rouz. The witchling adored Ilona, adored her pack; they named the wielder Betty. They hung decorations from her six horns, red as blood and the berries of the yew tree. She wielded magic on the triplemoons when the wolves turned skin. She learned killing magic from the wolves.

"And like many red wielders, the witchling was a center-heart, incapable of wielding magic that would defy the will of those she loved.

"When Betty was mature, Ilona brought her northwest to Wrenweary. Ilona brought her to the killing fields west of Gamma. And on the next triplemoon, Betty rode into battle with the wolves. When light came, Ilona took her back to safety; she never let the wielder look for survivors or loot at dawn.

"So it went for years. Slowly, the wolves pushed north under Betty's charge. Closer and closer to Septegeur, until the wolves finally pierced its fern-covered forests.

"During one battle in Septegeur, an enemy wounded Betty's wielding hand. She prepared for death, but the wielders who found Betty injured and disoriented didn't raise their hands to cast spells.

"Betty saw their horns—golden, but shaped similar to her own. She saw their faces, their features; she knew they were the same. They stared at her like a question with no answer, then set her free. She returned to Velm.

"Betty had questions; Ilona had answers. On the next triplemoon, Betty fought and killed. And when dawn came, Aloysius and Ilona could not convince Betty to stay back. She wanted to loot. She wanted to raid in the light of day. And when she did, Betty beheld all the destruction she had wrought. She counted the corpses felled by her magic.

"They were horned. Each of them.

"And when Betty turned and looked back, she raised her hands to cast killing magic against Aloysius and Ilona. But her magic wouldn't obey because, until that moment, she had loved them both as parents.

"It gave Aloysius and Ilona just enough time to kill the witch themselves."

I stare ahead at the marble walls.

Bloody Betty had sounded more intriguing as a child. Now it seems wildly dangerous to string along a powerful wielder.

I hate magic.

I shift again, moving the pillow that cradles my back.

My room in Bellator is taller than it is wide. The walls extend upward to a glass ceiling where snow piles and shifts. Past my bed sits a chest of drawers, a cushion for meditating, and a bowl for washing.

Mounds of white cotton sit beside the basin along with sanitizing supplies.

Despite my ongoing back aches and chest pain, the wound near my heart healed at a remarkable pace. Sometimes, I still look down in shock, prodding the scar tissue just to remind myself that it was real.

"Should we re-wrap it before you go to sleep?" Rex asks, following my gaze. "Or maybe..."

He trails off as heavy footsteps echo from the hallway. The next second, I register my father's ala. I sit up further as he nears my room, wincing as my spine aches.

I haven't seen my Alpha since I was injured. Our correspondences have been through letters alone.

Clearbold rushes into the room and stops at the edge of my bed. His black cape flares ahead as its momentum continues.

I swing my legs to rise and meet him, but he holds up a hand. "As you were, Samson."

He sits near my hip. He leans toward me, clasping my shoulder and drawing me closer. I flinch as pain shoots up my spine, but don't make a sound.

Clearbold bends his head to smell my hair, which hangs loosely to my shoulders.

I angle my neck to smell his hair, too.

He pulls back and holds my cheek with a hand. He smiles, brief and bright. "There's no killing you, my son. Not a wooly. Certainly not a witch." His hand tightens. "Welcome home."

I smile back.

It's good to be home.

CHAPTER 23

DEEP IN JAWS

HELISENT

I try not to roll my eyes at the Class's ridiculous posturing.

Six wielders stand with their hands clasped behind their backs. They wear prim white layers. The clean fabric is unsullied by even a speck of dust—despite the fact that the volcanic cones of Jaws are covered in black grime.

They stare at me with tidy white hair and unamused expressions.

I shimmy to sit farther up in bed. "You guys just let your-selves in? Rude. And do you practice standing like this? Oh, let's hear what you have to say. Will it be in order—and starting from which direction?" I point at the witch standing farthest to the left. A frown hangs across her wide face. "Do you start?"

Despite my animated tone, I'm trying to pull it together.

I fell asleep two hours ago with a bottle in my hand, then woke up to the Class ducking into my hovel. I sat up in bed and rubbed my eyes as they kicked aside the empty bottles on my floor, then opened my windows' shutters to blind me with sunlight.

Ideally, I'd get up and shuffle the Class outside and away

from my personal belongings. But I'm still teetering on the edge of last night's blackout drunk.

I tug my blanket over my shoulder as I switch to look at the witch farthest to the right. "Or is it you? Someone needs to start talking. As far as I'm concerned, I haven't broken the rules of my banishment. I haven't stepped foot into a city or tried to barter my dove for freedom or influence.

"*Wait*—are you guys here to beg me to sponsor Antigone again? My brothers said the lamps blink through the nights now without my dove. He also says residents on the eighth and ninth levels smell sewage at *all* hours."

"We're here to assign a caretaker for you." The tallest and oldest of the group steps forward. The warlock has a narrow face and a skinny frame. His white layers hang loosely from his shoulders and neck. "The villagers have reported a few distressing incidents since you arrived two months ago."

I can't hold back my eye-roll this time. "Why? Because I cursed at the oread in the market? She won't barter with me for clothes and has also shown disdain for my nudity. Riddle me that. Also, what the *fuck* do you think a caretaker will do for me?"

The Class stares at me in silence.

I go on, "I've been taking this banishment *very well*. May I state, *once again*, that I would have had no reason to harm the Kulapsifang. My goals were to kill Oko and Anesot, and—"

"How can you remember that?" a witch with neat braids asks. "Your panic magic decimated your memories, along with those of Samson 714 Afador. Neither of you can confirm what happened in Alita."

I throw out a hand. "Why are we assuming the worst, then?"

A fourth member answers, "Because Samson walked away with a serious chest wound, Helisent. He barely survived."

"And I slept for three days to recover from spending my magic. Why hasn't Samson been banished from Mieira? From

Velm? Maybe *he* killed Oko and Anesot and, in the process, was wounded."

The skinny elder shakes his head. "One day, you will remember the last four years of your life. One day, you will have better suggestions to offer us—ones that are based on your *full* memories."

I narrow my eyes. It's a surprisingly optimistic statement. "Fine, then. I'll snort all the grimoire in the world when I remember what happened, then I'll *prove* that everyone has been wrong about me. Maybe I'll even go to Bellator and tell the wolf *I told you so*."

What kind of Kulapsifang spends his time blaming others?

I highly doubt I dragged him to Alita and then tried to kill him with a metal ornament from my lilith.

I'm too powerful for that; any sort of spell could have downed the wolf so long as it wasn't the triplemoon or the doublemoon—which it wasn't.

"In the meantime, Helisent," the warlock goes on, "your caretaker has traveled from Luz to be with you."

I throw my head back. "I don't need a caretaker."

A skinny witchling cranes her head to stare through my opened door a few feet behind the Class's line. "Helisent? Hi. It's me. I guess you don't remember anything. I was your mentee. In Luz."

She steps into the room and tugs her red cloak tight over her shoulders. She glances at the tall warlock; she looks just as thin and stoic as the Class member. I stare between their faces and realize they must be related.

A caretaker or a spy?

"Right, well, why would I believe you?" I shrug as I study the witchling, then look back across the line of Class members. "I don't remember Luz. I don't remember any mentees. Also, I *don't* want a caretaker."

The warlock raises his chin. "She cares for you greatly, and someone has to make sure you don't step out of line here in

Jaws. Stop accosting the villagers, Helisent. We'll be forced to take action soon if you don't accept your banishment and reflect on your wrongdoing."

I gesture to the door behind the caretaker witchling. "Well, if that's it—goodbye. Thank you for stopping by."

Two wielders in the Class meet my eyes before filing out. The other four turn and leave, as though relieved to escape my hovel.

The ceilings are low, the light from the single window limited. The only thing more numerous than the empty bottles on the rock floor are the full ones stacked on my shelves.

Soon it's only me and witchling.

She gulps, then hustles to the edge of my bed.

She glances over her shoulder as though ensuring the Class is gone. Then she turns back and opens her bottomless bag. She shoves her hand inside, then she pulls out a tin container. "Simmy told me not to... but I think we can have a little fun today."

Simmy?

The last I remember, I was finding place and meaning in a warren in Alita. There was no one named Simmy there with me.

I let that go and zero in on the tin clutched between her skinny fingers. My heart leaps in my chest; I haven't been this happy since I woke up two months ago. "Is that fucking dextro?"

She clenches her jaw and nods.

I reach over and set my hand on her forearm. "You are... *so, so* perfect, little witchling."

A wondrous smile spreads across her face. "Really? You think so?"

"Yeah. Of course. Should we do some now?"

"Sure. I have to go get Simmy later today. They wouldn't tell us where you were banished, so he's waiting in Eupheme. Everyone in Luz has been asking for you—the warren,

Boonma, Itzifone, Gautselin, Elvira. Even Ninigone. There are
a few more that I can't think of, too. An okeanid that came
from the Deltas with her evil grandmother."

None of those names mean anything to me. I suppose I've
made a lot of friends in the last four years; all I remember now
is a filthy warren in Alita and the pain of losing my sister.

Vaguely, I wonder if this Simmy could be Onesimos. Of all
my warrenmates, the oread is my favorite. He's a friend, a
confidante, a lover.

Simmy. Interesting.

"Right." I raise an eyebrow. "And what the fuck is your
name?"

"Oh." She looks up at me, as though she forgot that I
forgot. Then she takes another minute—far too long to
remember her own name, but I don't call her on it. I don't give
a shit what her real name is, so long as she hands over the
dextro.

She says, "You can call me Esteban Luz."

"Alright, Esteban Luz. Let's get fucked up." I lean forward
and open my hand for the dextro.

She hands it over with another dazzling smile.

HI, READER!

It's over. (*Boooooo!*) Book 2 of the Sennenwolf Series, *Seed of Vex* (working title), will be released in late 2023. Until then, here are four suggestions to hold you over:

First, listen to Lazarusman. He's a real-life spoken word poet and music producer. His work inspires me constantly. If I had a cult (which I *don't*), I would make his music required listening.

Second, please review this book on Goodreads and the site where you purchased your copy. It helps me put a roof over my chihuahua's head.

Third, sign up for my newsletter. My subscribers (lovingly known as Tiny Dancers) have access to three bonus scenes from *West of Jaws*. Some of it is very smutty. All of it is canon.

Fourth, keep reading indie authors! We aren't as flashy as some big-name authors, but we make up for it ~~in bed~~ with inventive new plots.

GLOSSARY & WORLD

Feeling a little lost and confused? Hey, at least you found your way here! Take a few shortcuts with the information below.

Terms

- Ala: A wolf's scent. Alas are highly unique. They carry information on gender, health, generational count, family ties, and more. Only wolves can smell alas.
- Bitterroot: A bitter flavor preferred by wielders.
- Centerheart: A wielder who is unable to cast magic against those they love.
- Demigod: A very large and blue-glowing magical being that is tied to a specific geographic region in Mieira. Demigods are the source of elemental power that nymphs who are born in their domain can draw on. Demigods appoint kings and queens to help them with custodial duties related land-based resources. The only non-nymph demigod is Hetnazzar, who roams Velm.

- <u>Desita</u>: a state of ecstasy that the demigods and nymphs can energetically absorb. Wolves and wielders can feel desita, though it doesn't boost their physical and emotional health, as it does with nymphs.
- <u>Dextro</u>: Cocaine. Did anyone pick up on this? You guys, it's cocaine.
- <u>Driproot</u>: A sleep aid.
- <u>Dove</u>: A type of wild magic that wielders can store in order for other beings to use. Nymphs and wolves, though largely non-magical, can apply dove from a wielder for almost any purpose.
- <u>Fangself</u>: A wolf's form which is imbued with a secondary set of instincts and desires.
- <u>Form</u>: A true physical appearance. A wolf will phase into their form, a giant wolf, on the triple- or doublemoon. A wielder will use magic to hide their form so others can't see their horns or tails.
- <u>Highmoons</u>: Midnight.
- <u>Kulapsifang</u>: A title for the inborn Alpha of Velm, who is born from the previous generation's Male and Female Alpha. Often abbreviated as "kulapsi."
- <u>Lilith</u>: A cushion used by wielders for floating.
- <u>Mixed</u>: A wolf couple whose alas merge to form a separate third ala, mixed from their original alas.
- <u>Northing</u>: To move North into Mieira from Velm.
- <u>Pith</u>: To be magically powerless. Nymphs born far from their homelands and demigods are pith by distance. Some beings, like the offspring of wolves and wielders, are born pith.
- <u>Pitroot</u>: A contraceptive for male wolves.
- <u>Seething</u>: To be compromised magically by a witch's sexual ala. This occurs only between male wolves and witches. Seethings cause a wolf to dream of the witch in question.

- <u>Selkie</u>: A pink water-dwelling being. Selkies inhabit freshwater bodies, including rivers and lakes. When they transition into saltwater, they transform into seals. (Allegedly.)
- <u>Southing</u>: To move South into Velm from Mieira.
- <u>Torc</u>: A piece of jewelry that wraps around the necks and upper arms of wolves.
- <u>Unnumbered</u>: To live as a wolf without a generational count or pack.
- <u>Vagueroot</u>: A contraceptive for witches.
- <u>Waricon</u>: A wrestling match common to wolves. Waricons are designed for friendly competition, entertainment, and to resolve disputes of leadership.
- <u>Zhuzh</u>: A way wolves will finesse the truth without technically lying.

Moons

- <u>*M.* Marama, *V.* Vicente</u>: The largest moon that gives off a pink-gray hue.
- <u>*M.* Laline, *V.* Abdecalas</u>: The second-largest moon that gives off a green-gray hue.
- <u>*M.* Cap, *V.* Sennen</u>: The smallest moon that is blood-red and gives off little light.

Nymphs

(Nymphs are *loosely* based on ancient Greek beliefs. I am not a Greek scholar. This is not a work of non-fiction.)

- <u>Dryads</u>: Nymphs native to the **forests** across Mieira, including Septegeur, Rhotidom, and the Northern Deltas. Their elemental powers let them navigate the forest and its resources. They have olive skin and emerald hair.

- Hesperides: Nymphs native to the **plains** across
  Mieira, including Gamma and the Southern Deltas.
  Their elemental powers command certain crops and
  wind. They have speckled skin (based on vitiglio)
  and brown hair.
- Naiads: Nymphs born near Mieira's **freshwater
  bodies**, including lakes, streams, and rivers. Their
  elemental powers are tied to water; they can make
  any water supply potable. They have olive skin,
  slightly curly hair, and blue-green eyes.
- Okeanids: Nymphs native to Mieira's **saltwater
  channels**, including the Deltas bay and the coasts
  from Hypnos to Velm. Their elemental powers give
  them control over oceanic currents and tides. They
  have deep brown skin, tight black curls, and blue
  eyes.
- Oreads: Nymphs native to the **volcanic cones** of
  Jaws. Their elemental powers connect them to
  metal and fire. They can manipulate soil heavy with
  magnesium, calcium, and iron. They have deep
  brown skin and tight vermillion curls and eyes.

Words I Didn't Actually Make Up

- Ala: This means "wing" in Spanish.
- Cap: This means "moon" in Mongolian.
- Laline: this means "moon" in Haitian Creole.
- Marama: this means "moon" in Māori.
- Saiga: A species of antelope indigenous to the
  Eurasian Steppe; they are critically endangered.
- Zhuzh: This doesn't necessarily mean *to lie*, just to
  "fancy" something up. Some linguists think this
  weird-ass word came from Yiddish. Others think it
  might be Romani.

ACKNOWLEDGMENTS

Thanks to the Rat King for surviving all those brushes with death. Before your love, I was a plastic bag shaped like a human. Now I'm... just human? (More human than bag?)

On to all the homo sapiens who helped me write this book—

Bearclaw: How did we spend years in Brooklyn without connecting on our love of fantasy fiction? Thanks a million for taking a chance and reviewing this project. Someday, I will hurt Creepy Baby for you.

EV: I wish I could make your dreams come true like you've helped me do for mine. (What if I throw a one-woman talent show for you? Would you like that? I have many talents.) Thank you for being a Super Power Friend.

Mr. Capes: Wow, you finally read one of my books. And you liked it! And then you walked around the apartment quoting Samson and growling. It was 10/10 cute.

My Apple-Head-Ass-Dude: Our many misadventures in life inspired multiple scenes in *West of Jaws*. It's really nice to be farther ahead in our journeys of wellness than Helisent or Samson. It makes me feel like we really know what we're doing. (Is this the key to success? Narrating the past when we're a comfortable distance away from our worst mistakes?)

Lazarusman: Thank you infinitely for letting me include your work in this project. It was next-level world-building and fully blew my mind. And thank you for creating art with a spirit of warmth and thoughtfulness.

Jelena Gajic: Thank you for making this book cover a work of art in its own right! I'm obsessed—and I think Helisent would approve.

ABOUT THE AUTHOR

Capes is the pseudonym for author TL Adamms. She likes all things romantasy. And she likes spliffs. Mother Nature, too. As a queer artist, she aims to infuse a music festival vibe into adult fantasy fiction. All are welcome. The weirder, the better.

The Sennenwolf Series is her third project.

Other works by Capes:
The Decagon Series (*Decagon, Baphomet, Psychopomp,* 2020)
The Unburied Queen (shortlisted for Foreword INDIES, 2021)

Website:
WWW.CAPESCREATES.COM

Instagram:
CAPES.AUTHOR

Facebook:
AUTHOR.CAPES

Peace, Love, Unity, Respect... and Fantasy Fiction.

CPSIA information can be obtained
at www.ICGtesting.com
Printed in the USA
LVHW030724090323
741202LV00001B/21